J. EVAN JOHNSON

When It's TOO LATE TO TELL

A NOVEL

PROLOGUE

MARK stares at the paper, not sure of what to do next. His hand trembles as he focuses his attention on one sentence.

"Ninety-nine point nine nine percent accurate," he whispers to himself.

He then crumples up the paper and throws it against the windshield of his car. A few moments later, he grabs his cell phone to call his friend Craig. After only a couple of rings, Craig picks up the phone.

"She wasn't lying, man. I'm the father." Mark pauses. "She didn't, you know, get the procedure done."

A long and painful silence permeates the air. He knows Craig is unsure of what to say. In most cases, he would tell him God will make his circumstances right; to keep the faith and to pray for direction and guidance, but he doesn't say a word. Maybe those words Craig would say ring a bit hollow now. Nevertheless, when he needs him the most, Craig says nothing, forcing Mark to feel the effect of his actions even more.

"Just thought I'd let you know," Mark says. "I have to go."

Finally, it seems Craig musters up enough courage to say simply, "Stay strong, Mark. If you need me for anything, I have your back."

"Yeah" is all he says. He hangs up without saying another word. The small space inside his car is beginning to spin so he rolls down his window for air. Acting on impulse, throwing away any rational reasoning, Mark drives to Philadelphia.

Mark parks his burgundy nineteen ninety-two Pontiac Grand Am outside a three-story apartment building. Clouds begin to move in and the winds pick up speed, signaling a fierce storm approaching. He pulls out a picture from his wallet. A beautiful, smiling woman is sitting on a stool. She has milk chocolate colored skin accented by hazel colored eyes. Her shoulder length dark brown hair drapes down the side of her face. Everything about her seems perfect, even down to her straight and pearly white teeth. Mark stares at the picture without a sliver of emotion, eventually stuffing it back into his wallet and getting out of the car. Surveying the apartment building, he feels scared, even depressed. *This, by far, is the worst day of my life,* he thinks. A little boy walks out of the apartment building and runs across the street by himself, almost getting hit by a car that doesn't slow down at all. Mark shakes his head and steps into the building.

Inside the apartment building, it looks even more run-down than the outside leads you to believe. Something mysterious grows on the carpets, turning it different colors. The stench of cigarettes and urine rises to his nostrils and makes it difficult to breathe. With each step, the floor moves as if he's on sand. The wooden floors don't creak but sound off a high-pitched whine as he puts pressure on them.

He hurries up the stairs to get to the top floor and Apartment 3-A. The sounds of a baby crying, coupled with the sound of heavy raindrops pecking at the building, echo throughout the long and shadowy hallway. Mark puts his ear up to the door, being careful not to touch it, and tries to hear what goes on inside. All he hears is a baby crying. He puts his hand up to knock, but instead tries the doorknob and finds it unlocked. He cautiously enters the apartment. The air is thick and smells of marijuana and cherry incense; so much so, the apartment looks hazy. He hears laughing coming from one of the back rooms and does everything to avoid that area. He tiptoes into the second room to see a baby in a crib. Mark approaches the crib and the baby stops crying at once. Staring at the little girl, who now smiles at him, Mark goes to pick up the child.

"What are you doing?"

Mark straightens up and turns around to see the worst mistake he's made in his life: a buxom woman in her mid-thirties, almost a decade older than Mark. She squints her bloodshot eyes towards Mark while holding the door frame to keep from falling. She is wearing tight jeans one would have to peel off her to remove and a top that is a size or two too small to cover her large bust.

"I'm taking her with me."

The woman just stares at Mark. She scratches her arm a few times and the baby starts to cry again. Mark turns around and picks up the baby.

"Everything is going to be okay, baby girl," Mark whispers in the child's ear.

"You owe me some money," the woman says.

"I don't owe you a thing. You set me up."

"Where's my money?"

"Holly, I'm taking her and I'm leaving."

A short man covered in tattoos comes to the doorway. He stares at Mark and then at Holly.

"In your drawer," he says and leaves the apartment.

Holly twitches and leaves the room. Mark sees his opportunity to leave and slips out of the room. Through an open doorway, he sees Holly rummaging through several drawers in her bedroom. She whispers to herself but Mark can't hear what she's saying. She then flips her mattress and cushions, checking all the common hiding places, but at each location seeming more frantic.

"Holly," Mark says, but she ignores him. "Get some help."

She doesn't say anything and continues with her frantic search. Clutching the baby to his chest, Mark leaves the apartment but not before seeing a crack pipe lying on the coffee table.

As he exits the building, the sky is pouring rain so he covers the child with his jacket. In one smooth motion, he slides into his car and sits there still holding the child to his chest. He tries to think of his next move but doesn't know what his choices are. All he knows is that one day he was on top of the world, finishing school, with a beautiful girlfriend to whom he's engaged. The next day, not even a full twenty-four hours away, he's in Philadelphia picking up his five-month-old daughter, whose mother is a thirty-something-year-old woman addicted to every drug on earth. Mark stares forward as the little girl plays with his face. Tears force themselves from his eyes as he swallows down his sobs, trying not to disturb the baby. The child starts to laugh. Her laughs are light and soften Mark's heart. She smiles at him. Mark now considers the task before him. Nothing of what he decides to do will be easy. Mark turns on the car. Many parts of him feel mixed up, but his body moves with purpose, with intent. Putting the car in drive Mark drives off with almost a full tank of gas. To where, not even he knows.

☙❧

Craig wishes he were able to say something more to Mark, something profound. He puts down the phone, realizing he's running late for work. It is yet another weekend shift. Donna, his boss, is making life difficult for him. This is the third weekend in a row she set Craig up to work with her. Everything would be fine if she didn't find it necessary to hit on Craig at least once every hour. Although she is a beautiful young woman, Craig doesn't feel anything towards her. All he wants is to go to work and go home, but she wants . . . Craig. If it were a different time, Craig may have taken her up on her many offers of midnight rendezvous and midday flings. That is, if Craig wasn't a youth minister for a well-known church. A scandal like that wouldn't look too good if it were to get out in the open. He would be an embarrassment to the church, what's left of his family, and himself. Craig tries to prep himself for the long work night to come but finds difficulty doing so. All he can think about is the news Mark just told him and how he couldn't help him when it seemed like Mark needed him most.

Craig sits in the manager's office across from Donna, who is sitting with her legs crossed and her skirt hiked up on her thigh. Her hair is tied back into a ponytail, a usual for this time of night.

"So what are your plans for tonight?" she asks. She pulls the band from her hair, letting it unfurl down her back. She runs her hands through it and fluffs it out some.

Craig stands up and heads towards the door. "Sleep."

"Well, why don't you join me for a few drinks instead?"

"I don't drink. You know that." Craig grabs a stack of papers from the desk by the door and heads towards a filing cabinet at the back of the office.

"Yeah, all of a sudden, you decided to become super saint. But we had some fun times before then."

"I guess so."

Donna shifts her body to the side and rises from her seat while Craig has his back turned. She flips the top two buttons of her blouse open and eyes Craig, waiting for him to turn around. He doesn't. Taking a more direct approach, Donna slinks her way over, her hips swaying side to side.

"Come on, Craig. I know you had fun then too. But we nev—"

Craig snaps around and interrupts her. "Look, Donna. Seriously, drop it."

"But Craig, it's like starting a race and stopping before the finish." Donna crowds Craig up against the filing cabinet. "Don't you want to finish?"

"I'm running a different race now. Now, please, get out of my way."

Donna moves closer to Craig, clutching his sides.

"You don't find me attractive anymore?"

She begins kissing him on his neck and pulls on his belt buckle.

He nudges her away and says, "Stop it."

Craig hears a commotion of people outside the door. The closing workers are ready to clock out for the night and go home, and they need either Donna or Craig to log them into the store computers. The time clock at the store has been broken for weeks now, and the security technician who is supposed to fix it hasn't showed up, even after numerous calls. After a few warnings from Donna, the closing workers no longer barge into the office. Instead, they wait outside the door for either her or Craig to come out. Craig wondered if there were other motives behind Donna's actions then.

Craig grabs the sides of Donna's arms, trying to stop her pursuit. With deft movement, she unbuckles his belt. While leaning into him, she hikes her skirt up again, this time higher, and begins to slide her underwear down. Craig, concerned with someone deciding to ignore Donna's rules, tries to remain quiet in his attempts to stop her.

"Donna no," he whispers.

She smiles and tries to stop Craig from holding up his pants. Craig then slides to the side and moves her out of the way. With more force than he realized, he shoves her and she trips, falling into a table and to the floor with a thud. Papers fly everywhere as Donna lets out a short yelp.

Craig buckles his pants back up, but while he is doing so, people come storming into the room. A silence fills the air as the workers stand there stunned. There is Donna, lying on the floor with her purple thong wrapped around her knees, and Craig, straightening his pants. *I should say something; I should say something,* he thinks. Instead, he just grabs his jacket and rushes from the room.

CHAPTER ONE

"BOYS and girls, we are now in the finals of Trivia Fiesta Fridays. After a week of building up the prize pool and a whole day of question answering madness, it comes down to two contestants . . . ."

A classroom full of wide-eyed nine and ten year olds stare at their fourth grade teacher, Mark Cooke, as he stands behind two students sitting at the front of the classroom.

"Betty-Ann Lawrence and our reigning champion, Donald Francis. And now, the much-expected prize . . ."

Mark goes to his desk and pulls out a ribbon, a bag of candy, and an index card.

"A large bag of M&Ms and a no-homework pass good for one full day of homework, all subjects."

The children continue to stare at the two students sitting at the front of the classroom. Mark hears a few gasps from the room. A few others whisper words of disbelief, such as "No way" and "How can this be?"

"Okay, you two. You know the rules. I'm going to ask a question. Whoever grabs the Rubik's Cube and shouts the correct answer first is the winner. You ready?"

The girl with curly hair, pink shoes and shirt, and jeans nods her head. Mark looks over to the boy with a short haircut, glasses, and bushy eyebrows. The boy, who is a little shorter than the girl, doesn't nod but gives a smug look. Mark chuckles a little at the boy's confidence. He glances up to see a few of the other fourth grade teachers standing at the door to watch. He looks at the clock to see the bell is about to ring in a few seconds and decides to wait until it does. Right on time, the bell rings at three o' clock sharp. The whole classroom becomes antsy, not because they want to leave, but because they don't want to leave without finding out what happens.

"The capital of North Dakota," Mark says.

Donald snatches the Rubik's Cube from the table and says, "Bismarck, Mr. C. You gotta make this harder. I'm like a titan among average men here."

A bunch of moans and groans sound from the classroom, as many were hoping for a new champion.

"Congratulations, Donald. You are the champion for the week. This is the sixth in a row."

"Thanks, Mr. C."

"Good job today, Betty. You came out of nowhere to make the finals."

"Thanks. I knew the answer to that last one. I just couldn't get to the cube quick enough."

"That's okay. I expect you in the finals next week."

"I will be. I'm going to study my butt off."

"That's good to hear."

Kids, one by one, start to file out of the classroom. A few minutes later, as Mark is cleaning up, one of his fellow teachers steps into the classroom.

"You love this, don't you?"

Mark looks at the short, round man and smiles. "Of course, I love this."

"You know, word is that you single-handedly turned this school around." The man brushes over his thinning hair with his hand.

"I don't know who would say that."

"Well, me, for one. You've done the stereotypical impossible . . . taken inner-city youth and gave them hope."

"It's not that hard to do. And for the record, I didn't give them hope. I gave them an environment where they can hope."

"Whatever it is, you deserve teacher of the year again. And I'm not just saying that."

"Thanks, Earl."

Earl leaves the classroom as Mark packs up his briefcase. He looks at the clock to see that his daughter will get out of school soon as well. He snaps shut his briefcase and makes his way out of the school.

Mark swims his way through the stream of children rushing to leave the school. He waves to the music teacher, Mr. Benteed, a guy he knows from church, and continues on his trek to exit the school. Once outside, he glances back at the rough looking exterior of the school, and turns back with a smile. *Eight years,* he thinks. He gets to his car and throws his briefcase into the back seat.

Mark eyes his watch four times while inside the car. The thought of being a few minutes late drives him crazy, but at least he's late for a good reason. He drives up to a larger and better looking school than his own to see Kalina, his daughter, standing by the steps talking to a few of the other kids with their parents. She spots Mark and runs up to the car, waving good-bye at the others. She plops in and, with no delay, fastens her seat belt.

"Hey, Daddy."

"Hey, baby girl. How was your day?"

"It was good. Fridays are always good."

"Yeah, they are. Learn anything new?"

"Umm. Not really. We kinda just hung out with Mrs. Stanley. She gave us the day off."

Mark smiles as he puts on his turn signal. "The day off, huh?"

"Yep. It was fun. We just watched movies and read books."

"That's it?"

"That is it."

"I think I'm going to talk to her about that one."

"C'mon, Dad. Why?"

"You should learn something every day at school. Otherwise, why am I paying all this money? You could have stayed home and watched movies all day."

"You know, that isn't a bad idea."

Mark glances over at Kalina. "When you get in, you have to hurry and get ready for softball practice."

"Do I really have to?"

"Yes. I thought you liked softball?"

"I never liked softball. It's a boring sport."

"Well, what would you rather play?"

"I don't want to play a sport. You told me that I only had to do it for a little bit. It's been half a year now."

"I know, I know. This is good for you; trust me. You learn so many life skills by being on a team in a sport."

"Nothing that I couldn't learn outside a sport . . . and I know that's Mom talking, not you."

Mark chuckles. "That's me talking . . . and even if it wasn't, you're still going to practice."

"Fine, but you owe me a game."

"A game?"

"Yes. Our last one ended in a checkmate."

"Oh, you mean chess. Baby, they all end in checkmate."

"I know. But last time, I was closer. I had you on the ropes."

"You did?"

"Oh, come on, Daddy. You know I had you on the ropes. I would have won if it wasn't for one move."

Mark pulls up to the garage of his four bedroom, three and a half bathroom house. He stops the car and smiles at Kalina. "I'll play you tonight, after dinner . . . but for now, get ready for practice."

"This time, I'm going to annihilate you."

"Oh, that's a new word."

Kalina smiles, "You see … I did learn something at school today." She jumps out of the car and hurries into the house. Mark goes in after her.

Inside, Kalina rushes upstairs and Mark heads towards the kitchen to see Jade, his wife. She turns around and smiles. Mark gives her a peck on the cheek and goes over to the sink to wash his hands.

"And how are you, my queen?"

"I am a lot better now that I've seen you."

She comes up behind Mark and wraps her arms around his fit waist. Mark dries his hands on a towel and turns around to face her.

"Where's little man?" he asks.

"Upstairs getting ready for football practice."

"So, that means we have a few seconds."

"A few seconds for what?" Jade asks, smiling.

Mark places his lips on hers and kisses her with passion. He leans back on the counter allowing Jade to lean into him even more. He wraps his arms around her and pulls his face away from hers to look into her eyes.

"Need I say it?" Mark asks.

"Yeah. Say it in a deep voice, too."

In a deep voice, Mark says, "I love you."

Jade begins to giggle and acts bashful in Mark's arms.

"Get a room."

Mark looks past Jade to see Kalina standing at the front door in her softball gear, hands on her hips.

"Go get your brother," Mark says.

Kalina makes her way back upstairs, mumbling something under her breath. Mark looks at Jade.

"It's me and you later," Jade says.

"Why does that sound like a threat?"

"You are not going to kiss me like that and expect nothing to happen to you." Jade smiles even more.

"Don't we have something to do at the church tonight?"

"Nope. Told them we weren't going to make it tonight. I have everything already set up. The kids are going to the neighbors . . . I went out and bought a few things. Yup, you are mine tonight."

Mark smiles and redirects his attention towards the steps. He creeps up to the banister knowing that Kalina is sitting on the steps trying to hear the conversation.

"What cha doin!" Mark yells.

Kalina screams and runs upstairs laughing as Mark chases her.

⋙⋘

Craig Barlow, a financial advisor, sits at his desk reviewing an account he manages. His eyes are bloodshot and his face is unshaven. He looks like he hasn't removed himself from his office in a week. He gets up from his desk, holding a manila folder, and walks to the large floor-to-ceiling window. He looks out the window at the other buildings in the area. Being on the twenty-sixth floor with all the business owner and execs, he has a good view of the city. He hears Berta, his assistant, on the intercom.

"Craig, have you come up with a decision on the Rustinsky account?"

Craig walks over to his phone and clicks the intercom. "Not yet. I need a bit more information. Can you set up another sit-down with Mr. Rustinsky?"

"Sure thing. I also have a few other files for your review."

"Send them my way."

Craig gets off the intercom and sets the folder down on his desk. He looks at the clock to see that he has about an hour before a date at the restaurant down the street.

Berta knocks and comes into the office as Craig runs an electric shaver across his face.

"Oh, you didn't have to get all jazzy for me," Berta says jokingly.

"Ha-ha. I have a date tonight . . . well . . . I just remembered that I have a date tonight."

"That's the third one this week. Getting lonely?"

"You're just a barrel full of jokes tonight," Craig says as he lifts his head to shave under his chin.

"Just a few," Berta says as she lays a few more folders on Craig's desk. "So who is this one?"

"Met her in a flower shop."

Berta walks over to Craig and brushes the hair from his shirt. She then tightens his tie around his thick neck.

"Why are you working so late?" Craig asks with a confused facial expression.

"Why are *you* here so late?"

"I have to be. You don't. Your job description clearly says nine to five."

"I'm your assistant. That's my job . . . so for as long as you are in this office, I will be too."

"You're not getting a raise."

Berta laughs. "I don't want a raise. I'm just doing my job to the best of my ability."

"Does your job include getting me ready for a date?"

"It does when you look so terrible."

"Thanks for the compliment. You know … some people may take this verbal abrasion as jealousy."

"Jealousy? Of what? The airheads you date that can't put two and two together to get four? Or the money crazed ones who know about your status and want you to buy them diamond earrings on the first date?"

Craig squints a bit while looking at Berta. "Those aren't the only ones I date."

"Those are the ones I hear about."

"What about Blair?"

"She's a different kind of airhead. She is what I call a nutcase. She was power hungry . . . like a villain out of a comic book."

Craig laughs. "Yeah, I can see her now … just grinning from ear to ear with her little horns on the top of her head." After a few moments of laughing, Craig becomes serious. "My choices are slim, don't you think?"

"What do you mean?"

"I don't exactly have a normal past."

Berta sighs and pats Craig on the back. "You should get going. You don't want to be late for your airhead date."

"Wait up. Let me walk you to your car. Don't want anyone jumping out at you in the parking garage."

"Craig, no one is worried about me. I'm fine."

"Nope. It's eight-something at night and pitch-black outside. It's a horror movie waiting to happen."

"But I can run . . . and I carry a knife."

"Do you carry that with you to church?" Craig asks with a smile.

"No, I don't. What kind of question is that?"

"I don't know. Thought you would need it for that prison of a church you attend."

"You would know about prison really well, right?"

"Hey, hey, low blow. Fight above the waist."

"Sorry."

"Yeah, don't worry about it." Craig chuckles a bit as he grabs his gym bag from the corner of the office. Berta walks out of his office, and Craig shuts the lights out, sighs, and closes the door. He washes away the pained expression from his face with a conjured up smile.

ᘓᘔ

Alberta DeVries gets home, an average-sized apartment just outside the city, and throws her keys onto the coffee table. She's exhausted from a long day's work and flops onto the couch. She carefully slides her shoes off her aching feet and turns to lie on the couch. Closing her eyes, she takes in a deep breath and begins to pray. Every day after work, she thanks God for getting her through another day and for having a good job. In her prayers, she also mentions Craig, this being another everyday thing. Every day since her father's death, that is.

She then grabs her Bible and reads, picking up from where she left off yesterday, in Proverbs. A picture falls out of the Bible as she flips through the pages. Berta snatches it up and places it back in the Bible but not before catching a glimpse of it.

After her reading, she pulls the picture back out and stares at it. A woman with long brown hair is standing in front of a tree with the sun beaming on the side of her face. She is wearing simple clothing, nothing too extravagant. In shorts and a t-shirt, the woman still exudes beauty. You can tell the woman is a bit older from the slight wrinkles on her face, but the rest of her skin is next to flawless. Berta looks akin to her, having the same eyes, the same small nose, and the same wide mouth. Her father even told her that she acted like her, this woman whom she has never met, this woman whom she will never meet, at least, not in this life.

Berta slides the picture back into her Bible and sets it down on the coffee table. She gets up from the couch and looks at the clock. She figures she could still get to the gym in good time and no one would be there, so she goes to the bedroom to change into a pair of tights and a long t-shirt. She grabs her gym bag and heads out the door.

The gym is only a block away from her apartment, so usually Berta jogs down there as a warm-up. She steps in the doors to see it exactly as she thought it would be, almost deserted.

"Hey, Chad," Berta says, greeting the young man at the desk.

"Hey, Berta. Looking good as usual."

"Yeah. Thanks," Berta says unenthusiastically.

She keeps walking.

"Berta, when are you going to let me take you out?"

"When you grow a mustache. Isn't it a school night?"

"Funny."

Berta is at the back of the gym where she places her bag in a locker and then walks to a treadmill. She carries her MP3 player with her and sticks the ear buds into her ears. Listening to nothing but gospel music, she runs for a good three miles before stopping. Then she does some light weight lifting.

By the time she finishes her workout, the gym is just about to close. The young man that works the front desk, Chad, starts putting things up and cleaning things around the gym floor. Berta stares at Chad as he diligently works to shut down the gym for the night. She walks past him.

"Have a good night, Berta."

"I will. You do the same. See you tomorrow."

"So you're really not going to let me take you out?"

Berta turns around to face him. "Look, Chad . . . you're twenty-one. You're still a baby."

"I may have a baby face, but I surely know how to treat a woman."

"I'm not saying you don't." Berta smiles. "I'm saying that I'm way older than you."

"I've dated women older than me before. I'm sure I've dated women older than you as well."

"Well, that's a problem. What's wrong with the girls your age?"

"They aren't about much . . . and those that have everything in line aren't looking for a guy like me. The older ones at least give me some kind of respect."

"Stay away from those women. They're with you because they have issues. And it's likely they are using you for one thing."

Chad smiles. "But that one thing is what I am good at. I'm great at it, actually."

Berta shakes her head and continues to walk out of the gym. "Good-bye, Chad."

She gets home and drops her bag at the door. Right away, she unpins her hair and goes into the bathroom to take a shower. She eventually eats and relaxes for a few more minutes before finally getting into bed. That's how her day went. That's how her days always go; waiting for that day when everything changes.

ᘓᘔ

Jade Cooke sits on the edge of the bed strapping on her favorite high heel shoes, a pair of open toed black suede pumps. After a few seconds, she gets up to stand in front of a mirror, smoothing out a tight black dress that stretches over her curvaceous body. She examines herself, throwing away all points of doubt that she has in the way she looks. Her thighs are a bit large for her body, but that is expected after having a child. A smile comes across her face as she looks at the way her legs look in high heels. It's refreshing to dress up in something revealing, a halter top dress that comes to the middle of her thighs, as opposed to a modest pantsuit for church or the lab coat that she wears at the pharmacy. She turns to the side and nods her head in approval. She pats her hair, which is up in a bun, and does one last check on her makeup before putting on her earrings and misting herself with perfume.

She takes her time going down the stairs and into the kitchen. She set up this whole night for her and Mark, just so they could spend some time together. Lately, with the running around that they both have been doing, there has been little time for each other. Jade wants to change that. She wants to show Mark how much she loves him. She has to. Dinner is almost complete as Jade takes out the roast from the oven. She runs over to grab a lighter and lights two candles, setting them in the middle of the dining room table. As she grabs the dinner plates, she hears Mark's car pull into the garage. She smirks as she hears the car door shutting and she turns on some music, soft jazz … her favorite. She grabs two champagne glasses in one hand and a bottle of sparkling cider in the other and walks to the entrance. For a few seconds, she works out what pose she wants to have when he first sees her. She quickly decides on leaning against the wall. In her movement, her dress slides up her thighs a bit more. *All the more enticing,* she thinks.

෴

Mark shuts the door to his car and walks to the garage door to get into his home. Anticipation of this evening with Jade was more than Mark could handle. He thought about her during the kids' practices. He thought about her as he was dropping them off with their friends. He thought about her as he sped down the highway to get home. He places his hand on the doorknob, so excited that his mouth waters. He opens the door to see Jade leaning on the wall, gazing at him, ready to start off the night. A cool breeze blows in from the garage. Mark looks at his wife in awe. He doesn't remember the last time that he saw Jade in anything other than church clothes or pajamas. Adrenaline rushes through his veins and his heart beats even faster. As he turns his back to close and lock the door, he hears the sound of her shoes tapping across the kitchen tile. Mark follows close behind her, noticing Jade's legs giving off a luster under the dim lights. Jade pours sparkling cider into the two glasses and hands one to Mark. He guzzles it down as Jade leans back on the counter. He then moves in closer to Jade, whispering in her ear, "You aren't that hungry, are you?"

Jade purrs a bit as Mark nibbles on her ear. "I'm not, but I prepared this whole meal."

"Dance with me."

Jade puts up no resistance as she sets her glass on the counter. After leading Jade to the living room floor, Mark turns up the music. He grabs her and pulls her in close to him. Their bodies mesh with each other. Swaying back and forth, the two lovers dance. Jade's chest presses against Mark's enough to feel his heartbeat. With one hand, he holds hers, and with the other, he holds the lower area of her back, trailing it down her backside. They begin to kiss, pecking at each other at first and then more deeply as time passes. As the music intensifies, so does the way the two bodies intertwine, still moving along the carpet of the living room. Mark continues to move his free hand downward as he gets to the edge of her dress and the back of her thigh. She lifts her leg and wraps it around his side as the dress slides up even more. Mark slides his hand under her dress, caressing and squeezing her backside. Just as they plunge to the couch, the house phone rings. Both look wide-eyed at each other hoping that it isn't whom they think it is. They let the caller go to the answering machine.

"Mommy, Daddy," Kalina's voice comes through loud on the machine, "Charles is crying like crazy. He wants to come home. I want to come home, too. Ummm. Okay, bye."

Mark lays his head on Jade's chest. "We could ignore it," he says.

"We tried that before. Remember?"

"Oh, yeah . . . I forgot . . . Maybe we can do a little something on the way?"

Mark looks up at Jade to see her facial expression being anything but happy. Mark sighs and gets up from her. He helps her up and says, "I'll see you in a bit."

Jade stretches her dress back down and stomps upstairs. Mark cuts off the music and marches back into the garage. He kicks the empty trashcan, leaving the plastic can dented, and hops into his car to pick up the kids.

⊰⊱

Saturday morning, Mark is one of the first few in the local gym lifting weights. He lies flat on the bench and pushes up into the air a bar with more weights than normal. He sets the bar back on the rack, sits up, and grabs a towel to wipe the sweat off his face. For a moment, he stares at a skinny woman jogging on a treadmill. Her body is fit, tight. She isn't afraid to show it off, wearing long tights and a sports bra. Mark shakes his head and lies back down to do a few more reps.

"Four plates and some change, with no one to spot? What happened to you last night?"

Mark looks up to see Craig standing next to him. He places the bar back on the rack and sits up to shake Craig's hand.

"What's up, man?"

"I was getting ready to ask you the same thing. You're lifting like a man on PEDs, and I saw you stare at that woman over there." Craig

14

looks over at the woman. He bites his bottom lip and shakes his head. "Maybe there is a God."

"Hey, stop it."

"My bad. I just know it would take some being higher than I to create someone like that. She . . . man . . . good gosh."

"You sound like a man who is lacking some love as well."

"Man, I had the worst date ever last night."

"Ha-ha. So did I."

"At least you have a greater window of opportunity for a good one."

"You think? Try having kids."

"They did it again?"

"Yup. This time, right before things were about to jump off . . . right before. My hand was under her dress, on her thigh . . . and the phone rings."

"Noooooooooo."

"Yes. And you know it was over after that."

"I hurt for you, Mark, I do."

"You know what's really bad?"

"There's more?"

"She's the one who set the whole night up. She put on a little black dress, makeup, and earrings . . . everything. That ain't ever going to happen again." Mark lies back down to do a few more reps, grunting even more after each one. "What happened on the date?"

"Man . . . she was intelligent. She was gorgeous. She was fun to be with."

"And . . ."

"She drank too much."

Mark laughs.

"No, it's not funny. She took back too much and she started talking like crazy, but the only subject was the things that I could get her. I pretty much knew how it was going to go, so I took her home."

"That doesn't sound too bad."

"Yeah, it wouldn't have been if she hadn't thrown up all over the car."

"Inside?"

"All over the leather seats and dash. I have it in the shop getting cleaned now."

"That's disgusting."

"Yeah, it is. She then tried to get with me as I was carrying her to her room. I wouldn't have thought a girl who works in a flower shop would be an alcoholic."

Mark laughs again.

"But I really don't get it. There are so many women out there who complain about the lack of good men, but what about the good women? Where are they?"

"They're out there."

"Yeah, and you found them."

"You'll find one."

"I guess so. I mean, they deserve the utmost respect. I never disagreed with that. They just don't act like they want respect. They want a good man, but their number one criteria for judging a good man is money. Then some read this self-help book and think they have men figured out. They can try those tactics all they like, but what I want is someone to see me for whom I can be, whom I strive to be. That's the woman I will end up marrying someday, a woman who sees the potential in me and brings it out. Not the woman who sees the present-day money . . . or my not so good past."

"Sounds like the old day preacher coming out of you. Preach on, Pastor."

"Cut it out. I'm being serious."

"I am, too. The path to finding the right woman is a little bit easier when you involve God."

"No, it was easier for *you* when *you* involved God. I involved God in every aspect of my life. Remember? He then left me stranded. That is, if He really exists."

Mark gets up from the bench, ignoring Craig's last comment, and motions him over. "Lift."

Craig begins to do the bench press as Mark spots him.

"So what are you going to do?"

"Well, first I'm going to help you out. You and Jade set up a night tonight. I'll take the kids out. They have fun with me."

"Can't. Church."

"Tomorrow?"

"Church."

"Monday, after work?"

"She's probably staying late at work. I'll be at the church."

Craig stops lifting and sits up. "What time does your marriage get?"

"We do stuff together. It's just Jade is picky when it comes to certain things."

"When is the last time you . . . you know?"

Mark grumbles something Craig is unable to make out clearly.

"How long?"

"Five months."

Craig falls from the bench and curls up into a ball. Mark looks around embarrassed.

"I feel like someone just punched me in the gut. Mark, what the heck is going on?"

"Look. We both have busy schedules with work, ministries, and the kids. I have to catch Jade at the right time."

"At the right time? Man, you do have it rougher than me."
"Whatever. Jog?"
"Yeah, sounds like we both need to jog last night off."

CHAPTER TWO

"Y OU quit your job, didn't you?" Jade asks, talking into the phone.

"No, not at all," Mark says. "The kids are at lunch and I wanted to see how your day is going."

"This is a first. I must say, I am pleasantly surprised."

During his lunch break, Mark sits at his desk talking to Jade.

"I just want to make sure your Monday is going well."

"It is. Thank you."

A co-worker walks into the classroom and sits in front of Mark, staring at him until he gets off the phone.

"Baby, I have to go."

"Is everything fine?"

"I think so. I'll call you back in a few seconds."

Mark gets off his cell phone and stares back at Jolene, a short gray haired woman who teaches in the classroom right next to him.

"A new student is coming to your room," she says.

Mark nods. "That's always good. Why are you telling me?"

"I wanted to give you a heads up before they come in. He's a bright little boy."

"But all of my students are."

"No. He's very bright."

Mark looks at Jolene oddly just as the principal of the school and a little boy come into the classroom. Jolene immediately leaves the room.

Mark stands up and nods towards Principal Weaver. She smiles at Mark and talks to the boy.

"This is your new teacher, Mr. Cooke. Mr. Cooke, this is Timothy Langley."

The little boy doesn't say anything but puts his hand out for Mark to shake. Mark's hand covers the boy's entire hand.

"It is a pleasure to meet you, Tim. Is it okay if I call you Tim?"

The boy nods.

"Timothy comes from up north, Pennsylvania to be exact."

"Really? That's where I'm from. Most of my family still lives there."

Tim just stares at Mark.

"Timothy and his mother already went on the tour last week, so he already knows his way around the school."

"Cool."

Principal Weaver leaves with a smile on her face. She winks at Mark.

"Well, Tim, all the others are out for recess. Do you want to join them?"

Tim shakes his head.

"You sure? Recess just started and it's pretty good weather outside."

Tim just stands there. Mark tries to think of something to do but comes up with nothing. First, he needs Tim to talk.

"What do you like to do, Tim?"

Tim remains silent. Mark goes over to his desk to sit down. *Come on kid. Give me something to work with.* Mark watches him as the boy goes around the classroom looking at different pictures and projects that hang across the entire room.

"Our next subject after recess is Math. Are you good at Math?" Mark asks, trying to get Tim to talk.

Tim shakes his head, and he finally speaks. What Tim says is enough to make Mark angry and break his heart at the same time.

"My last teacher said I wasn't good at anything. He told me I was going to grow up to be a bum in the street."

He wonders why any teacher would say such a thing to a supposed, as Jolene puts it "bright" child.

"That's not true. You can be anything or anyone you want to be."

"Yeah," Tim says, looking down at the floor. He goes over and sits at a desk as kids begin to file back into the room.

After everyone settles, Mark introduces Tim to the class.

"Hey, kids, we have a new student joining us today. His name is Tim."

All of the kids greet Tim. One in particular, Frankie Simms, the rowdy one, makes his greeting louder than everyone else's.

"What's up, Tim dawg?"

Tim waves and looks down at the floor. Frankie looks over to Mark.

"Hey, Mr. C, this dude don't talk? What's up with him?"

"Shut up, Frankie," Betty yells from two seats behind him.

Not even a millisecond later, Frankie turns around in his seat. "You shut up. Imma get my double gang man on you."

"Hey, you two, cut it out. And it's doppelganger, Frankie. Stop watching all those sci-fi flicks."

Tim looks across the room at Betty and smiles shyly. For the rest of the day, Mark teaches the class, keeping a close eye on Tim. Tim doesn't raise his hand for any of the questions, but it seems as if he is giving Mark his undivided attention. Mark takes it as a good sign.

∞

Craig sits in his office with Berta floating all around him, handing him papers, taking others, and the like. He notices that she does everything with a smile. He notices he does everything with a stiff, almost glum look on his face.

"She was an airhead, wasn't she?" Berta asks.

He looks up at her and smiles. "For your information, she wasn't. She was very intelligent and has a lot going for herself."

"She was after your money?"

"It didn't seem like she was there for my money."

"She was missing a tooth."

"No. Her face was about perfect."

"So I guess that means you are going to see her again, huh?" Berta asks, still smiling.

Craig smiles even more and says, "Yes, indeed."

"Cool. Congrats. I'm happy for you. I'll be back with a few more files."

Berta begins to walk out of the door when Craig yells, "She's an alcoholic!"

Berta comes back into the office, laughing and jumping up and down, and says, "I knew it. I knew it."

"This lady took back, like, two bottles of vodka by herself," Craig pauses to laugh with Berta, who howls with laughter. "Then she threw it all up in my car."

Berta breaks from her laughing and holds her hand to her mouth. "Not in the new Porsche!"

"I forgot you were a car enthusiast. Yup . . . all in it."

"Were you drinking?"

"I started to, but stopped when I saw how much she was kicking back."

"You know, Craig, you sh—" Berta stops and leaves the office. She comes back in with a few folders. "You should really come to church with me. There are some nice women there."

"No offense, Berta, but none of those women put out."

"Wow. Good thing I've known you for years because I think that may have offended me in some other lifetime. Anyway, maybe you would find the one who's worth waiting for."

"I haven't yet. You know, I've always wondered something. How is it that you can work in this environment, work with me for all these years, and still hold tight to God? How did you work with Mr. Valencia for so long and still hold on?"

Berta stands there for a few seconds with a perplexed look. "I guess I always had hope for him. Just like I have hope for you."

"I'm not going back to the church, Berta. What do you hope for?"

"I don't hope you go back to church. I hope that someday you will stop blaming God for what happened to you . . . and that you will see that He was there for you the whole time . . . that He still is."

Craig looks at her as if she just took his heart away. He then looks out the window. Berta decides not to linger around and leaves. Craig sets his work aside and leans back in his chair.

CHAPTER THREE

MARK slams the top of his alarm clock to stop its gentle but annoying ring. He huddles back under the covers for a few moments before feeling around the bed. He pops up, noticing Jade isn't in the bed. Taking a few seconds to orient himself, he remembers that Jade works the early shift at the pharmacy today. He plods to the bathroom to shower and dress. He doesn't know why he was so panicky when he woke. Jade has left early for work many times in the past. *This day should be no different.*

Mark puts on his tie and runs downstairs to see Jade sitting in the dark staring at a wall.

"Jade, baby, are you all right?"

"Yes," Jade starts out in a deep hoarse voice. She clears her throat but her voice still sounds strained. "Everything is fine."

Mark walks up to her as she sits in the chair, still staring at the wall. "What's wrong?"

"Don't worry about it. Everything is fine."

Mark takes another step closer to see Jade in her work clothes. He then knows what is causing the strain in her voice. She was crying.

"I *am* worried about it. What's wrong?"

A long silence fills the air, making everything awkward between Mark and Jade. As the sun begins to come up, the house fills with a cool blue glow. Now, Mark is able to see Jade's face and the tears that are still forming in her eyes.

"You better go. You don't want to be late."

"I will just have to be late. I'm not leaving you here like this."

Mark steps even closer to Jade and gives her a hug. She doesn't hug back but instead pushes him away.

"Go to work, Mark. I'm fine."

Mark looks at Jade, unable to figure out what is wrong. Like a man defeated, he slinks out the door. He throws his briefcase in the car and starts the engine. Before he pulls off, he prays. He isn't sure of the problem, but he knows that God knows. That's good enough for Mark.

⋙⋘

Jade stares out the window as Mark pulls out of the driveway. She then glides across the floor and into the basement, trying not to wake the kids. The neighbors are picking them up today, and she should be at work. Instead, she sits at the bottom of the basement steps, holding her mouth to not let out any sobs until they leave.

⋙⋘

Mark sits at his desk as he waits for his students to file into the classroom. What plagues his mind is the way that Jade looked this morning. He doesn't know what happened but hopes that she will be fine. The bell rings to let the kids into the school and snaps Mark out of his daydream. His students rush into the room, hanging their coats and book bags on their hangers. Then, like clockwork, each student takes their homework out and places their papers on Mark's desk, all students, Mark notices, but one. He looks at Tim, who looks down at his desk. He doesn't have any school supplies with him, and he came into the classroom without a book bag. Mark observes him. It looks like he was crying. *Maybe it's an extreme case of Monday morning blues.* Mark goes over to Tim's desk and kneels down next to him.

25

"Did you do your homework, Tim?"

He shakes his head while turning red from holding back tears.

"It's okay. You just started on Friday."

"It's not okay," Tim whispers.

Mark looks at Tim shocked. "Don't worry about it. We'll get you caught up."

Tim nods, not even glancing at Mark.

For the whole day, Mark teaches with Jade and Tim on his mind. He keeps a constant eye on Tim, making sure he's good. The whole day, Tim pays attention, but Mark notices his attention waning towards the end of the day as if he's somewhere else.

"Tim, can you tell me what nine hundred thirty-one thousand, five hundred forty-five minus three hundred two thousand, six hundred eighty-nine is?" Mark motions to the class. "Can someone get him a paper and pencil?"

"Six hundred twenty eight thousand, eight hundred fifty-six," Tim answers.

Mark and the whole class looks at him shocked.

"That's the right answer," Frankie yells. "I just got the same answer."

"Good . . . job, Tim," Mark says. "Divide it by two."

Tim looks up at the ceiling and a few seconds later says, "Three hundred fourteen thousand, four hundred twenty-eight."

"Times five," Frankie yells.

"Frankie, stop. Yo—"

"One million, five hundred seventy two thousand, one hundred forty."

Everyone stares at Tim in complete silence. "Frankie, is that right?"

"I don't know, Mr. C. I can't write that fast."

Mark goes over to his desk to pull out a calculator and punches a few buttons before confirming. "He's right."

The whole class gasps and stares at Tim in awe. One of the students asks, "Is he a genius?"

Tim looks down bashfully. The only one in the class who looks at him differently is Betty. Her smile reaches from ear to ear across her face. Mark stares at Tim, remembering people telling him that he was very bright.

"Tim, you do all this in your head?"

Tim looks up at Mark and smiles shyly. Still not much for talking, he nods his head.

"So you're good at math, huh?"

He nods again. Mark smiles and begins to teach the class.

∽∝

Jade sits in her car, with Charles in the backseat, waiting for Kalina to come rushing out of the school. She stares at Charles, who is sound asleep. All day, she fought back tears, trying not to let on to what happened. She thinks about this morning and how Mark caught her in the middle of crying. *How could I tell Mark?* she asks herself. Part of her feels guilty for not letting him know what occurred. Other parts feel like she must hide what happened, so she can act normal. It is clear which side is winning right now. She still wears her work clothes. Usually on Tuesdays, she gets home from work with enough time to change, but that wasn't the case for today. Someone opens the car door and plops onto the passenger seat. Jade didn't see Kalina coming up at all and the little girl's entrance startled her.

"Hi, Mom."

Jade snaps a smile on her face, storing away the pain to come back to it later.

"Hey, Baby. How was school?"

"No complaints." Kalina scans Jade's appearance. "Why are you still in your work clothes?"

Kids. You can never hide anything from them . . . ever. "I got off late," Jade says.

"Was it old Mr. Oglesby again?"

"No, it wasn't him." Jade changes the subject. "You ready for some softball?"

"Umm, sure. Well, not really."

"Kalina."

"Mom, I hate softball. I don't like sports. Why do I have to play?"

"It gives you leadership skills, life skills."

"Did you play when you were my age?"

"Yes, I did," Jade says as she focuses on the road to hide that she just lied.

"Softball?"

"No. Tennis. Look, Kalina, if you want, you can quit after the season is finished. Keep in mind, though, you are going to do something. You aren't just going to sit around all day watching TV."

"I don't want to just sit around all day. I like things. I like chess. I like drawing and painting . . . creative stuff."

"We'll talk about it more when the time comes."

Kalina slumps in her seat.

"I like sports, Mommy," Charles yells from the back of the car.

Jade forces a smile at Charles through the rearview mirror, seeing he is wide awake from his nap. She hopes her smile didn't seem too fake.

⋈

Kalina looks at Jade, noticing the way she looks at Charles, the smile she gives him, thinking her mother's attitude changed completely when it came to Charles. Kalina knows that Jade isn't her real mother, but it never was so painfully obvious until now. For the rest of the ride, all three remain silent.

C8❧

"You've been in a funk all day. What's your problem?"

"What are you talking about? I'm fine."

Craig looks up at Berta from a stack of papers on his desk. She stands in front of him, hands on her hips. Craig looks her in the eyes. He feels a twinge, forcing him to blink his eyes a few times and look away from her.

"You've said two words all day. You look like crap."

"Don't I usually look like this?"

"I've never seen you like this. Dark circles under your eyes . . . in need of a shave . . . bloodshot eyes. Are you hung over?"

"No, I'm not."

"Then what is it?"

Craig gets up from his seat to grab a book from the bookcase. "I just didn't get enough sleep, that's all."

"What's stopping you from getting any sleep?"

"Don't worry about it. I can manage."

"What happened yesterday?"

"Berta, stop. Drop it."

"No." Berta grabs Craig's arm as he passes by her. "Sit. Talk." She pulls him over to the couch. Berta stares at him in concern. Craig sits a few minutes before talking.

"Why do you pray for me?" Craig asks.

Berta, shocked by the question, answers. "I always pray for those who are important to me. I want to see them do well."

"So it's a mass prayer that goes to God. Not, like a specific one."

"Why does it matter?"

"Because I don't understand what you think is going to happen to me."

"I told you that already. I hope f—"

"I know. I know. You hope for me to let go of all this pain I carry with me. Why does it matter?"

Berta looks at Craig and sighs. "You lost sleep over that comment?"

"No. I lost sleep over the crappy feeling I've had since you made it."

"Craig, do you understand who you are? I pray for you because I have so much hope for you. You are better than what you are in right now."

"But I was happy before you said anything."

"No, you weren't. You still hold on to your past. You still look for love from these women who aren't equipped to love you the way that you need."

"Now you're analyzing my life? Look, don't waste your breath. I'm fine the way I am."

Berta begins to show her anger. "I don't get you. You know what the truth is, but you turn your back on it every day. You were a youth minister, Craig. How is it that you led so many kids in the right direction but can't lead yourself in the direction that you know you should be going?"

"You want to know why?" Craig gets up from the couch. "I raped someone. Things don't go back to normal after that."

"But you didn't. Stop saying you did."

"Why? I paid the time for it. The church kicked me out for it. I lost five years of my life over it. I may as well say it. It doesn't matter if I did it or didn't. She said I did and they believed it; therefore, I did it."

"Stop it."

Craig walks up to Berta, almost glaring at her. "Berta, I'm a rapist."

Like a flash of lightning, Berta's hand comes across Craig's face, leaving them both looking at each other, stunned. Craig holds his hand to where she slapped him, speechless. Berta glares at Craig although there are tears in her eyes.

"That's not who you are!"

She then turns around and storms out of the office. Craig doesn't know what to do except watch her leave. He has never seen her that mad before today. What confuses him now more than ever is why she was so mad. He still doesn't get why it matters to her. He stretches his jaw a bit to numb the sharp sting that still pulsates through the side of his face. Eventually, he gets back to work.

☙

Mark pulls into his garage and stops the car. A million thoughts are running through his head and he is finding it difficult to rein them all into order. The joyous feeling he had after finding out that Tim could possibly be the most intelligent kid he has ever encountered is drowned out by what happened this morning. He doesn't know what was wrong with Jade earlier today, and part of him feels that he neglected his husbandly duties by leaving her to go to work. He steps out of the car with his briefcase in his hand. He stops just before the house door and takes in a deep breath. He chokes a bit from the fumes that still linger in the air. Slowly, he opens the door and steps inside the house.

As soon as he steps inside, Charles runs up to him and hugs his leg.

"Hey, Daddy."

"Hey, football star." Mark picks Charles up with one arm.

"Kalina got in trouble at school today."

"Oh . . . okay . . . and why are you telling me?"

"I don't know. She got kicked out of practice."

"Where's your mother?"

"Upstairs."

"Anything else you want to report on?"

"Something is wrong with Mommy, too."

"I know."

"Can you fix it?"

Mark smiles at his son. "I think I can. Tell you what," Mark says as he walks over to the TV and turns on cartoons, "Watch some TV. I'm going to see what I can do."

Charles slides from Mark's arms and sits in front of the TV. "Do you want my football helmet?"

Mark chuckles at his son's humor. Kids always know what to say without knowing what they are saying. "I think I'll be fine. But if I'm not back before dinnertime, come and rescue me."

Charles turns away from the TV. "Like in a secret mission?"

Mark nods and puts his finger up to his mouth to quiet Charles. He then starts upstairs. With each step he takes, he feels his heart sinking deeper into his stomach. He chooses to go to the easy problem to fix first and knocks on Kalina's door. It's a deep and hard knock, telling Kalina that it is Mark who stands at the door. The door cracks open slightly. Mark can barely see in the room but what he does see is that her blinds are closed and the room is dark. She opens the door even more with tears in her eyes. Mark walks in and gently shuts the door. Kalina sits at her desk and stares at the wall.

"What happened?"

Kalina doesn't say anything at first but knows that she had better answer Mark before he asks again. "I got into a fight."

"With whom?"

"Jessy Brinkerson."

"Why?"

"She said some things that ticked me off."

"So you fought her?"

"No. I walked away. She followed me, so I followed her with my fist. She wasn't going to back off otherwise."

"But you could have told the coach. You could have told your mother."

Kalina turns around in her chair to face Mark. "There was no one to tell. You weren't there."

Mark looks at Kalina. He motions her to come over and she does, crying. She sits next to him and he puts his arm around her.

"What is this really about?"

"Nothing."

"Kalina."

"I don't want to play softball anymore. I don't know why she is forcing me to."

"She as in your mother?"

Kalina nods.

"Look, I'll talk to her, but I think the team sport thing is still a good idea. How about another sport?"

"How about chess?"

Mark sighs. "There's nothing wrong with that."

"Yeah, but Mom thinks that chess will take me nowhere. She treats it like I'm going out doing drugs or something. Chess is a smart person's game. Smart people rule the world . . . not softball players."

"Softball players might not rule, but football and basketball players do," Mark says jokingly.

A smile slides onto Kalina's face. "I could use a sixteen million dollar paycheck."

"Yeah, me too."

Kalina looks up at Mark with an expression that makes his insides melt. It is a kind of look that isn't on purpose but comes up every so often. It's a look of admiration.

"Daddy, I really like chess. There are a lot of teams all over. And I don't like softball. I don't like the game. I don't like the team. I don't like any of it."

Mark gets up and goes to the door. "I'll talk to your mom. In the meantime, stop fighting people, stop crying, and for goodness sake, open your blinds."

Kalina smiles and wipes away her tears. She gets up and hugs Mark, holding him as tight as she can, her head resting on his stomach.

"Daddy?"

"Yes, baby girl?"

"What was my real mom like?"

Mark's face drops. Now, he almost regrets telling Kalina so much at a young age. The idea was to be honest with his daughter, but right now, it feels like that idea backfired. Not knowing too much about her mother himself, he answers, "She was an interesting woman but one with issues. She had major issues."

"Do you miss her?"

Mark's face shifts realizing that Kalina hasn't loosened her grip around his waist.

"That would be awkward, don't you think? To miss somebody after I have moved on."

"I miss her."

"You've never met her."

"I know, but . . ."

Mark now realizes what the real problem is, but that is only half the battle. He doesn't know what to say.

"It's going to be okay. Daddy will make it all better."

"K."

"Now, I want you to do your homework and then go downstairs with Charles."

"I finished it already."

"Well go check up on him. I'll be down in a few."

"Okay."

Kalina releases her grip on Mark and slides by him. "I love you, Daddy."

"I love you too, baby girl."

Mark walks to his bedroom door, which is closed as well. He taps and opens the door. Sitting in the chair closest to the window, Jade looks at Mark.

"Did you talk to her?"

"I did."

"So?"

"It's still the same story. She doesn't want to play anymore."

"What did you tell her?"

"That we were going to talk about it."

"There's nothing to talk about."

"I'm not going to continue to force her to do something she doesn't want to do."

Mark knows exactly what he is doing by having the sports discussion again. He is avoiding the real problem, the strained mother-daughter relationship between Jade and Kalina.

"She's eleven, Mark. They do as we say, not the other way around," Jade says in a bland voice.

"True. However, it is up to us to make sure that what we say and do is fair and allows them to grow."

"Fine. What would she rather do?"

"She wants to play chess."

"Chess. Don't they meet at the same time as softball practice?"

"Yeah."

"Oh, so that's why she is pushing so hard now."

"She has always pushed for it."

"What are you, her defense?"

"Defense? What are you talking about? Jade, what is your problem?"

Jade stares at Mark. "I'm sorry, Mark. Look, sit down."

Mark sits down on the bed. Jade sighs as tears begin to form.

"I . . . I got up to go to work this morning . . . nothing out of the ordinary. But I got a phone call just as I was about to pull out of the garage. It was my boss. He told me that . . . ."

Mark stares at Jade, figuring out what happened.

"He told me that I need not come in to work today. I thought he changed my shift or something, but he said that I had been let go. It wasn't his decision and so on. After seven years . . . they just end it. Just like that. He then said 'I'm sorry' in a fake sympathetic voice and hung up the phone."

Mark slowly takes in a deep breath. "I'm sorry to hear that. You do know everything is going to be fine." He goes over to Jade to give her a hug and she pushes him away. Mark notes that this is the second time she did that today.

"Is everything going to be okay?"

"Of course, it will."

"Well, I'm sorry for not signing up for the blind optimism."

"Jade, isn't that what faith is, knowing something will happen even though nothing in our present situation leads you to believe that it will?" Mark walks out of the bedroom, almost disappointed in the state his wife is in, finding it hard to understand.

Mark gets downstairs to see Charles and Kalina glued to the TV. As he walks to the kitchen, his cell phone rings. Mark grabs the phone to see that it is Craig calling him.

"What's up?"

"Hey, Mark . . . You good, man? You sound a little distressed."

"Yeah, I'm okay. Things are a little weird right now. A lot of stuff is going on."

"Do you want to call me back?"

"No. That's okay. What's up?"

"She slapped me."

"Which one?"

"What do you mean which one?"

"You're talking about a date, right?"

"No, I'm talking about Berta. She slapped me."

"Your assistant?"

"Yes. Her. She slapped the mess out of me."

"What did you do? Did you ask her out?"

"No. We were in a heated debate, and she hauled off and slapped me."

Mark chuckles.

"It's not funny."

"I'm sorry. Did you talk to her about it?"

"Nope. I haven't left the office since."

"Wait, wait. Are you scared of her? You scared to leave the office?"

Craig chuckles. "C'mon, Mark. Really?" Craig chuckles a little longer and then gets quiet. "Maybe a little bit."

Mark lets out a laugh. "I think I would be too. I've seen her before. She looks like she boxes or something."

"She is in the gym often. She is fit. She may even throw me out the window."

"She's not going to throw you out the window. Man up and leave."

"Thanks for all of your wonderful wisdom, Mark. I don't know what I would do without you."

"What do you want me to do? You're the one who is scared of her."

"I'm not scared of her. Man, I'm going to go."

"Don't get slapped again."

"Ha-ha. I'll talk to you later."

☙❦☙

Craig hangs up his phone and tiptoes to his door. He cracks it open to see that Berta isn't at her desk. In a hurry, he grabs his bag and runs out of the office. On his way out of the building, his cell phone rings.

"Hello."

"Hey. What's up stranger?"

Craig recognizes the voice to be Brett Cruz, a friend from college. "Brett, how have you been?"

"Man, things are great. I'm living the life, you know? Living the good life like there's no tomorrow."

"Yeah? What do you do now?"

"I'm a stockbroker now."

"Nowadays, I would suspect you being a bit more downtrodden than you are."

"Naw, man. I'm good at what I do. I'm so good at what I do that I don't need to cheat people out of their money. I always say that it's my ingenuity that gets me by. That's what people trust me for . . . my ways to make money in this terrible economy. That's why I'm still in business. Yeah, I'm the man, you can say it."

"Sounds like your confidence hasn't faded over the years."

"It hasn't, and it won't. Listen, I'm going to be in town for a couple days on a business trip."

"You mean in town, like, in my town, in town?"

"Yeah, man. You want to hit up a few clubs? I hear there's this one in your area that is always packed with some good looking women."

"Still haven't slowed down yet, huh?"

"Nope. Why should I? But seriously, we should take a night and run that club ragged. Party like we used to before you got all holy on me."

"Holy? That's what you call it?"

"Don't know what else to call it."

Craig chuckles. "You know what, that doesn't sound like a bad idea."

"I know it doesn't. Who doesn't want to party with the Brett-man?"

"When do you want to go?"

"I'm thinking Thursday night. I have to catch a plane back on Friday."

"Sounds good. I'm in."

"All right. I'm telling you, Craig. We are going to turn your city upside down. You are guaranteed to come back with at least three women."

"I'm good with one."

"One woman? I don't understand."

"I'm a one-woman guy."

"I guess the holy water hasn't fully worn off yet."

"Very funny. I'm being serious, though. I don't n—"

"Hey, Craig, I have to go. I'm about to step into this meeting with a super huge client."

"All right, Brett. I'll see you Thursday."

"All right, dude."

Craig hangs up his cell and gets in his car.

CHAPTER FOUR

MARK sits in the teachers' lounge, grading test papers, while Mr. Benteed, the music teacher, teaches the class. He has another five minutes before it is time to return to his class. Most of his students passed the math test he is grading. A few didn't do as well. Mark writes down in a notebook the kids whose parents he must contact for a quick parent-teacher conference. He gets to Tim's paper, expecting to mark an "A" on the paper. Instead, he puts a "F." Tim is the only one who failed the test. As if in pain, Mark writes Tim's name in the book. With two minutes left, Mark runs to the main office and talks to Annette, the principal assistant.

"Hey, Annette, can you set up a parent-teacher conference with the parents of these students?"

"Sure, Mark. Anything for you." Annette takes the list from Mark. "The new kid, huh?"

"Yeah, I'm not sure why. It may just be that he needs time to adjust. I still want to give the parents a heads up, just in case."

"No problem."

Mark gives her a wink and leaves the main office in a rush to get back to his classroom. Just as he gets there, Mr. Benteed is just finishing with explaining the different notes played in a song. Mark stands by the doorway, with test papers in his hand, and watches the class. He pays close attention to Tim, whose eyes light up when Mr. Benteed says the next lesson is about the piano.

After the music teacher leaves, Mark sits at his desk and stares at the class. They all already know what is next. Mark smiles and starts calling names so each student can come to the desk and get their paper. One by one, each student comes up, showing a scared facial expression. For some, the expression changes to smiles, for others, frowns. Mark calls Betty's name and she comes up nervously. Mark doesn't hand her the paper right away but instead stares at her. She looks him dead in the eye until Mark finally smiles and hands her the paper. She grabs the paper and looks at it, eventually smiling from ear to ear. She sticks her hand in the air and Mark gives her a 'high five.'

"Trivia Fiesta Fridays, Mr. Cooke. You're looking at the new champion."

Mark smiles as Donald makes a noise with his mouth. His face is skeptical.

Next, Mark calls Tim to his desk. Tim doesn't look at Mark at all. Instead, he just grabs the paper from Mark and goes back to his seat.

Frankie calls from the front of the classroom, "Whacha get, Tim?"

"Frankie," Mark warns.

Tim says nothing but holds up his paper for the whole class to see. Every person in the class sees a big "F" in the top corner of the paper. As if all at once, the class gasps. Tim sets the paper down along with his head.

"Dude, you know Mr. C. is going to talk with your parents?"

"Frankie, that's enough." Mark looks at Frankie with a stern face. He glances at Tim and then starts teaching the class.

Mark gets home after a long day. He has the kids with him and they run into the house and up the stairs as soon as they get in the door. Mark walks around the house looking for Jade but instead finds a pink piece of paper stuck to the refrigerator.

At church. Dinner in oven. Be back soon.

ങ്ങൽ

Jade takes a seat in the empty sanctuary of the church and begins to pray. She bows her head down for a few seconds, not exactly sure of what to say. "I need help," she whispers. Just as she was beginning to say more, someone sits next to her. She looks to her side to see that it is her mother. "Mama, what are you doing here?"

The short and stout woman is wearing fashionable clothing, complete with a new pair of shoes. Her face is round and soft looking, not a mark or blemish on it. Her lips are full and her eyes are warm. She slides closer to Jade, looking over her with a discerning eye. "I'm always here at this time. The question is, why are you here . . . looking all depressed?"

Jade turns away from her mother and stares at the deep burgundy carpet of the sanctuary. "I needed some time to pray."

"Is everything okay?"

"It is."

"Then why are you here instead of work?"

Jade hesitates before saying anything.

"Go on, child. Out with it."

"I lost my job."

Jade's mother takes in a deep breath and slowly exhales. "Well, think of it this way, you, Mark, and the kids are stable. Mark makes a good living. He does well in the provision department. Many people go through the same but don't make it out as clean."

"I know, Mama. Other people, this, and other people, that. I know we're fine, *financially,* but what about emotionally? Mentally? My self-worth?"

"Your self-worth? It's a job, baby. You can get another one." Jade's mother squints her eyes as if she is trying to look through Jade. "Do you want to tell me what is really wrong?"

"That's it . . . I'm worthless. Look," Jade says as she gets up from the cushioned seat, "I have to get home. Mark and the kids are probably getting ready for dinner. I'll, uhhh . . . I'll see you later."

Jade rushes to grab her purse and Bible. Before she is able to get away, her mother grabs her arm.

"You know you can talk to me."

"I know, Mama. I need to sort some things out in my head, first."

Jade pulls away quickly and leaves the sanctuary. She loves her mother but finds it hard to talk to her on this matter especially, although she knows that her mother is the one person who could give her any sound advice. She leaves the church and goes home. On her way out, she smiles at Pastor Brentwood, the senior pastor of the church. He looks like he has something to say, but Jade whirls by him.

☙❧

Mark sits, staring at a chessboard, with Kalina on the opposite side of it. Charles studies the board as well while waiting for Kalina to make her move. Kalina places her hand on a few pieces before grabbing a knight and placing it in the middle of the board.

Mark smiles. "Try not to touch so many pieces before moving. In some tournaments, the first one you touch is the one you must move."

Kalina nods and stares at Mark as he sits thinking. After a few seconds, Mark makes his move. "Check."

Kalina becomes fidgety. She, in a hurry, scours the board for her next move.

"Don't get so panicky, Kalina. The game isn't over yet. You can't think your way out of a problem if you're so wound up."

"But the game is almost over!"

"It's only over when you give up."

Kalina tries to calm down but to no avail. She scoops up a piece and move it a few spaces down the board. Mark moves one of his pieces across the board. "Checkmate."

She stares at Mark smiling. "I did it again, didn't I?"

Mark nods and smiles. "It's okay. Keep practicing."

"You played a good game, Kalina," Charles says.

"Thanks. Daddy, when can I play in a t—"

The front door shuts as Jade comes into the living room. "Hey guys."

Mark smiles but notices that Kalina's face changes into a slight frown. Charles runs up to Jade and gives her a hug. "Hey, Mommy."

"Did ya eat yet?"

"Nope."

Jade looks up at Mark with a questioning look.

"As soon as we came back, we got into the game."

Jade purses her lips and looks down at the ground. "Okay. Well, it's time to eat. You all hungry?"

The kids smile and nod. Jade tells them to wash their hands and goes into the kitchen to fix their plates. Mark follows in close behind her.

"How are you doing?"

Jade looks puzzled. "What do you mean?"

"How are you holding up?"

"How do you think?"

"I don't know. I know you were in pretty rough shape before . . . and that I wasn't the biggest help."

"So now you want to talk to me?"

"I just want to make sure everything is okay."

"Everything is fine."

Jade grabs a few plates and pulls out a knife. Mark continues to stare at her.

"I'm sorry."

"For what?"

"For how you feel right now . . . for the whole situation . . . for my insensitivity towards the situation."

"It's okay. Everyone thinks the same thing you do. I can get another one . . . my job isn't my life . . . we can still live good. But, baby, you know how much this hurts?"

Mark slides over to Jade and wraps his arms around her. She moves more into his embrace, allowing his warmth to comfort her.

"Everything is going to be all right. Tomorrow is a new day."

"Yes, it is," Jade says, tears welling up in her eyes. "Tell me about your week. Any interesting kids stories?"

Mark looks surprised that she asked about his week. "Well, it's been interesting. I have a new student. He officially started on Monday. There was this big hype about how smart he is . . . then he proved how smart he is. Shocked the whole class."

"What did he do?"

"He turned into a calculator."

"He's really good at math?"

"Yeah, he is. But ... then he fails the math test we had a couple days later. It confuses me."

"Maybe he has trouble with test taking."

"Maybe. Either or, I have to meet with his parents. I have to meet with a lot of parents tomorrow."

"A lot of kids failed?"

"Yeah. Looks like I need to review this topic again. It's going to be a long day."

"When are you getting home?"

"Probably around seven or eight. But anyway, that's the only downside to my week. Everything else was good. Betty wants to beat Donald so badly on Friday."

"I remember you told me she barely lost last time."

"Yeah, and she's coming back with a vengeance. I had to yell at her for leaving written threats on Donald's desk."

"What?"

"Yeah. She's trying to shake him up."

Jade laughs. "Donald is cocky."

Mark smiles. The kids come back downstairs ready to eat as Mark and Jade set the table for dinner.

CHAPTER FIVE

CRAIG sits in his top floor condo, excited for the night to start. He's trying anything and everything to keep himself excited and not think about what happened between him and Berta. He's unsure of why he feels the way he does, or why he felt the way he did, but knows that a night out on the town could help in relieving some tension. His cell phone rings.

"Yo, man."

"I'm in the lobby. Near the giant indoor waterfall."

Craig hangs up and heads to the lobby to see Brett throwing pennies into the twenty foot tall waterfall.

"Need some good luck?" Craig asks.

"Not at all. Just doing it out of habit. A guy like me needs no luck."

They shake hands and hug for a quick second before Brett asks, "So how are you doing?"

Craig starts walking out the lobby and to the elevators. "Doing well. You know ... nothing spectacular."

"Nothing spectacular? What do you mean? All this money ... every woman on Earth wants you ... what do you mean nothing spectacular?"

"I'm more than money and women. I need ... I need that one woman."

"You still talking about that? That's crazy talk, man. Stop it, right now. My ears are immune to that kind of talking."

"You haven't changed much."

"Ha. Listen, I found another club. A new one just opened. It's a lounge type place that's supposedly high-class."

"High-class?"

"Yeah. A bunch of sophisticated business and executive women."

"Sounds interesting."

"I knew you would like the sound of that." Brett smiles. "It's a ways away, though."

"How far away?"

"Maybe an hour and a half south."

Craig looks to be in deep thought. "Just opened, huh?"

"Yeah, maybe like a month or so ago. I heard from a friend that it's becoming the place for us rich bachelors to go."

"I'm in."

"I knew you would be. Plus, what's a couple hours drive in a Porsche, right?"

Craig smiles. "About five minutes if there aren't any cops on the road."

They both step into an elevator. An attractive woman steps in with them. Brett's ears seem to poke up when he sees her. He looks over to Craig and directs his eyes towards the woman's backside. Craig shakes his head and points to his ring finger. Brett shrugs his shoulders.

"Excuse me," Brett says to the woman. "I can't help but notice the perfume you are wearing. May I ask what it is?"

The woman turns around to Brett and smiles. She looks at Craig and smiles even more.

"Who's your friend, Craig?"

"Kelly, this is Brett, a guy I went to school with."

"Brett, huh? Well, I wonder—"

"How's your husband?" Craig asks.

The woman gives Craig a dirty look. He looks over to Brett and sees him doing the same.

"He's fine," the woman says. "He's coming back from Iraq in a few months."

"When you talk to him, tell him I said, 'Hey.' He's a cool guy . . . a smart guy . . . a devoted guy. I respect guys like that." Craig shoots a look over to Brett who looks away.

"I'll be sure to tell him," the woman says. A few moments later, they reach her floor, and she exits the elevator. She shoots a quick look at Brett, who smiles and winks at her.

Craig waits for the elevator doors to shut before saying anything. "You're disgusting sometimes, you know that?"

"I did nothing wrong."

"She's married."

"I didn't know that, at first . . . but she did."

"I told you she's married. You knew."

"I didn't believe you."

"I'm seriously questioning this friendship."

"Okay, okay. My bad. I was in the wrong, I know. I can take accountability for my actions . . . but what about her?"

"What about her?"

"She obviously cheated on her husband before."

"So?"

"So, why did you stop me from partaking in the festivities?"

"Because in some way, shape, or form, it will come back to me. I know it will."

"Okay. I'll give you that one. But at the club tonight, I don't want to see any of this blocking activity."

"I wasn't blocking. I was saving your life."

Brett laughs. "How so?"

"If her husband got a hold of you, he would eat you . . . literally, he would eat you alive."

"I'd take my chances. She was a nice petite one . . . real tight. I know she works out. How do you live here knowing you can get that at any time?"

"It's not on the forefront of my mind and . . . she's married.

Craig and Brett step off the elevator and into Craig's condo.

"Nice place."

"Thanks."

"So seriously, when are you going to give up on the 'one for the rest of my life' idea?"

"I'm not."

"You don't understand. You have the money and the cars . . . one woman couldn't handle you."

"Why is it that money is all you think about?"

"Because that's all they think about. If I didn't have the money, most women wouldn't even look my way."

"So what about the ones that would? What about those who would be in your corner no matter what?"

"Those are usually the ugly ones."

Craig laughs. "That's not right. That's not right at all."

"I'm telling you, Craig. I'm a genius at this. The ones who care all the time usually are the ugly ones because that's all they have to draw men towards them . . . personality."

"So you're telling me that I'm actually holding out for an ugly woman?"

"If you keep doing what you're doing, yes."

Craig laughs even more. "Something is wrong with your logic."

"Look, I'm going to end with this . . . women nowadays aren't too interested in long lasting relationships either . . . they all think they're players and so on . . . like, if men can do it, why can't they? All I'm doing is keeping from being taken advantage of because, when you think about it, what is the exact thing that is happening to you? What would happen if you were to marry one of these women?"

Craig thinks for a second before Brett says, "Can we please go to the club now? This talk is killing the mood."

"Yeah, but what if there's a woman who has money and is attractive?"

"You know the answer to that . . . she's stuck up and not worth anything more than a quick screw in the car."

"Wow."

"Hey, I'm an honest man. This is all truth and you know it. There's no such thing as finding the one. Not anymore."

Craig grabs his jacket and they both leave the condo.

"How's that sexy secretary of yours? You get to her yet?"

"Who? Berta?"

"Yeah, man. If I were you, I would lay her down and—"

"Brett."

"No, seriously, she would get the star treatment. I would oil her up so n—"

"Cut it out, man. She's good people."

They get back into the elevator.

"You know, Craig, you are real territorial. Don't talk to her because she's in my building. Don't talk to her because she's my secretary. It is a free world, you know."

"Yeah, yeah. Cry me a river."

The elevator door closes.

Craig sits on a cushioned round chair as he scans the inside of one of the hottest clubs in town. Both he and Brett have been in the club for a few hours now, and it seems like as time goes on, it gets more crowded. The air smells of stale cigarettes, liquor, and sweat. Maybe that's what desperation smells like. Most of the women are halfway naked with mini-skirts and tight tops that leave nothing to the imagination. Most of the men have open shirts and grind on the backs of the women. Craig quickly begins to wonder why he decided to go, now having an unsettling feeling about it. He knows this isn't quite his scene but tries to make the best of it. For most of the night, he tries to figure out what each person does for a living. He chuckles a few times while making jokes to himself about a doctor by day, pole dancer by night.

Interrupting his mental comedy show, a tan skinned woman approaches Craig with a smile on her face. She is wearing a red off the shoulder dress that comes to her mid-thigh. Craig glances at her strong looking legs and her high heels. She sits next to him.

"Not up for dancing tonight?" she yells over the loud music.

"Not quite."

Craig notices the woman doesn't hold a drink in her hand; the first he's seen all night.

"It's not really mine, either."

Craig doesn't say anything at first, allowing the bass sounds of the fast paced music to fill the air between them. "Then why are you here?"

"Probably the same reason you're here." She smiles again.

Craig becomes captivated by her wide and bright smile. *Why is she here? She doesn't fit here anymore than I do.* She smells sweet and moves elegantly with even the slightest of movements. She holds out her hand.

"My name is Maya."

Craig grabs her hand, noting how soft it is. "I'm Craig."

She leans over towards his ear. "So why *are* you here? You seem different."

"I'm here with a friend. He's in town for a few days. You?"

"I'm here with a bunch of friends. They thought I needed to get out."

"You don't go out often?"

"Not at all. I'm usually too busy. There's also a lack of places to go to nowadays."

"That's true."

Across the club, Craig sees Brett staring at him with a grin on his face, nodding his head. Craig snaps his attention back towards Maya.

"I guess that's who you came with."

Craig smiles and nods.

"Listen, I'm not going to bother you too much more. Just needed a quick break. It was nice meeting you, Craig."

"It was nice to meet you too, Maya."

Maya gets up from the seat, smooths her dress down, and walks away. Craig follows her with his eyes as she sits with a bunch of other females at a table across the club. Brett makes his way over to Craig and sits down beside him.

"It's just like you to be one of the only ones sitting down and still pull a hottie like her. You get her number?"

"No. I didn't ask."

"What? Where did she go?"

"Back with her friends. Listen, you about ready to go?"

"Not before you get her number. Come on."

Brett gets up and grabs Craig's arm. He scans the club to look for where Maya went. Craig reluctantly gets up as Brett pulls him towards the table full of women. They stop in front of the table.

"Excuse me, ladies."

Each of the five women, including Maya, turn around at Brett's voice. Maya has a slight grin on her face. Craig smiles a bit at her but then looks at who is sitting next to her. His face drops as he recognizes who sits next to Maya. The woman's face is tight and round with perfect proportions. Her eyes are gray, but Craig knows they are really brown. He tries to nudge Brett so they can walk away, but Brett continues flirting.

"Brett, we have to go."

Maya looks back and forth between Craig and the woman, picking up on their locked glances. Brett remains oblivious to what's going on, still campaigning for himself. The woman stares at Craig in just as much shock as Craig stares at her. She looks away for a quick second. Then she grabs her coat and gets up from the table. The other women call her name as she rushes out the club.

"Donna!"

Brett looks at her strangely and leans over to Craig's ear.

"Am I coming on too strong?" he asks.

Craig ignores the question as anger begins to boil from within him. All he can think about is the five years of his life he unjustly lost and could never get back. All he can think about is what happened in jail, the things that he saw, and the hate that he had learned to feel from and towards others. Craig storms out the club after her.

"Maybe they had too many drinks," Brett says, trying to ease away the awkwardness of the situation. Brett then walks away from the table and goes after Craig.

Outside, Craig looks for Donna. He sees her far down the street but notices another person following close behind her. At this time of night, in this city, Craig knows that is never a good thing. He jogs to catch up to her. Donna continues to press forward, trying to make it to her car as quickly as possible. Just as Craig reaches her, the guy who was following her grabs her arm. She screams, thinking it was Craig, and looks in complete shock when she realizes that it is someone else. She looks at the dingy looking man who is holding her arm, paralyzed by fear.

"Hey, baby," the man says, showing his broken and missing teeth. "Why don't you give me some of that sweet cream you got popping over there?"

"Get your hands off me." Donna begins to tussle with the man but he is stronger than he looks. Craig grabs the man's free arm and puts it behind his back, pushing it up towards the back of his neck. The man screams as Craig continues to push up until he hears a crack in the arm. He then lets go as the man falls to the ground, his arm falling limp by his side, and stomps on his face. The man lies on the ground, knocked out completely. Donna stares at Craig, not knowing what to do next. Craig shakes his head, not knowing what to do, either. He knows what he wants to do, and that is to beat her into a lifeless mess. Instead, he motions her over to the parking lot and walks her to her car. They both remain silent as she turns off the car alarm. Just before she gets in, she stares at Craig, who is already beginning to walk away from the temptation.

"I'm sorry," she yells.

Craig stops walking and turns around to look at her. He slowly walks up to her so they are face-to-face.

"Do you think 'I'm sorry' is going to give me five years of my life back? Do you think it will stop me from wanting to bash your face in?"

"I don't expect anything from you I ju—"

"I don't care." Craig begins to walks away from her.

"Then why did you help me?"

Craig turns around again. "Because I'm not a lowlife like you are. I actually care about people and their lives and their dreams." Craig pauses as he begins to calm himself down. "But you know something, Donna? You *almost* ruined me. Three years prison. Two probation. Yeah, you almost ruined me. But I'm still here . . . I am still here . . ."

Donna blinks her eyes a few times before tears start streaming down her face. Craig walks to his car and jumps into it. He hauls out of the parking lot to see Brett standing in front of the club. He steers the car over and slams on the brakes. Brett opens the door.

"Hey, man is everything okay?"

"Get in."

"Naw. I have a ride, if you know what I mean."

"Then close my door . . . and don't call me again."

Brett looks confused and shuts the car door. Immediately after, Craig screeches off, leaving a trail of smoke behind him.

⋈

Berta sits in a restaurant with Candace, her longtime friend, her best friend, for lunch. Candace chomps on a sandwich while Berta sips on her drink.

"I don't get him. I don't get him at all," Berta says.

"Wait, wait, wait, let me get this straight. You slapped him?"

"You're darn right I did."

"Why?"

"Because he is stupid."

"And you are just finding this out?"

"C'mon, Candace. I'm serious."

"I'm serious too. I'm getting near to the brim on all these stories of Craig and his issues. I still don't get why you deal with him beyond the boss–employee relationship."

"You know why."

"I know you feel something for him. I don't understand why."

"Because I do. Okay?"

"Fine." Candace takes another bite of her sandwich. "Just this last thing. I know I said this before," she wipes her mouth, "and I will say it again. You are too beautiful on the inside and out to put your entire life on hold for so long . . . for one man . . . who doesn't know where he's going."

"I know it doesn't make sense. Just trust me; I know what I am doing."

The waiter comes up to their table and sets down a drink. He tells Berta that a man across the restaurant ordered the drink for her. Berta looks to where the waiter is pointing to see a handsome man in a suit. He smiles at her. Berta then leans closer towards the waiter.

"Can you send this back to him and tell him thanks, but I don't drink."

Both the waiter and Candace look at Berta strangely.

"He looks good, Berta," Candace chimes in her opinion.

The waiter grabs the drink and goes back to the man's table. A few moments later, the man stands up with the drink and walks over towards Berta.

"And he's tall," Candace says.

Berta snaps her head towards Candace. "You shut up."

The man gets to their table and gently sets the drink back on it. In a deep and soothing voice, he says, "I'm sorry. Maybe I should have told the waiter to let you know this is iced tea."

"Maybe."

Berta feels Candace gently kicking her under the table.

"I'm Rodger. I ju—"

"Listen, umm, Rodger, I don't want you to waste your time but I'm not really looking for anything right now, and my friend here is married so . . ."

"Oh. Umm, I'm sorry to have bothered you." The man takes a step back. "Enjoy your lunch." He walks back to the other side of the restaurant.

Berta turns to look at Candace. She stares at Berta in shock.

"You're kidding me right?"

"What? I'm not interested."

"He was cute . . . and polite."

"So?"

"Forget it. I don't know what to do with you."

Berta smiles and takes another sip of her drink. "You get used to it after a while."

"Get used to what? I never got hit on as much as you do."

Berta smiles again.

"So how long do you plan to wait?"

"As long as it takes."

"And if he finds someone . . . that isn't you?"

"He won't." Berta smiles and gazes out the window.

CHAPTER SIX

MARK sits down at his desk and looks at Tim's file. He glances over the address, recognizing that he lives in a lower income area. He hears a few people walking down the hallway towards the classroom. He gets a glimpse of the parents' names, only seeing the father's name, Jacob Langley. He flips the file shut, sets it on his desk, and then stands up to greet Tim and his parents. Tim comes walking in with his head down. He looks up at Mark with a sad face. A few moments later, just his mother comes into the room and stands behind him. She stares at Mark with a plain look. Mark stares at her in complete shock. For a while, both stare at each other, not saying a word. Mark studies the woman's shoulder length brown hair, her hazel colored eyes, and her milk chocolate colored skin. Tim stares back and forth between the two, confused by what is happening.

"Mommy, this is my teacher, Mr. Cooke."

Both look down at Tim, dazed and confused. Eventually, Mark speaks.

"Hello, Mrs. Langley. Mark Cooke." Mark puts out his hand.

Tim's mother narrows her eyes at Mark but does not shake Mark's hand. Mark puts his hand back at his side without removing his eyes from hers. "Please, have a seat." He turns around to sit in a chair he pulled in front of them. Both Tim and his mother take a seat.

Mark feels as if he's out of his body as he sits down on the chair. Several questions run through his head with few answers. Mrs. Langley stares at Mark, seemingly to stare a hole right through him.

"Okay. Well, this meeting, as you know, is because Tim received a failing grade on his math test. I usually meet with the parents when this happens, but I fully understand that this is all new for Tim. I just wanted to let you know that I think your son is great and very intelligent. I don't believe there is a major cause for concern at this point."

Tim looks at Mark and smiles.

"Then why did you call this meeting, Mr. Cooke?" Mrs. Langley says in an annoyed tone.

"It's one of my policies. It also gives me a chance to know a little bit more about Tim and his parents."

She stares at Tim for a few seconds and then back at Mark. "Don't worry. He will be fine. Is there anything of any substance you need to talk about?"

Mark pauses and looks at the annoyed face of Tim's mother. "Nothing too serious, I guess. I just . . . wanted . . . this is . . ."

She begins to grab her things to leave. Mark stares at her in his bewildered state.

"Alicia."

She turns around to face Mark, shaking her head. "I'm sorry; do I know you from somewhere?"

Mark stares wide-eyed at the woman, hesitating for a while. "No. No, you don't."

"Oh, okay. Then, please, call me Mrs. Langley." She winks at Mark.

The woman grabs Tim's hand and walks out of the classroom. On their way out, Tim smiles and says, "See you tomorrow, Mr. Cooke."

Mark sits at the desk for a few more minutes. He grabs Tim's file to double check on his mother's name.

"Alicia Langley," he says.

Right after he reads her name, he grabs his cell phone and calls Craig.

"Hey, man you still meeting me at the gym?"

"You know it. I need to run about three marathons."

"You've been having a great week too?"

"Yeah, just dandy."

"Well, I'm headed over there now."

"No prob. I'll see you there."

Mark gets off the phone and rushes out of the school.

⚘

Craig hangs up his phone and thinks about his adventures of the previous night. Berta comes through on his intercom.

"Mr. Barlow . . ." Normally, Berta only uses his last name when someone else is present, but lately, she has been using it every time she addresses Craig. "I have a Maya Grange here for you."

Craig's ears perk up at the name. He clicks the intercom. "Thanks, Berta. Please, send her in."

A few seconds later, Maya comes into the office with a grin on her face.

"So you do remember me."

Craig gets up and lightly hugs Maya. "Of course, I do. What brings you here?"

"Well, this morning, I had a talk with my friend, Donna."

Craig steps back. "Okay."

"Apparently, you knew her?"

Craig nods.

"Well, she told me how great of a guy you are and how you're a great catch and so on."

"She told you what?"

Maya takes a step closer towards Craig. "Look, I'm very forward about this dating thing, so I'm going to just come out and say it. I had fun for the few minutes we were together. Do you want to go out to dinner sometime?"

Craig stares at her with his mouth wide open. "Donna told you I was a good guy?"

"Yes, she did. She told me about what happened outside the club. You're quite the hero."

"Oh?"

"Yes, indeed. If you weren't there, who knows what would have happened, and it's a shame because she's already been through so much."

"Been through so much?"

"How well do you know her?"

"Well enough."

"Then, you know about her situation?"

"Situation?"

"The sexual assault."

"Oh. Yeah, I know about that. What does she say about that?"

"Not much. It seems she was torn up over what happened at the club. Must have brought up memories. Anyway, Donna suggested that I come here . . . see if you felt the same."

Craig looks at Maya with a strained face. "No. This can't work. I'm sorry."

Maya's face changes slightly. She maintains her composure. "Well . . . it was worth a shot. If you ever ch—"

"I won't change my mind."

"I don't understand. Was it me?"

"No. Look, Maya, you are really nice . . . almost perfect, but Donna has misled you. I'm not some normal guy who came to her rescue."

"I knew it, you two used to date."

"No . . . it's not that at all. I . . . I am part of that sexual assault."

Maya stares at Craig, not fully understanding what he is trying to say. "What do you mean?"

"The case was against me, but I di—"

Immediately, Craig regrets saying anything as Maya's face shifts from blissfully happy and confident to angry and confused.

"What?"

Craig takes a step forward, but Maya jerks backward.

"The case was falsely br—"

Maya hurls the palm of her hand towards Craig's face and it lands right on his jaw. She slaps Craig a lot harder than Berta did, causing him to stumble back. After a few seconds of staring Craig in his eyes, she turns around and leaves.

Craig walks over to his desk, snaps up his briefcase, and snatches up his gym bag from the floor. On the way to the elevators, he passes Berta and shoots fiery darts with his eyes her way.

Inside the elevator, he yells, "Why am I always getting slapped?"

CHAPTER SEVEN

"**I** don't know. Is this 'slap Craig week,' or what?"

"You brought it on yourself."

"You think?"

Craig and Mark talk as they take a jog around the outdoor track at a local college campus. The sun is just about to go down, but the stadium lights are on still. Everyone else that was on the track heads towards the gym.

"Why would you claim that you are a rapist?"

"Why wouldn't I? Again, I went to jail for it."

"I know that but . . . you didn't commit the crime."

"But it still feels like I did."

"The fact is you didn't. Anyway, why did this other woman slap you?"

Craig and Mark stop jogging and walk to the bleachers.

"That's a long story, but to sum it up, I ran into Donna."

"Donna who?"

"Donna, Donna. Sexual assault Donna."

"Oh." Mark looks concerned.

"I saw her in a club that I went to last night."

"You went to a club? That's passé for you, isn't it?"

"It is, but Brett came down and wanted to hang out. You remember Brett, right?"

"Yeah, I remember him. He's a jerk. Why did you go out with him?"

"That's neither here nor there. Wont happen again. But Donna, in the club . . . is friends with this absolutely gorgeous woman that I also met in the club."

"Okay."

"Donna runs from the club, and for some reason, I follow her."

"Risky move."

"I know, but I had to, and then this guy tried to get her."

"Get her?"

"You know, get her. Take advantage of her . . . forcefully."

"Wait, wait," Mark says. He begins to stretch. "You're at a club, see Donna, and save her from someone who was trying to assault her . . . you . . . the same guy that she falsely accused of the same crime. How's that for irony?"

"Irony can take a jump off a cliff."

"So where in this do you get slapped?"

"Oh. So the woman I met at the club, her name is Maya, comes to my job today. Apparently, Donna talked me up to her. Now Maya wants me."

"And you want Maya."

"Yup. But here's the snag . . . she knows about the assault . . . so I had to tell her the case was against me. She was going to find out anyway."

"And here's where she slaps you."

"I mean, she took some of my skin with her hand, she slapped me so hard."

"Wow. So what are you going to do?"

"Leave it alone. I'm still trying to get over running into Donna."

"Well, it looks like we might be in the same boat."

"What do you mean?"

"I think I ran into Alicia today."

Craig stops in his tracks and stares at Mark. "No way."

"She acted like she didn't know me."

"Where did you see her?"

"She's one of my student's parents."

Craig stands still with a sick feeling deep in his stomach. "That doesn't sound good."

"I know, but I'm not too worried about it. We're all adults here. She's married and everything." Mark begins to laugh. "I didn't think when I asked you to come and live with me, all those years ago, that you would bring the past and everyone in it with you."

"Ha-ha. Very funny. Trust me, this is drama that I can do without. This world is too small."

"In other words, I didn't move far enough from PA."

"That too. Hey, how are Jade and the kids?"

They begin to walk back to the gym. "They're good. Well, the kids are. Jade lost her job."

"That stinks. Is she good?"

"Yeah, I think. She's been acting weird lately. They just let her go. No real explanation . . . nothing."

"You guys are good financially, right?"

"Oh, yeah. We're fine. I always saved for times like this. You may as well call me the Federal Reserve."

Craig chuckles. "Did she apply for unemployment?"

"No. We never really talked about it."

Craig glances at Mark. "Then I would go and fight for her job back."

"What?"

"I would go to that place and demand explanations . . . and her job back. I wouldn't take this one on the chin; especially the way times are now."

"I don't know. I'll talk to her some more about it."

They both get back inside the gym and go to the weights.

"I can imagine Jade having a real tough time right now," Craig says.

"Why do you say that?"

"Well, she has always struck me as independent. But you know what I really find strange?"

"What's that?"

"Is she taking this on the chin?"

"That's what it seems."

"When has that ever been Jade?"

Mark looks at Craig. "Never. She has more fight than any woman I have ever seen."

"Exactly. Something doesn't seem right here, man."

"You're right." Mark looks at the ground. "You think some foul play?"

"Maybe. But there's only one way to find out."

CHAPTER EIGHT

MARK sits at his desk at the school wondering if he should go to Jade's old job and ask for explanations and possibly her job back. On one hand, he believes it couldn't hurt, as there is nothing at stake. On the other hand, there isn't much point in trying. As each day passes, Jade is getting better and more comfortable with the way that things are. Mark gets a wrenching feeling in his gut. A few questions pop into his head. He doesn't understand why she would be fired after so long. She clearly was the most productive worker at the pharmacy. He doesn't understand why she seems to just take it. With those questions still raging in his head, he decides to go to the pharmacy on his lunch break. The art teacher is to teach after lunch, so he has a bit more time to work with. Mark wants answers. And he realizes that sitting back and watching life unfold won't do anything to help.

CZ80

"So to what can I say this visit is for?"

Jade steps into her parents' home, a mansion, and hugs her mother. She greets the butler and follows her mother to the sunroom. "I need to ask you for a favor," Jade says.

"What do you need?"

"Do you mind taking the kids for a weekend . . . this weekend?"

"Sure. Why?"

"I have something planned for the weekend."

"Oh. Yes, that isn't a problem at all. Your father would love that, too."

Both become silent, lounging in their chairs, relaxing under the warm sun.

"So," Jade's mother says, "You came all this way just to ask me that?"

"I was in the area."

"I doubt that. What else is on your mind?"

“”

Mark stands outside the pharmacy, Jade's old job. He takes a deep breath and walks inside the building. As soon as he steps in, he is greeted by Mr. Oglesby, who has his back turned towards him while writing a few notes. He doesn't notice that it is Mark in the store until he speaks.

"Hey, Mr. Oglesby. How are you?"

Mr. Oglesby turns around and smiles at Mark. "Hey, Mark. How are you?" He takes off his thick glasses to clean them with a cloth. Moments later, he pushes the frames back onto his face. "It's been some time since I've seen you. Everything okay?"

"Yes, it is. Do you have a few seconds to talk?"

"Sure, I do—Vanessa," he calls across the store, "Take the front for me for a few minutes."

A young woman comes from the break room to stand by the cash register. Mr. Oglesby then motions Mark to a different room, which looks like his office. "What can I help you with?"

"I came to talk to you about Jade."

"Jade," Mr. Oglesby sighs. "She was the best worker for this place, ever. How is she doing?"

Mark looks confused. "She's good. I was just wondering why she was let go?"

"Let go?"

"Yes, sir."

Mr. Oglesby gawks at Mark through his glasses, which make his eye look twice their size.

◯◯◯

Jade turns her head to look at her mother, who is reclining in her chair. "I'm having trouble in my marriage."

Jade's mother slowly sits up and stares at her. "What kind of trouble? What happened?"

"For the past few months, Mark and I haven't been on the same page with . . . anything. I think the kids should play sports, but he thinks they should get into the arts. I think we have too many obligations at the church, but he thinks we don't have enough. He wants more sex . . ." Jade looks at her mother, feeling a bit embarrassed.

"I'm guessing you don't?"

Jade nods her head. "I don't understand. Somehow we reached a point where there's a disconnect. I'm not sure how to fix it."

"Have you talked to him about it?"

"No. Mark is so blasé-blah about everything. It's always, 'Whatever you want, dear.' It makes me sick. He focuses more on his job and the kids than on me."

"But you haven't talked to him about it?"

"No. I haven't."

"So I guess that is what the weekend is for?"

"Yes . . . amongst other things."

"Is some of this stemming from you losing your job?"

"Oh, Mama, I didn't lose my job. I quit." Jade whips her face away from her mother.

Ϙ

"I'm sorry, Mr. Oglesby, I don't quite understand."

"We would never let go a quality worker like Jade. She handed in a resignation letter and that was that."

"Why did she quit?" Mark asks as he stares at Mr. Oglesby in confusion.

Mr. Oglesby takes off his glasses to clean them again. He now seems hesitant with his words. "I honestly don't know. The letter didn't say much other than when her last day would be. I thought you would know the answer to that one."

"Truth is … I don't."

"Oh." Mr. Oglesby leans back in his chair.

"So if she was to ask if she could work for you again, you would say what?"

"I would say, without hesitation, 'Yes, indeed.' No questions asked. But listen, I have to get back to work. I can't leave Vanessa out there too long."

Mark slowly stands up from his chair as Mr. Oglesby leads him out the office.

"Mark, whenever you see Jade, tell her I said hello."

"I will. Thanks for talking with me."

"Anytime, Mark. Take care."

Mark and Mr. Oglesby walk out the office, Mark heading out the pharmacy and Mr. Oglesby allowing the young woman, Vanessa, to take another break. Before leaving, Mark grabs a bag of candy for the kids in his class, and heads to the register. Mr. Oglesby rings him up and

71

smiles while doing it. Just before Mark leaves the store, Mr. Oglesby says, "Don't be a stranger."

Mark waves and walks out of the pharmacy as the bell on the glass door rings.

Down at the corner of the building, Vanessa is taking a smoke break. She sips in some smoke from her cigarette and stares at Mark. She gives him an odd look, motioning him to come over without ever doing so. Mark walks towards her. She only makes one statement and stamps out her cigarette before walking back into the pharmacy.

"She left because of Boley."

Mark stands there for a few seconds before walking to his car and driving back to school.

ᘓᘔ

"His name is Greg Boley. Married man with four kids. He is the biggest jerk I have met in my entire life."

"Isn't this the man who you worked with since you started years ago?"

"Yes, Mama, he is."

"I've met the man before. When did he become such a jerk?"

"He became a jerk when he kissed me. He became a jerk when he made me feel something that Mark hasn't made me feel in years."

Jade's mother becomes silent. Slowly, she lets out a sigh and shakes her head. "Jade, baby, what have you done?"

"I don't know. I'm so confused. One moment, I love Mark with all my heart and soul, but the next I want to be with Greg. It takes so much to get him out of my mind."

"How did it happen?"

"How do you think? We've been working together, side by side, for years, telling each other about . . . everything. We were each other's confidant. We had each other's back. He consoled me . . . I consoled him . . . and it turns out that our spouses do more harm than good."

"Now, you wait one moment. I've already heard enough. Hear this clearly; Mark is a good man, a devoted and loyal man. A man you married and made vows to. This isn't some guy on the street you're talking about. You are talking about your *husband*."

"Mama, I know."

"You don't act like you know."

"But, Mama, you don't understand."

"I do understand . . . and I can see the impending danger. So what is this weekend for, again?"

Jade doesn't say anything at first. "I'm going to tell him the truth."

"Wait. So, let me get this straight. When you first married Mark, you were upset about the way he was. You wanted him to do everything your way. Essentially, you wanted a butler, not a husband. But now that he has given in to some of your control, you're angry for what he has become. Because of that, you cheat on him with a man who gave you a fleeting feeling of infatuation. Am I correct?"

Jade stays silent at first. "I didn't cheat."

"How do you figure that?"

"I never slept with him."

"But you gave him parts of you, did you not? All it takes is the right opportunity correct?"

"Maybe."

She shakes her head vigorously. "If anything, your father and I should apologize to Mark."

"For what?"

"Because we have spoiled you rotten."

Suddenly, the warm air from the sun isn't enough to warm the cool space that exists between Jade and her mother.

"We will take the kids this weekend. What *you* ought to do is think about what you're going to do . . . if you still really want to be married, because your attitude about what's going on is appalling . . . like it is some triviality to be married. Own up to what you've done. Lying to yourself does no one good."

Jade's mother gets up from her seat and leaves Jade there sitting alone.

⊂੩੪⊃

Mark sits in his car in the teacher's parking lot trying to compose himself. He doesn't know any details, but he is angry with Boley. He believes that Boley forced Jade out so he could pull in more money. *He does have four kids.* He plays the entire story out in his head. *Sabotage . . . that's what he did. He set her up.* Mark assumes jealousy had a part in it as well. Jade was a hard worker that gained much recognition for her work. It would only be natural for a man to be jealous of a woman who does better work than him. Mark gets out his car and rushes back to the classroom. On the way, he thinks, *But why would Jade hide that? Why would she lie?*

Mark gets to the classroom just in time for the art teacher to leave. The kids look at him in anticipation, knowing that today is Trivia Fiesta Friday.

CHAPTER NINE

JADE eventually gets home and flops on the couch. She kicks her shoes off and lets them fly onto the wood floor. Sitting in silence, she stares at a picture of her and Mark and snatches it off the wall. She clutches it, pressing it to her chest, as in a hug, and begins to weep.

"Lord, please forgive me. I know this is not who you have created me to be . . . a soon to be adulteress. I know what I have to do. I know what I must do to make this right. Please . . . please . . . just give me the strength to do the right thing." She curls up into a ball, nestling herself into the cushions of the couch and falls asleep still clinging to the picture.

☙❧

"Okay, guys, for the first time in the history of Trivia Fiesta Fridays we have a three-way tie going into the final round."

The kids in the room stare at the three that stand at the front of the classroom with bright eyes.

"We have Betty, Donald, and our newcomer, Tim."

The class cheers.

"Mr. C," Donald says, "I think we should make this a bit more interesting. If my competitors agree, we should have harder questions this time."

"You want harder questions? Betty? Tim?"

Betty looks at Mark and then angrily at Donald. "Yeah. Give the hard ones."

Mark then looks at Tim. He puts his head down at first, but then says, "That's fine with me," in a quiet tone.

Mark nods his head and grabs a different set of cards for this round. "Okay, guys. This round is going a little differently. I'll ask each of you a question. You get one wrong, you are eliminated. We'll do that until we crown this week's champion. Donald, as our reigning champion, here is your first question."

For the next twenty minutes, Donald, Betty, and Tim answer questions ranging over many topics as the excitement from the rest of the class begins to build.

"Betty, here is your next question. Who painted the 'Mona Lisa?'"

"Leonardo Da Vinci," Betty says proudly.

"That is correct." Mark looks down to see he is out of cards. "It looks like we're at a stalemate here. We are out of cards."

"Go into the adult trivia," Donald says, looking for an advantage. Both Betty and Tim nod their heads.

Mark grabs another set of cards. "Tim, your question is . . . What are the holes in Swiss cheese called?"

The whole class, including Mark, looks dumbfounded. Betty and Donald, for the first time since starting the competition, look rattled. Tim looks down, deep in thought.

"Eyes?"

Mark pauses. "Correct." Everyone breathes a sigh of relief and claps their hands. "Donald, your question . . . How many quarts of blood does the average human body contain?"

Donald's eyes get wide. He takes a few moments before answering. "Seven?"

Mark looks at Donald. "I'm sorry, Donald, the correct answer is six."

The classroom erupts into cheers, knowing their long-running and sometimes arrogant champion has been dethroned. Donald takes his seat, shaking his head in disgust.

"Betty, your question is . . .Who invented the aero plane?"

Betty looks hard at Mark. She then smiles. "The Wright brothers, Orville and Wilbur."

"Correct. Tim, your question is . . . How many oceans are there?"

Mark notices Tim looking out the corner of his eye at Betty. He blurts out, "Six."

Long pause.

"Sorry, Tim. The correct *answers* are four or five, depending on if you count the Arctic Ocean. Which means, Betty, you are our new champion of the week."

Betty jumps up and down as the whole class cheers for her. Tim gives her a pat on the shoulder and walks to his seat. Mark notices Tim smiling on his way back. The school bell rings just as he sits in his seat. The class then begins to pack up their things to go home.

"Have a good weekend, everyone." Mark puts up his hand for Betty to give him a high five. "Good job today." Betty smiles and runs off with her bag of candy and homework pass.

After a few minutes, the entire class is empty and Mark grabs his briefcase to leave as well. He rushes out the school to go pick up Kalina and sees Tim still waiting for his ride home. He is the only one still waiting near the parking lot. Mark walks up to him.

"Good job today, Tim."

Tim turns around and looks at Mark. "Thanks, Mr. Cooke. It was fun."

"So you let her win, huh?"

Tim's face drops. "Am I in trouble?"

"No. Not at all. I'm just curious on why."

Tim looks Mark in the eyes for the first time. "She deserved it. Betty worked hard for it. You should get things for working hard like she did."

Mark smiles at Tim's generosity. He kneels down next to him. "So you like her, huh?"

"What? Me? No way. I don't like her. Ewww." Tim becomes fidgety.

Mark smiles as a car pulls up in front of the two. Alicia pops out the car and walks towards Tim, ignoring Mark.

"Hello, Mrs. Langley."

"Hello. Tim, we have to go."

"Mrs. Langley, do you have a few seconds?"

"No, I do not." Alicia gently moves Tim to the backseat of the car while getting back in herself. Mark moves to her window.

"I just wanted to tell you that Tim did great in class today."

"I know he did. Thank you." She buckles her seat belt and drives off, leaving a trail of dust behind her.

ಀಀ

"Mommy," Tim says, "Why are you so mean to Mr. Cooke?"

"I'm not mean to him, darling."

"It seemed mean to me. Mr. Coo—"

"Tim," Alicia says in a warning tone. "Mind your manners."

Tim sighs and stares out the window.

ಀಀ

Mark gets home with Charles and Kalina following closely behind him. He is exhausted from the day and even more drained from the thoughts that plague his mind. The kids begin to run upstairs when a voice comes from around the corner.

"Don't run up there yet. I have a surprise for you two."

Kalina comes back downstairs and walks out of Mark's view.

"Mom, we're going to be late for practice."

"No, you're not. You're not going today."

Kalina's mouth drops open. Charles jumps a few steps down and runs down the hallway out of Mark's view as well. Mark twists his face up in confusion and walks around the corner. He looks at Jade, who has a wide smile on her face.

"So where are they going?" Mark asks.

"Well, they are going to Grandma and Grandpa's . . . for the weekend."

Mark blankly stares at Jade as Kalina and Charles jump up and down in joy.

"Go upstairs and pack your things. Kalina, help your brother."

Both kids run upstairs and start packing. Mark continues to stare at Jade.

"What's wrong?" Jade asks.

"Nothing. What's the plan for the weekend?"

"Me and you time. I figured we were interrupted last week . . . so a weekend should give us time . . . we can still go to church for the marriage ministry and service and still have time to spend with each other."

"Oh. What's the occasion?"

"Does there have to be one?" Jade wrinkles her forehead.

"No. I guess not."

"Well, I'll take them there and then I'll come back and make dinner. Sound good?"

"It does."

Jade walks up to Mark and kisses him softly. She then goes upstairs to make sure the kids pack what they need for the weekend. Mark stands in the hallway feeling numb. The kiss was empty. It didn't feel like there was anything behind it. More thoughts run through his head. *She's hiding something, but I don't know if I want to know what it is.*

It doesn't take long for the kids to pack up, and they follow Jade downstairs and out the door to the car with their bags in hand. Jade gives Mark another kiss before she leaves. Again, Mark feels nothing. When they leave, he grabs his cell phone and calls the pharmacy. When Mr. Oglesby picks up, he disguises his voice and asks for Vanessa. She gets on the phone a few moments later. As soon as she says hello, he gets to the point.

"What did you mean she left because of Boley? What does he have to do with anything?"

Long pause.

"Take this number down. I'm almost off work . . . call me in ten minutes."

Mark records the number in his phone and waits as he sits on the couch. He feels the anticipation rise into his throat, making it hard to breathe. Another feeling mixes with the anticipation. It makes his whole body shake, something he hasn't felt in a long time. He feels fear and he isn't sure of how to manage it. A few moments later, he calls Vanessa back. A few rings later, she picks up the phone. She sounds like she has her speakerphone on while driving.

"Mark, I'm sorry for all of this."

"Just tell me what Boley had to do with this."

"Well . . . Jade . . . Boley . . . they had some sort of workplace relationship."

Mark's anxiety heightens. "What do you mean? Give me details."

"They always took lunch together. They would treat each other as if they were together. It made things awkward working there."

"So why didn't you tell your boss?"

"You think Mr. Oglesby would believe me? You think he would care either way? He wasn't losing his best two employees. No way. Plus, I didn't believe it at first."

"So what made you believe?"

Vanessa sighs. "I overheard them . . ."

Mark clenches his jaw. He doesn't want to hear what she ends the sentence with but listens anyway.

". . . Talking."

Some tension is relieved, but not for long.

"They were setting up a date . . . flirting and stuff like that. They thought I had left for the evening."

"So why did she quit?"

"I think she finally got a conscience . . . I'm sorry . . . I mean, I think she knew she was wrong and had to pull away. From the looks of it, she had only two choices: to go with you wholeheartedly . . . or him. She chose you, I guess . . ."

Mark sighs.

"I'm sorry Mark."

"Please, don't."

"No. You don't understand. You are a good man. And with all due respect to your wife, I hate women like her."

"Like what?"

"Women that aren't satisfied with what they have . . . women that have a good thing at home but decide to go elsewhere . . . it's hard enough to find a good man as it is . . . women like her make it ten times harder. Women like her d—"

"Okay. That's enough. I get it."

"Sorry."

"Boley is married, isn't he?"

"Yeah, he is, and his wife has no idea. She's pregnant with their fifth child."

Mark leans back in his seat. "Is there anything else?"

"I'm sure there is . . . but that's all I know."

"Okay. Thanks"

"Yeah. Again, I'm sorry."

"Yeah."

Mark hangs up the phone.

♞♞

Jade gets to the front of her parent's house and parks the car. Charles and Kalina bounce up and down in excitement. As soon as Jade parks, her mother and father come out the door. Kalina unbuckles her seat belt and runs out the car. Jade helps Charles out of the car and he runs behind Kalina. Jade's mother gives both kids a hug and a kiss on the cheek and meets Jade in the driveway.

"You decide what you are going to do?"

"I did. I want my marriage to work . . . and the right thing to do is tell him."

"And then what?"

"Hope for the best."

Jade's mother stares at her. She then gives her a hug. "I'm praying for you two."

Jade almost melts in her mother's arms. She begins to cry. "There's a chance that it's over, isn't there?"

"There is, but stay prayerful, child. Stay strong. If you feel that this is the right thing to do, do it wholeheartedly."

CHAPTER TEN

CRAIG sits in a small café that's down the street from his office building. He takes a big gulp of his lemonade before staring at a few papers in front of him. He had decided that he needed a change in scenery for the workday, so he took his work on the road. He still isn't saying much of anything to Berta, other than what is necessary for the job, and it seems that Berta is playing it the same way. Still looking down at some files, someone steps up to his table. Craig puts his hand over his cup.

"No more lemonade for me. If I drink any more, I'll burst. And I don't think you want that on your conscience." Craig smiles as he continues to look down. The person doesn't move at all, but stands there. Craig finally looks up. It's Maya.

Craig doesn't say anything and stares at her. He begins to pack up his things. She sits down.

"Please, don't leave," she says.

Craig continues to pack up his things, stuffing papers into his briefcase.

"Craig, please."

Craig stops packing and leans back in his chair. He just stares at her, as if he's becoming impatient.

"I went by your office today." She relaxes in her seat. "I wanted to apologize."

"Apology accepted," Craig says as he begins packing again.

"No. Wait. I wanted to apologize for me . . . and for women like Donna."

Craig stops in his tracks and stares intently at Maya. "What do you mean?"

Maya clears her throat. "I know . . . everything. Donna told me . . . everything."

Craig smiles in an attempt to hide his anger and embarrassment. "That's impossible. Not even Donna knows everything."

"Well, I know you were accused of something that you didn't do."

Craig waits for Maya to explain herself.

"I talked to Donna last night. Actually, we all talked to Donna last night. She told us what she did, accusing you of rape. Setting up her defense with other coworkers that were after you . . . the whole nine yards."

"Okay."

"She told us why she did it . . . and why she couldn't go on with it any longer. She told us about the good man you are . . . and why I was wrong for my actions."

Craig grabs his briefcase and gets up from the table. As he walks away, Maya follows him. They leave the café.

"I just want another chance," Maya says, still following Craig.

Craig abruptly stops and turns around to look at her. "So do I," he yells. "But life doesn't work that way. You make do with what happens to you and the decisions you made and go on from there. There aren't any second chances. Ever."

He turns around and storms away from Maya, leaving her standing there speechless.

Craig makes it back to the office with Berta staring him right in the eyes. He turns away from her and continues to his office.

"Maya left something for you," she says.

Craig stops and looks at Berta, whose soft and caring look still isn't enough for him to let down any defenses. She points at the end of the desk to an envelope. Craig snatches it up, throws it into the wastebasket next to Berta's desk, and storms into his office, slamming the door behind him.

✸

Mark sits, slumped in his seat, watching TV. With the remote control in his hand, he flips through the channels, not really watching any of them. He sits in the basement, his self-proclaimed "man room," trying to keep himself together. He doesn't fully believe the girl from Jade's job but recognizes that at this point, she has no real reason to lie. Of course, that has never stopped people from lying to him in the past.

He hears Jade enter the house and starts to go upstairs. For now, he will play it safe. He won't say a thing about it, but he will look for some change in the way she acts towards him. *But Jade is smart, so her behavior might not change at all.* Mark sighs and puts his head down at the thought. Walking up the stairs, with each step echoing in his head, he thinks a quick prayer. *Lord, I don't know what is going on here, but I trust you. I trust that you will reveal to me what I need to know. I trust that what is hidden right now will be uncovered. I need you now, Lord. This feeling in the pit of my stomach is getting worse, but I am listening for you. I am waiting for a move, Lord, and no matter what happens, I will continue to bless Your name. In the name of Jesus . . .*

"Amen," Mark says at the top step.

He sees Jade hang her jacket up in the coat closet and turn towards him. She walks over to him with a smile on her face.

"This entire weekend, it's just me and you, bud." She gives Mark a kiss.

Mark halfway smiles.

"There are also some things we have to talk about."

"Things that require the kids to leave?"

"Sort of. I figured that would give us more time together. We haven't had much alone time lately . . . and we should have that time."

Mark stares at Jade, who stares back with her soft eyes. He can read nothing from her face. "I see. What is it that we have to talk about?"

Jade whirls around, walks away, and starts digging through the kitchen drawer. "Us . . . our marriage . . . the kids." She pulls out a menu. "How's take out for tonight?"

"I don't have much taste for it. Can we talk about everything now? I don't want to wait a full weekend before we do."

Jade, with her back turned towards Mark, has a strained facial expression, which she changes as she turns around to answer him. "Sure. We can talk about things now. I'll make dinner afterwards." She walks over to the couch and sits down.

Mark follows but doesn't sit down immediately. He prepares himself for the worst. Jade looks at him with the same soft and gentle expression that made him fall in love with her six some odd years ago. He then sits down beside her. She motions Mark closer towards her and tugs on him to get him to lie on her. Mark leans back against her, resting his head on her chest and his torso between her legs. Jade rubs his shoulder.

"I know I haven't been the best wife in the world," she says. She feels Mark tense up, but what she doesn't notice is the scowl that Mark has on his face.

"And I know I have made some things difficult around here." Jade continues to talk, trying to talk herself into some courage to tell the truth. "That was mostly because I failed to see the bright side in things. I failed to see the bright side . . . in . . ." Jade sighs, realizing she is simply talking to avoid telling Mark of her infidelity. "Mark, I love you. I love you more than anyone in this world could know . . . and . . ."

"Jade, what's wrong?"

Jade looks up at the ceiling, trying to hold back tears. Like a ball bouncing off two walls, her thoughts go back and forth. One second, she believes that she should tell Mark about the real reason she isn't working anymore, but the next, she wants to keep it a secret. No matter the past, she knows she must become a better wife for Mark . . . for the kids . . . for herself . . . for God. She now isn't too sure of the benefit of telling him.

"Mark, I . . . you . . ." Jade shakes her head. She gently grabs Mark's face, turning his body to lie on hers, chest to chest, and pulls him closer to kiss him. Starting out as a quick peck on the lips at first, their kissing becomes more involved. Mark jerks up and leans back on the opposite side of the couch. He stares blankly at Jade. Jade stares back, not knowing why he stopped.

"Baby, I'm sorry," Jade says. "I will be different." She crawls over to Mark and continues to kiss him. With her head nestled on Mark's shoulder and her hand holding on to the back of his neck, Jade makes love to Mark. Mark still looks forward, showing no emotion. He's not exactly sure for what she's sorry. One thing is for certain: the main thought that pervades his psyche is how strangely disconnected he feels from his wife, even while making love. Something is wrong, and he doesn't know enough to fix it.

❧

Craig sits in his office, staring out the window, still fuming from his run in with Maya. The sun rises above the tall buildings to shine right into his office. Berta comes into the office to see the back of Craig's chair. She stands there silent for a few moments before pulling up a chair and sitting next to him. They both stare at the city streets below them.

"Mr. Shriner canceled his appointment today . . . rescheduled for next week."

"Oh," Craig says and continues to look outside.

A long silence shuts down the conversation. Berta glances at Craig, who appears to be in another world.

"Sorry about the slap," Berta says.

Craig finally looks away from the window, towards Berta, and smiles. "I've been over it for a while now. It's no big deal."

"You don't want to know why I did it?"

"What's to know? One of you best friends, who also happens to be the most handsome man you know, openly admits, albeit falsely, that he is a rapist. I should have been slapped."

"Oh. Well, I'm glad you aren't too offended."

"Yeah, and you can keep your job."

"My job?"

"I was going to fire you."

Berta laughs. "If you were going to fire me, you would have even before the slap."

Craig chuckles. "True."

"Oh, wait. Was that a laugh squeaking its way out?"

"I guess."

"It's about time. I don't remember the last time I heard you laugh . . . or saw you smile."

"I suppose it has been a while. You can blame that on the airheads." Craig stares at Berta with a huge grin.

"Are you calling me an airhead?"

Craig chuckles. "Well . . ." Berta's face becomes serious. "No. Not at all. I wouldn't dare. I might get slapped again. And then have to suffer through you calling me 'Mr. Barlow' again."

Both begin to laugh. "So what was this morning all about?"

"With what?"

"With Ms. Maya Grange."

"Oh. It turns out she's another airhead . . . a confused one." Craig grabs a business magazine from his desk and pans through it. "It was funny. I went out to this lounge or club . . . whatever it was, there were a bunch of stiff high status people. They all . . ." Craig begins to laugh.

"What's funny?"

Craig doesn't look at Berta but throws the magazine down on his desk and leans back in his chair. Moments later, he gets up and walks to Berta's trashcan to grab the note from Maya. He sets the note on his desk and picks up the magazine again.

"Maya L. Grange, a successful entrepreneur, shows that she has as much brains as she has beauty, running a chain of cafes all around the US." Craig shows Berta the full page picture of Maya and the article on the next page. "They wrote a whole two pages about her. The café down the street, she owns it."

"Wow."

"Maybe . . . she isn't much of an airhead."

Berta washes away her concerned look with a smile. She skims through the article for a second before saying, "Didn't all the people at that club own businesses?"

"I'm sure most of them did . . . or they had money from one thing or another . . . but there was something different about her."

"Oh?"

"I can't place it." Craig opens the envelope and smiles. "I don't know, Berta. We might be on to something here."

"We are?"

"Yeah. Give me a second, will ya? I'm going to see if I can smooth things over with Ms. Grange."

"Oh . . . okay." Berta walks out of Craig's office and gently closes the door behind her.

Craig grabs the envelope and reads it again. It's a short note with only a phone number on it. He grabs his phone and calls the number. After a few rings, Maya picks up the phone. The sound of Maya saying hello makes Craig's stomach jitter.

"Look, I don't know what it is, but I can't leave it the way that I did. I have no idea what it is about you, but I would like to know. That is, if you give *me* a second chance."

Long pause.

"We don't get second chances, remember? We do with the cards we are dealt, or something like that," Maya says in a monotone voice.

"I know. That's a bunch of crap. I was mad at what happened among other things. It isn't much of an excuse for yelling at you, so I'm sorry."

"No need to apologize, Craig. I'm a tough girl. I've been through worse."

Another long pause.

"Do you want to meet later tonight?" Craig asks.

"Why should I?" Maya asks, still not changing her tone.

Craig leans back in his seat. "I know you still wonder if this could be something. Things don't change that quickly. There's something about you, Maya. There's something about our moment in the club. And let me be totally honest, I don't want to wonder if you were it for me. I don't want to wonder what could have been. Heck, you already know more than ninety-nine percent of the women out there do."

Maya sighs. "I suppose I can clear my night."

"You didn't have anything to do. Don't lie."

Maya laughs.

"There we go. A laugh. Now, I'm headed in the right direction."

"We'll see. Meet me at the café tonight at eight."

"Tonight at eight, sounds . . . good."

"Good. I'll see you then."

Craig hangs up and hops out of his seat. He rushes over, grabs his briefcase and coat, and then bolts out the door.

"Hey, Berta, you can take off now if you want. I'm out of here early myself. Ms. Grange and I have ourselves a date."

"A date? Really?"

"Yup. Have a good weekend."

"Thanks. You too."

Craig rushes to the elevator, bouncing while waiting for it to open. As soon as it does, he jumps in and rushes out the building.

☙❧

Mark leans over a counter, staring at Jade, watching her cook dinner. Every five minutes or so, she looks back at Mark, and smiles as if she's putting on a show. This confuses Mark even more. *She looks like Jade. She acts like Jade. Actually, she acts like the Jade I married. So what is going on? If she is hiding something, she is doing a great job at it.* Jade turns around again with a spoonful of something in her hand and puts it to Mark's mouth.

"A white wine cream sauce," she says.

Mark tastes the sauce from the spoon. "It tastes good."

"Good. Dinner is almost ready. Can you stir the sauce a bit so I can finally put some clothes on?"

"Sure." Mark walks over to the stove, keeping his eyes locked on Jade, as her partially open silk robe cascades around her body. He stares at her hips. *She still walks like Jade, the same walk that hypnotized me years ago.* He even watches her as she carefully navigates her way through the clothes strewn out across the floor. Mark stirs the sauce, taking the spoon for a few turns before setting it next to the stove.

☙❧

Jade continues her way upstairs, picking up speed as she leaves Mark's sight. She gets to the bedroom and quietly shuts the door. She then rushes for the phone and calls her mother. The first sound she hears are the kids playing in the background.

"I couldn't do it. I couldn't do it, Mom. I couldn't do it."

Jade's mother sighs, "So what are you going to do?"

"Be a good wife," Jade says.

Long pause.

"I don't agree with what you are doing. I still think you should tell him . . . but if that's what you think you should do, go and do it. Get off the phone with me and tend to your husband . . . while I settle these kids."

Jade hangs up the phone and grabs a pair of sweatpants and a plain shirt. *That was the shortest conversation ever. The kids were going crazy, it sounded.* Jade thinks a bit more about what she is going to do. She knows what she did was wrong, but she believes she has the ability to make things better from here on out. She knows it will be some work, but she simply cant go through the shame of revealing how weak she was. She wonders why so little of her feels guilty, but she brushes all that aside. She skips back downstairs to the kitchen to see Mark on his phone talking. A few moments later, he hangs up and looks at her.

"Who was that, baby?" Jade asks as she starts preparing the plates.

"The church. Meeting Monday."

"Oh, okay. You ready to eat?"

"Yeah. Come here for a second."

Jade looks at Mark as she sets a plate down. Mark stares at her intently. For a quick second, Jade believes that Mark already knows, and she becomes nervous. Mark holds her hand and gets her to sit on his lap. With particular care, he caresses her body and eventually makes love to her. Sadly, unbeknownst to her, he only does it to numb the pain that he feels on the inside, hoping to somehow reconnect with his wife before it is too late.

CHAPTER ELEVEN

ERTA walks into her apartment and kicks off her shoes. The midday sun radiates through her large front window. She throws her purse on the couch and walks to the bedroom. She stands at the foot of the bed for a few seconds before diving headfirst onto the bed. Berta then grabs a pillow and covers her face with it, letting out a bunch of frustrations by yelling into it. She kicks her feet as she yells. For a few more moments, Berta looks up at the ceiling with a blank stare. Eventually, she changes into a pair of sweatpants and shirt and walks to the kitchen. She flings open the freezer door and digs around to pull out a tub of ice-cream. With a spoon already in hand, she flops on the living room couch and starts to dig into the sugar therapy.

After a few bites, Berta's cell phone rings. She rummages through her purse to grab it and sees that it's Candace. Berta sighs and answers it.

"You wanna do lunch today?" Candace asks.

"I . . . I can't. I'm not at work."

"Everything okay? You're not sick are you? I heard a nasty bug is going around. I had to wipe and spray everything down at my desk."

"No. I'm not sick. I just took a half day today."

"A half day?"

"Yes, a half day."

"For what?"

Berta sighs again.

"Berta, what's wrong?"

"Craig has a date."

"So?"

"Her name is Maya Grange."

"Who's that?"

"She's a rich businesswoman."

"Oh, I get it. You're threatened by this woman."

"Yes. I know Craig isn't my man . . . but she's taking my man."

"I thought he wasn't going to find anyone else? What happened to that confidence?"

"I don't know. She's not like the others. He even said so himself."

Long pause.

"You want my honest opinion?" Candace finally asks.

"I'm not sure I do . . . but I'm going to say yes anyway."

"I think it's time you move on."

"Move on to what?"

"Well, there's that nice fellow at the church who shows interest."

"Who? Brandon? Jeremy? Deacon Wells? There are a lot of *nice fellows* who are interested. None of which pique my interest."

"No, no, no. I'm talking about Daniel. You know ... the newcomer to our church."

"I know nothing about him."

"Then get to know something about him. He seems eager to get to know something about you."

"I don't know, Candace. What about Craig?"

"What about him? Craig isn't there yet. Daniel seems to have his stuff in order . . . a real man of God . . . not someone questioning if there is one."

"Hey, hey, now."

"I'm serious. You want to be with someone who you can have serious conversations with . . . someone you can study and pray with . . .

someone who feeds your soul as much as your heart. Craig doesn't strike me as that person."

"But he has been through so much."

"There's another sign. When the going got tough, he abandoned his faith. Look, Berta, this is the best advice that I can give you, and I say this because you are my dearest friend. Don't hold out for something that is likely to never happen . . . especially when you have something better right in front of your face."

"I still have faith in Craig," Berta says sheepishly.

"That's silly, Berta. You shouldn't put your faith in him . . . or Daniel for that matter. Your faith should always be in God and his will, no matter which way He takes you. You just have to make sure that it is Him that is taking you down a certain path . . . and not your emotions."

"I guess."

Long pause.

"I guess it's safe to assume that I won't be seeing you in church tonight?" Candace asks.

"Maybe. I don't know. I don't have anything else to do."

Candace chuckles. "Either way, I'll catch up to you. But as for now, my grilled cheese is getting cold. I'll talk to you later."

Berta hangs up the phone and sits there staring at the tub of ice-cream.

☙

Later in the evening, Craig parks his car in front of the café, which looks closed. Curtains cover the large front windows and darkness prevails behind them. He looks at his watch to see that he is ten minutes early. He leans back in his seat and waits for her to show. A million thoughts run through his mind as he laughs. This is the first date that he has been nervous on in quite some time. He even pulled out his thousand dollar suit he had made years ago. He rubs the palms of his hands on his lap to dry them. Out of the corner of his eye, he sees some movement around the front of the café. He turns to see Maya waving him in from inside the pitch-black café.

Craig hops out of the car and locks the doors. He struts over to Maya, who stares at him with a look of admiration. As he gets closer to the door, he can see a flicker of light come from behind Maya. She looks Craig up and down and stops at his tie.

"Fuchsia," she says. "My favorite color." She moves to the side to let Craig into the café.

It is at this point that Craig notices the flickering light was coming from the upper loft area of the café, where the live performances are usually held. He glances at Maya, who grabs his jacket and his hand, leading him up the steps to the upper level. Craig is captivated by the outfit Maya has on, a black open back halter dress that comes to her mid-thigh. His expensive dress shoes and her stiletto high heels make clicking noises as they make their way up the wooden staircase.

Once at the upper level, Craig sees the entire floor scattered with candles and in the center of the floor is a table with a single candle on it. Maya sits Craig down and hangs up his jacket. She then goes to the corner, grabs a wine bottle and two glasses, and comes back to Craig.

"So what do you think?" Maya asks.

"I am pleasantly surprised, I must say. I did not expect this at all, and what you have on is stunning."

"Thank you," Maya says as she pours the deep red wine into the two glasses and sits down at the table. She looks up at him, her green eyes giving off a strange glow under the light of the candles. "You are quite handsome yourself."

Craig smiles. For a brief moment, they both stare at each other, saying nothing. Maya grabs her glass and begins sipping on the wine. Craig lifts his glass and does the same. Neither knows what to say or even how to break the ice. Maya gets back up to grab a tray of various finger foods.

"Listen, I want to apologize again for ear—"

With ease, Maya places the tray down and kisses Craig before he could finish his sentence. She holds on to the sides of Craig's face as he tugs on her so she sits on his lap. They stare each other in the eyes for some time, noses touching.

"Stop saying sorry," Maya whispers.

⋄

Berta sits at the end of a cushioned pew during Bible study at her church. Candace sits next to her writing away in a notebook. For most of the time, Berta remains in her own world, thinking about what she wants to do with her life, particularly, her love life. She feels dumb for pushing Craig to someone else but now feels dumb for feeling anything towards him in the first place. Candace glances over to see Berta in deep thought.

"You're not even here, are you?" she whispers.

Berta looks over, annoyed that Candace interrupted her thoughts. "I am. I just can't stop thinking about everything."

"It's going to be okay."

Berta looks back towards the front. "I guess so." Out of the corner of her eye, she sees the newcomer, Daniel. As if he knew that she was looking, Daniel glances over at Berta and catches her eyes with his.

⋄

Mark and Jade sit on the living room couch watching a movie. Jade huddles up close to Mark to use his body for warmth. In front of them, at the foot of the couch, is an almost empty bowl of popcorn. Mark pauses the movie.

"We're almost out of popcorn," he says.

Jade looks down at the bowl. "Do you want me to go get some more?"

"No. It's already dark. I'll run to the market and grab some more."

"Can you grab some things from the list, too? I have a big breakfast planned for tomorrow."

"Will do."

Mark gets up and seizes the opportunity to get away from Jade.

On the way to the market, Mark drives by the pharmacy. He glances over at the parking lot to see only one car parked. He recognizes it to be Boley's. Quickly, Mark makes a U-turn and pulls into the pharmacy parking lot. He gets out of his car and enters the pharmacy, which should be closing in a half hour or so. The bell above the door clangs as Mark opens the door. He hears Boley greet him from behind the counter, though Boley doesn't see who entered the store since his back is towards him. Mark strolls to the counter and stands there waiting for Boley to turn around. When he does, he stares at him.

"I didn't come here for much," Mark says. "I just want the truth. I believe I know it already, but I just want to make sure."

"I'm not sure I know what you are talking about," Boley says. Boley is an interesting site to see, a tall, stocky man with dark chocolate skin, broad shoulders, and a perfectly shaped haircut.

Mark looks down to see that Boley isn't wearing a wedding ring. "So you don't wear a ring?"

Boley feels around his hand nervously. "Not while working. What can I do for you, Mark?"

"I already told you," Mark says in an annoyed tone.

Boley stares at Mark for a bit more. "I honestly don't know what you are getting at."

Mark gets even more annoyed. "Maybe I should talk to your wife. You think she would know something?"

Boley glares at Mark. "What? Look, Mark, you should get out of here."

"Why are you mad, Boley?"

"I'm not mad, but clearly, you aren't buying anything, and I'm about to close the store. I need you to leave."

"Okay, okay. But let me ask you this ... how far do you think I would go to find the truth? Better yet, how far would *you* go to find the truth?"

Boley stares at Mark for a few more seconds. He clenches his fist and bangs it on the counter. "Nothing happened."

"Oh, something happened. She didn't just leave for no reason."

"She didn't just leave. She was fired."

"Nope. I saw the resignation letter. So now a blatant lie. What are you covering up?"

Boley looks down and after much thought, he says, "I'm not a bad man."

"I don't care about who you are. I just want to know what happened."

Boley shuffles around a bit, seemingly battling within himself. He stares at Mark as if he is preparing for a fight and then snaps his gaze down. "Well, things were rough between my wife and I . . . Apparently, things were rough between you and Jade. A bunch of things led down this path. We kissed before . . . a number of times. We knew what we were doing was wrong, but—"

Boley looks up to see Mark heading out the door, swinging the door open wide, the bell clanging. Mark gets into his car and drives off, heading to the market.

Once in the market parking lot, he sits there and thinks. He doesn't know how far things between Jade and Boley went, but what he knows is enough. He can only assume she had sex with him. Disjointed thoughts run through his mind causing more confusion than healing. *This, I must keep close to chest. I can't tell anyone about what I know. I need time to figure this out, and if I reveal what I know, I have time for nothing. All I need is time.* Mark sits back and thinks even more as he tries to stop the tears from squeezing themselves from his eyes. Clearly, he could only see two options: One, get a divorce. Two, stay. Staying requires more effort and energy, both of which he doesn't want to give right now. Then, he thinks of the kids. *I forgot about the kids in all of this. What happens to them? I would have to get custody somehow.* But, then Mark fears breaking up the family. He knows Kalina might be able to withstand it, knowing that Jade isn't her biological mother, but Charles. . . .

"Charles," Mark whispers shakily. "My boy, Charles." Mark grabs the steering wheel and bows his head, those tears turning into out-and-out sobs. He cries even more realizing that he doesn't have the strength to say anything. He will take this pain on his shoulders and walk with it for the rest of his life for his children. As so many parents have done, he vowed to give his children what he never had, a strong and complete family. He may despise Jade at the moment, but he isn't going to break that vow to his children now, even if his marriage vows are broken. With grim determination, Mark gets out of the car and heads into the market.

☙❧

Back at the café, Craig and Maya dance to soft music. Maya's head lies on Craig's shoulder as he moves her around the floor.

"You are a very good dancer," she says.

"Thank you. You are good as well."

"So tell me, why aren't you off the market yet?"

Craig chuckles. "Probably for the same reasons you aren't."

Maya smiles showing all of her shimmering white teeth. "Someone looking to mooch."

"Or fame."

"Or those who have nothing going on upstairs but are too cocky to let on to it."

"I was just getting ready to say that. I dated one girl who got drunk and virtually told me all of that."

"Really? I dated a guy who was still living with his mother, but I didn't find that out until his mother showed up on the date."

"No way." Craig laughs. "Somehow, despite all the airheads—"

"And losers."

"Yes, and losers. Despite all the airheads and losers, it looks like we found each other."

"In a club no less."

Craig laughs. Maya's face flashes with seriousness. She stops dancing and looks up at Craig. "I have a confession to make."

Craig looks at Maya and smiles. "What's that?"

"I watched you for months . . . every day in this café. I would tell myself simply to go up to you and ask you out. It's been a while since I dated . . . a while since I've run into someone worth my time. Then I saw you at that lounge. I knew it was either fate . . . or some sick practical joke. Either way, I had to say something."

Craig looks at Maya and dips her as they continue dancing. "I'm normally not this open so soon."

"Neither am I." Maya bites her bottom lip. "Tell me something . . . would you like to come back to my place?"

Craig looks around to see most of the candles already burned out. "I think I would like that."

☙❧

"Berta, you are too funny," a man says as he laughs uncontrollably.

"You know you would have done the same thing. Don't lie."

"Okay, maybe. But not that way."

"Whatever floats your boat. I had my method and it worked quite well." Berta takes a bite of cheesecake and wipes her mouth with a napkin.

"Listen, I'm really glad you came here with me. It would have been boring had I come here by myself."

"No problem, Daniel. Unlike everyone else, I didn't have dinner before Bible study."

"Yeah, your friend seemed adamant that you go get something to eat."

Berta smiles while taking another bite. "Yes, it seems that way."

Sitting in a diner, Berta and Daniel talk, seemingly having a good time.

"So enough about me, where are you from?" Berta asks.

"Well, I'm originally from Texas."

"From Texas … but no southern drawl?"

"I travel a lot. Well, I used to travel a lot . . . for my job."

"Really? What do you do?"

"I'm a marketing consultant. I go all over the US for different companies and help them with their products and stuff. Nothing too exciting."

"Sounds pretty exciting to me. So what has you here in this town?"

"Two companies, one larger and the other smaller."

"So you're not going to be here too long?"

"I could be. It's entirely under my control. If there's a lot of business in Ohio, then I go to Ohio. Or, I could wait until there's business in Maine. It's up to me."

"So what are you deciding on now?"

"I'm thinking of staying. Nice home, nice church, nice people . . . ."

Berta pushes her plate from her and wipes her mouth again. "I better stop eating this before I explode."

"Full, huh?"

"Well, that and I don't want to put on too many pounds."

"Oh, stop it. You look fine."

Berta glances away shyly. Daniel looks at his watch. "It's getting late. We should head out of here."

"What time is it?"

"Eleven."

"Oh, my goodness. We were here that long? That's almost three hours."

"It didn't seem that long, did it?"

"Not at all."

Berta and Daniel pay their tabs and grab their coats. Daniel helps Berta put on hers and then puts on his. They both walk out to the street.

"This was fun," Berta says.

"It sure was. Here, let me walk you to your car."

"Oh, no, that's okay. You don't have to."

"Please, I insist."

"I can handle myself."

"That doesn't mean you *have* to. Come on. I'll even walk a few feet away from you if you want. I just want to make sure you get to your car safely."

Berta smiles at this man who isn't taking no for an answer. "Fine."

Daniel walks side by side with Berta. "Would you like to do this again sometime?"

Berta looks at Daniel. "Do what?"

"You know . . . this . . . umm . . . friendly gathering."

Berta smiles again. "We'll see."

☙❧

It feels like his insides are being pulled out through his mouth. The sharp tugging at his sides force him to hunch over as he begins to tremble. He feels nauseous but he ignores the feeling and begins to drive home. His mind races as he reviews his options. He jumps from pain to anger and back again so often that by the time he pulls up into the garage, he is a tenebrous version of the man that he once was. He gets into the house with the items from the list. He sees Jade huddled up on the couch sleeping. On the television, there still appears the frozen frame of the movie they were watching. As he packs things into the refrigerator, Jade pops up and walks into the kitchen.

"Hey, whatcha do, get lost?"

"Nope. Actually, I got this." Mark pulls out a bouquet of flowers that he picked up from the market. Jade smiles as he hands them to her.

"You know how much I love you?" she asks.

"No. I don't," Mark says, smiling.

"Let me show you," Jade says walking over to Mark. She sets the flowers down and kisses Mark. She then grabs his hand and leads him upstairs to the bedroom where they proceed to make love.

Mark's lips burn. His cheek and neck burns. His chest burns. All the places where Jade kissed him with her tainted lips, Mark imagines burns. He envisions her lips actually holding a poison and every place she puts them on his body turns black and blue. He envisions himself getting weaker because of the poison, but in reality, he is weaker because he is putting on the same charade that Jade has been putting on for quite some time. He is no better than her, but he considers himself valiant, preserving the secrecy for the kids' sake. He tells himself that for his own sanity. Otherwise, who knows what would happen. He doesn't think of Jade while making love to her, nor does he think of what she let Boley do to her. Instead, he thinks of the first person that comes to mind. He tries to switch off his brain. He tries to switch women, maybe to a celebrity or someone far out of reach, but he can't. Alicia remains scored on his mind . . . and she's just a teacher conference away.

CHAPTER TWELVE

"WE'VE been dating for a month or two. She's the total package, everything I've been talking about for years, smart, beautiful, knows what she wants . . . beautiful, I mean smoking hot. She wants me for me, you know?" Craig lifts a bar with weights, pressing it away from his chest and slowly letting it back down again. Mark stands over him, spotting him.

"Well, finally, some good news," Mark says.

"Yeah, even after all that other stuff. You would have known sooner if you came to the gym once in a while. I tried calling a couple times too. What's up? You getting fat and lazy on me?"

"Naw, not that. I just haven't had much time lately."

Craig sets the bar back onto the rack and sits up. He stares at Mark discriminately. "What's going on?"

"Nothing. Why are you looking at me like that?"

"Mark, we've known each other since grade school. I know when something is off, and let me tell ya, something is off."

Craig moves from the bench and wipes it off with his towel. Mark then slides onto the bench and points to the weights, signaling Craig to add more onto the bar. Craig reluctantly does so. Mark begins to lift when Craig interrupts with a question.

"How's the family?"

The clanging sound of the bar hitting the rack alarms Craig as Mark sits up and looks forward.

"Too much weight," Mark says. Craig pulls off some of the weight. Mark then lies back down and lifts again. "The family is fine."

"Jade?"

"She's fine."

"The kids?"

For the first time during the entire workout, Mark smiles, although it is a half-smile as he tries to push up the weighted bar.

"The kids . . . are fine . . . Kalina doesn't . . . play sports anymore . . . killing it in chess . . . Charles is a . . . football star." Mark sets the bar back on the rack and sits up, stretching his arms and chest. "They're both doing well in school. Love em' to death."

Craig notices the attitude shift and continues with the questioning. They both begin to walk to the boxing ring.

"So how's work?" Craig asks as he slides on a punching mitt.

"Work is great." Mark puts on boxing gloves. "I volunteered to be an assistant to the music teacher for this after school music program."

"So you're there way longer now."

"Yeah, hence the reason for not coming to the gym as much."

"Well, why didn't you just say that in the first place?"

"I told you I haven't had much time lately." Mark says, realizing that his excuse fit perfectly with the conversation. He hopes that ends Craig's interrogation. He begins punching into Craig's held up hands.

"You run into Alicia?"

Although Mark keeps punching, everything on the inside freezes at that question. "Nope."

"Her son is still in your class?"

"Yup."

"That's odd, isn't it?"

"Sort of. Her son's grades are up now. There's no need to meet with her. Actually, I'm not even sure anymore if it was her. Maybe I dreamed up that parent-teacher conference." Mark jokes. "Or that one day after school."

"One day after school?"

"Yeah. She was late picking him up and I waited—"

"For her?"

Mark stops and stares at Craig. "No, *with him.*"

Mark and Craig switch gloves. Now Craig starts punching into Mark's hands.

"I don't know, man. I would stay away from her at all costs. You haven't seen her at all really. I say good."

"Why do you seem so adamant about it?"

"Because, Mark, you have it all. A good wife, great kids, the house, the cars, the job you love . . . this is what people fight for . . . this is what people kill for."

"I suppose. But you know, not everything is what it seems. For some people, that's not enough."

"What more do you want?"

"Me?" Mark begins to laugh, knowing that it is not himself that he is talking about. "I want a lot more, Craig. A whole lot more."

"Well, stop being selfish."

Mark smiles again. "Look at you, giving me advice on life. This woman must really be under your skin."

Craig chuckles and sends a hard, sharp, right hook to Mark's padded palm.

ÃÆÈÉ

"It's been weird, Mama." Jade says as she talks to her mother on the phone while the kids stay glued to the television. She moves from the living room to the kitchen and lowers her tone. "He's been having weird dreams every now and again. Maybe once a week. He starts talking in his sleep. Nothing he says is audible except this woman's name."

"Whose name is he saying?"

"Alicia."

"As in the singer?"

"No. Well, I'm not sure."

Silence.

"Did you ask him about it?"

"And say what? Hey are you cheating on me in your dreams? Yeah, that would go over well, coming from a person who cheated in reality."

"I thought you moved on from that."

"How?" Jade looks around the corner since her tone was becoming loud. The coldness of her mother towards her issues is annoying her. She lowers her tone again. "How can I move on from it? How can I move on from something my husband, to whom I made vows, has no clue about?"

"I don't know, Jade. Have you been praying about it?"

"Of course. I never get an answer."

Silence.

"Why didn't you tell him?"

"Because I couldn't. That doesn't matter anymore."

"I suppose it doesn't. So what are you going to do now?"

"That's what I'm calling you for. I don't know what to do anymore. I call myself trying to save my marriage, but I fear I'm going to lose it no matter what. It has been two and a half months of this and it still feels the same as it did the first day."

"Jade, you need to tell him the truth."

"I told you already, I decided against that. I can't do it." Jade raises her tone again.

"That's the best th—"

"No!" Jade yells. She turns to the side to see Kalina and Charles standing in the hallway looking at her. Kalina looks at Jade with a confused face and points her thumb up in the air and then down towards the ground. *Just like her father*, Jade thinks. Jade gives her thumbs up, letting her know that everything is okay. Kalina then nods and goes back with Charles to watch television. "I'm sorry; I didn't hear what you said."

"I said that I highly doubt what I say has much bearing on what you do now. There isn't much point in asking me what to do because I'm not giving you advice on how to sneak around Mark."

Jade sighs. "So you think I should tell him?"

Jade's mother sighs louder. "Yes."

Jade thinks for a few seconds. "But, I'm already down this path. I had my chance and I blew it. It's too late to tell him now. I need to keep things steady. We can get through this."

"I don't know if I can help you, Jade. And as far as the dreams go, they're just dreams. Now, when he starts saying her name outside those dreams, then you worry. Until then . . ." She trails off until she's muttering something that isn't understandable. Jade ignores it.

"All right, mother. I have to go. It's getting close to the kids' bedtime."

Jade gets off the phone and leans over the counter.

CʒΒↄ

Berta rushes around her apartment looking for a good shirt to wear to church. She's tried on a few already, not liking any of them. She puts on a long sleeved blouse and stares in the mirror. A few minutes later, she shakes her head and starts digging in her closet yet again. She stops for a second to stare at her clothes. She has her work clothes mixed in with her church clothes and a set of different clothes on the side. These articles of clothing seem untouched. Berta pulls out a long black evening gown she once wore to a company networking dinner years ago. She throws it on her bed. Digging through more clothes, she pulls out a silk flower print sundress. *I wore this at the last barbecue Daddy had.* She throws it on the bed. Berta grabs another dress. She stares at it in admiration. *I never had the chance to wear this.* The dress is another evening dress but a more revealing one. It has a considerably low cut front and is formfitting with a slit going up the side. Berta holds the brown dress and sits on the edge of the bed. She doesn't remember the last time she went anywhere where she could wear a dress. She wears pants almost everywhere she goes . . . and that's only to work and to church. Her cell phone rings, but she ignores it, being in her own world. *All I do is go to work and go to church. I have no life outside the two.* Her cell phone rings again. This time she picks it up. It's Candace.

"Sorry, I missed you the first time," Berta says.

"What are you talking about? And why do you sound like a boy who lost his dog . . . in the rain."

"Oh. Never mind. I thought I missed your call, but it must have been someone else . . ."

"Berta, what's wrong?"

Berta sighs. "I have no life."

Candace tries to hide her laugh, but Berta hears it anyway. "What do you mean?"

"All I do is go to work and go to church. That's—"

"And out with Daniel after Bible study."

"Yeah, but . . . that's like friends going out to eat. I haven't ... I haven't been on a date in so long. I haven't dressed up or anything in so long . . . and Daniel doesn't seem all that interested."

"Are you interested in him?"

"Of course, I am. I wouldn't be going out with him after Bible study for so long if I weren't."

"I just think you're being impatient, and I don't care what you say, you guys are dating. Those Friday night dinners aren't just friendly get togethers. I mean, Berta, you two stopped inviting us weeks ago."

"I know but—"

"Nope. I will hear no more of it. Be patient. Let things grow. You'll get your chance to be all girly and stuff. Just sit back and wait. Enjoy the process for once."

Berta doesn't say anything but instead stares at the dress that she is still clutching in her hand.

"Berta?"

"Yeah, yeah. I hear what you're saying."

"Okay, good. Now, the reason I called was to see if you're going to church tonight."

"I'll be there."

"I'll see you there then."

Berta hangs up and looks through her phone to see who called her before Candace did. Her eyes widen when she sees it was Daniel who called. She quickly calls back. After only a few rings, Daniel answers.

"Berta, I'm so glad you called. Listen, are you going to be at the church tonight?"

"I am."

"Do you mind if I throw a monkey wrench in your plans?"

"It depends."

"Do you want to go out tonight? Rather, can I take you out tonight?"

Berta scrunches up her forehead and smirks a bit. "Sure. I . . . would love that."

"You don't sound so sure."

"I am. I just . . . had a bunch of thoughts going through my mind at once."

"Do you want to talk about it?"

"No, no, everything is fine. I would love to go out with you tonight."

"Great. I have everything set up already. All I n—"

"You knew I was going to say yes?"

"Well, no . . . and yes. I just prayed about it and moved forward as if it was so. If it didn't work out, then . . . oh well. I'd try again, though."

Berta smiles. "So where are we going?"

"I made reservations at Pierre Romano."

Berta jerks her neck back. "That expensive Italian restaurant?"

"Yeah. I thought it would be a different kick from the diner we always go to."

"How did you get reservations there? There's usually a two month waiting period."

"Faith, my dear. That's all I can say. Is eight a good time to pick you up?"

Berta looks at the clock. She only has two hours to get ready. "I have to go now if you want me to be ready."

"That's fine. I will see you at eight."

Berta smiles even more. "Okay. See you then."

Berta rushes off the phone and calls Candace back.

"Ummm, Candace. I don't think I'm going to church tonight."

"Okay. Everything cool?"

"Yup . . . I'm going on a date with Daniel tonight."

"Wow. I knew Jesus worked fast, but I didn't know that fast. That has to be a record somewhere."

"A record?"

"Yes, a record of how fast Jesus answers a prayer. As soon as I got off the phone with you, I prayed for you, and BAM, there it goes . . . anyway, have fun, and . . . where are you two going?"

"Pierre Romano's."

Berta hears a rustling on the phone so loud that she has to pull the phone from her ear. She still is able to hear Candace yelling at her husband, Jack.

"Jack, Berta is going on a date tonight. . .. Yup, Daniel. . .. Yup, and guess where they are going . . . Pierre Romano. . .. Yup, I'm not lying. . .. Yup. . .." Candace's voice becomes stern. "So my question is, how come you never took me there. . .. Oh, is that right? After three years of marriage. . .. Oh, I have to wait until we reach twenty. . .." Now Candace is yelling. "Berta and Daniel just started dating. . .. I see, well guess where you're sleeping tonight. . .. What. . .." Candace comes back to the phone. "Berta, congrats. I have to go and slap up my jerk husband. Have fun and tell me all about it."

"Thanks. I will."

Berta gets off the phone and stands up as she looks at the brown dress she is still holding. She opts to wear it on her date. She skips around the apartment pulling out jewelry and things to get her hair ready. "You do work fast," she whispers.

CHAPTER THIRTEEN

"SO this is it, huh?"

Berta stands in front of the elegant facade of the Italian restaurant holding Daniel's hand. They stride to the front door as Berta continues to observe the building. Walking into the restaurant, she sees a pianist playing in the corner. Amazed, she looks around to see the romantically lit area filled with people, each one dressed to impress. She grips Daniel's arm and huddles close to him. Filled with excitement, everything becomes a blur until the two are seated. Daniel sweeps around Berta, pulling her seat out for her. As she sits, he slides the chair in so she can be at the table. He then moves back to his seat.

For hours they talk and have a good time, with Berta feeling more comfortable in the restaurant and with Daniel.

"Berta, I have to say this. I've been holding it in for the longest now and I can't any longer. Please don't be offended in any way when I say this, but . . . you look exquisite. I have never seen you like this . . . and I like it."

Berta smiles and looks down in front of her. She then rolls her eyes to look up at Daniel as she brushes a strand of hair behind her ear. "Thank you. It's not too much, is it?"

"No. Not at all. You look very classy." Daniel whispers. "Why do you think all these other guys are staring at you?"

Berta giggles but soon stops realizing that she sounded like a little kid. "I'm not sure why they stare. I'm not sure why their wives stare too."

"Jealousy. The dress looks like you are ready to accept the award for best actress in a movie."

"Thanks. It was a gift."

"A gift? From whom?"

"My fath … ummm, my previous employer. He got it from France."

"You were getting ready to say your father."

"No, I wasn't."

"You were."

"I wasn't," Berta says in a harsh tone.

Daniel stares at Berta for a second and then looks down at the table. "Okay . . . you weren't. You up for some dessert?"

"I'm sorry. I'm not."

Daniel looks around the restaurant for the waiter and calls for the check.

On the ride home, Berta remains silent. Afraid to say anything wrong, Daniel remains silent as well. Daniel pulls up in front of Berta's apartment building. She looks out her window, almost dreading returning to the place alone. She turns to Daniel.

"Listen, I had a great time. I appreciate you setting this up for us."

"But you don't want to do this again."

"I do. I really do. I just …"

He grabs her hand. "What happened? I thought we were having a good time."

"We were. I . . . we just have to slow things down a bit." She winces at what she just said.

"That's fine. No pressure." Daniel kisses her hand.

Berta then slides out of the car and walks to the front door as Daniel waits for her to get inside. She jams her key into the door and pauses. She then pulls the key out of the door and walks back to the car. Daniel rolls the window down as Berta leans in to talk.

"Can you come in with me? Just for a little while. I . . . I don't want to be alone right now."

Daniel nods curiously. He parks the car and walks with Berta upstairs to her apartment.

Inside, Berta takes off her coat and takes Daniel's. She stuffs them both into the closet and then puts some hot water on the stove. "Would you like some tea?"

"Yes. That would be good."

Berta takes out two cups and sets them on the counter. She then walks back to the living room and sits on the couch. She turns her legs to the side and removes her shoes. She breathes a sigh of relief as she flings them off to the floor. Daniel smiles.

"Your feet hurting?"

Berta rubs her heels. "Sure do."

Daniel reaches down and touches her foot. "May I?"

Berta gives an unsure nod. She presses her thighs together and sticks out one leg. Daniel begins massaging her foot. After a few seconds, Berta feels a tender and warm feeling throughout her entire body. She closes her eyes but then snaps them back open as what she saw behind her eyelids reminded her of a late night movie on cable television. She stretches to tap Daniel on his forearm.

"Okay, cowboy. That's enough."

"Everything okay?"

"Yup. Sure is." She gets up and walks to the kitchen. She grabs the hot water from the stove and pours it into the tea-bagged cups. She then brings the two cups to the coffee table. The two sit and sip on their tea in silence.

Berta looks at Daniel and smiles. "Why is it that no matter what happens, whenever I'm around you, I am completely comfortable?"

Daniel places his cup of tea on the coffee table after taking a sip. "Because that's my goal. To make you as comfortable as possible."

"No, it's not."

"It's one of them."

"Well . . . good job."

"Thanks."

Berta looks Daniel in the eyes. He stares back, confused at first, but then settling into her gaze.

"I did get this dress from my father," Berta says, "who was also my employer . . . at the time."

Daniel nods in understanding. "Well, the man has good tastes."

"Had. He had good taste."

Daniel stares blankly.

"He died years ago."

"I'm sorry to hear that."

"It's okay. I had more than enough time to cope. Anyway, he was a good man . . . Raul Valencia."

"Wait . . . I thought your last name is DeVries."

Berta smiles and pulls a pin out of her windblown hair. She lets it fall to the sides of her face. "It is. Raul wasn't my biological father . . . but he took care of me. People though it was weird, you know, this old guy always around this young woman. People thought I was a gold digger and everything. They didn't know that he had taken care of me since I was twelve years old."

Daniel rubs his brow. "If you don't mind me asking, what happened to your biological father?"

Berta stares into Daniel's eyes again, almost reading him to find a reason not to tell him. She turns away. "Turns out he wasn't much of a father at all."

Daniel gives that understanding nod he gave before, but Berta knows he doesn't fully understand what she is saying.

"So he adopted you? Raul, I mean."

"Not exactly. But, he took care of me, yes. My life is so different because of him. I knew God was throwing me a rope . . . and it was him."

"The situation with your real father was bad, wasn't it?"

Berta nods. She tries to stop herself from saying any more. She tries to stop herself from feeling any more, not about the situation, but for Daniel. She looks into his eyes again as if hypnotized and continues. "He raped me."

Those three words put some distance between her and Daniel, she feels. Daniel shows no sign of being uncomfortable even though Berta feels the gap widening.

"Where was your mother?" he asks.

"She jumped ship years before. She had an affair with her golf instructor, which isn't anything major to her. Of course, she wasn't exactly a beacon of light if you know what I mean."

"What was wrong with her?"

"She was one of those stuck up people that thought everything was owed to her. She wouldn't have defended me anyway . . . her own daughter . . . So when that sorry excuse for a woman was gone . . . it started. That loser would come home from his business trips and do what he did to me. He blamed me for Mom leaving."

Daniel slowly nods. "Sorry for not understanding, but how did Raul get to you then? How did he know?"

"That's a good question. I don't know. I just remember the day he took me away. I remember it vividly." Berta pauses and breaks the attention from herself. "What about your parents?"

"My parents?"

"Yes, your parents . . . since we're on the subject of family."

"My parents have been married for about thirty years. They live back in Houston." Daniel makes a face. "There isn't much else about them."

"Oh."

Things get quiet for a while as the two of them sip on their tea. At this point, Berta feels that she has revealed too much.

"Listen, I better go," Daniel says.

He and Berta get up from where they were sitting and Berta walks him to the door.

"Thanks for dinner," Berta says.

"Of course. I would love to take you out again . . . if that's okay. I know you want to take things slow."

Berta smiles at Daniel and shifts her glance to the floor. "I would like that."

Daniel smiles and gives her a hug. "I'll call you tomorrow."

"Okay."

Daniel leaves Berta's apartment and Berta closes the door behind him. She leans on the door smiling but still feeling extremely vulnerable.

Ϙ⁊

Craig rolls around in his bed trying to wake from his slumber. He leans over the edge of the bed to make out what time it is and then plops his head back onto his pillow. He flops his arm onto the opposite side of the bed and feels around. In a fast jerking motion, he flips out of bed looking around the room.

He and Maya went out last night and this time ended the night at his place so Craig fully expected her near him when he woke. He pauses for a second to hear music coming from outside the bedroom. A few moments later, Maya glides into the bedroom holding a tray in her hands.

"Good morning, sleepyhead. Or should I say good afternoon?"

"Morning, sweetheart."

"Sit back so you can enjoy this luxurious meal I have prepared."

Craig quickly props himself up with a pillow. "Luxurious?"

"Yup. Just you wait." Maya places the tray of food in front of Craig. "Taste it."

Craig smiles. "I've never had breakfast in bed before. It feels kinda weird."

"Well, get used to it." Maya lies on the bed at Craig's feet. She lies on her side resting her head on her hand, her long tendrils of jet-black hair covering her face like a protective shield.

Craig begins to eat. Sensing Maya's need of approval for the good meal, he says, "Best tasting eggs ever."

She brushes the hair away from her face and smiles. "Are you lying?"

"No, I'm not. This is a good tasting omelet. Those years of culinary school have paid off."

Maya lets her hair fall back down over her face. "Thank you."

Craig stuffs more food into his mouth and then takes a big gulp of his drink. "I had a good time last night," he says between bites.

"I did too. I can't believe it has only been a few months."

"Yeah . . . what time did you wake up?"

"Nine."

"Nine?" Craig laughs. "And four hours later, I wake up."

"So much for church."

Craig stops eating. "Church?" He stares at Maya, causing her to brush her hair back again and sit up straight.

"It was a joke. My mother always said it when I was younger. Dad always slept until one on Sundays. Mass was at eleven. She was always mad at Dad . . . every Sunday . . . and she would yell 'so much for church.' Then Dad would say simply, 'so much for it.'"

Craig smiles and finishes his food. He then moves the tray from his lap. Maya scoops up the tray and takes it to the kitchen. Craig rises out of the bed and walks into the bathroom to take a shower. While in the shower, he hears Maya brushing her teeth. He yells over the sound of pounding water on tile.

"So what did you do during all that time you were awake?"

With a muffled voice, she says, "Looked at you."

Craig laughs. "What? You mean you stared at me for hours?"

Maya spits. "Not for hours. Eventually I made breakfast. You have enough for tomorrow by the way."

"Thanks."

Steam floods the air in the bathroom making it impossible to see anything past the shower glass.

"What is that scar from?"

Craig stops in his tracks. Placing his hands onto the shower wall and letting his head fall between his shoulders, he lets the water pound on his back. The water flows on his back like little snakes, tracing along the long scar that reaches from his top left shoulder down to where his right kidney is. Craig doesn't answer at first. He hears the shower door slide open, and then shut once again. Craig shivers as he recalls how he got the scar. Breaking him out of his trance is Maya's soft hand on his back feeling around the scar. The feel of her touch becomes too much as every muscle in his body tenses. Though no one could ever tell, Craig's eyes fill with tears.

"I've always wanted to ask. I guess I just got the courage to do so."

Craig's silence becomes Maya's answer. She traces her finger along the scar a few times, not wanting to pry, but ultimately curious about Craig and this part of his past. "What was it like . . . in jail?"

Craig raises his head. The water runs down his back faster and makes less noise now that it isn't pounding on his neck. "Do you know what a demon looks like?"

Maya shakes her head. "I don't."

"I do . . . Imagine facing them every day . . . every night . . . Imagine being trapped in a cave where everyone wants to kill everyone else for no reason . . . where you eat, drink, sleep, read, and smell hate . . . Imagine being trapped in hell . . . for doing the right thing . . . for doing those things . . . that He wanted . . . Him . . ." Craig shakes his head. "I prayed so much . . . at first . . . to be released . . . My prayers later turned into pleas . . . to be put out of my misery . . . then . . . I became one of them"

"One of whom?" Maya whispers, somewhat afraid of the answer.

"One of those guys that I was imprisoned with. I had to live out my entire sentence . . . for something I didn't do . . . He didn't come to my rescue. How can a being so great let something so bad happen to someone whom He calls son?" Craig bangs his fist hard on the tile of the shower wall, hard enough to send a deep roar throughout the bathroom, as if the room were growling itself. "It comes down to but two reasons. Either He hasn't and never will love me . . . or He isn't that great at all."

Being filled with Craig's emotion, Maya grabs his arm and turns him around to face her. She hugs him, resting her head on his shoulders. Her nose nuzzles up against his neck, the splashing water dripping from her chin. "*I* love you . . . and I won't leave you alone."

Initially, Craig is thrown off by the statement. He places his hand on her head and strokes her now silky looking jet black hair. After a few minutes, Craig settles into Maya's statement and finds a bit of comfort. Still, there isn't any amount of 'I love you's that could heal the scars that aren't so visible. Secretly, Craig hopes Maya realizes that.

CHAPTER FOURTEEN

IN the middle of Monday morning, Mark sits at his desk cramming into his mouth the small lunch he made for himself. Each day around this time, his mind becomes plagued by various thoughts on his life, most of them negative. He looks around the empty classroom. The kids are out at recess for another fifteen minutes. Soon, the art teacher is coming to help the kids with some more drawing techniques. Mark figures he has maybe an hour of free time and gets up to walk to the teachers' lounge. Stepping into the room with gray carpeting, he finds no one there. Most of the teachers must have gone out for lunch. He stands in the room and listens to the low hum of the refrigerator across the room. A beam of light shines in and spotlights a potted plant in the corner. Other than that, there's nothing interesting in the room. Mark leaves the room and stands in the hallway. He can hear the kids playing outside, but he hears nothing inside the building. Around this time, he would usually hear one of the teachers' radio playing classical music or another teacher talking on the phone, but today . . . not a peep. He continues down the hallways to see if anyone is in their rooms and only finds one, a substitute teacher. Mark waves and continues along his way. He heads towards the main office, desperate to find someone he knows. As he makes his way to the office, he hears the squeak of sneakers on the tile floor and a few snickers. Mark looks around the corner to find no one but continues towards the auditorium. Just as he gets to the door, he decides against going in immediately. Instead he goes through the back of the auditorium towards the stage entrance. As he creeps through the strewn about stage props and items, he hears a tune coming from the piano that sits in the middle of the stage. Mark gets to a curtain and hides himself behind it as he sees Tim playing the piano with his back turned towards him. Mark twists his face up into a smile as he listens to the boy play a tune he has never heard before, a beautiful tune, a tune that brings a tear to his eye. Mark steps out onto the stage. Tim, hearing footsteps jerks around to face him. Mark looks to the back of the auditorium to see two girls trying to escape the crime scene.

"Hold on, you two," Mark yells to the back of the auditorium. He points down in front of him and motions them to the stage. He looks back at Tim, who stares back at him in shock. "I'll talk to you in a second."

The two girls make their way to the front of the auditorium as Mark stares at them the whole way. He glances at Tim, who lowers his head.

"You two . . . you two," Mark pauses. "You two, hurry up and go back outside."

The two girls look at each other, astonished that they didn't get into trouble or sent to the office, and run off out the auditorium. Mark turns towards Tim and stares at him for a few seconds. Tim looks him right in the eyes.

"I didn't have a piano like this at my old school."

Mark doesn't know what to say. He smiles for a second but returns to his stern face.

"Where did you learn to play like that?"

"A bunch of places."

"You took lessons?"

Tim shakes his head. "Mommy always said we don't have the money for lessons . . . so I taught myself."

"You taught yourself to play like that?"

Tim nods.

"How long have you been playing?"

Tim shrugs his shoulders.

"Can you play something else?"

Tim's eyes light up in excitement. He nods his head vigorously. He swings around in his seat and begins playing again. He plays a different song, a more upbeat song for a few seconds before Mark interrupts him.

"I have never heard these songs before. Who composed them?"

Tim smiles. "Me."

Mark is taken by surprise by one, the child's outburst of energy, and two, by the fact he plays his own music.

"No way."

"Yuh-huh, Mr. Cooke. I made the songs."

Mark sits on the bench next to him. "I bet your parents are very proud of you."

Tim nods but doesn't look him in the eyes anymore. He traces his finger along the keys of the piano. Something about the way Tim acts now bothers Mark. Through the years of teaching and dealing with kids, Mark knows he has hit on a sensitive topic for Tim. His body language says it all.

"What do you think of staying after school for a few days out of the week to practice with the school orchestra?"

"That would be cool."

"I'll get the permission slip and you get your mom to sign?"

Tim looks up at Mark and gives a half smile. "She won't sign it."

"Your dad?"

"Daddy is . . . gone."

Mark lifts his head up and looks at the multicolored lights above the stage. His stomach turns a bit, feeling sorry for this boy genius.

"If I could get your mom to sign, would you like to join? That way you can show off what you know . . . and learn some more stuff."

"Mommy doesn't like you too much . . . so I don't know how you're gonna get her to sign."

The bell rings throughout the school signifying the end of recess. Mark gets up from the bench.

"I'll get her to sign. But you have to give her the papers first. C'mon, let's get to the classroom."

Mark paces out the auditorium with Tim following. He pulls on Mark's sleeve. "How are you going to get her to sign?"

"I don't know. Maybe if I ask really nicely, she'll say okay."

Tim smiles. "Good luck with that."

Mark laughs.

"Can I still spend my recess in the auditorium?"

"Only if I don't get her to sign."

Tim smiles and runs to get to the classroom. The hall monitor tells him to slow down as they both disappear around the corner.

For the next few days, Mark tries to do everything in his power to get Alicia to give Tim permission to join the school orchestra. At the end of the day Monday, Mark sent Tim home with the permission slip, only for it to come back on Tuesday with a big red "NO" written on it. That afternoon, Mark convinced the music teacher to call Alicia at her job to try to convince her. On Wednesday afternoon, Mark learns the plan failed miserably. He figured that left him with one alternative, and that is to talk to her himself.

Thursday afternoon, after the final bell rings, Mark walks Tim outside to find his mother.

"I told you she wasn't going to sign."

"Yeah, yeah. I didn't give up yet."

Mark and Tim wait by the front of the school where the parents pick up their children for a few minutes before Alicia drives up in her vehicle. She's one of the last parents to arrive as she rushes out of her car and rushes Tim into the car.

"Mrs. Langley. I know we seem quite persistent with the school orchestra, but—"

"You called my job," Alicia says as she motions Tim to the back seat. "And it wasn't an emergency."

"Yes. I know. We only did that because your son can seriously benefit from joining the club . . . he plays very well."

As Alicia closes the car door, she stares at Mark. "There is no benefit to him joining. It is a grand waste of time."

"Please, Mrs. Langley."

"Look, Mr. Cooke, I don't know what you are trying to do, but we are just fine without you or your little orchestra."

"Have you ever heard him play?"

"It seems I must tell you again. Tim—"

"Have you ever heard him play?"

"What does it matter?"

Alicia starts to walk away from Mark to get into her car.

"What is wrong with you?"

She pauses at the question. She walks back around the car and stands face-to-face with Mark. "What's wrong with me? Here's what's wrong with me: My son's teacher is some crackpot with the idea that he can benefit from some school band when I, by myself, helped him to where he is. We are just fine without any help from you. All you are doing is hyping his head up only to be let down later, leaving me with the shattered pieces to pick up and deal with."

Mark gets a feeling that they aren't talking about Tim anymore, at least, not just about Tim.

"Don't do this."

"Don't do what?"

"Don't punish your own son for something that happened years ago. Something that has nothing to do with him."

"I beg your pardon."

"I'm not beating around the bush on this one. I know who you are. You know who I am, and we have a history, but somehow we both are moving on without recognizing those simple facts."

"I'm sorry, do I know you? Really? Do I know you? Have I met you before?"

"Alicia."

"Mr. Cooke."

"Alicia." Mark stares at her. "Just let him play."

"No."

"I'll . . . I'll step down as assistant. You won't see me at all. Please, just don't let this opportunity pass him by."

"Opportunity?"

"Yes, opportunity. Look, Mr. Benteed and I came up with this program to meet a need. We have had a bunch of musically talented students over the past years but none of them had the place to explore that talent. For some kids, yes, it just gives them something to do, but for others, it opens big doors."

Alicia looks confused.

"About a five-hour drive west from here is a school for the musically gifted. Delori School of Music. Mr. Benteed and I were able to set up a partnership with them so each year two or three students are chosen to get full scholarships to this private school. Tim, from what I heard already, is a shoe in. This band, as you call it, could easily write him a ticket towards a better future."

Alicia looks at Tim, who stares back and forth at her and Mark from inside the car. She turns back towards Mark.

"When is the first practice, if that's what you call it?"

"Tomorrow."

She looks down and purses her lips. "And you will step down?"

"Yes."

Alicia looks back at Tim again, seemingly trying to figure out what to do. She faces Mark.

"I hate you."

Mark smiles. "Is that a yes?"

"Yeah," Alicia says as she walks to the driver side door.

"Wait. I still need you to sign the permission slip. It will only take a few seconds."

Alicia looks around and sucks her teeth. "Where is the slip?"

"I left all my stuff in the auditorium."

"Mommy, I have to go to the bathroom."

Alicia goes into the car and talks to Tim, likely trying to determine if he can hold it. A few seconds later, she pops back out from the car.

"He has to use the bathroom."

"Well, you may as well come to the auditorium and sign this slip. Again, it will only be a few seconds."

Alicia ducks back into the car to say something to Tim. Tim's eyes light up as he hops out of the car. He grabs his mother's hand pulling her back into the school and towards the bathrooms. Once inside the school, Tim still clutches his mother's hand but grabs Mark's hand, now pulling both of them along. Mark glances at Alicia, who smiles at the happy-go-lucky attitude of her son, but snaps his head away so he doesn't get caught staring at her. Tim then lets go of both of their hands and runs into the bathroom.

"Be right back," he says.

Mark and Alicia stand outside the bathroom, looking around awkwardly. A few seconds later, a toilet flushes and Tim comes running out the door.

"Did you wash your hands?" Alicia asks.

"Oh, yeah." Tim runs back into the bathroom.

A few seconds later, Tim comes running out, flapping his hands trying to dry them. They all walk to the auditorium and then to the back booth that's behind the stage.

"Mommy, can I?" Tim asks, pointing at the piano on the stage.

"No, Tim, we aren't staying long at all."

"Please?"

Alicia stares at Tim. "For only a few seconds."

Tim runs to the piano and begins to play. He plays the same sad tune that Mark first heard him play. Mark and Alicia take a seat in the booth.

Within the first few seconds of Tim playing, Alicia begins to cry. Her face is emotionless, but tears constantly stream down her face. Mark sits there unsure of two things: what her tears are really for and what to do next.

Mark says nothing. Every muscle in his body tenses as he hears in his head what he feels compelled to say next. His throat tightens as if his body is stopping him from saying anything, but somehow he gets out, "I'm sorry."

The corner of Alicia's mouth turns up a bit, not in a fashion of a smile, but a snarl. "You've apologized already, albeit over the phone and from miles and miles away. I don't need any apology from you."

Mark insults himself in his head and remains quiet.

"You know what I always wondered? Why, Mark? Why did you leave me?"

More insults in his head for opening this floodgate. He digs in his pocket for his wallet. He pulls a picture from it and hands it to Alicia. She takes the picture and looks at it for a few minutes.

"She's beautiful . . . your daughter?"

"Yes. She's eleven."

Alicia stares at the picture even more as her face changes from confusion to realization. "So you cheated on me?" she asks in a monotone voice.

"I did. There's no excuse for it. I was drunk at a frat party. We went to a club after the party and I met someone. Still drunk, I . . . I slept with this woman . . . an older woman. She got pregnant. I asked her to get an abortion, but she had a different idea in mind. She wanted money . . . She didn't know I was just a college kid . . . so she didn't get the abortion and planned to take me to court for child support . . . She was already a few months old when I got to her . . . but I got to her . . . and took her with me. At that point . . . I wanted to get away from everything . . . from . . . from . . ."

"Me?"

"No, not you . . . but I didn't know any way that I could tell you what happened."

"But you could have simply told me, Mark. You could have told me. I would have been mad, hurt, upset, everything under the sun, but I loved you . . . and I would have been there right by your side . . . we could have fought through it . . . we were engaged . . . I was your wife to be . . . we could have made it . . . if you would have just given us the chance."

"I'm sure we could have made it . . . but I panicked . . . and I was ashamed." Mark slumps in his seat. "And now . . . and now . . ." He laughs. "I guess what goes around comes around."

"What do you mean?"

Mark sighs. "My wife cheated on me . . . with a guy she worked with."

Alicia remains silent for a moment, trying to find the words to say while trying to sort through her own feelings. "I'm sorry to hear that."

"Don't be. I deserve it."

Mark grabs the picture from Alicia and slides it back into his wallet.

"What's her name?"

"Who? My wife or my daughter?"

"Your daughter."

"Kalina."

Alicia nods. "That's a pretty name."

Mark nods, almost embarrassed at mentioning it to her. "Look, here's the sheet. It just needs your signature on this line." Mark points at a place on the half-slip of paper.

Alicia scribbles her signature on the paper and gets up from her seat. She calls Tim and pulls him from the piano.

"See you tomorrow, Mr. Cooke," Tim yells.

Mark comes out the booth and smiles at Tim. "I'll see you in class tomorrow." He pats him on top of his head.

"What about practice?"

Mark looks at Tim and then at Alicia. "I, uhhh, I might n—"

"He will see you there," Alicia cuts in before Mark could finish. She stares at Mark as she says it.

Tim jumps up and down and mumbles something to himself, visibly excited. Alicia moves Tim along as they both exit the auditorium. Mark catches himself watching her as she walks away. Just before she walks through the door, she looks one last time at Mark and then lets the door close behind her.

೦೩೮೦

"Check, Mommy."

"Check what?"

"No, I put you in check."

"What am I, out of line or something . . . and you can't put me in check, I'm your mother."

"No. The game. I made a move putting you in check, meaning your king is in danger, meaning you are in danger of losing the game."

"Oh." Jade looks intently at the chessboard in front of her as Kalina sat on the other side of the board awaiting her move. Charles sits as a spectator as with all of Kalina's games.

"How does this piece move again?" Jade picks up a horse looking piece.

"It moves in an L-shaped direction. It can skip over other pieces, but remember, once you touch it, you have to move it."

Jade looks at the piece she holds and back at the board in frustration. "Can you make an exception this one time?"

"Sure. Move whatever piece you want to move."

Jade puts the horse piece back and grabs the one that looks like a castle. "What's this piece?"

"A rook."

"Right." Jade takes her rook and moves it in a straight line across the board, taking one of Kalina's pieces.

"Good move."

Jade smiles at her own game play. Kalina stares at the board in deep concentration. After a few seconds, she smiles and moves a piece. "Check."

"You know ... if this was poker, your face would have given everything away . . . and you'd lost already."

"Well, it isn't poker . . . and you're about to lose."

Jade can only see one move initially but stares at the board even longer. She still only comes up with one move and makes that move. Kalina grabs a piece and moves it in a dramatic fashion across the board. "Checkmate!" She places her hand out over the board. Jade slowly shakes her daughter's hand.

"You know, you are good at this game."

"I know."

"A little modesty goes a long way, though."

"Sorry." Kalina wrinkles her forehead. "Want to play again?"

"Sure do. Do you two want a snack first?"

"Yes, please." Charles also nods his head.

Jade gets up and goes to the kitchen. As she rummages around the cabinets for a snack for the kids, she hears Mark finally coming home from work. She looks around the corner to see Mark coming in the door from the garage. The kids run up to him and give him a hug. He looks at the board.

"Who's playing?"

"Me and Mommy."

Mark looks at Kalina with a twisted smile on his face. "You and your mother . . . playing chess?"

"She wanted to learn to play."

Mark gives another twisted expression and looks at the board. "Well, it looks like you took her through the ringer. No such thing as going easy on the beginners, huh?"

"Nope."

Mark smiles and starts his way upstairs without saying anything to Jade. Jade simply stands in the kitchen staring at an unnoticing Mark. Kalina follows him. Once upstairs, Mark begins to change his clothes but notices Kalina staring at him.

"You didn't say hi to Mommy."

Mark stops in his tracks. "I will. Don't worry."

Kalina stares at Mark again, as if she's trying to understand something. She eventually turns around and heads out of the room. "Daddy, you smell like perfume. I don't think Mommy would like that."

Mark follows Kalina with his eyes as she leaves to go back downstairs. The first thought that enters his mind is that he has done nothing wrong. All he did was talk. What right does a child have to talk to him in such an accusatory fashion? But no matter how Mark felt about what his daughter said, he knew she was right. He also knew the conversation with Alicia finished in a way that left more questions than answers. Not only did it finish with more questions, it ended with a desire to find out more.

CHAPTER FIFTEEN

CRAIG gets into his office the next morning and sees a vase of roses sitting on Berta's desk. As he stares at them, he hears Berta coming from the elevator and heading to her desk. Craig turns around and smiles at Berta.

"This guy must really like you."

Berta smiles and looks at the bouquet of roses she received from Daniel a few minutes before she left the office last night. "They're just roses."

Craig chuckles at Berta's shyness. "So you like him too, huh?"

"Maybe." Berta sits at her desk.

"When do I get a chance to meet him?"

Berta stares at Craig for a moment before answering. "You want to meet the guy? Is overprotective big brother Craig coming out again?"

"No, no. Nothing like that. I just want to meet the guy who could eventually take your hand in marriage."

"Whoa. Hold on one second. You're moving us kinda fast, don't you think?"

"I'm just saying. Not that I'm rushing things . . . it's just good to see you've found someone . . . someone good. For a moment I thought —" Craig pauses, feeling like he has said too much.

"Go on."

"I just thought you stopped looking, that's all."

"Why would I stop looking?"

"I don't know. I just . . . Look, when can I meet the guy?"

"He's coming to pick me up for lunch. You can meet him then."

"Hey, you know what. I was going out to lunch with Maya. Why don't we make it like a double date?"

Berta snickers. "We aren't in high school."

"Sounds like a bunch of fun to me. I don't know."

Berta sighs. "I'll ask him to see if he's interested."

"See? I knew you liked the idea. I'll call Maya now." Craig walks into his office.

After they both make their phone calls, lunch is set for the two couples. They decide to meet at a steakhouse a few blocks away.

Craig, Berta, and Daniel wait for Maya to make it to the steakhouse before they enter. From across the street, Craig spots Maya and smiles. A few moments later, she runs up to Craig and gives him a kiss. After everyone introduces themselves, they all go into the restaurant. The four are seated and Craig is the first to strike up a conversation.

"So, Daniel, I've heard some good things about you."

"Really?" Daniel asks while smiling.

"Well, no, not really, but Berta's face says enough. Over the years I've worked with her, I have never seen her this happy."

"I guess I'm doing something right."

"I'd say so."

Berta remains silent, looking back and forth between Craig and Daniel but really trying to sneak a few glances at Maya.

Daniel looks at Maya. "You're Maya Grange, aren't you?"

Maya looks at Craig for a second and then back at Daniel. "Yes, I am."

"That was a great article done on you in 'Power Business' magazine."

"Oh, thank you. Are you a businessman yourself?"

"Yup. I'm a consultant. Big business marketing strategy."

"Sounds like fun."

"It is. Just a lot of travel that's all."

"What kind of businesses do you consult?"

"All kinds. I've done consulting for three of the top five."

"That's impressive. How long have been doing it?"

"Maybe eight years . . . ten if you count the jobs I did while getting my Masters."

Maya nods her head and turns to Berta. "You're quiet over there."

"Oh, me? I'm just listening to the business talk. I mean, I've only had one job since college . . . and I'm still there so not many stories from me."

"But you do a great job," Craig interjects.

Berta smiles shyly. "Thanks."

"And if it helps any, I only had one job since college too," Craig continues.

"Oh, no," Maya says. "You've been stuck with him for that long?"

Berta chuckles. "He's not that bad."

"How long *have* you two been working together," Daniel asks.

"How long has it been, Berta? Seven years, maybe?"

"Yeah, I think seven, going on eight."

Daniel gives a perplexed look that Craig notices.

"Craig dear, eventually you have to let Berta go and spread her wings. You can't keep her hostage forever. With the experience she has, she can write her own ticket."

"She sure could," Daniel says.

Craig chuckles believing that Maya is a bit uncomfortable now as well. "If Berta wanted to leave, she surely could . . . and I would write her the best recommendation known to man."

"Actually, I know of a bunch of people looking for an executive assistant with experience. It would be as e—"

"I don't want to leave. I'm fine where I am."

"I'm sure you would like to move up in the world," Maya says.

"Moving up in the world isn't much of my concern. I love my job, and I don't need for money . . . so what's the point?"

Daniel now shifts his perplexed look towards Berta.

"I would think that something you do day in and day out you would want to perfect. I would think you would want to get better at it, maybe not for others, but for yourself . . . you know . . . taking pride in what you do."

Craig glances at Maya as Berta answers.

"People get that confused many times," Berta says. "What I do is so much more than being an assistant . . . my self-worth isn't tied to me being an assistant . . . or status . . . or anything else that comes or goes like the wind."

"So what is it tied to?"

"The measuring stick is Jesus Christ Himself. I don't worry about moving up and gaining status, or gaining money, or things . . . all I worry about is how I follow what was given to me . . . how well I treat people . . . because when all is said and done . . . the last thing that will be talked about is what top executive I've assisted."

"I told you she is a spiritual woman," Craig boasts.

"I get all that," Maya says. "But I don't get just slouching your way through life here on Earth because some God gave you a few rules to follow."

Craig grimaces and he places his hand on Maya's lap to get her to be quiet.

"Slouching?" Berta asks in a louder tone. "Some God?" She feels Daniel's hand on her lap as well and shakes her head. "You have a very interesting outlook on life," she says in a calmer tone.

Neither Maya nor Berta says anything for the rest of lunch. The conversation becomes dominated by Craig and Daniel talking about sports.

⚜

That night, Craig lies on his bed talking on the phone with Maya.

"I don't like her. I don't like her at all."

"Come on, Maya. You tried to attack her philosophy . . . you attacked her religion . . . what did you think was going to happen?"

"That's not the part I'm really mad at."

"That's the only part."

"No. Did you notice the way they both sat there like they were better than us?"

"No, I didn't. Look, Maya, you're still mad. Take a few minutes to calm down and we'll talk about it then."

"No. I want to talk about it now. The nerve of them. Together, we make more than they could ever dream of. All I was doing was giving some advice. And did you hear the way she talked to me?" Maya starts mocking Berta's voice. "'I don't need for money so what's the point.' Arrogant."

"You did come off like you knew more than they knew . . . or at least more than Berta knew."

"I was just giving advice, and are you defending them?"

"No. I'm just looking at the si—"

"Are you defending her?"

"Maya, I'm just looking at the situation logically. She had a different view than you did and that angered you. You were wrong. Big deal. You own up to it, apologize if needed, and move on."

"Good-bye, Craig."

"What?"

142

"I'm getting off the phone now. Good-bye."

Craig sighs. "All right. Talk to you la—"

The phone clicks.

The next day, Craig gets to work to see Berta diligently working at her desk. He stands there for a few seconds before approaching her. When he does, she looks up at him and gives him a smile that stops him in his tracks. Craig doesn't understand why he stopped. It's the same smile she always gives him. Nonetheless, there he stands, staring at Berta.

"You okay?" she asks.

Craig shakes off whatever feeling he had. "Yes, I'm fine. Good morning."

"Morning."

Craig sits on the edge of her desk. "So I guess no more double-dating for us, huh?"

Berta snorts. "That's what it looks like."

"Well, first let me apologize for Maya's actions. She . . . she . . ."

"She doesn't like me too much."

"Well, no. It's not that. It's just . . ."

"Don't make up some story. I know for a fact she doesn't like me. I'm fine with that . . . I'm not too fond of her either. She reminds me of my mother."

Craig looks past Berta at the wall. "Ouch. At least your guy is cool. I had no problems with him."

Berta winces. "Well . . . He doesn't really like you too much."

Craig chuckles. "What did I do? I only said a few things."

"Do you really want to know?"

"You may as well tell me."

"What he read from you is that you're a selfish person . . . and arrogant."

Craig laughs and leans in to Berta. "He's right, you know. That's me all the way." He slides off her desk and walks to his office door.

"Who did she say I was?"

Craig turns back. "Snobby and stuck up. You think you're better than everyone."

"I am," Berta laughs. "Aren't I? Aren't I better than everyone else?"

Craig laughs. "Yup, you are. Together, we are a pair of the worst people alive."

Berta laughs even harder. "Get to work, you selfish loser."

"Get back to work, you snobby prima donna."

Craig walks into his office and shuts the door behind him. He throws his bag in the corner, shuffles to his chair, and plops right into it. He tries to understand Berta and her smile as if she were some math equation.

"I don't get it," he whispers moments later just as he digs into his pocket to grab his vibrating cell phone. He looks to see that Maya is calling and decides to let her call to go to his voicemail.

CHAPTER SIXTEEN

"YOU told her what?"

"I told her that I would step down as your assistant so he could play."

"Mark, why would you do that?"

Mark looks at the music teacher, Mr. Benteed with a twisted look. "The kid can play."

"I understand that, trust me, I do. What I don't get is why you would put something like that on the table."

"I don't know. That doesn't matter now. It worked you see." Mark pulls out a half cut piece of paper from his briefcase. "She signed the slip."

"Yeah, but at what cost?"

"None. I don't have to step down. I just said that to show how serious I am about her son."

"So you lied to her?"

"No. At the time I was serious, and she agreed to me stepping down, but after we talked and she saw how I am with her son, she changed her mind."

Mr. Benteed smiles. "So why didn't you say that from the beginning?" he shakes his head. "So you laid it all on the line for this one child to play?"

"Exactly. It's what I do for every child."

"Are you trying to get teacher of the year again?" Mr. Benteed says smiling.

"No. That's not my concern. I just don't want Tim turning into a statistic. He has something going for himself. He just needs a little guidance." Mark gets up from his seat. "I gotta run. My case is exploding with test papers to grade, and I need to come up with next week's lesson plan."

"No problem. Is Tim coming today?"

"He sure is." Mark smiles. "Teacher of the year for the third year in a row would be nice." He begins to walk away.

"Well, that isn't out of the realm of possibility, Mark. You've got everyone's respect, including mine."

"Just make sure you get the kids ready for the recital." Mark waves and continues out the door toward his classroom.

In the hallways, the after school rush is just starting to die down. He gets to his empty classroom and opens the door wide. Setting his briefcase on his desk, he pauses to look around him. In a practiced set of motions, he closes the shades and turns on his desk lamp. Then he pulls out a bunch of pens and notepads before sitting down to start grading.

For hours, Mark sits at his desk grading papers and forming new plans. He does this without taking a break. Over time, each teacher and student shuffles from the classroom section of the school until Mark is the only one left. He pulls open the shade to see it getting dark outside and looks at the clock.

"Six twenty-five."

Mark looks down at his desk, proud of the work he completed and begins to pack. He hears a faint noise in the hallway that gets louder as the seconds pass. Mark begins to pack slower, trying to hear what the noise is. Soon enough, he recognizes the sound as someone in dress shoes coming down the hall and assumes it's a teacher picking up some papers. To his surprise, the footsteps stop at his door as a soft knock on his door raises his head.

"Hey, Mark," Alicia says.

Mark stares at her confused. "Hi?"

Alicia smiles. "I was told you don't help out with the orchestra on Thursdays."

"Yeah. I usually take Thursdays to grade papers . . . come up with lesson plans . . . other stuff."

"Oh. Well, I won't take too much of your time. I ju—"

"I'm finished now," Mark blurts out before she could finish.

Alicia smiles again. Mark notices that she smiled twice in this short conversation, more than she smiled in any recent conversation they had.

"Well, I just wanted to stop by and thank you . . . and apologize. I have been acting like a two-year-old and I almost messed up a big opportunity for my own son."

"Don't worry about it. Your apprehension is understandable af—"

"Was."

"Huh?"

"Was understandable. You said 'is understandable.' I'm not too apprehensive anymore."

Mark stares blankly at her. "Your apprehension was understandable . . . after everything that happened between us."

"Yeah, well sometimes you just have to cut your losses and move on, right?"

"Yeah." Mark, feeling uncomfortable, changes the subject. "Where's Tim?"

"Still with Mr. Benteed. In his words, he is 'doing piano.' He wanted extra lessons to try to learn the notes before the recital."

Mark thinks for a second while picking up his briefcase from his desk and grabbing his jacket. They both then walk out of the classroom. Mark closes the door behind them and they both walk down the hall.

"A lot of people respect you around here, Mark."

"You sound surprised."

"I am . . . but not at you. I'm rather surprised at myself."

"I don't think I follow."

"People always respected you. You have always been a respectable person. I thought that somehow changed."

"In other words, you judged me on a mistake, well a chain of mistakes."

Alicia nods. "But you're the same Mark. The same Mark . . ."

Mark looks to the side eying Alicia as she looks down in front of her feet and shakes her head. "Don't worry about it, Alicia. What's done is done."

"I missed you."

"Alicia this—"

"No. Wait. Let me finish."

"This isn't a good idea. We shouldn't be talking, at least not about this."

"Wait, Mark. We're both adults here . . . married adults. All I was saying was that I missed you *back then*."

"Why are you telling me this?"

"I don't know, Mark. I don't know. I had in my head everything that I was going to tell you. I was going to tell you how worthless you are . . . how you are the scum of the planet . . . how inconsiderate . . . how selfish . . . how completely idiotic you are . . . and instead I could only think about the good times we had. All I could think about is what we were setting up for . . . the lives we planned . . . and how good it feels just to walk side by side with you again. It's all taking me by surprise . . . too many emotions coming up . . . ones that I thought I suppressed."

Mark finds himself unable to say anything as they make it to the doors of the auditorium. They walk in to see Tim concentrating hard on learning his piano notes. Mr. Benteed sits next to him pointing and talking to him. He sees the two and motions them over there.

"He's picking up on this quickly," he yells.

Mr. Benteed hops off the stage and meets them in the middle of the auditorium. He begins to talk of how well Tim grasps the concepts of playing a piano. Mark hastily takes the opportunity to excuse himself from the conversation and leave. Alicia gives him a look before he is able to escape. Running out the school doors and looking at his watch, he realizes he is already late for his workout, but it isn't until he's on the road and almost at the gym when what Alicia said hits him.

Mark comes out the gym locker room looking for Craig. He feels someone nudge him on the shoulder.

"I'm already done. I'll spot if you want."

Mark turns around to see Craig unwrapping tape from his hands. "Sorry. I got caught up again."

"You okay? You look out of sorts."

"I'm fine. Just a load on my mind. I was just going to hit the heavy bag and roll afterwards."

"The heavy bag? The gym is closing in a half hour and it takes just about that long for you to wrap your hands."

"I'll go bare-knuckle."

Craig looks impatient. "Man, what's been going on? You haven't been acting yourself lately . . . and don't give me that, I've been thinking a lot . . . or I'm okay . . . things are fine. Clearly, things aren't fine."

Mark stares at Craig for a few seconds before leaning his head towards the heavy bag. He then taps his knuckles and starts to walk over to the bag.

For the first fifteen minutes, both remain silent as Mark gives it to the defenseless bag. A few of his hits were enough to send the bag and Craig jerking back. Craig meanwhile stares at Mark, trying to understand what is going on in his head. Finally, Mark begins to talk, although he pauses to send another haymaker into the bag.

"Alicia. Alicia . . . is . . . here . . . and she . . . did everything . . . from cuss me out . . . to telling me . . . she missed me."

As Mark finishes his sentence, Craig notices that Mark's knuckles are starting to bleed. He immediately tells him to stop. Mark drops his hands to his sides and walks back to the locker room.

"I don't know what the heck is going on," Mark says.

"Well, all I can tell you is this: stay away from her at all costs. It sounds like nothing but trouble from where I stand. I hate to say this, but Alicia is a bitter and scorned woman. Dangerous territory if you ask me . . . and Mark . . . what about Jade?"

Mark scoffs at Craig's comment. "What about her?"

Craig is shocked by what Mark just said. "What do you mean? She's your wife."

"She stopped being that some time ago."

Craig is stunned into silence.

"There's a lot you don't know, man. That's all I care to say right now."

Craig nods. "Fair enough, I guess. That's more than you've been telling me."

"Yeah . . . you know what else? I'm scared, man. I don't know which direction I'm going . . . and even worse . . . I don't know where God is in all this . . ."

"Did you pray about it?" Craig says awkwardly.

"Nope. What am I praying for? I know where my heart is . . . and it isn't in a good place to ask for anything."

"I don't get it."

Mark stares at Craig with a serious look. "I miss Alicia too . . . and, other than the kids . . . I'm not sure what's keeping me with Jade."

"Mark, what happened?"

Mark shakes his head, knowing he can't tell Craig the whole story.

"She's going to be at this recital for the school." Mark feels around his knuckles. "I'm trying not to look forward to it . . ." Mark looks up at Craig.

Craig shakes his head but says nothing. Mark shrugs his shoulders, his face looking glum. "Let's get out of here, man. I'm not much in the mood for working out."

こげ

Jade sits in front of the TV, curled up under a blanket, waiting for Mark to come home. She senses even more separation than before, even though the dreams when he whispers another woman's name are less frequent. She feels him slipping away no matter how hard she tries to maintain the norm. Part of her believes that he knows of her infidelity, but the rest of her remains in denial. *How does he not know?* she thinks. *Either he is so far removed from our marriage . . . or he has taken a vow of silence.* There's something tearing her marriage apart, she knows this much. What that something is . . . or even what those some things are . . . .

Finally Jade hears Mark's keys at the front door and sits up as she smooths down her hair. Mark steps in and gives her a weak smile.

"How was your day," Jade asks.

"Long."

Mark throws his bag by the steps and walks upstairs out of Jade's sight. Jade turns the TV off and follows him upstairs. Mark stops by Charles's room and peers in to see him sound asleep. He looks into Kalina's room to see her sound asleep as well. He then walks into the master bathroom and closes the door. A few seconds later, Jade hears the shower running.

What would a good wife do right now? Jade thinks of things she could do, not for the sake of being a good wife to Mark, but to continue to cover up what is wrong in their marriage. She walks over to the bedroom door and closes it. She then presses the button on the handle to lock the door. She goes to her dresser and grabs a bottle of oil and sets it by the bed. *Long day equals massage.* She sits on the edge of the bed and waits for Mark to come out the shower, calculating her every move. She crosses her legs and props her chin up in her palm. She stares at her nightstand and the leather cover Bible under the lamp. She begins to daydream while looking at it, imagining a better life, a life without her mistake. Mark comes out the bathroom. She didn't realize she zoned out for so long. Mark looks at Jade with a blank stare and shuffles his way to his side of the bed. Jade walks to Mark and tugs on his towel. He looks at her and eyes the bottle of oil on Jade's nightstand.

"Baby, I'm pretty tired. I just need some rest."

Jade lets her hand drop from his towel as Mark shuffles around clothes in his drawer. His back is towards her and she stares at him for a few seconds before leaving him be and sliding into bed. Moments later, Mark gets in bed and pretends to go to sleep.

They both lie there, backs turned towards each other, pretending to sleep. There's a space between them. It is possible there always was a space that they never noticed. It's hard for them not to notice now, for the once empty space is flooding with lies and pain. They both know that no marriage can truly survive ignoring what really resides in that space: a growing parasite. All the parasite will do is grow until it takes over and sucks away what love they have left for each other. They also believe their marriage won't survive exposing the parasite, either. The secrets and faults, the emotions and the lack thereof would render their marriage defeated. So for now, denial is the best way to go. Denial is their defense. If no one says anything about the parasite that is killing their marriage, then it isn't there. That is, until it rears its ugly head. Then, they will have no choice but to face it and deal with the aftermath.

CHAPTER SEVENTEEN

SHE'S had nightmares every day for weeks now. None of them are about anything in particular. She just knows that she is waking up in a cold sweat. When she does wake, she prays until she falls asleep again. She thinks something is wrong. Being the person that she is, Berta tries to pray her way through whatever this struggle is, but as time goes on, things get worse. Something doesn't sit right in her spirit although everything in her life is golden right now. Great job. Great boyfriend. Great church. Great friends. Berta goes over everything and comes up with nothing but good things, yet she sits in her apartment trying to understand why she feels so empty.

All Saturday morning, Berta sat in her chaise thinking and praying. By noon, she'd become tired of herself and called Daniel. After a short conversation, Berta asked him to stop by to talk. Now, they both sit staring at each other, Daniel waiting patiently for Berta to say something.

"Everything all right?" Daniel finally asks.

Berta sighs. "I don't know. I think so."

"Okay . . . well what's wrong?"

"Nothing. Nothing is wrong at all."

Daniel grabs hold of Berta and embraces her.

"I'm sorry," Berta says into his chest.

"Sorry? What are you apologizing for? You didn't do anything wrong."

Berta thinks for a second, knowing he is right. "I don't know, Daniel. I don't know."

"Have you prayed about it?"

"I've been . . ."

"And?"

"Nothing."

Daniel takes a deep breath that Berta hears from his chest. "So there's a chance you are missing something. Maybe. Maybe there's also an equal chance that you're not missing anything but you need to be stronger . . . to endure."

"I guess."

"Whatever this is that's going on . . . is that why you didn't come to Bible study last night?"

"Maybe."

"I'll tell you what. I'll cook dinner for you tonight and keep you company. Maybe we can pick up a movie or something and just hang out. What do you think?"

Berta doesn't say anything right away.

"Or we could go out," Daniel says. "We could go to the movies."

"Do you always know what to say and when to say it?"

Daniel looks at Berta with a frown.

"You always have the right words. You always do the right things."

"I don't know if I have an answer to that."

"Seriously, you are such a good man. Sometimes I wonder what you see in me. I'm a head case at best."

"Hey, hey, now don't start talking like that. You are a beautiful and unique person. You're not the average woman, and you're definitely not a head case."

"Thanks but—"

And just like that, Daniel kisses Berta in the middle of her sentence. A million thoughts run through her head as they share a long and engaging kiss. Berta is the first to pull away, and they both stare into each other's eyes for a few seconds.

"Sorry. I just had to k—"

Berta cuts Daniel off by leaning into him for more. They kiss again, this time more heavily. No thoughts run through her head except one, and that is how much she wants Daniel. He isn't shy about his want of her either as he slides his hand up under her shirt. They begin kissing each other wherever there is exposed skin, moving like ferocious animals.

Too fast, Berta. Too fast, girl. Too soon, girl. Slow it down. Slow it down.

Daniel tugs on the front part of her jeans as if asking permission to continue. Berta arches her back, pushing herself more into him, while coaching herself against it. Daniel begins to unbutton her pants.

Stop, Berta. Stop now, Berta. STOP.

"Wait." Berta says as she tenses her entire body. She puts her hands on Daniel's shoulders, not pushing him away, but not letting him advance.

Daniel looks at her, coming out of his trance as his face melts into one of shock.

"I'm sorry," he says. "I better leave. I . . . I'm so sorry."

"No, it's fine," Berta says sliding her shirt back down and readjusting herself. "I, ummm, well . . ."

A few moments after adjusting, Daniel leaves. They are barely able to say good-bye to each other without wanting to continue what they were doing, so he rushes out the door. Berta takes a few moments to calm down and steady her breathing. *What was I about to do? What was he about to do?*

CB80

Mark hasn't seen Alicia since that one Thursday after school. Since then, it has been nothing but him and his thoughts. So when he finally sees her in her work suit, a smile makes its way onto his face. It's as if the smile sneaked its way onto his face without him knowing, and it forces him to realize that he is elated to see her.

"Hey," she says with an even wider smile on her face.

"Good evening. You about set to go?"

"I am. Is my little man ready?"

"Nervous, but ready, yes."

"When is his solo?"

"Towards the middle, after the intermission."

"Okay, good. I have my tissues ready."

Mark chuckles. "Me too."

"Awww. Is big strong Mark going to cry?"

"Are you poking fun at me?"

"Nope." Alicia gives Mark a sarcastic look.

"Whatever. Your seat is down in front with all the soloists' parents."

Alicia looks strangely at Mark. "You're not going to sit with me?"

Marks heart stops at the question. "Ummm, no. I have to do a few things in the background. Why? You need someone's shoulder to cry on, ya big baby?"

Alicia laughs. "I'm a proud parent. I can cry like a blubbering fool if I want."

"Well, I'm his teacher . . . I'm like a proud parent."

Alicia smirks and turns away to walk to her seat. She turns her head back and says, "You are." She smiles at him again before walking down to her seat.

Mark stares at her as she walks away from him leaving a trail of a sweet smell behind her. He rapidly shakes his head and continues to greet and direct parents to their seats.

∞

Back home, Jade puts the finishing touches on dinner while Kalina sits on a stool and watches. Their relationship has improved over the last few months, mainly because Jade took more interest in Kalina's interests. Kalina feels more open to talk about things with Jade now and for the first time in her life, she feels like she has two parents, a mother and a father, as opposed to just her father. Jade starts to place food on dishes and sets one plate aside.

"That's Daddy's plate?"

Jade glances up at her. "Sure is. I made his favorite tonight. You think he's gonna be surprised?"

Kalina gives Jade a twisted look. "I think so. But I thought Daddy was going to eat at the school."

Jade stops preparing the plate. "Why would he do that?"

"Remember, Mommy? The recital is tonight. He said he was going out to eat afterwards."

Jade looks down. "Oh, yes. I forgot. Well, I guess he has a big lunch for tomorrow." She wraps up the food-filled plate with aluminum foil and sets it in the refrigerator. She then prepares the kids' plates and finally her own. Her entire face feels hot as if she has a fever. *He never told me about a recital. He didn't mention one word about it.*

Jade begins to combat the number of questions she has that run through her head. She doesn't know why he wouldn't say a word about it. It's like he's trying to hide something. At least, that is what her intuition is telling her. In the middle of her meal, she sets her plate down and walks to the garage, pulling the hanging keys from the wall. She swings open her car door and hops in the vehicle.

CogoD

Mark stands towards the back of the auditorium listening to the children's orchestra. A lump forms in his throat as he becomes nervous for Tim, who is to play soon. Someone in the front row stands up and starts walking to the back doors. As the person gets closer, he sees that it is Alicia leaving the auditorium. Mark remembers distinctly that he said Tim was after the intermission. She walks right by him and out the double doors. Mark follows. In the hallway, he sees her on the phone and decides not to call her name to get her attention.

"Okay, I get it," Alicia says to the person on the phone. "Umm hmm. Yes, okay. Seriously, I have to go. *My* son is about to play." She looks up at Mark and smiles a faint smile. He can hear that the person on the other line is angry. "What do you mean, what do I mean?" She turns away from Mark. "You haven't shown your face for years. Don't act like you care now."

There is more yelling on the phone. Mark begins to walk away, but she grabs his arm. She looks at him with tear-filled eyes. Instinctually, Mark grabs the phone from Alicia and hangs it up on the stranger's angry words. He then hands it back to her.

"I don't need to know what's going on. I just came to get you because your son is about to play. Nothing is more important than that right now. He needs to see you there so . . ."

Alicia wipes the tears from her eyes and nods. She takes in a deep breath and exhales slowly. Mark nudges her a bit and smiles at her. Alicia gives Mark another faint smile and heads back into the auditorium.

⚭

Jade still sits in the parked car in the garage. She hasn't moved since getting into the car. Tears begin to stream down her face as she continues to talk herself out of going to the school. *What are you thinking? The kids are still home, wide-awake. What do you think is going on?* Jade clutches the car keys in her hand and gets out the car. She walks back into the house to see Kalina and Charles staring at the television.

"You two, time for bed," she says exhausted.

They look at each other and back at Jade. They know at this point not to say anything to go against her order, so they both run upstairs. Jade plops onto the couch. More questions run through her head. *What right do you have to question anything? Even if he is out there cheating, you started it. You brought it into this household.* She silently cries again but this time with Kalina secretly watching from the stairs.

Once the tears stop flowing, she stares at the television with blurred vision. She feels hurt and betrayed but knows not why. She finally determines that she's reaching her breaking point. She can't keep this secret from Mark any longer. She's guilty and part of her wants to believe that Mark is guilty, just so she can shift the blame. But Mark is blameless. He goes around being the best father and husband a woman could want. *And I just threw it all away,* she thinks. Jade gets up from the couch and goes to the kitchen, where she opens a bottle of wine, a wedding gift from years ago. She pours some into a glass and begins to drink. At first, the bitter taste does anything but calm her down, but after a few glasses, she becomes relaxed, almost somber.

❦

The recital is finished. Proud parents have already taken their children home. Tim played an excellent piece that had everyone in the audience moved to tears. Parents, children, and even faculty gave Mark and Mr. Benteed a standing ovation for the well put together night, but there Mark sits, in the middle of the auditorium, by himself. He was supposed to go out and celebrate a job well done. Instead he sits in the auditorium questioning everything in his life. The cool blue lights of the stage give everything a memorable look. It reminds Mark of those black light parties he had in college. He hears the doors open behind him. He doesn't move because he knows who it is. After all, he is the one who asked Alicia to come back.

She comes down to Mark's row and slides into the seat next to him. For some time neither say anything, but Mark can feel her staring at him.

"I know it might have seemed silly, asking you to come back. I just wanted to know . . . Why are you here? Like, it is already out on the table why I am here . . . why I left, but it was never clear why or how you ended up here."

Mark hears Alicia tremble out a breath. "I came for Tim." Alicia shifts her body to face Mark more. "Look, I have to come clean about something."

Mark simply looks at her.

"I knew about the school . . . Delori . . . I knew about their acceptance programs and the way it worked and how you have to be in the area for acceptance. We came down here to get into that school."

Mark stares at Alicia. "Is that the only reason you came down?"

Alicia hesitates. "I . . . I don't know. I guess I came here to get away from you. It sounds laughable, I know, but I came here to somehow get you out of my mind . . . out of my space."

"But you knew I wasn't even in the same state as you. I was already gone."

"You never left, Mark. You may have been gone physically, but you were still . . . you were still there with me. Yeah, you were there, taunting me, telling me that I was worthless. You were there to ruin my marriage. You really have no idea what it was like, do you? Do you know what it was like to fall in love with a man who you knew would never compare to your first love? Do you know what it is like to settle because everyone around you thought that the person standing in front of you was a catch?"

"I can't say I do know. I know that I've apologized a billion times over for my actions though. I know that if I could do it all again, I would. I know th—"

"Wait, wait. Mark, this is turning into another argument." Alicia calms the tension while internally reveling in the last few words that Mark said.

Mark takes a deep breath and begins talking again. "So, I ruined your marriage. How?"

"You didn't. I just said that." Alicia sighs. "You see, I blamed you for everything wrong in my life, yet I compared everything good to you. So when my husband decided that he couldn't live life to beat you, a man he has never met, he left. Tim was three then."

"I'm sorry."

"You don't have to apologize anymore."

"I'm not really. I feel sorry for the man that left . . . Tim is a great kid."

Alicia smiles. "He is great."

Long silence.

"So why do you keep the last name?"

Alicia winces. "We aren't divorced . . . just separated I guess."

"So you two have been trying to work it out I'm guessing."

"For far too long."

"I see."

Alicia gets back on topic. "So, I came down here to get away from your memory. But I run right into you. Ironic."

"Irony can take a jump off a cliff."

Alicia looks at Mark confused.

"Just something I picked up from a friend. You remember Craig?"

"I do." She leans back into her chair and crosses her legs. "Tell him I said hi."

"I will."

Silence.

Alicia nods. "So now what?"

Mark thinks. "You're Tim's mother. I'm Tim's teacher," Marks says, not really knowing what to do next but figures stating facts will help them to a conclusion. But after a long pause, he realizes that it didn't help. "Where is Tim?"

"He wanted to stay the night over at a friend's house."

"Oh."

Alicia interrupts, "Mark, I don't expect anything from you. I know you have things on your mind and a family to deal with. I feel bad for acting the way I have. I was so childish."

"I can't blame you."

"Well, just do me this favor. Just keep being the great teacher that you are . . . for Tim's sake."

Mark understands what she is really saying. He understands that it is best for them to focus their energies on Tim. Otherwise, there would be nothing to stop them from focusing on each other, two bitter and dissatisfied spouses with a connected past. At least, that is the way he understands what she is saying. He gets up from his seat.

"I better get back home . . . make it in time to tuck the kids in."

Alicia grabs his hand. Just the sheer warmth of her hand alarms Mark. "Just . . . one more question . . . and I'll leave it alone for good."

"What is it?"

"It's just so strange that I run into you while trying to run away from you." She lets go of his hand. "Do you think . . . that God . . . I mean, when we were younger, we knew that we were soul mates . . . but . . ." Alicia shakes her head. "Never mind. You better head home. Tuck your children in."

Mark stares at Alicia for a few moments before leaving her side and going to the control panel to cut off the lights. As she makes her way to the back door, he cuts the lights off and turns on one spotlight that is still aimed at the door. Alicia looks at him and smiles.

"Just lighting the way," Mark yells.

"You always did," Alicia yells back to him. She then leaves the auditorium. Mark shuts the spotlight off and stands in total darkness. He takes a few breaths and a few moments to think. *There goes another one of those comments. I think she's actually starting to warm up to me again. Wait, that's not a good thing. Come on, Mark. You're married man. What happened to your vows? What happened to your plan? What happened to . . .* Mark doesn't finish his thought. Instead he leaves the building and heads home.

☙❧

Jade sits on the kitchen floor, leaning on the sink cabinet with a wineglass in her hand. Half of the bottle of wine she started earlier is gone. She sees a reflection of herself on the dishwasher. Little by little her reflection turns into a monster. She shakes her head and attempts to stand up but stumbles and falls. She lays her face on the cool tile floor and rests. Just as she begins to fall asleep, she hears the clicking of men's dress shoes on the floor. The footsteps stop right in front of her face. She reaches up and grabs the leg of the mystery man. Instantly, she is scooped up in his arms. She tries to adjust her blurred vision to focus on the man's face. After a few moments, she figures the man to be Boley. He smells like a mixture of cologne and sweet perfume. *It has to be Boley,* she thinks. *He smells like his wife.* Jade rests her head on Boley's chest and closes her eyes, allowing herself to be carried away to some unknown place. One moment she feels the movement of Boley's strong arms carrying her upstairs. The next, the movement stops.

"No . . . don't stop . . . take . . . me away, Greg" Jade says in a slur. She groans a bit before resting her head again and closing her eyes. Everything thereafter becomes a confusing mesh of her senses.

☙❧

Mark gets home and throws his keys on the coffee table. He grabs the remote to the television and clicks it to shut off the TV. He hears a gentle noise in the kitchen and heads there to see Jade face flat on the kitchen floor. He steps right up to her face and stares at the half empty bottle of wine. For a few seconds, Mark stares at Jade in disgust. He is even tempted to leave her there, but his better judgment kicks in and he lifts her off the cold floor and into his arms. He begins to walk upstairs with her in his arms when he sees Kalina huddled up against the banister asleep. Mark figures that she watched Jade for a while. He grits his teeth trying to eliminate the urge to throw Jade out the door. She mumbles something that is mostly inaudible, but one name.

Greg.

He realizes she thinks he's Boley as he lays her on the couch. He then steps to Kalina and lifts her up from the stairs.

"Is Mommy okay?" she murmurs.

Mark kisses her on the forehead. "Mommy is fine. Now you need to get some rest. It's a school day tomorrow." He takes her to her bed and gently lays her down, tucking her between the sheets. He stares at her in admiration.

"I love you, Daddy," she says.

Mark blows her a kiss and leaves the room. He checks in on Charles to see him tucked in and sleeping soundly and figures Kalina to have helped in that department. At least, that is what he hopes happened. He gallops downstairs and lifts a passed out Jade. He carefully takes her up to the bedroom and lays her on the bed. He removes her shoes and throws them to the floor. Jade groans again. Mark, disgusted with his wife, sets the alarm clock to wake up Jade, grabs everything he needs for tomorrow, and heads to the basement. For some time, he sits in the dark and cold basement attempting to pray but to no avail. Eventually, he takes a shower in the basement bathroom and sleeps in the chair that sits in front of the TV.

CHAPTER EIGHTEEN

CRAIG gets to work to see that he made it in before Berta and goes to his desk to listen to his phone messages. Most of them are from clients. One of them is from Maya apologizing for her actions from earlier in the week. Craig figures that Maya finally cooled off and realized her actions were childish. He decides to call her back later.

He hears Berta coming from the elevator and to her desk and gets up to greet her. When he looks at her, he can see the sadness on her face.

"What's wrong?" he asks before ever greeting her.

Berta looks up with bloodshot, glassy eyes. "Nothing much. Everything is fine."

"You sure? Because either you've been crying or getting high just before you came to work."

Berta smiles a bit.

"Okay. A smile. That's a start. Now the next step. What's going on?"

"Please, Craig. Don't." Berta looks at him, pleading with her eyes.

Craig twists his face into an awkward expression, but backs off for now. "I won't bother you, but if you need me, just call."

Berta nods.

ⓒ⋈ⓓ

In the middle of her lunch, Berta hears the beep of the elevator reaching the floor. She waits for a few moments but sees no one come around the corner. After a few more moments, she hears the elevator doors closing, but still, no one appears. Berta gets up and walks towards the elevators. Just before she gets to the corner, a woman appears strutting into her view. She wears a hat, sunglasses, and a long trench coat. At first, Berta thinks it is Maya, but wait . . . a wedding ring. . ..

"Jade?"

"Hey, Berta, girl. I haven't seen you in ages. How have you been?"

"I've . . . been . . . good. What brings you around these parts?"

"I came to see Craig. Is he around?"

"He is. I'll call for him. Please, take a seat."

"Thanks."

Berta goes back to her desk and tells Craig that Jade is visiting. He asks for a few moments. Jade stares at Berta through her sunglasses.

"Too bright?" Berta asks.

"Huh? Oh, no. Just a headache right now. I get those every now and again . . . from the light."

"You might want to get that checked out. You might need prescription glasses."

"Yeah . . . maybe. Berta, can I ask you something, woman to woman?"

"Sure. Anything."

"Have you," Jade pauses. "Have you ever had something to tell someone you loved . . . but couldn't."

Berta looks in confusion, and tenses up on the inside.

"It could be serious . . . or not . . . but it's something you have to tell that loved one . . . or . . . or bad things could happen. But you know if you did tell that person, it would surely mean bad things."

"I'm not sure."

"Well, what would you do if you were presented that situation?"

Berta continues to tense up. "I would first seek God. From there . . . anything could happen."

"Have you ever been too embarrassed . . . or guilty to go to God?"

"At times . . . maybe embarrassed. Never really guilty. Why? Everything okay?"

"Yeah, everything is fine. I was just curious. Kalina presented me with another of her philosophical questions." Jade smiles.

"Oh. How are the kids?"

"They are great. Kalina is into chess now . . . although, I think it's a game of perverted little nerdy boys who don't socialize . . . but I'm warming up to it, I suppose. Football season is over, so it's basketball for Charles."

"That sounds great. Craig should be . . ."

The elevator comes up to the floor yet again, but this time, the person coming off it flounces right around the corner. Berta's face drops. Jade turns towards the woman who is standing next to her in a defiant stance. She smiles at Jade and turns directly to Berta. For a few moments, she says nothing as both Jade and Berta stare at her. She finally sighs.

"Berta, I'm sorry. I know I came off wrong, and I didn't mean anything by it," Maya says in a practiced speech.

Jade snickers a bit.

"That's fine," Berta says. "I was over it a while ago. Ummm . . . Craig is busy right now but—"

"Oh, no," Jade says. "She can go. I'll wait."

Berta keeps her eyes on Maya.

"Thank you. I actually just wanted to run in really quick just to say hi," Maya says moving towards the door. She goes in to see Craig on the cell phone and closes the door behind her. Craig's face drops when he sees her.

❦

"You see what you did, man," he yells into the phone. "Now Maya is here. I better not get slapped. I have triple the chance of getting slapped . . . I am calm . . . that's it . . . I'm gonna get slapped."

Maya trots over to Craig and grabs the cell phone. She closes it, ending the call. She then kisses him deeply on the lips. He stares at her wide-eyed as she kisses him.

"I just wanted to see you," she says, wiping the corner of her mouth.

Craig looks at her confused after she releases his lips. "Is there another woman out there?"

"Yes, she let me go ahead. I wasn't going to take long but if you want …" Maya removes her coat and flings it to the ground. She begins kissing him on his neck.

"No. Wait. It's important that I talk to her."

"I know somebody that needs some talking to," Maya purrs.

"She's my best friend's wife."

Maya stops.

"So do you want to slap me now . . . or later?"

"Later … if you really want me to." She starts on his neck again.

"Wait. What? Why are you acting like this?"

"Like what?"

"Forget it. Look, me and you tonight, okay? We can talk and all that good stuff later. I just really, really have a bunch of stuff to do with very little time to do it."

"What time tonight?"

"Ten, maybe? At my place?"

"No, ten at my place."

"Fine. I will be there."

Maya grabs her coat from the floor and puts it back on her shoulders. "I'll see you tonight, baby."

Craig gives a wry smile. "See you tonight."

Maya leaves, being cautious in closing the door. Craig, in a frenzy, rushes over to his fridge and grabs a bottle of water, gulping half of it down before shoving it back into the fridge. He loosens his collar and paces to the door. He opens it and smiles.

"Hey, Jade. What brings you by?"

Jade gets up and smiles at Berta. "Thanks for listening," she says.

"Sure, no problem. Seriously, if you need to, call me," Berta says with a strained face.

"Thanks. I will." Jade looks to Craig. "How are you, Mr. Big Time?"

"Big time? I'm anything but," Craig says, giving Jade a hug. "I work with peanuts."

"If that's what you want to call millions of dollars, okay."

Jade walks into his office and Craig glances at Berta, noticing the concerned look on her face. He shuts the door and offers Jade a seat. She sits and seemingly stares at Craig through her sunglasses.

"Can ya see me through those things?" Craig asks.

"Pretty well actually."

"Why don't you take them off? It freaks me out."

"I'd rather not. But listen—"

"Wait a minute. I know that look anywhere. Have you been drinking? Are you hung over?"

"How do you know that look?"

"Let's just say that at one point in my life, I conditioned myself to know that look. The real question is why were you drinking?"

Jade looks out the window. She sorts through her thoughts trying to find the right way to present this issue to Craig without seeming like the worst person on the face of the planet. "Things aren't so good between Mark and me."

"What do you mean? What happened?"

"A lot." Jade takes off the sunglasses and grabs a tissue from the desk. "But I came to ask if you've noticed anything different about Mark. Has he been acting strange lately?"

Craig leans back into his seat. He doesn't want to lie, but he's not too keen on the truth right now either. "I've noticed a few things, but I assumed it's because of work."

"Work related, huh?"

Craig nods. "I mean, he doesn't come to the gym as much because of the school orchestra, but other than that," Craig cringes on the inside, "nothing out the ordinary." Craig's mind is flooded with thoughts of Mark when he talks of Alicia and the lost expression he wears on his face whenever talking about her, but it is Jade's next question that sends chills up and down his spine.

"Who is Alicia?"

Craig looks at Jade, who looks at him with purpose, attempting to read him.

"She's an ex-girlfriend."

Jade nods. *He was dreaming about an ex-girlfriend*, she thinks. "So wh—"

"Look, Jade. I'm not totally sure what's going on with you two, but I do know that you ought to have this conversation with Mark. For as long as you have known me, you have known me to be straightforward, correct?"

"Yes."

"Then talk to Mark. I think that would do a whole bunch more good. Talk to your husband."

Jade listens to Craig as he stresses the word "husband." She nods again and shoves her sunglasses back on her face.

"Everything will be all right. Just talk to him."

"I will. Thanks, Craig." Jade gets up believing that Craig knows something, but not knowing what. She hugs him and leaves. On the way out, she hugs Berta. Craig notices that they hug for some time as the twinkle of tears appear on her cheeks.

A few moments after Jade leaves, Craig goes out the office and sits in front of Berta's desk. He sighs and Berta sits shaking her head.

"They're in serious trouble, aren't they?" Craig asks.

Berta nods solemnly. Craig bangs on the table in anger.

"Mark is messing up, big time."

"Mark?" Berta says. "What did Mark do?"

Craig stares at Berta in confusion. "What do you mean? He's the reason things are so weird."

"Is that what she told you?"

"No, that's what I know. Wait, what did she tell you?"

"Craig, I can't."

"Berta, seriously. Tell me."

"It's not my place . . . it's not yours either."

"What are you talking about?" Craig raises his voice in anger. "Mark is my best friend. If there is something Mark should know we should tell him. Period. We can't just let a marriage fall apart at its seams."

"God will fix it."

Craig laughs. "Every time som—" He stops himself.

"Do you trust me?" Berta asks.

"I do, but I think you're wrong."

"Just trust me on this one. God will fix it."

"Well, how much worse does it have to get before He does?"

"I don't know. I just know that He is able . . . and He will."

Craig laughs and gets up from his seat. "I remember when I had your type of faith. The faith that doesn't make any sense."

"You will again . . . one day."

"Yeah, I doubt it. Jail has a good way of breaking you out of that habit."

Berta flips the subject. "So what did Maya want?"

"Ummm . . . nothing really . . . just to see me. It was weird . . . the way she was acting."

"She missed you, I suppose."

"I guess . . . but I dunno Berta. She isn't . . . she isn't ... she isn't it. I don't think she is it for me. I could be wrong but . . ."

Berta looks at Craig with increasing interest. "What prompted this?"

"A lot . . . but I guess we better get back to work."

C3&80

Berta nods and looks down as Craig plods back into his office. He quietly shuts the door. When she hears the door click, she leans back in her seat and rests her head. She gets excited knowing that Maya and Craig are on the rocks but is put off by her own selfishness. She quickly reminds herself that she is with someone now anyway. She then shifts her thoughts to all Jade had revealed to her while Maya was in with Craig. All she can think is *she cheated on him twice.*

C3&80

Jade leaves Craig's office feeling good about her talk with Berta but not so good about her talk with Craig. Craig alluded to an issue with Mark as opposed to herself. *Maybe Mark does know. Or maybe he is doing what I had already done.* Jade gets into her car and drives to the market. During the whole drive, she thinks about what she told Berta, that she cheated on Mark, but Mark doesn't know, and that she doesn't know how to tell him. For a quick second, she thinks she should had clarified that it wasn't physical really, but knows she's just looking for a way to make her seem better than she is. Berta's advice was sound but none too likely to happen. She said that holding in the secret would eat her alive and that she should tell Mark. Jade laughs at the notion but contemplates on it again. Telling Mark would eventually allow them to move on, because divorce is not an option for her. Divorce is embarrassing. Divorce signifies failure and she isn't one to fail in something so great. *Maybe it's too late,* she thinks. *Maybe our marriage is already over.* Jade thinks of Kalina and Charles and how they would become another sad statistic. She read somewhere that there are more kids with single parent or separated parent homes than kids with both parents around in the same home. She doesn't want her children to be like everyone else. She doesn't want to be like everyone else.

She gets to the market and picks up a few vegetables for the dinner she has in mind when she hears a woman call her name. She looks to the side to see a short pregnant woman waddling her way towards her. Behind the woman is Boley, and closely following, their four kids. Jade freezes. Staying calm, she plays their presence off as normal.

"Hey, Tabby," she says, giving the pregnant woman a hug. She turns towards Boley and gives him a quick jab in the arm. "What's up, ya big goof?"

Boley smiles. "Same ol, same ol. How have you been?"

"I've been good."

"I'm still so sorry for everything that happened at the pharmacy. During these times, ya know, people are losing jobs left and right," Tabby interjects.

"Yeah. I'm not worried about it. I'm about used to the not working thing . . . although I may start up again soon. Either way, things are fine."

"Well, that's good. That place isn't the same without you. They hired all these young people that don't know what they're doing."

Jade smiles. "Yeah. So how are you? You look like you're set to go."

"I am. Any day now."

"Any day? Why are you walking around?"

"I'm trying to speed this process up. I'm about sick of being pregnant."

"I see." Jade smiles again and begins to shift away. "Well, listen, I have to go. Gotta pick up the kids."

"Oh, Jade, you and Mark should come by sometime. We have to catch up."

"Definitely. I'll give you a call."

Boley awkwardly says, "Yeah, I saw Mark a few some odd months ago. He came to the pharmacy not too long after you were let go."

Jade stops in her tracks. "He did?"

"Yeah. He came by to pick a few things up . . ." Boley looks at her with an expression his wife couldn't see. His attention is then drawn to one of his kids running away down an aisle. He smiles and waves. "I'll see you around, Jade. Tell Mark I said hi." He gives her one last look before chasing after his little girl. Tabby waves and motions with her hand to tell Jade to call her. Jade smiles again and walks away.

Over the years of working together, Jade and Boley had formed their own form of silent communication. Easily, Jade knew what Boley was trying to say. That tidbit of information outrages her. *Mark knew. He knew. He knew this whole time. He was pulling an act. But why wouldn't he say anything about it? Why the charade?*

Chapter Nineteen

THAT night, Mark gets to the gym and rushes to look for Craig. He looks all around the building but doesn't find him. He walks to the front desk and asks the attendant if he has seen Craig.

Nothing.

Mark waits on a bench for a few minutes before leaving the gym. As he steps outside, he sees Craig's car parked down the street. He hustles his way over but notices that he isn't there. Down the street a bit more, Mark sees a small corner church. Standing in front of the tall standing cathedral is Craig. He simply looks up at it, almost in admiration. Mark makes his way over to him. He calls his name, seemingly startling him. Craig pivots away from him, wiping away at his face.

"Craig man, what's up?"

"Oh . . . nothing . . . some old lady wanted me to walk her to the church. They're having some event. Apparently, I have 'backslider' written all over my forehead." Craig finally turns towards Mark. "How long have you been waiting?"

"Not too long, I guess. You okay?"

"Yeah, I'm fine. The wind was blowing . . . making my eyes tear up."

"Oh." Mark looks at the front windows of the church, noticing that none of the lights are on inside the building. "You ready to hit the gym?"

"Yeah. I can't stay for too long. I have to meet with Maya tonight."

Mark nods. "Would you rather not do the gym thing tonight?"

"Naw. It's cool . . . we can st—" Mark surprises him by throwing his gym bag on the steps of the church and sitting down on the cold stone. Craig goes to the other side of the steps and sits as well. Neither says anything as they watch the nightlife starting to pick up around town. Streetlights come on and more people begin to walk the streets.

"You remember . . . back in the day . . . we used to do this all the time," Mark says.

"I remember," Craig says. "Life was easier then. Then we had time to sit out on the steps and look around aimlessly. Now . . . life doesn't leave much time for anything really."

Mark nods. "What did Jade want?"

"I'm not a hundred percent sure. She asked me if I noticed you were acting strange."

"And you said?"

"I said yes. I wasn't going to lie to her. But I said it's because of work."

"You don't sound so sure about that one."

"Come on, Mark. I've known you for too long now. You don't have to play these games with me. I know your plan . . . even if you don't know your plan. I know how Alicia fits into the plan . . . and I can tell you now, she isn't going to bring you happiness."

"Thanks for the advice, but I'm fine. There's no plan. Trust me."

Craig looks directly at Mark and chuckles. He shakes his head and faces forward again. "She talked to Berta too. It was clear that her conversation with her was deeper than hers with me."

"Did Berta give any hint on the subject?"

"Not really, but we both agree."

"On what?"

"You two are in trouble . . . and if you don't talk to each other . . . it will only get worse."

Silence.

Craig looks at Mark, who is now leaning back against the steps. A tear traces its way down his face.

"She cheated on me," Mark says. "And she's keeping it a secret from me."

"Jade? No way, man. Jade wouldn't. You sure you have the right story? I mean, I can't pi—"

"She did. *That's* the reason she *quit* her job. She was never let go. She quit to cover her tracks. Her and Boley."

"Boley? Did you confront him about it? We ought to go handle this right now. Is he still in the picture? We can easily make sure he gets erased."

"Craig, don't worry about him. He's nothing to me . . . plus I don't think he seduced her or anything. I think it was Jade who pursued him . . . so there's nothing to say to him . . . he's just a man. She started all this."

"So why don't you say something to her about it?"

"Why? So we can get a divorce and end up another broken family? I can't put the kids through that . . . so I'm keeping quiet."

"Do you see what keeping quiet is doing?"

"Nothing to me."

Craig stares at Mark in astonishment. "That's a lie . . . and you're telling yourself this lie . . . for Alicia. You think you can just ease Alicia in or something?"

Mark gets angry. "No. I don't." He stands up suddenly. "I said nothing for the kids' sake, then BOOM, Alicia appears. Now . . . now . . . I just want to be happy. Don't I deserve that? After giving nearly my entire life to others who take what I give to them and trash it . . . don't I deserve this?"

"What about Jade . . . your wife. What about the vows you made to her."

"Vows? She made those same vows. She made those very same vows. Screw Jade. She can go to hell." Mark walks away towards his car.

"She's your wife, man. If that's where she ends up, you'll be right next to her. You can fix all this," Craig yells.

Mark stops. "What do you know? You've never been married . . . what can you tell me about marriage? What do you know about vows . . . about promises . . . nothing. Stay in your lane."

"How blind can you be?"

"Blind? Man, screw you too. I'm out." Mark hurries to his car and speeds away.

Craig stays sitting on the steps for a while before moving. He calms down and continues his prayer that Mark had interrupted a few minutes ago.

附

Berta sits across from Daniel in the same diner they have been going to for months after Bible study. After a long talk about ways to control their own urges for each other, Daniel drops a bombshell on Berta.

"You what?" she asks.

"I have been asked to return to Texas. Three startup firms. I would make enough to retire on . . . it would be enough for us to retire on."

"Us?"

Daniel clears his throat. "Berta, I want you to come with me."

Berta's face hasn't changed. She still wears the look of complete shock. "I'm not sure what to say."

"Say you'll come with me. We can start a new life together . . . and it would be easy for you to find a new job down there . . . if you wanted to work . . . you don't have to."

"No, Daniel, I can't just up and leave."

"Just think about it. I haven't officially accepted the offers yet . . . I still have time."

"How much time?"

"Maybe two weeks."

"So you think two weeks is enough time to consider everything for this move?"

Daniel doesn't say anything.

"I grew up here. This town happens to be very important to me. The people in this town happen to be very important to me. My church is here . . . my . . . my . . . you talk about us as if we are married, but I didn't hear any proposal."

"That would eventually come."

"Wait. So you want me to move with you to another state and live with you until you ask me to marry you?"

"I just don't want to lose you."

"Then stay. You once told me that you could live wherever you want to live. You don't have to take those jobs."

Daniel takes a deep breath. "Please, just think about it. You can stay at my place and I can find a new place down there if need be . . . just give it some thought."

Berta begins to gather her things.

"Are you mad?"

"Maybe."

"I don't get it. At least tell me why."

"Because, Daniel. You made me think I was worth staying for. You made it seem like your job is just a job . . . but in reality, your job is your love."

"That's not true. I think you're taking that a bit far."

"Am I? You wouldn't have brought it up if you knew you were staying. If it isn't true, then stay. Simple."

Berta gets up from the table and leaves the diner. Daniel springs up and follows her.

"Berta, wait."

Berta keeps walking. *I knew something was off. I knew it.*

Daniel finally catches up to her and says a few things, but Berta doesn't hear him. He grabs her arm.

"Get off me," Berta says as she flings his hand off her.

"Berta, I didn't mean to offend you."

She keeps walking and ignoring his words again. This time, there's nothing he can say to smooth things over with her. Berta gets in her car and drives off angrily. Immediately, she dials Candace.

"Okay, Berta, I love you but why are you calling me on a Friday night this late?"

"You weren't doing anything. Otherwise, you wouldn't have picked up."

Long pause.

"So what's up?" Candace says.

"He plans on leaving."

"Who?"

"Daniel. He's taking a job in Texas. It's offering enough for him to retire."

"What? What about you?"

"He wants me to go with him . . . to Texas."

Candace sighs over the phone. "So I take it you are mad?"

"I am . . . and embarrassed. I fell so easily for him."

"I honestly don't know what to say. I mean, it is a little soon to ask someone to move with them . . . especially to another state. On the other hand, it is a bit romantic. Think of it this way, at least he asked you to come with him. At least you're important enough for him to want you with him."

"I guess so. What do I do, Candace? What do I do?" Berta asks in a whiny voice.

"I don't know. If it were me . . . I . . . I . . . I don't know. Talk to him some more. See where his head is."

Berta hears a beep over the car speaker. "That's him now. Let me go. I'll call you tomorrow."

"All right. Good luck."

"Yeah. Thanks."

Berta presses a button on her cell phone to have Daniel come in over the speaker.

"Yes, Daniel."

"I didn't mean to make you mad. I was just asking. I haven't decided yet . . . well until a few moments ago."

"What do you mean?"

"I decided not to take those offers. I'm sure they're going to sweeten the deal a bit more to get me to come . . . but either way, I'm staying . . . with you."

"And what brought you to this decision?"

"Berta, I love you."

Berta's head jerks back. She pulls the car over to the side of the road. "Daniel, you don't love me. You don't even know me enough to love me."

Daniel sighs. "You know those things in life, those rare opportunities that come up, that put your entire life into perspective? I've had one in the diner. There we were, sitting there talking about moving to another state . . . for a job. I've done it many times. But for a job, I was asking you to throw away your entire life . . . it was so stupid . . . but it made me realize that I don't want you far from me. I need to be able to get to you someway, somehow. No one before you was that important. No one ever will be. So if that isn't love, so be it, but I know for sure that is how I feel."

Berta sits in the car unable to say anything.

"Berta, you still there?"

"Yeah, I'm here. I just . . . I just . . . I'm headed to my place. I'll talk to you tomorrow."

Daniel sighs again, this time a more dejected one, and agrees, soon getting off the phone and allowing Berta to her thoughts.

⋇

Mark gets home, surprising everyone because he is earlier than usual. Kalina and Charles run up to him and give him a hug. He enjoys this moment, the moment of seeing his kids again, every day. Jade pops from around the corner and stares at Mark blankly.

"No gym today?" she asks.

"Nope. We just hung out for a few."

"Oh. So how was the recital yesterday?"

"It went great," Mark says in an impersonal tone. "Thanks for asking."

Jade nods. "I didn't know there was a recital until Kalina told me," she says in a laughing way. "What? Was it no wives allowed?"

Mark stares at Jade with a simple look but a disgusted smile. "No. Nothing like that. I just figured you wouldn't want to come."

Jade narrows her eyes. "I don't remember you asking."

"Next time, I'll ask. I just thought that you wouldn't be interested. I mean, it isn't the first school event I had to go to . . . I don't see why this is the one to remember."

"Well, I was interested. Just let me know next time."

Mark chuckles. "Sure. No problem." He walks by her and goes upstairs. Following closely behind him is Kalina.

"Daddy?"

"Yes, Munchkin?"

"You wanna play a game of chess? I learned some new openings today."

"New openings, huh? Set it up. I'll come back down after I change."

Kalina jumps up in the air and yelps. She then speeds downstairs.

Mark begins to change his clothes when Jade marches into the room. She gently closes the door and locks it. She then turns around and faces Mark, arms crossed.

"We need to talk," she says.

Mark looks up at her as if everything is good with the world. "Okay. Talk."

"What's going on?"

"What do you mean?"

"You've been acting distant lately."

"Really? I haven't noticed." Mark slides a shirt on and begins to walk past her.

"Well, I have . . . and I don't like it."

Mark stops walking and cocks his head to the side. He turns around and stares at her. "I'm not sure I know what you are talking about."

Jade narrows her eyes. "I think you do."

Mark gives Jade a strange face. He isn't sure what else was said at Craig's office so he continues with his positively fake attitude. "Baby, there's just been a lot at work. It's been a bit more stressful than usual, that's all. I'm doing everything I can to give these kids a few open doors. It's just a bit hard, that's all."

Jade stares at Mark. She begins to say something but nothing more than a sigh comes out as her chin begins to quiver.

"Work?" Jade's voice shakes.

"Baby, you okay?"

Jade still says nothing although she knows this is another opportunity to come clean, to release herself of the secrets that plagued her for months.

Mark walks over to her and wraps his arms around her. Jade pulls away and sits on the edge of the bed, tears welling up in her eyes. She cries for a number of reasons, including her failure to admit her wrongdoings. For Jade, it isn't much a question of consequences, but one of accountability. Can she come to terms with the fact that she committed adultery? Can she free herself of the guilt and shame that has taken over her life? Can she fight for her marriage by exposing herself in the worst way? Right now, as it was before, the answer to all three is a loud and resounding no.

Mark sits next to her and grabs her hand. With his finger, he wipes away some of the falling tears. Jade looks at Mark, into his genuine looking eyes, and cries a bit more. Mark finds himself simply going through the motions in comforting his wife, but what he doesn't know is that by doing this, he is also convincing Jade that he doesn't know of her dark secret. This makes Jade cry even more because she feels even guiltier for getting angry with him and allowing her paranoia to take over her life.

"Just leave me to myself for a few moments," she says.

Jade keeps her distance from him, and Mark doesn't try to advance any further. Emotionally, he feels numb, so he walks away from her until he opens the door and leaves.

Chapter Twenty

THE air is cool, but every now and again a warm breeze blows through the barren trees leading up to Maya's house. Soon, the trees will bud and new growth will come through. Indeed, springtime is almost here. Craig drives down the winding private drive that leads to Maya's house. A bunch of thoughts run through his mind, the least of which being Maya. Instead, he thinks of Berta and of Mark, the two people he prayed for, and quite frankly, the two most important people in his life. Craig isn't very religious and hasn't been for years, praying only sometimes before eating, but something in Berta's resolve, something in her faith sparked something anew in him. It amazes him that even through the toughest of times, he has never seen her truly worried. She always had a silent faith, not loud and boisterous. She was never obnoxious, never quoting every verse of the Bible just to say hello. Her actions say it all.

He wouldn't be able to explain it if someone asked what's different about him. He just knows that something is indeed different; he is feeling like he did when he was a youth pastor. The rest of his day was filled with memories of those days, those great days of teaching kids to properly deal with everyday issues, those days of preaching the gospel of Jesus Christ to kids who soak it up like a sponge, those days of helping Mark to his path. It is there where Craig stops all thought. His friend, a person he has been friends with since childhood, needs help. The problem is that Mark doesn't know it or want it. Craig realizes that Mark now looks like what he looked like for years, lost. But Craig also realizes that there isn't much he could do but pray.

He gets to the front of Maya's house and parks the car. Maya comes outside to greet Craig and flies into his arms a few yards from the house.

"Hey, baby," she says, kissing him.

Craig halfway smiles. "Hey."

"What's wrong?"

Craig grabs her hand and leads her back to the house. "A bunch of stuff on my mind . . . but I'm good."

"Do you want to talk about it?"

"Not really. So what's the plan for tonight?"

Maya looks at Craig strangely. "The . . . plan," she claps her hands lightly, "just a quick dinner and a movie. Then maybe I can ease some of those things that worry you."

Craig smirks, but it is clear his mind is somewhere else.

They get into the house and Maya takes Craig's jacket. "Have a seat."

Craig sits on one of the sofas. After a few moments, Maya comes whirling around the corner. She sits next to him with her feet under her and stares at Craig. "Something is wrong. I can tell. Look, if this is about the lunch with Berta and her man, I am sorry . . . and I'm sorry for hanging up on you."

"What about for barging into my office?"

Maya narrows her eyes. "I didn't know that was a problem."

"There was somebody waiting for me . . . and I was on the phone. It was rude."

"Hmm. Well, I'm sorry for that too. I didn't know it bothered you."

Craig shifts in his seat. "It's fine. What movie did you pick out?"

Maya doesn't say anything. Craig looks at the perplexed look she has.

"Something bothering you?"

Maya faces Craig. "The woman at your office . . . that came to see you."

"Mark's wife."

"Yes. Her. Are you two close?"

"Close? I'd say so. She's the wife of my best friend."

Maya nods. "How come I never met Mark before? And it took me to storm into your office to meet Jade, to whom I was introduced by Berta."

"I don't know. I guess the opportunity never came up."

"But they're important people in your life, correct?"

"Yes. What are you getting at?"

"I just thought I would have met them by now."

"Under different circumstances, you may have . . . but I'm a bit skeptic now only because of how you treated Berta."

Maya gets up and stares down at Craig. "So Berta is important to you?"

"Yeah. She's my assistant. We've been working together for—."

"Years, I know. I already apologized for my actions. There's nothing else I can say. How long are you going to penalize me for that?" She snaps her head to the side. "I just don't understand. Why is Berta one of those important people?"

"Are you jealous?"

"No. I'm asking you a serious question."

"You are jealous. Maya, she's a coworker."

"But you just said she is important to you. Did you two date?"

"Date? No. We never."

"Did you have sex with her?"

"Maya, no. She's a church girl. She doesn't get down like that."

"The church girl thing means nothing. I've seen plenty of *church women* ready to drop their panties to the floor for someone high up in the church . . . so don't shovel that stuff towards me. What makes her so important?"

"Maya, I'm only going to ask you this one time. Stop this."

"No. I should know. I'm not going to set myself up to be cheated on."

"First, there's nothing to know. Second, if you don't calm down I —"

"You'll what? All I want is the truth."

Craig coughs out a nervous laugh. "I really don't believe you. So this is what the strong businesswoman really acts like, huh. Some crazed, jealous lunatic." Craig gets up from the sofa and starts walking around Maya's house, looking for the closet in which his jacket is hanging. She follows him, still yelling.

"I'm not the lunatic, Craig. Nor do I live in some made up world."

Craig ignores her and finally gets to the closet. Before he can open the door, she grabs hold of his forearm. He flings her hand away and flips towards her. He then grips her on the sides of her arms but not enough to hurt her. He wants to push her through the wall, but instead he does the only thing he knows will shut her up for a while. He kisses her. Maya recklessly pulls away and flies backwards into the wall.

"Get out," she says. "Now you're just playing games with me. Get out, now."

Craig grabs his jacket and begins to walk out the door. He turns around and stares at Maya one last time. Her eyes well up with tears as her entire face turns beet red. She continually flips her hair back behind her ears. Craig then stomps out and Maya slams the door.

⚜

The weekend for Mark was uneventful. He decided against church on Sunday for the sole reason that he is tired of putting on a show for the church folk. He needed time by himself to recharge. Of course, Jade and the kids still went. The first few days of the week were just as uneventful. Go to work, teach, orchestra, go home, play house, go to sleep, and awake the next morning to do it again.

Mark now sits behind his desk on a Thursday night, under the solo light of his desk lamp, grading test papers. He fiddles with his pen, twitching from the lack of use. *Either I'm becoming a better teacher or these kids are cheating their behinds off*, Mark thinks. *Heck, who am I kidding? I wasn't even paying attention.* He flips through the papers seeing most of them marked with large red "A"s. Even Frankie had a large "A" on his paper. *Someone's cheating.* He leans back into his seat and tries to think of anything suspicious he saw while the kids were taking the test.

For some time, he tries replaying the entire test-taking period in his head but comes up with nothing. *Outsmarted by fourth graders.* Annoyed, he collects the papers and throws them in his briefcase, snapping it shut. *Pop quiz, it is*, he thinks, smiling. Getting up from his seat, he grabs his case and jacket. The echo of footsteps resonates throughout the empty halls of the school. Mark freezes. The steps sound light but he hears them clearly. A few moments later, Alicia appears at the door of the classroom. She smiles at Mark. Mark now realizes why his weekend and early week was so blasé. He smiles back at her, noticing she that is carrying a paper bag.

"Headed out early?" she asks.

"Yeah. I plowed through everything fast. So it's to home I go." He starts to put on his jacket.

"Darn. I brought you this thinking you would be hungry." She pulls out a few Tupperware containers filled with food.

Mark looks in astonishment. *Jade never brought me food on any late night . . . ever.* He sets his briefcase down and flings his jacket onto a chair. "Whatcha got?"

Alicia smiles. "Some lasagna and a few rolls . . . and a couple of drinks. You can take it with you if you'd like. I just figured you would be hungry, you know, missing dinner and all."

Mark stares at Alicia and then back at the food. "Looks like you have enough for two, maybe three?"

"I made a lot, I know."

"Did you eat?"

"I did have a little to eat before I came."

"Good," Mark says, grabbing a bunch of paper towels and covering his desk. "That means you're hungry enough to join me."

Alicia doesn't move an inch. "I suppose."

"You suppose? Don't act all shy now, like you didn't used to throw down back then."

She smiles and begins taking the rest of the food from the bag with a couple plates and forks.

"I hope you learned to cook though," Mark says smiling.

"What? I'm better than before."

"We'll see." Mark takes a fork and scoops out an already cut piece of lasagna and sets it on Alicia's plate and then one on his.

Alicia takes a roll and places it on Mark's plate and sits down in a chair next to his desk. Mark sits in front of his desk and starts to dig into the food. Alicia stops him.

"You didn't bless it," she says.

Mark pauses and glances at her. He never knew that it could even feel awkward to say grace. "You do it," he says, knowing that it is likely he shouldn't be having this meal with her.

Alicia bows her head and blesses the food, and they both begin to eat.

"It's still piping hot," Alicia says.

"You know what?" Mark says with a full mouth. "This is really good. You may have gotten better over the years."

"May?"

"Okay. You definitely are better than you were before."

Alicia smiles. "You remember the first thing I made for you?"

Mark sits up, slowing down to enjoy the food a bit more. "I do. That nasty stuffed chicken. You gave me food poisoning, you know."

"I know. I felt so bad," Alicia says laughing. "I thought you wouldn't want to ever see me again after that."

"Yeah, but somehow I went back to you . . . just call me a glutton for punishment."

"Okay, glutton. It took a while to convince you to try anything else of mine."

"It sure did. It took a year or so, didn't it?"

"Yeah, I think it was somewhere around that. Oh, and do you remember that week we were the only ones snowed in at the dorms."

"We weren't the only ones there."

"Yeah, there was that guy Brad downstairs."

"You know he's in jail?"

"No, I didn't. What did he do?"

"Drugs."

"Wow. I wouldn't have thought that."

"I would. Hey, you remember when you broke your ankle?"

"You mean when you broke my ankle?"

Mark starts laughing. "I didn't break it. I just accidentally fell on it. It was a freak accident."

"Yeah, okay. I still have the scars from the surgery. I remember having to explain it to my mother . . . I came up with some lie. I know she didn't believe me."

"How is your mom?"

Alicia changes her tune some. "She died a few years ago."

The room gets silent. "I'm sorry to hear that."

"Yeah. Me too."

More silence.

"We had a lot of fun back then," Mark says quietly.

"We sure did."

Mark grabs his plate and Alicia's to throw them in the trash.

"Mark," Alicia whispers. "Why did you tell me about your wife?"

"What do you mean?"

"One of the first things you told me, even when we weren't so ami-cable, was that your wife cheated on you. Why?"

Mark throws the plates away and plops back down in his seat. "I don't know. I guess for a quick moment, I felt like we were the same people we used to be. Close."

Alicia looks down at the table. "If you don't mind me asking, how are things now?"

"Worse. She still hasn't confessed. She still runs around playing wife . . . I just let her."

"Why don't you confront her about it?"

"Why should I? I mean, at first I stayed quiet for the kids' sake. Now . . . I don't know. It hurts a lot."

"I'm sorry. I truly am . . . and I hate to see the pain on your face. It seems like you wear it every time I see you."

"I'll try to look better next time you see me," Mark says chuckling.

"That's not what I meant."

Mark gets up from the desk. "Don't worry about it. I'll be fine. I fought through against worse odds."

Alicia stands up now as well. "That doesn't mean you have to."

"What choice do I have?"

"I don't know." She looks at the floor. "I don't know."

"Look, thanks for the sentiment, but like I said, I'll be fine." Mark cleans the paper towels off his desk and refolds the clean ones.

Alicia grabs her bag and carefully watches Mark as he grabs his jacket and briefcase.

"Thank you for dinner. It was great." Mark looks at his watch. "Tim should be getting out of practice soon."

Alicia continues to stare at Mark, saying nothing.

"You good?"

Alicia blinks her eyes a few times and looks away. "You said you deserved it. When we first talked about it, you said you deserved your wife cheating on you."

"I deserve all this. At the very least for what I did to you."

Alicia looks down. "Did to me? No one should have to suffer in the way that you are."

"Knowing that I left you was worse. Again, I can manage."

Mark walks past Alicia.

"Did you miss me?" she asks.

Mark stops in his tracks and stands still for a few moments. When he turns around and looks at Alicia, he sees tears in her eyes. His heart pounds harder than ever and his neck throbs. "Like crazy."

Alicia sweeps her way to Mark and stands in front of him. She touches his face with one hand, seeing if he would move, then the other when he didn't budge, and kisses him. At first, Mark pulls away, staring at Alicia for only a moment before kissing her back. A surge like a powerful electrical current runs through his body. Alicia's lips taste sweet, and that pushes Mark even further. He picks her up while still kissing her as she wraps her legs around him and carries her over to the desk. Alicia sits on the desk with her head tilted up as Mark kisses on her neck. Tears stream down the side of her face as Mark continues to explore. She untucks his shirt just so she can get her hands on Mark's skin, his skin being something she hasn't felt for years. She feels his chiseled abs and his strong back. The feel of Mark surrounding her makes her bite her bottom lip. For Mark, each place Alicia touches him feels a surge of pleasure. He slides his hands under her shirt and lifts it off her, feeling her soft skin. He continues to indulge in the taste of her lips, tasting his way down her body. Alicia then leans back onto the desk as Mark kisses her bellybutton while undoing the button to her pants. Mark's heart races so much that he gets dizzy, but out of the corner of his eye, he sees a picture of him, Jade, and the kids. He closes his eyes, but the picture is burned into his vision. He slows down and finally stops, leaving Alicia on top of the desk panting.

"I can't do this. I'm sorry. I didn't . . ."

Alicia stops him from talking and slides back into her clothes. "It's my fault. I kissed you. I'm the one who's sorry. Ummm ... I have to go get Tim."

And just like that she rushes out the classroom. Mark stands there confused. For a brief moment, he actually felt . . . happy. He gets himself together, grabs his things, and rushes home.

જ

Jade sits at the dining room table talking to her mother on the phone. Charles is already in bed asleep, but Kalina stays up in her bedroom and waits for Mark to come home. She has been doing that every school day for the last few weeks; however lately, she has had to stay up later and later. A few times, she fell asleep waiting for him to come home.

Jade remains downstairs waiting close to the door to the garage as she whispers to her mother on the phone. "I'm back and forth on it," Jade says.

"So what do you think this man Boley was trying to tell you?"

"I thought he was trying to tell me that he told Mark everything that happened, but I don't know. Mark doesn't seem like he knows at all . . . and I don't know if I can trust Boley. He could be trying to get back with me."

"You sure it isn't an act?"

"If it is, he is doing a great job."

"Look, why don't you just talk to him?"

"And say what? Every time I try, I freeze. The right words simply don't come."

"Try, 'I cheated on you.'"

"Sounds simple doesn't it? It isn't that simple. If it were, I would have told him a long time ago."

"Somehow, I don't think you would have."

"What do you mean?"

"Exactly what I said, I don't think you would have told Mark earlier. It seems like you want somebody else to solve this problem for you."

"Whatever." Jade is annoyed. "And I think something is up with this Alicia thing. I found out that Alicia is a person he knew. She was his girlfriend at one point."

Jade hears her mother sigh over the phone.

"I know what you're thinking, mother. You think it isn't a concern, and that it was just a dream . . . or that my guilt is eating me alive and forcing me to think that he may be cheating."

"I didn't say a thing."

"Okay . . . so what do you think?"

"I told you several times already. I think your ought to talk to your husband about all of this . . . and stop expecting me to give you some deep insight on this issue. I can't bail you out of every situation in life."

"Who said I was asking you to?"

"I know you are asking me to, so let me tell you even clearer, I'm not going to bail you out of your marital problems. It is about time you take to that 'leave and cleave' thing. It isn't my marriage, it's yours. I can't tell you what to do, you're grown . . . and you've made your choices."

Jade remains silent for a second. "So you're so much better than me that you can't even offer a listening ear? Is that it?"

"That's not what I said either. I sa—"

"I heard what you said . . . and it all sounds like you put yourself up on this pedestal. You're better than me, huh? A woman who did the same thing I did, twice."

Jade's mother laughs. "Mind your manners, Jade. You don't know what hole you're digging yourself into."

"No. I'm tired of this holier-than-thou attitude you have. I need someone to talk to . . . someone I trust . . . I thought I could get some advice from some—."

"Advice? You aren't asking for advice. You are asking me to solve the problem. And before you go on any further, let me tell you this. I was woman enough to tell my husband of my mistakes. I talked to him and we worked on our marriage . . . with no one's help but God's. I wasn't sulking around trying to catch your father cheating. I was honest with everything. Period. That's the advice I am giving you, talk to your husband."

Jade knows she struck a nerve with her mother.

"You know what, Jade? You made this screwed up decision to turn your back on your husband. You made the screwed up choice to not tell your husband. Now you expect me to solve the problem. Life doesn't work that way . . . and call it my fault for allowing you to think that growing up . . . for spoiling you so. But for your own good, I have to ask that you not call me about this again."

"So that's it?"

"I'm sorry, Jade. You have the power to fix this . . . I suggest you do."

And just like that, her mother hangs up the phone leaving Jade still holding the phone to her ear. A few moments later, she hangs up and Mark gets home but comes through the front door instead of the garage door. He waves to her, smiles, and runs upstairs. Jade starts to follow him but stops in her tracks once she gets to the door. She picks up a light smell that doesn't smell at all like Mark's cologne. She takes a few steps upstairs and she recognizes the smell to be that of roses. She skips upstairs to get to the bedroom and hears Mark in the shower. She looks around for his work clothes but finds nothing. *He must have taken them in with him*, she thinks. Interestingly enough, Jade sees a dozen roses on the bed with a card that has her name on it. She opens the card and reads the handwritten note.

Hey, Jade. I just wanted to tell you that I love you. I hope everything is okay, and whenever you want to talk, you know I am here for you.

Mark

Jade takes the note and sets it on her dresser. She picks up the flowers and smells them, soon finding herself to be undeserving of them. She sets them on the dresser as well and crawls under the covers to go to sleep.

಍ಞ

Mark gets out the bathroom to see Jade already asleep. He breathes a quiet sigh of relief. Though he isn't sure what happened tonight, he knows he feels awkward even in his own skin. For the rest of the night he thinks of Alicia, even when he doesn't want to think of her. He dreams of what it would have been like had they went further.

Chapter Twenty One

CRAIG gets to the office, his mind filled with many thoughts yet again. He sees Berta, who greets him with a smile, again this one a weaker one than usual.

"Okay, Berta," Craig says. "Tell me now. What's wrong with you? I'm not doing a lick of work until you do."

Berta looks at him with a simple but powerful look. "Don't worry about it, Craig. I'm fine. Seriously."

"That's fine, but I'm still going to sit here until you tell me the truth."

"Craig."

He looks at her and the serious look she gives him and decides to back off a bit. "Fine. How was your weekend?"

"It was fine."

"How are you and Daniel?"

"Just fine, Craig . . . nothing is wrong" Berta looks at Craig with an annoyed expression.

"Okay, I get it. Sorry." Craig continues to stare at Berta.

Berta sighs. "Look, when I'm ready to talk, I'll be sure to let you know. Deal?"

"Deal."

"So, how was your weekend?" Berta asks, getting back to work.

"I wish I could say just fine."

"What's wrong?"

"Maya, that's what's wrong. She's crazy."

Berta looks at Craig with a smile as to say, *I knew that already.*

"I was over at her house having a somewhat good night. She kicked me out . . . for no real reason."

"You two got into an argument?"

"Yeah."

"Over what?"

"You."

Berta looks at Craig asking for more explanation.

"She's jealous of you . . . of our workplace relationship . . . or whatever you want to call it."

"Workplace relationship?"

"Yeah . . . or whatever you want to call it."

Berta nods. "I figured that out quite some time ago."

"Yeah, well her jealousy just boiled over . . . I tried to tell her nothing was going on and that you don't play games like that, but she still kicked me out. And before that, I got into it with Mark."

"You didn't."

"I did. He pretty much cussed me out and left."

"What did you say?"

"The truth. Jade came by asking questions. He better get his marriage in line, stuff like that."

"Craig, why would you—"

"Hold on a second. Let me finish. He told me that Jade cheated on him. Is that what Jade told you?"

Berta nods. "He knows?"

"Apparently. It seems he has known for a long time now."

Berta shakes her head. "This isn't good."

"I know . . . but that's not it. Mark is thinking of doing the same."

"No, he's not."

"He is. They're treating each other like mortal enemies. It's a shame."

"Jade, when she talked to me, seemed distraught. I hope she took my advice."

"What did you tell her?"

"I told her to tell Mark. She has to talk to him. That's why we shouldn't mettle. We'll do nothing but mess things up."

"Even though we have more information on their marriage than they do?"

"But God has more information than us both."

Craig nods. "Is that why you're taking the vow of silence with me too?"

"No it's not. I just . . . I . . . ."

Berta pauses, trying to figure out a way to word how she feels without saying anything brash. "Have you ever felt unimportant? Like, people can do without you?"

"Of course, I have, Berta, you know that. Jail doesn't exactly give off the warm and cuddly feeling of importance. I was a number, nothing more, nothing less."

"I know, but . . . you were at least still important to Mark. He checked up on you every chance he could."

"True. So what are you getting at? Do you feel unimportant?"

"I don't know. I guess so."

"Berta, you are important to a lot of people."

"But it doesn't seem like I am important to the right people. Let's say I moved to a different state, there wouldn't be anyone to tell me I shouldn't move."

"Daniel would. Right?"

Berta nods again. "Yeah. He would. Maybe . . . I'm worrying about nothing."

Berta glances at Craig, presumably getting the answer to a question that has rolled in her head since Daniel asked her to leave with him. It was a last ditch effort to make sure she isn't about to make the wrong decision. She wants Craig to say that she is important to him. She wants some inkling that she should stay, that moving away from Craig isn't as big a mistake as it sounds. Although she is with Daniel still, she was looking for something to pull her away from him and into the arms of Craig. Essentially, that is what is bothering her. Everything looks good on the outside, but she knows that Daniel is second-best to Craig. Daniel is really a Craig substitute because she's tired of waiting. She has already done so for so long. Craig puts his hand on her shoulder.

"Why don't I take you out to lunch? Maybe it will take your mind off things."

"I can't. I have too much to finish today but thanks for the offer."

Craig nods. "If you change your mind, just let me know."

"I will."

CS&SO

Craig moves from Berta's desk and into his office. He shuts the door and taps his head against the wall. *Why didn't you say anything? You choked! You choked! She is important to you, you idiot. That's what you should have said.*

Craig flops into his chair and tries to muster enough courage to say what he really thinks, that he got into this argument with Maya because Berta is that important to him, that he doesn't know what he is feeling, but he is feeling something for her. Unfortunately, he never does.

CS&SO

That night, Berta calls Daniel. He answers the phone as if he's excited to hear from her.

"Did they sweeten the deal yet?" she asks.

"They did. They made three more offers after that, but I turned them down. It takes a bit for them to realize that I'm serious."

"Call them back, all three. Tell them that you accept their offers."

"What? Berta, I'm staying with you. I already—"

"No. Listen. I will go with you."

"Are you serious? Are you sure? This is a big step for us."

"I am sure. I rethought everything, and I am sure this is the move for me to make, for us to make."

"Berta, you don't know how great this is. I know a few churches in Texas, and until we get you on your feet, you can stay in my house . . . or I'll rent an apartment or something."

"Wait, Daniel. Slow down. First, call those companies back. Tell them you accept their offers and we'll talk specifics tomorrow."

Berta gets off the phone with Daniel and immediately calls Candace.

"Don't yell at me and don't try to talk me out of it," Berta says. "But I decided to go with Daniel to Texas."

Candace says nothing.

"Are you going to say anything?"

"You told me not to yell or talk you out of it."

"So you don't have anything else other than that to say?"

"I guess I'm curious as to why, but I'm sure I know."

"Candace, I need to move on with my life."

"I thought that's what you were doing by dating Daniel."

"No. That's what you thought I was doing by dating Daniel. What I was doing was filling a void. No matter what I do, no matter how I do it, Craig—"

"I knew it."

"Listen. Craig is in my system and I can't get him out. I have to get away from him. If Daniel and I are going to get any further in our relationship, I have to get away from Craig."

"But it's clear that Daniel isn't who you really want. Why would you leave with him?"

"Are you trying to talk me out of it?"

"Sorry."

"I'm not important to Craig . . . at least not as important to him as I am to Daniel. Daniel is a great man. He is a great man."

"Why does it seem like you are trying to convince yourself?"

"Talking me out of it again."

"Stop it, Berta. You need someone to talk some sense into you. You're panicking right now, but when you least expect it, God is going to give you exactly what you need. You know that. But moving far away isn't going to solve anything. At least not in this panicked state. Obviously Daniel is second to Craig. Maybe, that won't ever change. Daniel would be second-best even if you moved to China. I mean, Daniel is a good man, a man who is all for you, who wanted to whisk you away to another state so he can continue to grow with you, but he simply may not be the one for you."

"I'm not panicking. It's confusing, I know, but I am tired of waiting. I'd rather live my days with someone who loves me than with someone who doesn't even notice me. It is about time my life becomes my life, and not Craig's . . . or Dad's."

"I'm telling you now, it won't make you happy."

"So what do you think I should do? If you were in my shoes, what would you do?"

"Berta babe, I would sit back and pray. I would seriously pray. You made an impulsive decision. Did you tell Daniel yet?"

"I did."

Candace groans over the phone. "Why, Berta? Why? Okay. Look, do this. Pray. Pray some more. Then I want you to figure out if you are moving to be with Daniel or to get away from Craig. Then pray even more."

"But I've trapped myself. No matter what, Daniel is going now. He's not going to change his mind now that I said I will go with him. So it's either stay here or go with him."

Tears start to make their way out of Berta's eyes. Her voice changes as she tries to keep in the tears.

"Berta, are you okay?"

"I'm not. I feel so bad and confused. This isn't me making all of these crazy decisions. But it hurts every day now, just seeing him. It hurts every day knowing that Dad's last wish is going unfulfilled . . . and what he promised me meant nothing. I just can't keep going on with life like this. I've lived the past eight years according to a stupid promise. And he hasn't changed one bit since. And then there's Daniel . . . a good man whom I can't seem to really connect to beyond the carnal level, whom I just told I would pick up all my things and leave with."

"Wait. What are you talking about? Last wish? Promise?"

"Dad asked me to do some things before he died."

"Okay . . ."

"I don't want to talk about it. It hurts too much. I . . . I have to go."

Berta rushes off the phone and curls up in a ball on her couch.

CHAPTER TWENTY TWO

IT has become easier for Mark to play house. At first, the devastating news of his wife's infidelity sent him into a depression of sorts. Now, he has a whole new routine of self-sufficiency. Of course, he still depends on Jade for certain things to make it seem like he is still her husband, but in his mind, she is simply an acquaintance. Now, he holds his cards to his chest even tighter, because revealing to Jade what he knows about her would end what could happen with Alicia. He once felt sick at the thought, turning his back on God, committing adultery, and becoming one with his wife, but this time, in hell. He knows he has become nothing more than a hypocrite, but his actions became easier after a while . . . almost natural. His marriage was suffering, and he had no urge to fix it. Mark found his happiness. Though fleeting, he found something other than the pain and torment of an adulterous wife. The only ones who truly seem to benefit are the kids. Because of this whole ordeal, both have become better parents in efforts to cover their tracks. Both think, the better they treat the kids, the less the other would suspect anything. Mark uses that notion as a form of solace for his actions. At one point, a sick part of him even blamed the kids. If it weren't for their happiness, he wouldn't have to sneak around like the devil himself. If their happiness weren't at stake, he would have left a long time ago, potentially even before this entire ordeal. It wasn't long before he snapped out of that line of thinking. For a brief moment, he reminded himself of his mother and that made him sick to his stomach.

He's off from the school today. The end of the year approaches and the kids received their report cards yesterday. The only things left for Mark are the parent-teacher conferences next week. In front of him sits Kalina as they play a game of chess.

"Daddy, I have to tell you something."

"What's up, sweetheart?"

"Some boy at school touched my butt yesterday."

Mark freezes. He looks at Kalina, who still concentrates on the board. This day is one of the days he feared on the list of many. Kalina is a bit more developed than any of the other eleven-year-old girls in her class, being top heavy. He knew hormonal little boys would start to notice her soon. He was just hoping not so soon.

"Are you okay?" Mark asks.

"Yeah. It didn't bother me much."

"What do you mean it didn't bother you much? You know stuff like that is wrong."

"Yeah, I know," Kalina says, still looking at the board. "I punched him in the nose and that was it. He won't do it again."

"Who was it?"

"Everyone calls him Smooth."

"Smooth?"

"Yup, Smooth. I don't know his real name."

"Did you tell the teacher?"

"Of course."

"So you're okay?"

"Yeah. It was kinda funny actually. He ran off holding his nose. I think I made him bleed."

"And that's funny to you?"

"Not the bleeding part. Just the part about him running from a girl. He acts so cool, but he's really a wimp."

"Did you tell your mother?"

"Nope. I thought she was going to get upset. She seems upset a lot lately. Your move."

Kalina stares up from the board at Mark. Mark looks down at the board to make his move.

"Well, you did the right thing by telling a teacher and by telling me."

"And by punching him."

"Especially by punching him. You don't have to accept anything like that if it makes you uncomfortable, no matter who it's from."

"I know."

Mark moves a piece across the board. Just as he does, he gets a text message. He pops his phone up and reads it. It's from Alicia. It reads:

Do you think you can be at my place tomorrow night? 8pm.

Mark looks at the message strangely but replies, "Sure."

"Who is that, Daddy?"

Without flinching, Mark answers, "Your uncle Craig."

"Oh. Tell him I said hi."

"That's what I'm doing now, sweetheart." Mark continues to press buttons on his phone and sends another message to Alicia asking her if everything is okay. She quickly responds with a "Yes."

"Check."

Mark looks at the board again to see that Kalina is about to win the game and, for the first time, beat him in chess. He looks all over the board for a move to make but finds nothing. As time goes on, Kalina's grin turns into an all-out smile. Eventually, Mark knocks his king over, resigning the game and taking the first loss to his daughter. Kalina puts out her hand as she grins from ear to ear. Mark shakes her hand.

"I can't believe you did it, but you beat me."

Kalina gives a giggle and rolls onto her back, kicking her feet in the air. "I did it," she says repeatedly. She jumps up from the floor. "I got to tell Mommy. I can't believe Charles missed this too."

She disappears upstairs.

Mark goes through his phone and erases all the calls and text messages from Alicia that are still on his phone. Ever since that Thursday night when they kissed, they have met up in various private places just to be with each other, always while Tim was at practice. They would always be back just in time for no one to suspect anything strange. Alicia would get Tim and they would go home. Mark would go home as if nothing happened. During their trysts, they kissed a few more times, but never took it any further than that. Now that the school year is over, he wonders what kind of cover-up they can come up with. Even more so, he wonders what she has planned for tomorrow night. First, he has to come up with a way to get out the house without Jade suspecting anything.

Mark eventually comes up with an elaborate scheme to get out the house, and he plays it out with precision. The night before, he tells Jade about going to the gym with Craig. The night of his "date", he leaves for the gym at seven o' clock. He gets there at seven thirty and parks out front. He signs in at seven thirty-five. He sneaks out the back door at seven forty-five to see Alicia parked on one of the side streets. They get to Alicia's house at eight o' clock sharp, and by five after, they rush indoors to not be seen by anyone.

Mark get inside and scans her home, a well-decorated townhouse. "You have a beautiful home." He continues to scan the home, expecting to see pictures of Tim hanging all over, but finds none. Not one. "Where's Tim?" he asks.

Alicia shakes off the trench coat she was wearing to reveal a skintight emerald green mini dress. "He's with his father until next week . . . back in PA."

"Oh," Mark says, staring at Alicia's body. "You look great . . . and I am totally under dressed."

"Don't worry about it," Alicia says. "I knew when I was picking you up from the gym you were going to be in workout gear . . . so I picked you up some clothes . . . and a new pair of shoes. They're upstairs . . . the back bedroom."

"Oh. Thanks, I guess."

"Now, go get dressed while I set things up down here."

Mark walks upstairs and heads straight to the back bedroom. A sweet aroma fills the air the closer he gets to the bedroom. He gets to the bedroom and cuts on the light. He assumes the bedroom to be a guest bedroom since the other two doors in the hall are closed. On the bed is a white collared shirt and black slacks. On the floor is a shiny pair of dress shoes. Mark begins to put everything on to find that it all fits nicely, not perfect, but good enough. Mark slides on the shoes and makes his way downstairs. The first thing he notices when he returns is that the lights are dim. He then sees a few lit candles scattered around the room. In the middle of the floor, he sees Alicia holding two champagne glasses filled with a dark liquid.

"I figured you ate dinner already."

Mark nods. "I did." He grabs a glass from Alicia.

Alicia walks to the stereo to turn on some music. Mark stares at her as she kneels down to see the station. Her skin shimmers under the candlelight. He gets a good view of how strong her legs look as her not so modest dress slinks high on her thigh. She plays with the radio for a few seconds. At this time of night, nothing but love songs play. Mark takes a sip of his drink. After swishing it in his mouth, he swallows and laughs.

"Grape juice?"

Alicia laughs. "I thought you would get a kick out of that." She stands and walks over to Mark.

"Yes. Very funny."

"Well, I couldn't have you going back home drunk, could I? At least not off alcohol."

Mark smiles. "I suppose not."

Alicia grabs his free hand and leads him to the couch to sit. "I'm so happy I have this time to spend with you, Mark"

Mark waits for Alicia to sit down before taking a seat. "Very happy."

"Seriously, there's so much I want to tell you."

"Well, I'm here now. You can tell me anything." Mark sets his glass on the table in front of him.

Alicia smiles and looks into Mark's eye with admiration. "Things weren't the best with me before we met up again. And one day, I remember this day distinctly, I prayed. And this is already after I moved. I prayed that God would give me a sign or something. Something to know that I had done the right thing by moving down here, for Tim's sake especially." Alicia sets her glass down and huddles up closer to Mark. "Maybe even something to tell me that my life is worth more than it seems. The very next day, Tim comes home talking about Mr. Cooke and how great a teacher he is. He says I have to meet him."

"Tim is a good kid."

"Yeah, he is." Alicia lays her head on Mark's shoulder. "But anyway, I asked around about this Mr. Cooke and find out that this Mr. Cooke has a first name of Mark. At that point, I'm mad and disbelieving. I didn't get it at all. But I get it now. Mark, you are my sign."

"Is that what you think?"

"It is. I also think God is shifting things around so we can be together again. I'm so sorry that you have to go through so much pain for it to work. I hate what that woman has done to you."

Mark says nothing at first. A single thought presses itself onto his mind. "So what about your husband?"

"What about him? He made his choice."

"But you still keep his name, right?"

"It makes things easier . . . at least until we get this divorce."

"Do you still love him?"

Alicia pulls away from Mark and gives him a look. "No . . . but I still love you."

They stare at each other for a while.

"Mark, I know we don't have much time tonight . . ." Alicia looks away and then down at her glass. "I want you to feel better. I want to end the pain you go through . . . even if it is for a moment."

Mark doesn't know exactly what she is indicating. In one smooth motion, Alicia turns her back towards Mark and lifts her hair from her neck. Mark stares for a second, not confused, but not willing to admit what is about to happen.

"Can you get my dress for me?"

The question forces Mark to tense every muscle in his body. He thinks for a brief moment, not about what he faces right now, but about Jade. He wonders what Jade felt when she was kissing Boley. Joy? Anger? Disgust? Lust?

"Mark?" Alicia snaps him out of his thoughts.

"Sorry." Mark inches closer to her. He raises his hands to the zipper of her dress, his mouth watering, and with care, pulls down the zipper. Unable to resist the urge, he leans in closer and kisses her on the nape of her neck. She lets out a slow and trembling breath, her body shivering.

Alicia holds the front of her dress and stands up, the back fabric of her dress now hanging off her shoulders. She lets go of the dress and lets it drop to the floor. With her dark green shoes still on, she steps out of the dress and turns to face Mark. Mark blinks a few times ogling her tight figure in a green thong set. She straddles Mark and kisses him.

"I just want to make you happy," she whispers. "Let me make you happy."

Mark hears her whispers as he continues to kiss her on her body. He places his hand on her back, leaning her back so he can kiss her on her stomach. She smoothly slides off Mark and stands up in front of him. With her pointer finger, she motions Mark to follow her and sashays her way up the stairs, giving him one last seductive look before leaving. Mark watches her go upstairs, seeing her legs disappear last. Mark gets up and takes a deep breath. He wants to stop, but his body is forcing him to continue. Like a lamb to the slaughter, he goes upstairs. He sees her shoes sitting at the top of the steps. As he reaches eye level with the upstairs floor, he sees the main bedroom door open with Alicia sitting in the middle of the bed. She holds a sheet to her chest to cover her body. Mark keeps going up the steps, now unbuttoning his shirt, and finds her thong on the floor just outside the bedroom. He then sees her bra hanging on the doorknob to the bedroom. He tries to tell himself that he has gone too far, but he is still unable to stop. He feels nauseous but can't tell if it is from nervousness or if he is flat out sick of himself. The sweet aroma, which he smelled earlier, rushes his nose. He now realizes that the aroma came from the bedroom.

He grunts, throws his shirt off, and swings the door shut behind him.

CHAPTER TWENTY THREE

JADE wakes up early in the morning to make sure the house is straight. She slides out of bed, puts on a robe, and heads to the bathroom to wash her face. Everyone in the house is still asleep so Jade takes a few moments to relax. Although her relaxation is short lived, it is enough to get her moving on house chores. She grabs some of her dirty clothes and Mark's gym bag and goes downstairs to the laundry room. Along with other piles of clothes, Jade throws the clothes in her hands to the ground. She then zips open Mark's gym bag. Immediately the smell of fabric softener rises to her nostrils. *Fabric softener? Why do his clothes still smell like fabric softener?* Jade puts Mark's shirt to her face and takes a deep whiff to still smell fabric softener, not sweat. Jade thinks back to last night and how tired Mark seemed and throws the clothes to the ground. She looks into the bag for any other clothes and finds his cell phone. She grabs it, sets it on the washer, and throws the bag to the side. For a few moments she stares at the phone, debating on if she should go through it. She never had to before but believes there's reason to now. Maybe it will give her what she wants. Jade grabs the phone and begins to search through the call logs. Everything is empty, completely cleaned out of even normal numbers. She looks for text messages but finds none of those either. After searching the phone a bit more, Jade sets it down on a shelf and continues to sort clothes. Just as she starts the first load of laundry, the phone begins to make a humming noise on top of the shelf. Jade snatches it to silence the loud vibration. She sees that there's a new text message on the phone from an unnamed number. She opens the message to see the words "Good Morning." Jade's hands trembles as she replies to the message with a

"Good Morning." Within a few moments, she gets back a response. What she sees is enough to send a chill raging up and down her spine. "I hope I didn't wake you," the message reads. "But I had to tell you that I had a great time last night. I want to see you again soon." Jade begins to shake even more. She now knows there's another woman. The question that remains is, what for? In a frantic rush, Jade texts back, "How soon?" and waits, still shaking and tapping her foot. A few moments later, "After last night, ASAP" appears on the phone. Jade clutches the phone tighter in her hand and thinks. Instead of texting back, Jade calls the number and waits for someone to answer. After only a few rings, a woman picks up and starts talking.

"You must really want to talk to me. I take it you want to meet again soon?"

Jade quickly hangs up and grits her teeth. She wants to throw the phone across the room. Instead, she goes back to texting. "Sorry, everyone just woke up."

Jade thinks she only has a few minutes before everyone actually does start to wake up and want breakfast. The phone buzzes in her hand, but she ignores the message and calls the number again.

"I think you just wanna hear my voice," the woman says. "Sitting here talking to me while everyone else floats around. You're a bad boy, Mark."

Jade takes a deep breath and finally speaks, not knowing what to say. "Actually, I did want to hear your voice. And you are absolutely correct," Jade continues as if she growling, "Mark has been a very bad boy."

Silence.

Jade listens for any sound coming over the phone but hears nothing. Jade knows she's still there. Somehow, she can feel her.

"Hello, Jade," the woman finally says.

"Oh. I see that you know my name. Funny thing is … I have no idea who you are. But that doesn't matter. Tell you what. Let's just say you won't be seeing my husband any longer." Jade hears movement up-stairs.

"I don't know if it is my choice to make," the woman says.

"It isn't. It is mine to make . . . and I'm making it. Stay away from my husband."

The woman laughs. Jade becomes upset. "I didn't know I said any-thing funny."

"Oh, you did," the woman laughs more. "The nerve of you to try to call the shots. Your husband, as you call him, is virtually a free man. You made sure of that some time ago."

Jade's eyes get wide. She hears more movement upstairs. "Since you're so bold, why don't you meet me? I have a few questions that need answers."

"You know what? I think I will have to take you up on your offer. I have a few questions that need answers as well."

"The Crabtree Laguna . . . 2 pm," Jade says and presses hard on the screen to hang up the phone.

She goes through the phone and clears all messages and calls. Then she sets the phone back on the shelf. She flips modes and starts packing clothes into the washer.

A few moments later, Mark appears in the doorway. Jade turns and gives him a faint smile. "Morning," she says.

"Good morning."

Jade squeezes by him to grab the laundry detergent. "I almost washed your phone with the clothes. I set it on the shelf."

Mark walks to the shelf and grabs the phone, clutching it like it's a piece of gold.

"I'm going out today," Jade says. "Do you mind looking after the kids?"

"Sure. What time?"

"Sometime around two."

"I guess. Church stuff?"

"Nope."

"Oh. So what's the occasion?"

Jade thinks, *I don't have to tell you anything.* Instead, she says, "It's a nice day out. I was going to go window shopping . . . maybe grab a bite to eat. Take a walk around the park. I just don't want to be inside all day."

"Oh." Mark shuffles his way back upstairs to change his clothes.

Jade pours some detergent into the washer. All her thoughts are about this mystery woman. *What kind of woman is she? It seemed like she knew about me . . . and the kids. What kind of woman is she to claim someone who is clearly a family man, as if he were a free man? Why does she act like she has a right to my husband? How did Mark meet her? What happened last night?* Jade stops her thoughts for a second, slams the washer door shut, and starts the washer.

Jade sits in a small restaurant awaiting her guest. She got to the restaurant an hour early, just to calm her nerves. What she doesn't want is to blot out what dignity she has left by making a fool of herself in front of her husband's supposed mistress. That was the exact reasoning behind suggesting the Crabtree Laguna, hoping this mystery woman wouldn't want to make a fool of herself in public either. Too many thoughts run through Jade's mind, all ending with her beating this woman into a lifeless mush. For her to act "ladylike," as her mother would call it feels like a stretch. A young waiter comes over every fifteen minutes or so to ask her if she ready to order. Each time, she says she's waiting for someone and the waiter returns to the back. She thinks to herself that she doesn't even know what this someone looks like and begins to laugh.

Fifteen minutes before two, a woman slides into a chair at her table to sit across from her. It only takes a few seconds for the waiter to show back up for their order. He asks if they would like anything to drink. Both women order diet sodas.

For some time, the two women stare at each other, observing the other's outward appearance, trying to gain whatever information they can. Therefore, Jade made sure she wore her pleated dress pants and blue blouse with matching stilettos. She looks at the mystery woman who is wearing a nice set of diamond stud earrings, a sundress, and heels.

"So what do I call you?" Jade asks.

"My name is Alicia," the woman states.

Jade's breathing becomes hard as even more thoughts run through her head. "Alicia . . . as in Mark's ex-girlfriend Alicia?"

"So I guess you have heard of me."

"Not from him," Jade snaps back. "But … I must say you are one bold woman, Alicia."

"What did you call this little rendezvous for exactly?"

"I needed to see you. I needed to see the woman who is taking part in the destruction of my marriage."

"The destruction of your marriage? You yourself caused that. I never cheated on him. You did."

"What?"

"I think you heard what I said."

Jade thinks quickly. "I never cheated on Mark," she says simply to look less foolish.

Alicia shakes her head. "Nope. Not buying it. I know the look of pain on Mark's face when he said it. A look like that, no man can fake. It's the look of a man's heart being taken out and stabbed over and over again."

Jade thinks some more. The waiter comes back with two sodas and Jade takes a sip of hers. "So he told you I cheated on him? What other lies did he tell you?"

Alicia stares at Jade in disgust. "I know quite a bit about you . . . things that aren't so flattering."

"So you take this as an opportunity? Like some scavenger?"

"No, no, no," Alicia says, remaining calm. She then takes a sip of soda. "I'm just taking back what is mine."

"Do you run around chasing all your ex-boyfriends?"

Alicia laughs. "No, but I am going after my ex-fiancée."

Jade slowly takes another gulp of soda, but the information she is gaining from Alicia is becoming too much to bear.

"I guess that's another thing he didn't tell you, right?"

Jade doesn't say a word.

"Don't you have any morals?" Jade finally asks. "You think you can just take whomever you please? I am married to Mark. We are married. Does that mean anything to you?"

"It didn't mean anything to you."

Jade stares Alicia square in the eyes. "Answer the question. Does it mean anything to you that you and Mark are committing adultery?"

Alicia sits back in her seat, finding herself unable to say anything.

"Are you two so caught up in what you had that you don't even bother to think about what sins you commit . . . things you will have to answer for?"

"Don't preach to me. Your marriage is over. It was over when you opened your legs to another man."

"First of all, that is not what happened, so I suggest you keep your mouth shut about things you have no clue about. Second, my marriage is not over. I still wear my ring . . . he still wears his."

"You see, that's your problem. You're too focused on the outside appearance, the clothes, the hair, the ring. I bet you really liked showing off something that wasn't a reality."

Jade stares at Alicia in contempt. "But weren't you able to touch him and kiss him and Lord knows what to him with that ring on?

Weren't you able to rehash all those old feelings while he still had a significant and plainly visible connection to me?"

"I never said any of that happened."

"So what did happen?"

"I don't have to tell you anything. That's between me and him."

Jade takes a moment to calm down and decides on a different approach although she wants so badly to cry, kick, scream, and punch her way through the issue. "Look, maybe things weren't the best between Mark and me, but he is still my husband. I am still his wife. If you don't understand that, there's nothing I can do to get you to do so. All I want to know is what is going on. I mean, haven't you ever found yourself in a situation where everything is happening around you but you don't know what's going on?"

Alicia props herself up in her chair and looks across the restaurant. She takes a sip of her soda and begins to tap her finger on the table. She doesn't look Jade in the eyes. "I didn't plan on any of this. I know that won't change your viewpoint of me, but I have to mention that. I didn't plan to run into Mark. I didn't plan to have any feelings for him again. I didn't plan . . . It all just happened."

Jade remains silent and lets Alicia speak.

"We didn't do anything major, I suppose. We kissed sometimes . . . but nothing more."

"That was until last night, right?"

"What do you think?" Alicia says in a non threatening manner, as if she really wants to know what she thinks.

"I don't know. Again, I'm trying to understand."

Alicia looks up at Jade showing a break in her hardcore demeanor. "Last night was different. We had dinner . . . we kissed . . .."

"And?"

"What do you want me to say?"

"Tell me exactly what happened."

"I just did. It went no further."

"That doesn't make sense . . . and I don't believe it one bit. Did you sleep with him?"

Alicia looks down and brushes a few strands of hair back behind her ear. "No."

"But you wanted to . . . and so did he."

Alicia nods.

"So let me ask this again, does it matter to you that Mark is a married man?"

Alicia, appearing more solemn by the moment, looks at Jade. "Of course, it mattered. But I found myself so caught up in him that it started not to matter. The more pain I saw on his face, the more I wanted to help him . . . to heal him . . . and the more I resented you. I didn't understand it. I still don't to an extent. How could a woman be so uncaring . . . so foolish . . . so disgusting to treat a great man like Mark like trash? How could someone cheat on him?"

Jade looks down in shame.

"Jade, I love Mark . . . I always have . . . I'm afraid I always will . . . and I'm not saying that to condone any of my actions . . . but I am saying that I will continue with my actions . . . until he says stop." Alicia gets up from the table. "He has to be the one to stop it."

"So ultimately, you're telling me that marriage . . . our marriage means absolutely nothing to you."

"I'm sorry." Alicia starts to walks away, but Jade follows her.

At this point, Jade doesn't care about drawing attention to herself. She follows Alicia all the way to the door.

"What do you plan to do? Being with him . . . then what? Marry him? Live the rest of your lives in fear of the same thing happening again? Of some woman coming along and taking him from you?"

Alicia stops walking and turns around towards Jade. "You know, I haven't thought that far." She laughs a weak laugh. "I really don't know."

"How can you call yourself a woman, knowingly doing this? Yes, I have made my mistakes . . . but what you are doing is taking the role of judge of my marriage . . . and that role doesn't belong to you. You are condemning my marriage by taking him away from me. You are condemning it, don't you see that?" Jade begins to cry. "I love Mark too . . . and I'm not just going to let him go. And if you think I'm just going to let this all happen right in front of me, you have severely underestimated me and how far I'm willing to go."

Alicia looks at Jade sadly and walks out of the restaurant. Jade looks around to see everyone around her gawking at her. She trots back to her seat, grabs her purse, and storms out of the restaurant.

Chapter Twenty Four

CRAIG gets to the office later than usual. Everything about his morning was normal, getting to the office, passing Berta, and greeting her, but he finally gets into his office and sees a piece of paper in his chair. He picks it up and reads. A few moments later, he storms out of his office and to Berta's desk.

"What is this?" he asks, flapping the paper around in front of her.

"It's my resignation letter." Berta promptly responds.

"Is this a joke?"

"It's not. I know this is all of a sudden, but it is something I have been thinking about for a while now."

"Did you find a new position?"

"Not quite."

"I don't understand."

Berta looks at Craig for a second and then turns away from him. She finds it difficult to stare him in the eyes now. "I am leaving with Daniel. We're going to Texas."

Craig tries to hide his shock. "What?"

"He has a few big jobs lined up that are offering a bunch of money. We would be set for life."

"But you don't know the guy that well . . . do you?"

"I figured that if things don't work out between me and him, I could easily get a job down there . . . but that isn't the main plan. Things are working out very well between us now . . . it seems like the right choice."

"Are you sure?"

"I am absolutely positive."

Craig grabs the back of his neck and sighs. "Does anyone else know about the big move?"

"One other person. You remember Candace?"

"Vaguely."

"She is one of my best friends."

"Short church girl?"

"Yup."

"I remember her. Every time I saw her, she was fussing at her husband. What did she say?"

Berta pauses for a second trying to make up something to say. "She thinks it's a good idea."

"She does? What about the church?"

"I haven't told the church yet."

"Oh." Craig continues to play it cool. "Well, is anyone having anything for you . . . like a going away party or something?"

"No. I'd rather not have one."

"I see." Craig looks at the paper and then back at Berta. "Look, how about this, since no one else is doing anything, let me take you out to dinner or something just to celebrate. Is that okay?"

"I suppose. Where to?"

"I don't know yet. How about we go right after we leave here tonight?"

"Sure, I guess. We—"

"Wait, no. Let's go later tonight. This is a big occasion that requires a big celebration. I'll take you somewhere really nice."

"As long as it isn't Pierre Romano's, I'm fine."

"Pierre Romano's? I haven't been there in years. I was talking about somewhere really special. Somewhere out of town. I know you're going to like it."

Berta's purses her lips to avoid smiling. Craig gets up and nods his head.

"Yeah, I know exactly where I want to take you. You're going to like it."

Berta finally smiles.

"Look, Berta," Craig says. "I don't know what has been going on with you lately. I'm not even sure I can really help. I just ask this: make sure this is the right move to make and that you aren't making it out of some place of pain."

"Why would I make such a decision based off pain?"

"I'm not saying you would. I'm just saying that even the best of us don't know when we are sometimes. Take me for example. I've done it for years." Craig chuckles. "Don't be like me." He then walks into his office, and shuts the door.

Later in the night, Craig gets to Berta's apartment and knocks on the door. He hears a rustling behind the door and moments later, Berta opens it. She has a toothbrush hanging from her mouth and pulls it out to speak. Muffled, she says, "Is that what you're wearing?"

Craig looks at the black slacks and black button up shirt he is wearing. He then taps his shiny dress shoes on the wooden floor. "What's wrong with what I have on?"

Berta runs to the bathroom and spits out the foamy toothpaste muffling her speech. "I still have my work clothes on."

"I told you I was taking you somewhere special."

"Somewhere like where?"

"My hometown."

Berta pops out of the bathroom and stares at Craig. "Craig, that's like three hours away."

"I know . . . so you better hurry and change."

⊰⊱

Berta runs into one of the back rooms and closes the door. She spent the last few hours prepping herself for this outing, not physically, but emotionally. With little time, she had to learn how to turn off certain parts of her feelings for this outing to go well tonight.

"Enjoy the moment," she tells herself. She yells from behind the door. "I don't know what to wear."

"Something comfortable . . . but sexy."

Berta laughs. "Like you're taking me out on a date?"

"I'm just trying to make sure you look at least half as good as I do."

Berta laughs again. "Where are we going, you arrogant jerk?"

"I already told you . . . my hometown."

"I'm only going to ask once more before I lock myself in this room and we go nowhere. You taking me to a strip club?"

Craig laughs. "Not at all. I'm taking you to a jazz club I used to go to all the time . . . in Center City."

"A jazz club? Sounds interesting. Why there?"

"I don't know. It's the first place I could think of . . . one that I thought you would like."

⊰⊱

Craig hears the sound of high heels hitting the wooden floor as Berta makes her way out of the bedroom wearing a burgundy strapless cocktail dress. Craig's mouth drops as he stares at Berta and what she is wearing.

"What? Is it too much? I'll go change," Berta says and turns around to go back into the bedroom. Craig reaches for her arm.

"You look great." Craig stares her in the eyes for a second. "And if you change again, you'll force me to take you to a fast food joint instead."

Berta smiles. "Well, let me put on a shawl or something . . . then off we go."

Berta starts rummaging through a closet and pulls out a black shawl. Craig gently grabs it from her. "Please, allow me."

Berta turns around and allows Craig to place the shawl over her shoulders. For a brief moment, Craig pauses and observes Berta's body. He finds it strange, this attraction he feels towards her. He starts to feel guilty as his eyes slide down her body to her backside. Berta turns her head to the side as she adjusts the shawl over her shoulders.

"You okay?" she asks.

Craig snaps out of his trance. "Oh, yeah. I'm fine. You ready to go?"

"Indeed, I am."

Berta grabs her keys and purse from off the dining room table and follows Craig out of the apartment. Craig then walks ahead of Berta as she walks down the stairs and opens the car door for her when they get to it.

"So I finally get to ride in the Porsche."

Craig laughs. "I'm surprised you didn't ask to drive it yet."

"Craig, it's a hundred thousand dollar car . . . the way I drive, I would give you a heart attack."

"Yeah, you would." Craig starts the car.

Berta jumps up in her seat. "But listen to her purr."

Craig smiles. "So Daniel is okay with this?"

Berta hesitates for a second. "Well, sure . . . he just doesn't know that he's okay with it."

"You did tell him I was taking you out . . . right?"

"Not quite. He doesn't need to know. It will probably cause some unnecessary drama."

Craig pauses to think. He looks at her. "Are you still sure you want to leave with him?"

Berta ignores the question and asks one of her own. "Is Maya okay with you taking me out? Wait, I know she isn't."

Craig nods and smiles a weak smile. "Actually, I haven't talked to her since she kicked me out of her house."

"I still can't believe she did that."

"Neither can I, but she's jealous . . . and insecure. It was expected."

"So when are you going to end it?"

"A little forward with that one aren't you? I don't know when I'm going to bail out. I'm not so sure why I haven't already."

"The sex must be too good. I told you that always clouds your judgment."

"No. Actually, we haven't done anything in quite some time. I haven't really wanted to. Strange, huh?"

"That is kinda strange . . . at least for you."

"You would be surprised at how many strange things have been going on, my dear."

Berta stares at Craig as he focuses on the road.

◌৪৩

For most of the ride, both remain silent, Berta watching the scenery and Craig trying to get to the jazz club as fast as possible without being pulled over by the cops. When they finally do get there, they both take a few seconds to stretch and make their way into the club. Almost immediately, they are seated and offered menus. Berta studies the interior of the restaurant. The lighting is low and romantic, and there are a bunch of people waiting for the live performances to start. Many people are dressed like they are, in a dressy causal way. Some women wear dresses a bit more revealing than hers. Berta frowns but straightens her face when Craig looks at her.

"So what do you think so far?" he asks.

"I like it. Very bluesy."

"Well, let me tell you, the food here is great and the music is even better. Only in Philly can you get a great combination of both."

"I'm sure you can get it elsewhere."

"Are you insulting my city?"

Berta laughs. "Not at all, sweetheart. Not at all."

Craig looks at the stage for a moment trying to shake the feeling of this outing being a date. "You know … I've been praying lately," he announces.

Berta looks at the back of Craig's head in shock. "No, I didn't know."

"Yup."

Both of them become silent. Craig still stares at the stage. Eventually he turns around to see Berta staring right at him. He looks into her eyes without flinching. Somewhere in her eyes, Craig finds comfort. He guesses he always did find that comfort in her eyes, but he never took notice until now.

"Not that you praying is bad . . . but what sparked that? Not too long ago, I was slapping you because you called yourself a rapist."

Craig nods. "A lot sparked it. Maybe even desperation sparked it. My right hand man is on a path of destruction . . . and I know there's something wrong with you . . . you just aren't saying what . . . but to see you so confident in God making a move to fix things . . . I don't know. It made me confident . . . again."

"I'm not as confident as you may think."

"You seem confident when it comes to Mark and Jade."

"Maybe."

"Well, I wanted to ask you something."

"What's up?"

"Do you think you would like to come to church with me? You know … it's been a while . . . and I really didn't want to go in alone."

Berta looks at Craig and smiles. "I would love to." She pauses. "So, I take it Maya isn't the church going type."

"Nice joke. She really isn't, though. But even if she were, I wouldn't ask her to go with me."

She nods. "So where is this church?"

"Just down the street from the gym I go to."

Berta doesn't say anything more. Their waiter comes to take their orders. Craig insists that Berta order first and then orders his food after her.

Out of nowhere, Berta asks, "Why are you still with Maya?"

Craig, taken back by the question, takes a sip of water. "Well . . . I see a bunch of potential, I guess. I don't know."

"But she isn't a very nice person."

"I know. But that could change."

"Do you think you would marry her?"

"What kind of question is that?"

"A simple one to answer."

"I guess . . . I mean, right now, I don't see that for us. I don't know. I did at one point but . . . Why do you ask?"

"But you still see potential in her? Even though you don't see marriage for you two? That doesn't make sense."

"I don't know, Berta. Why does it matter?"

"I'm curious, that's all."

"Okay, well answer me this, why are you leaving with a guy you have known for maybe four months?"

"Because I know in my heart that it's the right thing to do."

"So you love him?"

"What?"

"In your heart, that is what you said. It is a matter of the heart."

Berta doesn't say anything and looks down at the table.

"Berta, do you love him?" Craig stares at Berta with furious intent.

"I do. Why else would I leave with him?"

"I don't know." Craig looks down and thinks. "Do you think Mr. V. would have liked him?"

"Oh, wait one second. Daddy would have told you to kick Maya to the curb a long time ago, so let's not go there."

Craig looks away from Berta. Berta gets up from the table.

"I'm going to the ladies room for a sec. I'll be right back."

Craig nods and motions his hands as if he's opening the way for her to go. Berta marches her way past him.

☙❧

Berta enters the fancy looking restroom and goes into one of the stalls. She slams the door shut and stares at the back of the stall door. She grabs a piece of tissue to dab at her eyes as tears try to push their way through. *What are you doing, girl? Keep your cool.* Berta wipes away more tears. *Oh, what does it matter, you can't have him anyway. You just permanently pushed him away by telling him you're in love with another man. Way to panic, way to freaking panic.* As Berta continues to tell herself to keep it together, a group of women enter the restroom. She hears a few of them talking as others enter the stalls next to her. One of the women talks about something of particular interest, a man in all black who was sitting in the back. Berta looks through the sliver of an opening on the sides of the stall door to see three women, seemingly younger than her, talk while putting on makeup.

"Did you see him? I'm not going to tell you what I want to do to a man like that."

"I know. He looked big and strong—"

"And distinguished," a woman yells from the stall next to her.

Another woman starts to laugh. "Distinguished? Who cares about if he's distinguished? I'm more worried about what fires he can ex-tinguish with his … you know what I mean."

The entire bathroom erupts into laughter. Berta sees two women giving each other a high five.

"But I think he is with someone," someone yells from the far stall on her right.

"True. I did see this bangin' chick with him."

"Yeah, but she looked old."

"If she is, that's what I want to look like when I'm old."

"I wanna be like her when I grow up," a woman says in a whiny mocking voice. A few of the others giggle.

"I'm just saying. Obviously she's doing something right, to catch a man like—"

And just like that, Berta opens the stall door as the toilet flushes on her movement. Berta walks to an open sink to wash her hands. She knows the young women were talking about her as she feels three sets of eyes stare at her. She looks to the side and smiles.

"Good evening, ladies."

In unison, each of the women says, "Good evening."

Two more toilet flushes sound from the stalls behind her as she now feels all five sets of eyes staring at her. One of the young women walks up to Berta. She's a short woman that Berta now realizes is one of the girls that she was frowning at earlier in the night. The woman has on a tight red spaghetti strap shirt and a black miniskirt that comes up too high by Berta's standards. She wears heels that are at least five inches high. *She's a beautiful girl,* Berta thinks, *but she doesn't have to show so much.*

"Ma'am," the woman says in a soft voice, "Your shoes are really nice."

Berta smiles as the rest of the women nod in agreement.

"She got them get em' girl shoes," one of the other women say.

They all begin to snicker.

"Well, thank you. Be safe tonight, ladies."

All of them nod. Berta walks out the restroom as the women begin to talk again. After the door closes, Berta stands by it for a second to listen.

"I think I do want to be like her when I'm older."

"How old do you think she is?"

"She has to be in her late thirties, early forties."

Berta jerks her head back and returns to her table. She sees Craig waiting patiently for her as two plates of food sit on the table. Berta slides back into her seat as she smooths her dress over her thighs.

"How old do I look?" Berta asks.

Craig twists his face up a bit. "You look like you're in your thirties. Why?"

"Just asking."

A few moments later, Berta sees the group of women walking towards one of the tables in the front. They all stare at Berta and smile. One of them says, "Get him, girl," and they all burst out into laughter. Even Berta snickers a bit.

"So it looks like you made some new friends," Craig says smirking.

"Apparently." Berta looks down at their plates. "You could have started if you wanted."

"No. I'd rather have waited for you." He looks down. "Listen, things got a little heated a few minutes ago, and I just want to say sorry. That's not at all what I intended for this night. So, no more Maya and Daniel talk. Agreed?"

She smiles. "Agreed."

She continues to smile but realizes that this get together has, beyond any shadow of doubt, become a date.

A short bald man walks onto the stage and announces the forthcoming main live performances. Craig shifts around in his seat and starts to tap his foot.

"This is what I brought you here for. You're going to love it."

Berta smiles and blesses her food. Craig bows his head at the same time and waits for Berta to raise her head before he says, "Amen."

⊰❦⊱

For the rest of the night, Craig and Berta enjoy each other's company and the live music. One of the saxophone players even played right at their table. A couple times, Craig finds himself huddled close to Berta, taking her in with all the senses that he could respectfully use. Craig even enjoys the three hour ride back to Berta's apartment although she was sleep for almost the entire ride and it rained the entire way. He would look over at her every so often to see if she was okay and smile at how beautiful she looks even while sleeping.

At five o' clock in the morning, Craig finally gets them both back safely and parks the car. He caresses the side of Berta's face to wake her. She first shifts around and then lifts her head. She opens her eyes and looks directly at Craig and smiles.

"What time is it?" she asks while stretching.

"Five thirteen."

"Wow. I guess we are two party animals."

"Not quite. I haven't been out this long for some time."

"Neither have I. Not since my unsaved days."

Craig smiles. "Listen … don't worry about coming in to work today."

"Don't you have that meeting with Mr. Goldman?"

"Sure do. Ten o' clock."

"Nope. I'll be there. It's still my job to be there . . . even if it's only for about a half week more."

Craig nods and looks out the window. Abruptly, he unbuckles his seat belt. "Let me walk you to your door."

Berta begins to stop him, but he moves too fast and is out the car, in the rain, walking to her side. He slowly opens her car door and holds her hand as she steps out, while holding an umbrella over her. They both navigate around the puddles on the ground to the main door of her building and stand there looking at each other.

"I . . . really appreciate this, Craig."

"No problem. I'm glad you had a good time."

Silence.

Berta shivers.

"Hurry up and get in." Craig begins to walk away. "I'll see you in a couple hours."

Berta smiles. "Hey, Craig?"

Craig turns around to look at her.

"Seriously. Thanks."

"It was my pleasure, my dear." Craig takes a bow.

"Call me when you get in? So I know you got home okay."

Craig smiles. "I'm a big boy, Berta."

"Yeah. You're also in a Porsche at five o' clock in the morning."

"I'll give you a call . . . but you better not pick up. You better be asleep."

Berta smiles and walks into her building. Craig gets into his car and leaves the complex. On his way home, not even a few blocks away, he calls Berta.

"You're not even home yet."

"I know . . . I . . . I . . . just wanted to see if you were serious about the church thing. I'm probably going on Saturday."

"Is that why you really called?"

"Yeah, it is."

"I'll go with you. It's not a problem. Now get off the phone … on the road … in the rain."

"Okay. I'll see you later."

"Bye, Craig."

Berta hangs up and throws her cell phone on the couch. She kicks her heels off, sending them flying across the room, and walks to her bedroom. She changes her clothes thinking of how much fun she had. She tells herself that she likes Craig, she loves Craig, and she hates Craig, all at the same time. She goes to the bathroom and looks in the mirror while tying up her hair. She yawns and eventually flops into the bed to go to sleep.

CHAPTER TWENTY FIVE

SINCE the meeting with Alicia, Jade has spent her remaining hours at the park just down the street from the restaurant. She, at times, broke down in tears, and at those moments, she had to run back to the car to avoid public embarrassment. She went back three times before she decided to stay in the car.

Now, she sits in the car, thinking of what to do. Little droplets of water speck the windshield. Jade knows that soon it would rain and that soon it would get dark. Since she doesn't like driving in either condition, she decides to go home.

When she gets home, it is dark and rainy outside. Jade pulls up into the garage and presses the button to close it. She steps out of the car and enters the house to see Mark and the kids watching a movie. The kids run up to her and give her a hug. She hugs each and gives them a kiss, but she looks at Mark in disgust. Mark notices and squints his eyes as if trying to understand something she said.

"Go back and watch the movie," she says to the kids. She goes to the kitchen and grabs a small glass and that bottle of wine she was working on some odd days ago. Mark comes around the corner to see Jade pouring herself a glass.

"No," he whispers and grabs for the wine bottle. "The kids are right here."

With more strength that she realized she had, Jade shoves Mark away. Mark stumbles back into the refrigerator making a loud and thunderous thumping noise. The wine bottle falls from his hands and shatters on the floor. Mark stares at her in total shock. Kalina and Charles come running around the corner.

"What happened?" Charles asks.

"Nothing," Mark says as he goes to clean up the glass. "I was trying to throw it away . . . looks like I missed the trashcan."

"Yeah, Dad, you missed it by a mile," Kalina says.

"I know. Listen, why don't you guys finish watching the movie downstairs in the basement?"

"Are you coming to watch it?" Charles asks.

"Yeah, little man, I'll be down."

The kids run to the living room to grab the DVD from the player and run downstairs to the basement. Jade stomps past Mark while he cleans the broken glass. She marches her way to the bedroom and paces back and forth as she waits for Mark to come upstairs. She's trying hard to contain her anger but seeing Mark this night changed something within her.

"What is your problem?"

Jade looks at the doorway to see Mark staring at her with an angry gaze.

"I'll tell you my problem. Alicia. There's my problem. That is my problem, Mark."

Mark closes his eyes. He walks over to the dresser by the door and sits on it. "What about her?" he asks in an uncaring fashion.

"What do you mean, what about her? You're sleeping with her. How about that one? Or how about she's your ex-fiancée, someone you never told me about?"

Mark takes a deep breath and remains calm. "I really don't know what you are talking about."

"I met with her, dumb ass. There's no need to cover anything up. It's all out. All of it. How could you?"

"How could I? You brought this into our marriage, not me."

"I made a mistake. I tried to make amends. You . . . you . . ." Jade gets louder. "You knew the whole time. The whole damn time you knew, and you said nothing. You played games. You intentionally kept things to yourself . . . so you could run around like some super husband and teacher. You're an even bigger whore than she is."

Mark stands up from the dresser. "Why should I have said anything to you? Tell me. Why should I have said a damn thing to you? You made the wrong move. You were the one who didn't have the guts to tell me. You kept it a secret . . . while playing house. All the pain you felt, you deserved. All the pain you feel now, you deserve."

"You know what, Mark I—"

"No. Screw you and how you feel and what you think. You did all of this. I have done nothing but love you. I changed who I was for you," Mark pounds his fist on the dresser. "And it still wasn't good enough for you. So screw how you feel."

Interrupting their yelling, a vibration noise comes from Mark's nightstand. He realizes that he left his phone in the nightstand after he took a shower earlier in the night. He walks for it, but Jade stomps on top of the bed to get to the nightstand before him. She grabs the phone and easily recognizes the number. She looks at Mark with tears in her eyes. The phone continues to vibrate in her hand.

"Give me the phone," Mark says getting closer to her but not close enough to grab the phone.

"No." Jade answers the phone and simply begins talking. "Listen to me, you dirty whore. If you call my husband but one more time . . . I will kill you." Jade hangs up the phone puts it into her pocket.

"Jade, give me the phone."

"You never even made an attempt," Jade says crying and shaking her head. "You never even tried to make it work. You ran right to her."

"Jade."

"What?" Jade yells.

"Give me the damn phone!"

Jade begins to walk past Mark, ignoring his command, when Mark grabs her arm. Without thinking, she cocks back her free hand and sends it flying into the side of Mark's face.

❦

Mark steps back and turns his torso sideways. He looks at Jade for a second, who glares back at him with the most defiant stare a woman could give. For a brief moment, Mark thought he had control. However, the weight of the events of these past months have put so much pressure on his psyche, he finally snaps. He grabs Jade on the side of her arms and slams her into the wall. Jade yelps in pain, but being one who never backed down from a fight of any kind, she sends a barrage of punches and slaps towards Mark. He grabs her hands to stop her from hitting him and throws her onto the bed. He then pounces on her and leans his whole weight down on her, not allowing her to move. He wraps his hands around her neck and begins to squeeze. Jade squirms under him and screams, likely loud enough for even the neighbors to hear, but Mark keeps his grip around her neck and puts more pressure on her throat. Her screams turn to raspy whispers for help as Mark keeps his grip, restricting her airways. Jade looks up at Mark, her face turning red, as Mark presses her entire body into the bed. Her eyes begin to shut. She kicks a few more times, trying to get Mark off her, with each successive thrust weaker than the one before.

"Daddy!"

Mark snaps back and lets go of Jade's neck, looking at her as if he didn't know what he was doing. He gets up off her as she gasps for air. Mark looks to the side to see Kalina standing in the doorway with tears coming from her eyes. Mark looks back at Jade just in time to see her swing something at him. Then for him, everything goes black.

☙❧

Jade drops the lamp she hit Mark with near her side. Her mind is filled with images of how Mark looked. There was a chilling emptiness in his eyes. She crawls over to Kalina and hugs her.

"Get your things, baby." She coughs. "We're going to Grandma and Grandpa's."

"Mommy wh—"

"Just get your things. Where's Charles?"

"In his room."

Kalina runs to her room and Jade careens to Charles's room to find him curled up into a ball in the corner of the room. He rocks back and forth whispering something. The closer she gets, the more she realizes what he is saying. He whispers, "Help them, Jesus."

"Charles," Jade whispers, as to not frighten him, but also because it hurts to speak.

He looks up with tears in his eyes and crawls to Jade, hugging her tightly around her neck.

"We have to go, baby." Jade says as she shifts Charles's arms from her hurting neck.

"Why, Mommy? Why were you screaming? What's wrong with Daddy?"

"Everything is going to be all right, love. I need you to pack your things. We're going to stay somewhere else tonight."

Charles slides from Jade's grip and starts throwing clothes into his mini suitcase. Jade rushes out of his room and back to the bedroom to see Mark still face flat on the floor. She walks to the mirror to see bruises and cuts all around her neck. She grabs the house phone and dials her mother.

"Mommy," Jade gets out in a trembling voice.

"Jade, what's wrong?"

"Mark—"

"Jade, baby, I alrea—"

"No, Mom," Jade wails. "Listen, please. Me and the kids . . .." Jade begins to weep. "We . . . need to come over . . . now. We need to come over right now. We need somewhere to stay. Please."

"Of course, Jade. What happened?"

Jade gets off the phone abruptly and rushes to get the kids. Both children stand at the top of the stairs waiting for Jade.

"Let's go," she says, wiping her nose.

The kids rush ahead of her to the garage and get in her car. She makes sure that Charles is in his seat properly and kisses him on his forehead. She looks at Kalina, who is looking blankly out into space. Jade hurries to get in the car and start it. A few moments later, she is on the road headed to her parents' house.

CS80

Mark groans and squirms slowly on the floor. He feels a ticklish feeling on his forehead and feels for it. As soon as he touches the area, a shot of pain rages through his head. He pulls his hand away to see blood. He rises to his feet, reorients himself, and lurches to the bathroom. He looks in the mirror to see a giant gash on his forehead, one that will require stitches. He bumbles around the house looking for any signs of life but finds that he is in the house alone. Jade left and she took the kids. Mark leans over the railing and begins to cry. Burned into his mind is the look of fear on Kalina's face. His head continues to spin as he makes his way downstairs. All he hears is Kalina's scream . . . and the screams of Jade. His family is broken, and he will forever be haunted by the sound of those screams. He goes to the garage and sees the garage door still open. He walks back in the house.

243

Addictions come in many forms. Some are addicted to drugs, some alcohol. Others are addicted to pornography, maybe even sex. For Mark, his addiction has easily become Alicia. She has become his escape without him ever really knowing it. He grabs the house phone and dials her number. It takes a while for her to pick up, but when she does, all feels right with Mark.

"Hey."

"Mark, is everything all right?"

"I'm leaving her . . . but I need somewhere to crash tonight. I need to get out of here."

"Come over, but be careful, it's raining hard outside."

"I'll be over in a few."

"Okay."

"Alicia?"

"Yes, baby?"

"I love you."

"I . . . I love you too."

Mark hangs up the phone and rushes out the door.

ఇ౪ు

Jade gets to her parents' house. The kids quickly unbuckle their seatbelts and hurry out of the car.

"Hold on guys." Jade rushes out of the car and to the front door. Kalina opens the unlocked door and races inside, both her and Charles running crying in the arms of their grandparents. Jade walks in and stands at the doorway. As she walks inside, both her parents look at her in shock. The bruises around her neck are darker now; her face wet from the rain. Her eyes are bloodshot and she walks with a limp. Jade's father walks up to her with tears in his eyes. It is obvious to them now what happened to their daughter.

"Baby," Jade's father says and hugs her.

Jade wants to cry in his arms, but she gathers her strength.

"Daddy, I need the key to your desk drawer . . . the bottom right one," Jade says into his chest.

In a deep gruff voice, he says, "Baby, you know I can't do that."

Jade begins to cry. "Please." She feels him take a deep breath.

"That isn't wise, baby."

"Daddy, please. Please." Jade pulls away from him. "Look at my neck. Look at me. Look at what he did to me."

A tear traces down his face. Reluctantly, he digs into his pocket and hands her a small desk key. Jade's mother looks at her husband in complete disbelief.

"Are you serious?" she says. "Jade, this is going to do no good. You hear me? No good."

"You wanted me to deal with this myself, right? Well, I'm handling it." Jade leaves to go to her father's study. She scrambles to the bottom right drawer and jams the key in, twists it, and pulls open the drawer. She digs in it and pulls out a shiny silver handgun and sticks it into her purse. She slams the drawer shut and leaves the study. Jade's mother took the kids upstairs. She hears Charles crying for her but ignores it and steps outside. Standing in the rain at her car door is her father.

"This isn't going to solve anything," he yells over the pounding rain.

Jade doesn't say anything.

"God set your marriage together . . . you two let man tear it asunder . . . it takes God to bring it together again."

Jade's hair is matted to her face and she can barely see anything. "How Dad? There's no going back to the way things were. It just doesn't appear out of thin air."

"Like anything, it takes work. It took work for it to be torn apart . . . ." Jade's father steps out of her way. "Why don't you stay? It's too dangerous out there."

"No."

"What are you going to do?"

"I don't know."

"Jade."

Jade gets into the car and drives off, tires screeching in her wake. Her father stands in the rain for a few seconds before entering the house again.

☙

Mark can barely see the lines on the road to drive straight. He took the only route that he knows to take to get to Alicia's home, most of which consisting of back roads. This particular road Mark knows is a little traveled one, one that is dangerous in bad weather, but one he takes every day. He avoids thinking of the kids . . . or Jade . . . or anything that would be related to them. He avoids thinking of the school . . . and the kids there. All he thinks about is Alicia and making it to her. Without realizing it, he speeds up. Everything around him is a blur. He starts to feel a rumble as if somehow he is veering off the road and tries to slow down. He taps the brakes but he hits one hard bump and his entire car starts spinning down the road. Mark grasps the driving wheel to try to straighten out the car, but before he knows it, he feels a hard jerk and hears a boom, then a pop and breaking glass.

Mark sees nothing but white. He looks around to see nothing but white and hears a ringing in his ears. The smell of chemicals fills his nose. His body feels numb and he feels as if he is paralyzed, but in reality, Mark is in shock as he gets out of the car and starts to walk down the road aimlessly. He limps along the edge of the road, falling to the ground a few times. The ringing begins to fade away, but he still doesn't know where he is. He can't tell if the flashes in his vision are from lightning or if it is himself, having suffered several blows to the head. He makes a wrong step and he ends up falling off the side of the road. He slides and rolls down into a heavily wooded area and finally into a ditch, receiving yet another blow to the head. This one knocks him unconscious. He lies face up in a ditch as the rain pounds on his face. The rain starts filling up the ditch, enough to have the water completely cover Mark's ears. The muddy waters mix with the blood that streams from his head and his now bloody nose. Like being under the water in a bathtub, Mark is able to hear his heartbeat and its slowing pace. He then hears people's voices. He hears Craig . . . and Jade . . . Kalina . . . Charles . . . Tim . . . and Alicia. Then he hears laughing . . . it's his own voice. He can't move a single muscle, and he hears himself laughing . . . but not as if he's happy. It's an evil laugh. Finally, he hears one thing that makes even his soul shiver.

Checkmate.

CHAPTER TWENTY SIX

JADE pulls into her garage and sees that Mark's car isn't there. She pulls the gun out of the purse anyway and gets out of the car. She closes the garage door and enters the house, gun drawn. She gently closes the door behind her and stands there, listening for any movement. She hears none. Her feet hurt. She realizes that she has been in heels all day and kicks them off, sending them flying into the back of the couch. Then she goes on her search. She tries to keep her breathing steady as she checks the basement and the main floor. She heads upstairs, taking each step with caution, and checks the rooms. The entire house is empty. Jade stands in her bedroom doorway imagining what Kalina saw. She imagines what it looked like, her father set to kill her mother. Jade shakes her head to shake away the chill that goes up and down her spine. She walks over to the bloodstain on the carpet and stares at it for a few seconds. She then stares at her neck in the mirror. The bruises are darker and her entire neck is swollen. She begins to cry but holds herself together. Right at her foot, peeping out from under the dresser, is Mark's cell phone. She picks it up and clutches it, almost breaking it. She takes one last look in the bedroom, the place where so much love was, the place where they were always guaranteed to have time for each other, and the same place where she almost lost her life. Jade shuts the lights off and slams the door. She gingerly walks down the stairs to the kitchen, swinging the hand with the gun at her side. She throws the cell phone on the counter and notices that the house phone has dark fingerprints on it. Jade takes a closer look to see that it is blood on the phone. She places the gun on the counter, wipes the phone off, and looks at the last number called. Jade recognizes the number but checks it with the one that is in Mark's phone anyway. Jade calls the number from the house phone. Almost immediately, Alicia picks up.

"Is he over there?"

"Jade, Mark—"

"I thought I told you that if you talked to him again, I would kill you," Jade says in a drained but menacing voice. "Do you not think I am serious?"

Silence.

"Do you?" Jade yells.

"Jade, I don't know where he is. Yes, he was on his way here . . . but that was a long time ago . . . and in this rain . . . I'm across town and the only roads he could have traveled are already washed out from the weather. Jade, I think you should call the police."

"Call the police?" Jade hangs up the phone and out of rage throws it against the wall. The plastic casing of the phone shatters into a bunch of small pieces. Jade looks at the gun that she set on the counter. *What if something bad did happen to him?* She shakes her head and begins pacing back and forth along the cold tile of the kitchen floor, telling herself not to panic. The rain hasn't let up at all since it started. The numerous drops sound like drills on the roof of the house. She remembers seeing on the news about flash flood warnings for the entire area and remembers knocking Mark out with the lamp. He is likely to have a concussion. After a few more moments, Jade runs to a closet and grabs her sneakers. She pulls them on and rushes out the door, grabbing only her keys.

CB&ED

Mark's twisted body lays in a muddy ditch. He lays there thinking to himself, feeling trapped. *Okay, Mark. Stay calm. Your mind is running all over the place. Someone will come for you. No one will come for you. What? Stop it, Mark. What is wrong with you?*

Mark tries to keep his thoughts straight, but every time he finds something calming, another thought comes through . . . but he's not so sure it's him. *Okay. Move. Come on, Mark. Move. MOVE.* Mark remains in the ditch, not having moved a single muscle. His eyes remain closed. *This is where you will die. Both of you. In a ditch. Both of you will die in a ditch. No. Yes. No. Jesus. Jesus? He's not real. Jesus. You can keep calling. He doesn't hear you. Kalina, I'm so sorry. Jade, I'm so, so sorry. It's too late to apologize now. No one hears you, Mark. But wait, aren't you going to apol-ogize to Alicia?*

More laughter.

Lord, Father, God . . . please forgive me. Suddenly, the laughter stops. Mark doesn't hear anything, not even his heartbeat, and he is overtaken by a feeling of peace. He doesn't feel cold anymore and his body doesn't ache, but he still is unable to see. There's nothing but darkness around him. Again, he hears himself talking. *In a ditch, you find yourself, Mark. In a ditch, you have been for quite some time. How easily have you fallen into a trap of the enemy.* Mark tries to stop his thoughts, but again, it is as if he is being spoken to as opposed to speaking to himself. *How easy it was for your marriage to fall apart. How easy it was for you to let go of hope . . . of your faith. It hurts to see something so good become so rotten, but there is hope. My strength and power are enough to help you. My grace is enough to cover you. My love is enough to pull you through and to heal your mar-riage. Start anew, for My light will shine through the both of you.*

Long pause.

Father? I don't want to die here.

⋇

Jade knows of only one road that would take her across town, a long and winding back road. She's sure this is the way Mark took because this road is the most familiar to him. He takes it every day to get to work. She creeps along the road, finding it difficult to see past a few feet in front of the car. She sees a set of headlights on her right. She quickly pulls over and tries to make out what the car looks like, but the streams of water that cascade down the car make that task nearly impossible. Jade sneezes and looks around for an umbrella. She doesn't find one but she does find a flashlight. She grabs the large bulky flashlight and tests it to see if it still works. The light illuminates the entire car. Jade takes a deep breath and exits the car into the pouring rain. She sneezes again and runs up to the car that is leaning on a tree. The back is crushed and it looks as if the airbags have deployed. Jade crawls into the car and opens the glove box. She sifts through a few papers, sneezing more often, and finds that the car is Mark's. Without hesitation, she jumps out of the car and aims the flashlight down a steep hill.

"Mark!"

She hears no answer. She runs back to her car to look for a phone but finds nothing. She remembers that the only thing she brought was the keys to her car. Jade sits in her car shivering. She closes the door and turns the heat on for a few moments to warm up again.

She knows Mark is somewhere close. She feels him. The problem is that she doesn't know exactly where he is, and at this rate, he could be anywhere from where his car crashed to three miles down the road. Now, fear begins to take over her mind. Jade leans over the steering wheel and starts to cry. Hopelessness settles on her shoulders like a two-ton weight.

"Lord," Jade says sobbing. "Please . . . please . . . take me to my husband. Bring us together again . . . please." Jade sits in the car as if waiting to hear something. She looks out of her window to see it rain harder. Rushing waters now cover parts of the road. Jade reopens her car door and clutches the flashlight. Her entire body is stiff coming out of the car. She walks to the edge of the road and begins to navigate down the side of the steep hill.

"Mark!" Jade yells in a hoarse voice.

No answer.

Jade continues down the steep hill as she waves the flashlight around and tries to scan the ground for her husband . . . or at the very least, a sign. She continues down the hill, navigating her way past shrubs and fallen trees, and comes to a landing. She waves the flashlight again and still finds no one. She notices that the slope is now mostly mud, as it is hard for her to keep her footing. Jade takes a quick step to climb back on solid ground and falls to the ground. The flashlight flies out of her hand and slides down the slope to another landing. Jade adjusts her vision to see an outline of something where the flashlight landed. *It looks like . . . Mark!* Jade slides down the hill, getting cut by jagged rocks and sharp branches, to get to the bottom of the steep slope. Water pools in the area as she grabs the flashlight and aims it at the outline. In front of her, Jade sees her husband, cut up, bruised, and lips turning blue. His body is halfway in the pool of muddy water. Immediately, she kneels down to lift her husband out of the ditch and drags him to a less muddy part of the landing. She feels his neck to feel a faint pulse. She leans back onto the slope and grabs him under his arms to attempt to lift him up the slope. She can't get good enough footing so she slides back down at each try. On her third try, she falls backwards with Mark landing between her legs. She remembers lying like this very well. This is the way they had lain together on their couch all the time. Mark always would lay the back of his head on her chest and act as a blanket for her. This is the way they had lain when she first attempted to tell him of her infidelity. Lying like this holds some significance for Jade. Back then, she would secretly pray for him. She would pray for their marriage. Somehow, it fell out of practice, praying for her husband. This night she makes it a practice again. This night is the most important night to do so.

"Baby, don't you leave me," Jade whispers in his ear. "Just hold on." Jade then bows her head and prays. She prays for her husband to live. She prays for her marriage to live. As time goes on, her prayers turn into tears. All strength is gone from her; so much so, she can't even move from under Mark. She pulls him close to her, though in pain, not wanting him to slide back into the ditch. The rain starts to let up, but not enough to stop the pain when it hits her cold and rigid skin. Jade cries harder. She feels Mark's pulse. It's slowed down even more. Out of desperation, anger, and sadness, all at the same time, Jade screams. Coming from deep inside, she releases a primal sounding scream. She screams until she can't anymore and bows her head. She now knows that this is where they will both die. In her head, she hears herself talking, saying the same things over and over again. *This is where you will die. Both of you. In a ditch. Both of you will die in a ditch.* She nestles her face in between Mark's neck and shoulder and closes her eyes.

A short amount of time passes before the rain slows down to a drizzle. Jade faintly hears a noise that becomes louder as time continues. It's the sound of sirens, a bunch of them. She looks up towards the road to see the beams of flashlights waving through the air.

"Hello," Jade calls in nothing louder than a whisper.

After a few more moments, the shining lights start to beam down the hill around the two of them. Jade tries to move but finds herself unable to budge. Finally, a beam of light shines in her face for a quick second. Then the beam shines in her face again.

"Here! I found something," a man yells.

A bunch of other beams shine in her face. She squints her eyes and bows her head to Mark's ear again. "Baby, please be with me still. Everything is going to be okay. Everything is going to be okay."

Chapter Twenty Seven

"I don't believe you."

"What do you mean?"

"I don't believe you are ready to go."

Berta and Candace have lunch on a warm afternoon outside of a restaurant not too far from where Candace works deeper into the city. People walking and enjoying the good weather fill the streets.

Berta yawns. "I am ready," she says.

"Okay, hold on. That's the fifth time that you yawned in the last minute or so. What's up? Am I a bore?"

Berta smiles. "Late night last night. Real late night last night."

"What were you and Daniel doing last night?" Candace asks with an inquisitive look on her face. She smiles.

"Nothing. I wasn't with Daniel last night."

"Something wrong?"

"Nope."

"So why the late night?"

"I went to Philly."

Candace twists her face up in confusion. "Philly? What's in Philly?"

"This really nice jazz club that I think I will go to again someday."

"You went by yourself?"

Berta hesitates and considers lying. "No . . . I went with Craig."

"What? You two went out on a date?"

"It wasn't a date. It was a going away celebration."

"Well, who else was there?"

"Ummm, a live band."

"No. Who else was celebrating with you two?"

"No one, I guess."

"So it was a date," Candace yells, almost cheering. "Wait, isn't he with someone too?"

"It wasn't a date . . . and yes, he is with someone."

"You two . . . I'll tell ya . . . you two are sneaky. So what happened?"

"We weren't sneaking around . . . and nothing happened. We ate, listened to music, and went home."

Candace smiles. "I'm sure that's the way it went. Anyway, I was pretty sure before, but now I'm absolutely positive, you aren't ready to go."

"There's no way of convincing you otherwise, is there?"

"Nope. Seriously Berta, have you been praying about it?"

"I have."

"And?"

"All I keep hearing is 'look.'"

"Look?"

"Yes, look. That's it."

"Look at what?"

"If I knew, I wouldn't have such a confused look on my face, now would I?"

Candace smiles. "Well, maybe you should stay still until you figure out what that means."

"Meaning don't go?"

"Exactly."

"I'm still going."

"But don't you see? This is so impulsive. This isn't like you at all."

"I know it looks weird. I know it looks silly. I just can't take it anymore. It's too much."

"What is? You're not telling me anything."

"I told you already. To be around him . . . and not be with him . . . it's such a tug of war on my heart. I can't take it."

Candace looks perplexed. "And if he said he's madly in love with you and he doesn't want you to go? What if he ditches that other chick and pursues you until no end? Will that make things better?"

"Honestly, no. I sound crazy, I know, but this whole time, for years, all I have been doing is living in the shadow of this . . . of this promise. I want to be free."

"This the promise that you rarely ever talked about that you apparently made to your Dad?"

Berta nods. Both women remain silent as they watch the crowds move along the city streets.

"So you don't want Craig to love you . . . but you do? You can't stay, but you have to?"

Berta looks at Candace but says nothing.

"Look, Berta, I'm sorry."

"For what?"

"As a friend, I gave you advice that may have caused all of this."

"What?"

"I told you that it would be a good idea to date Daniel . . . to forget Craig . . . to move on. But look at how much trouble that has caused. I just feel bad. I shouldn't have said anything."

"None of this is your fault. I made the decision . . . you didn't force me to. Where is this coming from anyway?"

"I don't know. I just . . . I'm starting to think you and Craig are destined to be together."

Berta jerks her head back and laughs. "I don't know how you see that." She plays with a strand of hair. "It doesn't matter now, anyway. I'm leaving in a few days."

☙

Mark wakes up and hears beeps all around him. Without guessing, he knows that he's in a hospital bed. All the lights are off in the room, almost forcing him to believe that he is still asleep. Only a shine from the streetlights outside light a corner of the room and gives that part of the room a dim orange glow. His body feels numb, and he feels weak. He takes a few moments to try to adjust himself over the stiff hospital bed. He winces in pain as he tries to sit up. He hears some rustling other than his own and stops moving. He sees a silhouette of a person moving in the chair across from the bed. The figure flows closer to him. He still only sees an outline of the person and believes the person to be Alicia. She touches his face.

"Welcome back," she says in a stuffy voice.

Mark recognizes her to be Jade, not Alicia. He continues to try to sit up. Jade moves to help Mark prop himself up and cuts on a small lamp next to the bed. Mark looks at Jade under the light of the lamp and repeatedly asks himself what he has done. Under the single light of the lamp, he sees large and dark bruises around Jade's neck and is ashamed. He puts his head down before she turns from the lamp to look at him.

"You've been out for a day," Jade says, looking for Mark to say something. "The doctors treated you for moderate hypothermia. They treated your wounds too. They were worried about infection, though." Jade waits again for Mark to say something, but Mark keeps his head down. "You had a fever for a couple hours." Jade sniffs. "But you came back strong."

Mark continues to look down even though he knows Jade is looking for a response. He simply can't bring himself to say anything. He has never been so ashamed of himself in his life. He looks at Jade for the first time since waking up. She looks tired, almost completely broken down. Tears well up in his already bloodshot eyes. Jade realizes that Mark isn't going to say anything and leaves the room to grab a nurse.

⚮

A few moments later, a nurse comes in and cuts on the bright overhead fluorescent lights of the room. She examines Mark while Jade watches attentively. The nurse then turns to Jade, not looking her in the eyes but at her neck.

"The doctor will likely check on him tomorrow. Looks like he'll be okay to go home by tomorrow afternoon."

Jade thanks the nurse and the woman leaves, eying Jade as if she suspects something. She stares at Mark for a bit longer.

"Well, you'd better get your rest. I'll be back in the morning."

Jade makes her way to the door when Mark says, "I heard your prayer."

Jade stops at the door and turns to look at Mark, who is staring out the window.

"Word for word," he says. "I thought I died. I didn't hear anything. I didn't see anything. I thought it was all over, my time here . . . but then I heard your voice . . . I heard your cries. I didn't want to die . . . but then it seemed inevitable . . . and I eventually looked forward to it. But your voice . . . your voice . . . ."

Jade stands there for a second holding back tears. The effort hurts almost every part of her face so she gives up and lets the tears stream down her face. Her nose was already stuffy, but now breathing through her nose is next to impossible. "I love you," she says and slowly leaves the room, not waiting to hear anything else from him.

Jade leaves the hospital and drives home thinking of all the things she must do to get the house ready for Mark's return. Not for a second does she think of getting any rest herself although the doctors that treated her suggested she do so. She looks at the clock to see that it's almost midnight.

She finally gets home and steps into the house, being cautious to not make any noise, as if someone else were there other than her. She sets her purse down on the dining room table and reaches under the kitchen sink to grab a bucket and a bunch of cleaning supplies. From there, she marches upstairs and to the bedroom. When she got home yesterday afternoon, she made sure that she didn't step foot in the bedroom because she wasn't ready to step foot in it yet. She took a shower in the kids' shower and found some clean clothes in the laundry room. She avoided the room at all costs. Tonight, that all changes.

Jade slowly opens the bedroom door and turns on the lights. Her attention is caught by the large bloodstain on the carpet right by the bed. She walks past it and goes into the bathroom. She fills the bucket up with water, pours in a lemon scented cleaning chemical, and grips a scrub brush. Kneeling at the stain, she sprays the stain with another chemical, dips the brush into the water, and starts scrubbing. At first, the stain looked as if it was going to be easily removed, a brownish red foam forming around the edges of the treated area, but after some time of scrubbing and rinsing, a light brown stain remains.

The reason for her not going into the bedroom the previous night starts to creep up on her, as she plays over in her mind what happened just a couple nights ago. Jade sits on the floor and leans against the dresser as she contemplates what to do now. For the first time since her infidelity, Jade truly considers divorce. *This marriage has become so toxic . . . so, so toxic.* She begins to cry. *He put his hands on me. He tried to kill me. If Kalina hadn't come, he would have. Get out now. That's what I should do. Get out and get custody of the kids. No. I can't take the kids away from him. I can't do that.*

Jade continues to think to herself, eventually reminding herself that those very hands that Mark laid on her are the same hands that would touch her so passionately in all the right places. Those are the same hands that massaged any and all of her tense muscles after a long day at work; the same hands that would hold her close almost every time she needed it. His hands, hands that put bruises around her neck, are the same hands that once held her face as he looked into her eyes and told her that he loves her. His hands are the same hands that would grab hers and stroke them as they prayed together. Prayer. Jade leans her head back against the dresser.

"What do I do, Lord?" she whispers. "I know what I asked of you when we were stuck in the storm . . . I wanted to salvage something of my marriage . . . but is that the right thing? Is that Your will? Is it too far gone?"

❧

Craig lays in his bed unable to go to sleep. He stares up at the ceiling thinking about his plans for tomorrow. Every thought he has turns to thinking of Berta. He wants to call her but knows that he can't. His cell phone vibrates on the nightstand. Quickly he grabs it and picks it up, hoping it is Berta, but knowing the chances of that are slim.

"Hello."

"Hey."

Craig pauses, hearing the person that is the exact opposite of Berta. "What's up, Maya?"

"That's it? What's up? We haven't talked in some time, Craig."

"As I recall, that was your choice."

"I've called. I've called a number of times. Look, I'm sorry. I overreacted—"

"Again."

"Yes, again. I'm sorry I overreacted again. I . . . I—"

"You are jealous of Berta."

Long pause.

"I am jealous of Berta," Maya says simply as a triviality.

"Why?"

"What do you mean why? You've worked side by side with her for how long? You can't tell me there aren't any feelings of anything between you two."

Craig sits back and thinks for a second. "Even if there were, it doesn't matter."

"Why doesn't it?"

"She's leaving in a few days. She and Daniel are moving to Texas."

Everything becomes silent. Craig can almost feel Maya smiling over the phone.

"I'm not going to lie, that's the best news I've heard in a while."

Craig winces at her comment. "Yeah."

"So what does that mean for us?"

Craig sits on the edge of the bed and rubs the back of his neck. "Nothing."

Maya sounds stunned. "Wh-what do you mean?"

"You're insecure . . . and I know that there's always going to be a Berta somewhere for you. I'm not looking for that type of relationship . . . where you question every step I make."

"I promise, Craig, things will be different."

"I don't believe you. Honestly, I don't even want to believe you. One of the closest people to me is leaving and all you can say is that it's good news to you. You're selfish." He clears his throat. "I understand why we worked so well at first. I was acting selfishly too, but now . . . I don't think we're on the same page."

"So what are you saying?" Maya growls. "Stop talking in riddles and be up front about it."

"I'm saying that I'm no longer in. I can't do it anymore."

"Look, Craig, how about we do this—"

"There isn't anything to do. I've made up my mind. That's it."

"So after everything we've been through, that's it?"

"We haven't known each other that long. We really haven't been through anything."

Long pause.

"You're in love with her, aren't you?"

"What?"

"You're in love with Berta. That's why all of this is coming up."

Craig pauses. "Once again, you're letting your jealousy get the best of you. You're being ridiculous."

Maya laughs. "I'm not. She's with someone, Craig . . . and you just told me that she's leaving. Why are you throwing away what we have for something that will never happen?"

"It doesn't seem like you get it, Maya. Sadly, when you do, I will already be out of the picture."

"Not quite. I don't think you get it . . . but that's fine. You're a grown man. Do what you want, but don't think you can just hop back to me when you get rejected."

Craig laughs. "Good-bye, Maya."

Maya hangs up without saying good-bye. Craig throws his phone onto the bed and stands up. He walks to the window and stares at the city skyline.

CHAPTER TWENTY EIGHT

THE next morning, Jade wakes to a beam of sunlight shining in her face. She fell asleep on the floor by the dresser and feels it in her neck and back. She rises from the floor, ambles to the bathroom, and takes a shower. After her shower, she walks to her bedroom window and opens the blinds wider to allow in more sunlight. Then she walks to the mirror. The swelling around her neck has gone down significantly and the bruises are next to invisible. *Good,* she thinks. She walks to the closet to find something to wear and decides on jeans and a short sleeve shirt, an outfit that is a rarity for her to wear outside the house. She glances at the clock to see that it is already one in the afternoon. She turns away but snaps her head back suddenly. Realizing that she was supposed to be at the hospital early in the morning, she runs to the phone to see a few missed calls, two of them being from the hospital. At once, she calls the hospital and asks the receptionist to put her through to Mark's room.

"Mark, I'm running late, I was … I was. . ."

"It's okay. They're going to keep me here until tonight. Take your time."

Jade pauses, listening to Mark's voice, and hears the solemn bass coming from him. After everything they have been through, even this makes her heart hurt, to hear her husband so distraught.

"I'll be there tonight."

Mark sighs. "Okay," he says, sounding like he is about to cry. "I'll see you later."

"Okay," Jade says and hangs up the phone. Somehow, saying bye just didn't seem right at the time. She paces back and forth in the bedroom before going through her nightstand and grabbing her Bible. She sits at the edge of the bed and stares at the faint bloodstain in front of her. She starts to read and pray. For a couple hours she sits in silence until she grabs the phone and quickly dials a number she has dialed many times previously.

"Hey, Claire," Jade says. "This is Jade Cooke. How are you?"

The woman on the other side of the phone is a kindhearted older woman who is Pastor Brentwood's assistant. After a few minutes of small talk, the woman asks what she can do for Jade.

"I would like to set up an appointment with the pastor, if possible."

"Of course," the old woman says. "You know he will always make time for you."

"It's for both me and Mark. Is that okay?"

"That is fine," the woman pauses. "Is everything okay?"

Cʒʒɞᴑ

Berta drives past the church to which Craig gave her directions and finds Craig patiently waiting in front of the large doors. She continues to drive down the street until she finds a parking space nearly a block away. Once parked, she rushes out of the car and skips her way to Craig. When he sees her, he smiles.

"Hey. I thought you were standing me up."

"No. Not for such a momentous occasion." Berta smiles.

"Well, thanks for coming. I really appreciate it."

Berta observes the tall standing building with its stained glass window front. She looks a bit more at the design of the building.

"Come on," Craig says. "Let's grab some seats."

Berta and Craig walk into the church with a crowd around them. Almost every person says hello to both of them. Berta looks around noticing the many types of people who attend this church. As they walk down the rows of pews, a decent sized choir sings a song that Berta immediately recognizes. The choir sings it differently than Berta is used to, but she is still mesmerized by the sound. Berta follows Craig towards the front of the church and smiles. She thought, since this is Craig's first time back in a church, he would want to ease back into it and sit where most newcomers go unnoticed, in the back. She looks at him in admiration, knowing that Craig is rarely afraid of those situations from which most would shy away. He gets to a row and moves aside to allow her to slide in first. She thanks him and Craig slides in next to her. Berta looks to her other side to see that she sits next to an older woman. She smiles at Berta and looks forward. She hums along with the choir.

Berta then looks at Craig who is smiling just as much.

For most of the service, Berta sits there thinking of Craig, noting his every move. She hasn't seen him like this before, so . . . happy. Eventually, a plump man walks up to the altar carrying a large book and stands behind a podium. He sets the book down and grabs a microphone that was sitting on the podium and begins to speak into it.

"I first want to thank all of you for packing this place out on a Saturday afternoon . . . not a Sunday morning, but a Saturday afternoon." People clap. "God moves in wonderful and mysterious ways. Today, this service was sort of a last minute decision. In my study and prayer time last week, I asked God if there's anything new I could do. I asked if there's something I could do that would shake some things up in this area, something that would allow us to reach even further into our community." Some people begin to nod their heads. Berta can easily tell who is a member of the church and who is visiting; although, Craig acts just like one of the members.

"I didn't hear anything," the plump man says. Berta now assumes him to be the pastor of the church. "But this past Tuesday morning, I woke up with this thought on my mind. Have a Saturday service. On Tuesday I thought this." The pastor smiles. "That left no time to tell anyone really. That only left time to print up a few signs and post them around town. But somehow we have packed this one thousand seat church to capacity." He becomes more animated with his gestures. "If I may, can I get all our first time visitors to stand."

At first, one by one, then more as each person stood until almost the entire back of the church stands. A few sitting in the middle section stand, and then Craig and Berta, the only ones up front, stand.

"Just look," the pastor says loudly. Berta snaps her head forward. "Look at what God has done. Come on church; let's give them a round of applause."

The people who are sitting begin to clap for those who stand. A few people around Berta and Craig clap proudly, as if they were their children. This goes on for a few minutes before the clapping dies down and they are asked to be seated.

"Listen, you are the reason for this Saturday service. Now, I know some churches do this to gain members . . . but you can ask any member here, that isn't our style. After this service, you don't have to set another foot in this place if you don't want to, but I do urge you to get into a Bible teaching church . . . a Holy Spirit filled church. We are all in this race together, and this service is just our attempt at making sure we all make it to the finish line together. Amen?"

The church answers, "Amen."

"Now if you can, please turn your Bibles to the book of Genesis . . ."

Berta looks at Craig as he pulls out a Bible from a holder in front of him and opens it. She realizes that she didn't bring hers and slides closer to Craig to read. Again, Berta finds herself drifting off and thinking of

Craig. She thinks of him during the entire sermon until the pastor yells out "Just look" again.

At the end of the sermon, the now sweaty pastor speaks softly to the church. "We're going to do something different this time," he says. "Normally, this would be an altar call and we would invite anyone who wants to join in on the life of the church to the altar. Today, we are going to pray two prayers at our seats. You can pray as you feel led. The first prayer is for salvation, saying that you give your life to Christ. This says you live for him now." The pastor wipes the sweat off his forehead with a towel. "The second is a prayer of rededication. This is if you were living for Christ, but you lost your way. Up front here, while you pray, a few of our church members will pray for you." He lays the towel on the podium. "Now, if we can, let us all bow our heads."

Berta bows her head as the pastor recites a prayer of salvation. A few people from far off begin to cry. Immediately after the pastor says "Amen," he prays a prayer of rededication. Berta listens this time. She keeps her head down but opens her eyes and looks towards Craig to see him remaining still, saying nothing. Berta snaps her head back down and shuts her eyes tightly. Part of her is disappointed, wanting so badly for Craig to believe again. Another part understands, knowing it has been so long for him, that he may never want to go back. That last part is the one that hurts her the most. She feels like a failure.

⁂

After the service, Craig and Berta walk out the church, side by side. Craig playfully bumps into Berta and she smiles. They stand on the sidewalk as people file out the church.

"Do you want to do lunch?" Craig asks.

Berta looks at Craig contemplating his offer. The wind blows her hair in front of her face and she quickly brushes it aside. "I can't. I have to pack."

"What about dinner?"

Berta winces. "Can't do. Daniel is taking me out tonight."

Craig looks across the street and nods. "So . . . I guess this is . . ." He finds himself unable to finish the sentence.

Berta looks at Craig slightly confused. "I'll come back and visit."

Seemingly out of the blue, Craig states, "I broke up with Maya."

Berta nods and smiles. "She wasn't much a fit for you anyway. Her loss."

"Yeah." Craig expected more from her. He didn't quite expect a party but he thought she would be a bit more excited about it.

Long silence.

The two stare at each other, not knowing what to say next. Craig moves closer to Berta and gives her a hug. She almost melts into him, enjoying a brief moment of what she once believed to be her destiny.

"Good-bye, friend," Craig says.

"Good-bye."

Berta moves away from Craig. Both then turn away from each other and walk to their cars. Tears stream down Berta's face.

Craig walks away with a pained expression on his face. He feels his heart tearing from him the farther away Berta moves. Quickly he turns around. He isn't able to take it any longer. He looks for her to tell her that he doesn't want her to go but finds a large crowd blocking his view. He walks back to the front of the church and tries to search her out but still doesn't find her. Eventually, he gives up and walks back to his car.

ଔଓ

Jade gets Mark home after he was finally released from the hospital. For some time, he sits in the living room, resting on the sofa. He's afraid to go anywhere inside the house. Jade sets two glasses of water on the coffee table in front of Mark. She then sits on the sofa across from him. She stares at him for a few moments before saying anything.

"The kids are at my parents'."

Mark nods.

Jade stares at Mark for a few more moments. "I'm going to stay with them as well."

Mark still says nothing.

"I'll let you get your rest." she gets up from her seat and grabs her drink.

"What are we going to do?" Mark asks.

Jade stops in her tracks and sits back down. "Well first, I think we need to talk."

Mark nods and lays his head back on the headrest.

"I called Pastor," Jade says and awaits Mark's reaction. Mark does nothing but continue to stare up at the ceiling. "I set up an appointment for us. I figured that would be the best thing to do right now." Mark still says nothing. Jade becomes impatient but keeps her cool. "Look, all I need to know is that you want this to work. I know that it seems crazy . . . to want to stay married. I know there's a great chance that it will never work, but I'm willing to try. I just . . . I need to know that there's something there . . . that you are willing to try as well."

Mark finally looks at her. His face is emotionless, and he doesn't say anything for a while before looking back up at the ceiling again. Jade becomes more frustrated and stands up again to leave the room. Just before she goes upstairs, Mark speaks.

"When is the appointment?"

Jade stands at the steps and looks back at him. "In a couple days."

Mark rubs his face. "I'll go."

Jade looks at Mark for a bit longer, hoping he would have more to say, but eventually goes upstairs to pack her clothes.

◌⃝

Berta gets to Daniel's house. She is still thinking about Craig and the service from which they just came. She's already packed up and ready to go, at least physically. Mentally and emotionally, she feels unprepared but presses forward anyway. She pulls up to Daniel's house and gets out of her car. She sees that Daniel hasn't picked up his mail yet. *He probably has been so busy packing as well.* Berta grabs the stack of mail from his mailbox, flipping the handle back down, and walks to the front door. She rings the bell.

"Door's open," he yells from inside.

Berta opens the door to see a bunch of boxes lying all around and hears music coming from the kitchen. She sets the mail down on a stack of boxes and walks to the kitchen to see Daniel packing up plates and kitchen utensils. He stops for a second and smiles at Berta.

"Hey, baby," he says and walks over to her to give her a kiss.

Berta smiles at him, noticing how excited he seems. "Hey. How are you?"

"Tired, but good. You?" Daniel goes back to one of the boxes and closes it. He begins to tape it up but doesn't have enough left to cover the opening. He sits on the kitchen floor and looks up at Berta to listen to her response.

"I'm good. I just packed up everything."

"You've been packing all day?"

Berta pauses to think. "Yup. I only have what I need to survive the night."

Daniel gets up and hugs Berta. "Tomorrow, tomorrow. Big day tomorrow."

"Sure is."

"Look, I ran out of tape. I'm going to the store down the street. I'll only be a few minutes. Then we can head out to dinner afterwards. Sound like a plan?"

Berta nods.

"The living room, for the most part, is untouched, so make yourself comfortable." He grabs a jacket. "I'll be back in a few."

"Okay."

Daniel leaves. Berta walks around the entire house, many rooms completely empty. In the quietness of the house, her mind roams. She sits on a sofa in the living room.

She begins to fall asleep when she hears it. It was soft but not in any recognizable voice. However, it is enough to get her to move. She gets up from the sofa and looks around the house again, but nothing seems to be out of the ordinary. She hears it again, this time louder.

Look.

Berta moves around the entire house for a third time looking for something, anything. She stops at the front door, where she put Daniel's mail. For a quick moment, she stares at the stack of mail. Slowly, she picks it up and looks through it, finding bills, offers, and ads, but nothing ultimately important, until the last piece of mail. It's a beige envelope with a return address in Houston, Texas. She squints her eyes.

"Justine Davis," she says, reading who sent the envelope.

Everything in her tells her to open the envelope, but she doesn't know why. She believes it to be her nosiness at first, but then feels an even greater urge beyond that forcing her to open the envelope. She sets the other mail back down and holds the envelope in her hands. She opens it and as she does, a sweet smell of roses rushes her nose. It's a letter. She pulls the letter out and notices a picture still in the envelope. She slides it out to see a woman lying sideways on a bed full of roses, posing in lingerie. Berta's eye twitches. She grabs the letter, opens it, and reads. The first thing she notices is that it is dated early last week.

Danny,

Hey, baby. I just got off the phone with you and I was feeling really mushy, so I wanted to write you. There are so many things I want to tell you and I figured that this was the best way to do it. First, let me tell you how excited I am that you are coming back to Houston. I know this long distance relationship hasn't been the easiest for us, but I know now that things will get better.

I remember the night you were leaving and we talked for hours. We went out to eat and got back to your place, which you had covered in boxes at the time, and sat around some more. Then you made love to me. I knew I should have felt some guilt afterwards, but it felt soooooooooooo good. After all, what the church doesn't know can't hurt them, right? Anyway, that was one of the best and worst nights of my life. It was the best because I knew even before then that you were the one for me, but it was the worst because you were leaving me. But you made it a bit easier to manage with the nightly calls and texts. Talking to you has become the highlight of my day (especially all those dirty things you said you wanted to do to me). When you come back, I want to make love to you. I know that's a line we shouldn't cross again, but like you said, it's all good since we're getting married. Oh, I can't wait until you come back to me. To feel your skin again is something I long for. To have your hands touch . . .

Berta crumples up the paper, but not before reading the explicit details of what this woman wants Daniel to do to her. Several questions run through her head although she is clear on one thing. She isn't going anywhere with Daniel. She takes the picture out of the envelope and sets it on the boxes with the letter and then stuffs the envelope into her purse. Soon after, she marches out the house.

CHAPTER TWENTY NINE

HE misses her already. It's only been but a couple of hours and Craig sits slumped in a chair. He looks out at the skyline and wonders when he may see her again. He battles with himself in his mind about if he should have said something to her, something that would get her to stay, but each thought brings him to the same conclusion. Yes, he should have said something, and he should have because he loves her. Craig slumps deeper into his chair, looking at the bright skyline in anger. For the first time in many years, he feels alone, and he can't help but feel despair. He feels he has come full circle. The last time he felt so alone was when he was in jail. He gets up from his seat. Walking to his nightstand, he begins to grumble to himself. He digs in the nightstand and finds a Bible. It has ragged edges and torn pages, but he holds it carefully, as if it were a piece of gold. He flips through a few pages, not looking at any in particular, but eventually puts it down. He thinks of Berta again. He also thinks of Mark. *He would know what to do.* But then Craig realizes that he can't ask Mark anything. Mark needs help himself, likely more help than he needs. He gets up and walks back to the window.

"Why does it always end like this?" Craig says seemingly to himself. "Why whenever I start to trust you again, something bad happens?" He places his hands on the window. "Why is it that no matter how much I trust you . . . no matter how much I trust you, I still wind up failing . . . and being alone?" Craig grits his teeth and clenches his Bible in his hand. He looks around the room as if he is looking for a person. In a rage, he cocks his arm back and throws the Bible against the wall.

He ambles to his bathroom and opens his medicine cabinet. He grabs a bottle of pills. He stares at them, pops the top open, and then shakes a few into his hand. Truly, Craig has now come full circle. He remembers those things he hasn't told anyone, those times in prison when he tried to kill himself, when he tried to force God's hand. He remembers starting a fight with a bunch of people from various gangs just so they could retaliate and end his life. That's really what caused the scar. Yes, he was cut in the back, but he provoked it and tried to lie there afterwards so he would bleed out. He remembers those times well, and the main reason behind them all. He remembers his parents abandoning him when he was six, the pain he felt because they thought him to be a "demon child." He remembers the church abandoning him because they thought him to be a rapist, and finally, he remembers feeling abandoned by God for reasons he still can't figure out. He knows the source of his pain. He knows in part it is the fear of being utterly alone. He also knows that on the inside, he is a failure at everything he does; a man that is inferior in every way. He starts to take the pills, one by one. Now, he's thinking of Berta. How cruel is God that He would place someone like her into his life and then remove her just as quickly. Craig begins to wobble. He continues to take the pills but swallows none of them. Then suddenly, with a knee jerk reaction, he spits them all out in the sink. He pounds his fist on the edge of the sink before lying on the floor of the bathroom and crying.

"I don't want to be alone," he whispers.

He feels lightheaded and dizzy. He crawls to the corner of the bathroom and cries, sobbing loudly. It is at this very moment that Craig feels something. It feels warm, as if someone is hugging him from behind, and he hears this single statement: *I will never leave you . . .* Craig knows the end to that saying, to that verse, but for some reason, all he hears is: *I will never leave you . . . .*

Craig then spends his time praying for anything and everything; most importantly, he prays for his own salvation, his own once abandoned walk with God.

After sitting in the corner of the bathroom for hours, Craig finally gets up. He notices the sun going down and knows that he has been in the corner for more than half the day. His phone rang a few times in that time period, but he left the calls unanswered. He walks to the bedroom and grabs his cell off the nightstand to see who called. Mark, Maya, and Mark again. Maya left a voice message, one that Craig listens to first. As he listens, he picks up his Bible, which made a dent in his wall when he threw it, and sets it on the nightstand. In the message, Maya told him that she was leaving to one of her startup stores out of state. Craig sees it as an attempt to get him to rush to her and stop her, but he already knows the person he should have stopped is already leaving. He thought about rushing and stopping Berta many times, but would immediately decide against that. He knows she loves Daniel. She's in love with Daniel; at least, that's what she said. He could try to convince her otherwise, but he cares too much for her to do that. He wants for her to be happy. Craig erases the message Maya left, without hearing the rest of it, and takes a deep breath. He then calls Mark back. After only one ring, he answers. No one says anything for a while. Mark finally speaks.

"Hey, man, I just wanted to apologize, you know. This whole Alicia thing . . . it's . . . it's . . . ."

"Don't worry about it, man. I came off kinda harsh."

"Naw, you didn't. You were right. I gotta make things work with Jade." Mark pauses. "We're going to get some counseling." Mark laughs. "I never thought . . . never in a million years . . . ."

Long silence.

"I know, man . . . I know."

"I don't know how I allowed this to go this far. I was over at her house."

"Alicia?"

"Yeah. We . . . we . . . ."

"No, you didn't."

"Hold on. Let me explain."

For hours, Craig and Mark catch up on what has been going on in their lives. Interestingly enough, their conversation ends on a prayer.

Jade pulls up in front of her parents' home, feeling nervous to see them and the kids. She gets out and grabs a large duffel bag from the backseat. Very few thoughts run through her head as she lugs the large bag to the front door. She rings the doorbell. A few moments later, Jade's father opens the door. He smiles, gives her a hug, and helps her with the bag.

"Either you're staying with us too or the kids are staying a whole lot longer."

"Both."

He smiles a wry smile. "I haven't run around this much in years." He sets the bag a few feet from the front door. "Charles runs around nonstop. I don't know where he gets the energy from. And Kalina . . . she is one smart cookie. C'mon, let's go upstairs. They're up there with your mother."

"Wait," Jade says softly. She looks at her father and opens her purse to show him the shiny silver gun. He nods and motions her to his office.

Once inside, he closes the door and Jade gives him the gun. He examines it for a second before setting it back into his drawer.

"Just so you know, I didn't use it," Jade says.

"I know," her father says smiling. "There weren't any bullets in it."

Jade looks surprised. "Why did you give it to me?"

"Because you asked for it."

"So?"

"That's it."

"What if I were pulled over by the police . . . what if I went to jail? What if I threatened Mark with it?"

"Didn't you think of that beforehand?"

"No."

"Well, why not?"

"Because he choked me. I wasn't thinking at all."

Jade's father looks down. "I wasn't going to meddle . . . not like your mother."

"What? That makes no sense. Your daughter comes to your doorstep with your grandkids and crying, in need of help, with bruises all around her neck, cold and wet . . . and you send her back out with an empty gun? This has nothing to do with meddling or mother."

Jade's father walks over to the window and stares at the garden outside. "So what does it have to do with? A decision to let you be you . . . to not solve everything for you?"

"What are you talking about? You never solved anything for me."

Jade's father stares out the window and doesn't say another word.

"Dad . . . Dad?" Jade gives up and leaves the office.

She goes upstairs to see her mother lying on the floor in the bedroom with the kids watching a movie. Jade steps to the doorway and stands there for a few moments before anyone notices her. Jade's mother looks back and smiles at her. She nudges the kids and they look up at her. Charles is the first to see Jade.

"Mommy!" He runs up and hugs Jade. Kalina sits up and stares at Jade's mother for a few moments. She then stands and steps to Jade and gives her a hug.

"You okay, Mommy?" Kalina whispers in her ear.

Jade nods. "Of course, I am. Are you?"

Kalina doesn't answer. She simply holds tight to her mother.

"We were praying in the closet, Mommy," Charles says.

"You were?"

"Yup, and we prayed for a long time."

"How long were you in there?"

"We were, like, in there for a year."

"A whole year?"

"We weren't in there for a year," Kalina says. "It was a few minutes."

"Well, it could have been a year," Charles says, giving Kalina a look. "Hey, Mommy, are we going home now?"

Jade looks at her mother for a quick second. "Not yet, sweetheart." She looks back at Charles. "But soon. Very soon. Why don't you two go play with Grandpa? I'm going to talk to Grandma for a second."

They both stand in the doorway, not wanting to leave. Jade moves them along. "I'll be down with you in a few." They reluctantly leave. Jade waits a few moments before speaking.

"I hope you don't mind . . . I need to stay a few days. Mark's at home . . . I just don't think . . ."

"Don't worry about it. Those are our grandkids . . . you are our daughter . . . we don't mind."

Jade mother sits up on the edge of the bed and pats the space next to her. Jade walks over and sits down next to her.

"Kalina told me what she saw . . . what happened between you and Mark."

Jade takes a deep breath. "How is she?"

"Torn. Her hero turned into her worst enemy in a matter of seconds. She's scared. If you don't mind me asking, what really sparked everything that night?"

Jade turns to face her mother. "He cheated."

Jade's mother lifts her head and lowers it, seemingly in deep thought. "So what are you two going to do now?"

"Counseling. Pastor Brentwood is meeting with us on Tuesday."

"This is something you both agreed on?"

"It is."

Jade and her mother look each other in the eyes for a moment.

"Are you sure there is something worth saving at this point . . . something that hasn't become toxic?"

"I still love him. Right now, that's all I can stand on."

"Does he still love you?"

"I'd say so. He agreed to the counseling."

Jade's mother gets up from the bed. "It's an uphill climb from here on out . . . and there's a good chance he will never be the same Mark that you married."

"I know. But I have faith."

Jade's mother starts to walk out of the room. "And I hope that you are doing this because you truly want to stay married to Mark and not out of the guilt of your own actions."

"It's not out of guilt."

"Good, because that is a terrible mistake to make," Jade's mother looks down. "A terrible mistake." She leaves the room.

⋆

On Monday morning, Craig sits at his office desk doing nothing but staring at the wall. He checks his emails a couple of times, most of them being potential candidates for Berta's replacement. Craig laughs thinking that there isn't anyone who can replace Berta, but he sent out an ad anyway. It surprised him how many people had responded. Today, he has already had two interviews. He is informed of the last one's arrival by the receptionist downstairs. Craig reluctantly gets out of his seat and goes to greet the next applicant.

She's a young girl, fresh out of college, meaning she has no experience. Craig stares at her, almost bored out of his mind, as she unsurely answers the first and the easiest question on his list: Why are you here?

After a few more answers, Craig decides that he has heard enough and sends the young woman on her way. He stands corrected. There is no one to replace Berta. A few moments later, Craig's work phone rings.

"Craig Barlow, speaking."

"Craig?"

"Yes?"

"Craig, this is Candace. You remember me? Berta introduced me to you at a company dinner years ago."

"Sure. I remember. Your husband is the construction worker, right?"

"Yup. Listen, I'm going to cut right to the chase. I need you to stop Berta from making the biggest mistake of her life."

"What?"

"She leaving for Houston . . . she doesn't want to go to Houston . . . so stop her from going to Houston."

"If she doesn't want to go to Houston, why is she going?"

"You still don't get it, do you?"

"Clearly, I do not."

"Craig, Craig, Craig. You're as dumb as a brick. Berta is going to get away from you."

"Okay . . . so why am I stopping her?"

"Because she loves you."

"What? She's with Daniel . . . and she loves him . . . and if she did love me, as you say, then she would have said something . . . right?"

"No. That's not how Berta operates, you know that . . . at least you should know that. Daniel is second best. Daniel always has been second best. She wanted you. I guarantee that she still does, which is why I need you to stop her. Proclaim your love for her and she will stay . . . then I don't have to lose my best friend."

"So this is more about you?"

"Craig, if you don't go to her apartment and stop her . . . I'm going to hurt you. Her plane is leaving tonight."

"You are pushy. I don't know how your husband does it."

"I can explain all that later when we're double dating at some fancy restaurant, but right now, go get Berta."

"What if I don't love her?"

"You do. I know you do. If you didn't, you wouldn't have let me talk this long about it. Now, I need you to go get her and call me back when you do. I tried calling her all day and she hasn't picked up at all. Here, take down my number."

"Seriously, being this pushy isn't attractive." Craig grabs a pen and paper.

"Yeah, and I'm sure my husband thinks the same. You ready?"

"Go ahead."

Candace gives Craig her number and sends him off with a final warning. "You better call me back," she says.

Craig gets off the phone and heads to Berta's apartment.

Craig quickly gets to Berta's apartment and parks in the lot. He jumps out and gets to her building. He rings her bell but no one answers. Not knowing what to do next and feeling a bit desperate, Craig rings someone else's doorbell. A few moments later, a man's voice comes over the intercom. Craig asks for Berta, but the person doesn't know who she is. He hears nothing else afterwards. Craig leaves the building front and calls Berta's cell phone while he walks back to his car. He sits in his car and tries calling Berta three more times, leaving messages each time. Eventually, he stops calling and throws his phone on the passenger side seat.

"Come on, Lord," Craig whispers. "Just one more chance. I know at this rate I don't deserve it, but please just one more chance."

He gets out and walks to the door again to ring the doorbell. Just as he gets to the front someone comes out the building. A woman opens the front door and smiles at Craig. She's a slim woman, one who Craig would easily ask on a date. The woman holds the door for him and continues to examine him. He slides by her and thanks her for holding the door as she leaves. Quickly, he runs up to Berta's apartment and knocks on the door. Nothing. He knocks again and calls her name. Still nothing. Finally, he tries the doorknob. Strangely, it is unlocked and he walks right into the apartment. His feet make a scuffing noise as it echoes throughout the empty apartment. He walks around the entire apartment finding nothing. No furniture. Nothing. Not even a speck of dust. He grabs his phone and calls Candace.

"She's already gone."

"What? She wasn't supposed to leave until tonight. Where could she be?"

"Try with Daniel," Craig says, sounding irritated and dejected. "I should have never let you talk me into this." He quickly hangs up the phone and leaves the apartment, slamming the door behind him.

CHAPTER THIRTY

"SO, why are you two here?"

Mark and Jade stare at Pastor Brentwood, unsure of how to answer his question. There are many reasons they sit in front of him. The old man wearing glasses looks back and forth between the two of them, awaiting an answer. Still, Mark and Jade say nothing. Pastor Brentwood starts flipping through papers on his desk and pulls out a piece of paper.

"Look, you two. You came to me because your marriage is in dire straits but that's not the reason you are here. That's just a circumstance for right now. You are here because, even though your marriage is in a rough patch, you still want to be married. Somewhere, deep inside the both of you, there's much love, love that we have to put to practice again." He sets down the paper. "This will only work if you both come to the table humbly, ready to make this right. I'm here to help you communicate and lead you to a greater understanding of each other and this thing that God put together called marriage. Know that my prayers will never cease for you two, but to make this work, you two are going to have to work if you know what I mean." Mark and Jade nod. "These sessions are, of course, geared towards Biblical teachings, but I'm not going to ram this book," the pastor grabs his Bible, "down your throats. You've read and studied before. I'm sure you know what is in it. But I will send you home with an assignment out of it." Pastor Brentwood takes a deep breath and nods his head. "You two . . . God will shine his light through you two ... bright enough even for others to see. This marriage isn't over . . . not by a long shot." The pastor stares at them for a few moments. "Now, let's start from the beginning. What has your marriage in such turmoil?"

Jade looks at the pastor and then at Mark. Mark looks down at the floor and says nothing. Jade begins to speak. "Well, I guess I started all of this," she says. "I cheated on Mark."

Pastor Brentwood looks at Jade plainly, allowing her to continue speaking.

"I fell for this guy at work and I . . . cheated on him."

The pastor then looks at Mark. Mark doesn't look him in the eyes.

"I cheated. I put my hands on her." Mark says nothing more.

"Okay. Jade, why did you cheat?"

"I," Jade pauses, "don't know. I was stupid."

"Mark, why did you do the things you did?"

"Happiness. Relief. Respect."

The pastor leans back in his chair. He thinks for a moment while observing Jade's reaction. "Is it fair to say that you both gave certain things to these people that you should have given each other?"

Both nod.

"What were those things?"

Jade looks at Mark, expecting him to answer first, but Mark stays silent.

"I gave my time," Jade says. "I gave my respect. I gave my dreams . . . maybe even my fantasies. I gave my heart." Jade stares at the floor as once again, she realizes how much trouble her marriage is facing.

"Mark?" The pastor looks at Mark.

"I don't know."

"Mark, for this to work, you need to be a bit more open."

Mark looks at Pastor Brentwood, then at Jade, and finally back at the floor. "I gave my time, my energy . . . my thoughts . . . details of my marriage"

"You see both of you," the pastor pauses. "Both of you gave away something. Think of those things as water, and your marriage is the plant. Your marriage, the plant, with proper watering bears fruit. Instead, you sent water to barren grounds and got nothing for it, and the plant, your marriage, was dying. Never give something that belongs inside your marriage to something or someone outside your marriage."

Both nod.

"I want to go back to before any of this happened. Take me back to the beginning. Mark, you start."

Mark looks up, being content with keeping quiet for most of the session. Jade glances at Mark but then fixes her eyes on the pastor. Mark straightens himself up in his seat.

"What do you mean? Like, the beginning, beginning?"

"Start where you think it would be best. Start at a time that is most important to you."

"You mean when we were dating?"

Pastor Brentwood leans back in his chair and folds his hands under his chin. He stares at Mark. "Tell me about when you first met Jade."

Mark, knowing his attempts to stall weren't working, picks a point and starts talking. "I first saw her in this church. I wasn't consistently attending then . . . I didn't believe much in the love that God has for me. I was actually going for food . . . and for Kalina. Back then, the church ran a free day care program to help those who needed it. You remember, right, Pastor?"

"I do."

"Well . . . I needed it. After my credits in school transferred, I still had a few classes to take before I could graduate. So I went to school during the day and worked part-time after class. Then took care of

Kalina at night . . . just to get a few hours of sleep and do it all over again. I did that for a year or so until I got my degree. From there, I became a full-time teacher, and even though I had the money to take her to a day care, I kept Kalina in the church. Maybe it was taking advantage . . . maybe not. Anyway, one day, I see this woman taking care of Kalina and . . . it just seemed like she was her mother . . . like she should have been her mother. She was this beautiful woman . . . one like I've never seen before. Something about her was so . . . different. I walk up to her and introduce myself . . . and she told me her name was Jade."

Jade shifts in her seat as she also relives the moment.

"Everything about her was so different, even down to the way she dressed. I couldn't help but try to find out more about her."

The pastor stares at Mark, listening attentively. He glances at Jade who stares at the floor with the same expression Mark once had. "So what happened?"

"I asked her out on a date. Of course, she said no, but I remained persistent. Truth be told, she's the reason I came to accept Christ."

"Wouldn't be the first time I heard that one, a guy coming to Christ for a woman." Pastor Brentwood laughs. For the first time in the session, Mark smiles.

"At first, I started going to church to get closer to her. But then I saw things in her . . . in the church ... that had me baffled. Back then, I thought no one could be that happy all the time, to smile every time I saw them."

Jade whispers something.

"What was that, Jade?" the pastor asks.

"I smiled because I was around him."

Pastor Brentwood smiles and nods his head, looking for Mark to react in some positive way, but Mark just stares blankly at the floor. "Mark, tell me something before we continue. What makes you tick?"

Mark looks at the pastor. "What do you mean?"

"What makes you get out of bed each day?"

Mark thinks for a second. "Honestly, I don't know anymore."

"What was it before?"

"Kids . . . my family . . . God. Of course, not in that order."

"Well, if you had to put it in order, what would it be?"

Mark pauses and looks down. "I don't know."

"Here's what it should be. God should always be at the top of your list. All things come from Him. The most important thing here is your relationship with God. Without that intact, all other things fail. Second should be your family. After all is said and done, your family falls under your responsibility. God placed the souls of those people under your stewardship first. Then it should be other kids, whether it's your job or the ministry."

Mark nods.

"Jade, do you agree?" the pastor asks.

"I do."

"Good, because your priority list is exactly the same."

Jade nods.

"Mark, you must stick to that order. You have to . . . or this won't work." The pastor writes a few things down on a notepad. "Please continue."

"Eventually, I gave my life to Christ. Jade was right next to me when I did. She helped me the entire way. From there, we actually started dating. As I got to know her more, I knew she was the one for me. There wasn't a doubt in my mind."

Pastor Brentwood looks at Jade. She stares blankly at the pastor.

"So eventually, Mark, you asked her to marry you."

"Yes. Then we went to the premarital counseling and all that fun stuff . . . then we got married."

The pastor looks at Mark for a second, reading his body language. He waits for a long time before saying anything. Both Mark and Jade think he has run out of things to say, but then he asks a question that seems from far left field.

"Mark, why did you come here?"

"Pardon?"

"You're originally from Philadelphia, but somehow you end up here already with a daughter. What forced you out of Philadelphia?"

Mark sighs and looks over at Jade, who he notices stares right at him.

"Me. I forced myself out of Philly. At first, I panicked. When I finally got hold of Kalina, everything became real to me. I knew I needed a change, not for my sake, but for hers . . . and I didn't want her to grow up in the same environment that I grew up in. Kalina deserved a clean slate. She didn't deserve to be caught up in my personal drama. So, I left. I didn't know where to go so I just drove away. I left everything and everybody without as much as a simple good-bye."

"But eventually you went back, correct?"

"Yeah, to pick up my things from my dorm . . . to talk to a few of my professors . . . but for nothing more than that."

"What about your parents?"

"What about them?"

"Did you talk to them about the move . . . about your decision?"

Mark looks down and shakes his head. He twists his face into a look of contempt. "No. There was no need." He looks up at them. "I'm sorry, but what does this have to do with Jade and I?"

Even Jade looks at Mark in confusion.

"I'm sorry, Mark. If this is too uncomfortable—."

"I'm not saying it is uncomfortable. I'm just asking what this has to do with us."

Pastor Brentwood crosses his legs behind the desk. "Your past seems to be an interesting one; one that likely holds some major events that could have lead up to this. But if you would like to move on, we can."

Mark thinks for a second. He glances at Jade again and then out the window, past the pastor. "I haven't talked to my parents in years. As soon as I left for college, I considered that to be the last time I acknowledged them as such."

"Why?"

Mark's forms his mouth into a snarl. "Because I hate them. Wherever they are, I know they are somewhere screwing someone over someway, somehow."

"Hate is a strong word."

"I know . . . and I mean it. When you wake up each day to a different guy to call Dad ... My mom . . . didn't care one bit about me . . . or my brother."

Jade's face is now one of shock. The pastor writes notes while Mark talks.

"If she cared . . . if she cared, she wouldn't have let them abuse her the way they did. It seemed like every week, there was another guy."

"What about your real father?"

"What about him? He ducked out a long time ago. Last I heard was that he shacked up with some eighteen year old."

Pastor Brentwood nods. "So your mother, she slept with all manner of abusive men?"

"Yeah. The things we saw . . . no child should see."

"And where is your brother . . . I'm sorry, what is his name?"

Mark bites his lip. "His name . . . was Bernard . . . and he's dead."

"I'm sorry to hear that."

The pastor looks at Jade. Jade plays with her wedding ring, seemingly to keep herself from crying.

"If you are comfortable enough, please continue."

Mark nods. "After a while, the abuse wasn't just towards Mom. It turned towards us . . . and one day, Bernard got a beating . . . for putting the remote to the TV in the wrong place. Bernard, of course, ran to me . . . as if I was his protector . . . but I couldn't do anything. The guy at the time . . . his name was Jack . . . beat Bernard so bad. He cried so loud and Jack seemed to get madder that Bernard was crying . . . so he beat him some more." Tears flow from Mark's eyes. "I ran to Jack and started punching him, but then Mom grabbed me and locked me in my room. Minutes later, Jack throws Bernard into the room and locks us both in it. I grab Bernard and ask him if he's okay. He looks at me and simply says no. That was the last thing I heard him say. I was five then. I really didn't know that Jack murdered Bernard until I was Kalina's age. By then, it was so buried deep inside me that I didn't care."

"So when exactly did it come back up again?"

"When Kalina saw me choking Jade. I turned into one of them, one of those guys Mom used to sleep with. Right at that moment, I realized that I had failed in everything I was trying to accomplish. Everything." Mark has a pained expression on his face.

Pastor Brentwood doesn't say anything at first, but he looks at Jade, who already has a tissue in her hand to give to Mark. Mark shakes his head vigorously at her offer. Jade's entire demeanor changes as she slumps into her chair. The pastor notices and writes more on his notepad.

"Would you like to move on?"

Mark nods.

"Tell me about this Alicia woman."

Mark takes a few seconds to compose himself. "She's an ex . . . an ex-fiancée."

"One that you never told Jade about. Why?"

"I couldn't. I thought that if I did, it would hurt my chances with her . . . and . . . and bring up questions of if I still loved her."

"Well, did you?"

"Yes, I did . . . but I was too ashamed to try to make things work with her. She then became part of the past that I needed to get away from."

"Do you still love her?"

"No." Mark answers quickly.

"But she so happened to end up here?"

"That's what it seems."

"So you didn't send out any kind of invitation or anything of that sort?"

"No. I was shocked and didn't know what to do. I thought at first she wanted to kill me or something crazy, like off the movies. But no, her son is in my class. She came down here to better his chances of getting into this prestigious music school. Quite honestly, I understand that. Her son is gifted."

"And you didn't tell Jade about her then because?"

"Because I wasn't saying much to Jade. I no longer trusted her . . . and I wanted to keep things steady . . . for the kids' sake."

"And then?"

"And then it turned into what I wanted . . . and I wanted her because despite all this mess that was going on inside my marriage, within my family, I was happy . . . and it was whenever she was near me."

"She has a son. Is she married?"

Mark hangs his head even lower. "She is."

Jade shakes her head and starts to laugh. The pastor looks at Jade and sees her also twitching her leg.

"It was a perfect slope," Mark says.

"What do you mean?"

"I mean . . ." Mark thinks for a second. "I didn't know I was going downhill. I had an idea . . . but there were so many other things in the background working. In retrospect, it looks like Satan pulled off a miracle. What would you call that?"

"A trap," Pastor Brentwood says. "I would never call that a miracle." He collects the papers from his desk and sorts them into a neat pile. "Let's take break. I'll see you two here in a half hour. Okay?"

Both nod as the pastor leads them out of his office. As they get to the large main hallway of the church, Mark and Jade go in opposite directions. The pastor stands in the hall looking back and forth at the two people who are determined to do their own thing.

"Okay, Jade, earlier Mark told us some pretty deep things. At this point, how do you feel about everything he has said so far?"

Jade sits with her legs crossed and looks at Pastor Brentwood. "I don't know how to feel. He said some things that I never knew about him. I guess that makes me sad. After seven years of marriage, I feel like I don't know who I married."

"And you felt like you knew before?"

"I did."

The pastor scribbles some more notes on his notepad. "So tell me, where does it all begin for you?"

"You know that already, Pastor. I was in here for the beginning."

"I know that, but from your eyes, tell me what it was like when you first met Mark."

Jade sighs and brushes her hair behind her ears. "It was my mother's idea to join the day care ministry. She said that if I didn't know how to take care of children, I would be of no use to any man. Momma was way more harsh back then. So I joined and helped wherever I could. My first few days there, the other women would teach me a few things and I soaked it all up. Eventually, I was placed in the room with the two years olds. They were terr-i-ble. But there was this one little girl who never threw a tantrum, who always smiled. Her father dropped her off early so she was always the first one there . . . and she was always the last to get picked up. She was the cleanest little girl I had ever seen. She always had new clothes and her hair was always done nicely, but I never met her father. At the time, I was living with my parents and I wasn't working. Even though I had my pharmaceutical degree, I stayed with them and focused on the ministry. If it were up to them, I would still be with them. Anyway, I finally met him, he introduced himself to me. His name was Mark and he was a teacher. I wasn't too fond of him at first. Everyone knew that he was taking advantage of the ministry we had in place. There's no way a teacher can dress like he did and put nice clothes on his daughter like he did and not be able to afford day care. The ministry was on a slot basis, meaning that we had a limited number of spaces for children. He took a slot from someone who really needed it. That's why my parents didn't like him too much either. They thought him to be selfish."

"I see. Mark, what do you think of this so far?"

Mark shrugs his shoulders. "They were right."

Pastor Brentwood nods.

"But then, I got to know him. Reluctantly, of course. But I found out that he was a nice guy, just misguided . . . and then he asks me out on a date."

"And you said no."

"Exactly. I've already heard too much of that unevenly yoked thing from my parents. I wasn't up for hearing it again. He was a great friend. That was it."

"So then what?"

"He was persistent. Boy was he persistent . . . and then him giving his life to Christ. I thought that to be an act of God, not him still trying to get with me."

"So you dated him."

"Yeah. But my parents were still against it. They thought Mark to be beneath me."

Mark's eye twitches a bit.

"And I got to know him more . . . and I grew to love him."

"Then he asks you to marry him."

"Yes. And I said yes. But . . . I didn't want to."

A flash of shock comes over Mark's face, but he quickly returns to his blank look.

"I mean, I loved him. I just didn't love him for marriage. I didn't think he was the one for me."

"But you said yes. Why?"

"To spite my parents. I didn't know that before, but it is clear for me to see now. Then my parents got to know him. They liked him and admitted they misjudged his character . . . but that left me stuck. I was still married to a man who I didn't feel was for me."

"So you tried to change him."

"No. I convinced him to change himself."

The pastor gives Jade a skeptical expression. "What was this ideal man you had in mind?"

Jade looks down. "Someone of status . . . within the church or outside of it . . . someone who didn't just take life as it came but went out and created opportunities . . . a man who changed his environment as opposed to being subject to it . . . someone who commanded the attention of everyone in the room. I suppose that's how I got caught up with Boley."

"Because he was all of those."

"Exactly. Even after all the changes that Mark made, I still found him to be a replica of Boley."

Pastor Brentwood notices that Mark has an angered look on his face. Mark flexes his jaw muscles but remains quiet. For a few moments, everyone in the room remains quiet.

CHAPTER THIRTY ONE

LATER in the night, Craig puts on his gym clothes and heads to Mark's house. After their last conversation on the phone, they both decided to go to the gym tonight, but Mark needed a ride. During the conversation, Craig readily agreed to pick up Mark, but now, he doesn't feel like doing anything but lie in bed. Work was terrible today. All he could think of is how Berta is in some other state and not returning any of his phone calls. He believes that she landed sometime earlier in the morning but has no way of knowing. He had to convince himself that this is for her happiness, and if she's happy, he ought to be happy. He ought to be happy, but clearly, he is not. Nevertheless, Craig gets to Mark's home and picks him up, saying nothing more than hi to his good friend. Craig found himself drifting away, thinking of Berta about five or six times before they even set foot in the gym. On the last time, Mark catches him.

"You okay, man?" Mark asks.

Craig signs a paper at the front desk and walks to the weights. "I'm good, I suppose."

"You still battling with God on some things?"

"Actually, I'm not. I'm good in that respect."

"So it's Berta."

Craig starts to warm-up on a treadmill. "Yeah, it is."

Mark steps on the treadmill next to him and turns it on for his own warm-up. He begins to jog but has to raise his voice so Craig can hear him over the motor of the treadmill. "Have you prayed about it?"

"Tons. I've been praying nonstop about it." Craig presses a button on the treadmill. "I know it's been a while since I was a willing participant in my relationship with God . . . a long time since being able to pray and listen and hear what He wants me to do . . . so I'm not sure what He is saying. I just get that gut feeling. I'm missing something."

"Yeah, I had those feelings . . . I ignored them though . . . and look at me now. No wife . . . no kids . . . miserable."

"How are you holding up?"

"Okay, I guess. I just can't believe how stupid I was."

"Yeah, we all have those moments."

"Yeah. We had our first counseling session today."

"And?"

"I don't know. Jade said some things that I didn't know . . . I said some things I knew for a fact that Jade didn't know. I'm not so sure this is going to work. I mean, it was rough. Real rough."

"Do you want it to work? I mean, do you still love her?"

"There's no question about either of those. I love her, even after all of this. I still want her by my side."

"Let me ask you this: Are you still willing to be that person who pulls the best out of her and guides her with love to be the person whom God wants her to be?"

"Of course. Her and the kids—"

"Take the kids out of the situation for a second. Just focus on Jade. No one questions if you love your kids. Everyone who knows you knows that you love your kids and would do anything for them."

"Maybe they don't know that."

"Even so, all it would take is a couple talks and you're back. What you should really ask yourself is if you can be her husband again."

Mark stops the treadmill and steps off it. He smiles at Craig. Craig looks back a few times and stops his treadmill as well.

"What's up?" he asks.

"You sound like the old you."

"I know. I'm right . . . right?"

"Yeah, you are."

Mark and Craig go to the bench press.

"I gotta run in about ten minutes," Craig says. "But I'll be back to finish the workout."

"What's up?"

"The church down the street," Craig points. "You know ... the one I started going to."

"Yeah."

"They're having this meeting. What it's about, I don't know."

"Already going to church meetings?"

"Yeah. There are a few people that I said I would meet with. They're part of the men's ministry."

"I see. Well, I should be here."

"Yeah, it should only take a few minutes. I don't plan to stay too long."

"Do what you gotta do. I think I'm going to be here til close anyway." Mark stops in his tracks while Craig sits on the bench. "I know it might not seem like it, given everything that is going on with me, but I am proud of you."

Craig smiles. "Thanks." He lies flat on the bench. "But cut it out with all this sentimental stuff while I'm trying to lift."

⊂ℬ⊃

Mark and Craig continue to lift weights until the time Craig said he had to leave. He quickly makes his way out the gym and runs down the street. Mark moves on to the leg press machine and lies down in the metal contraption. He does one set and rests. After a few seconds, he begins another set when he sees the shadow of someone behind him.

"So how was the meeting?" Mark asks.

Craig doesn't answer.

"That good, huh?" Mark says, pushing the stack of weights up again. "Everything cool?"

Craig still doesn't say anything.

Mark lets the weight fall and turns around in his seat to see Alicia. She stands there looking down at her side with a confused expression on her face.

"I tried calling you," she says.

Mark doesn't know what to say as he simply stares at her.

"What happened to you?" she asks. "I knew you were coming over that night . . . but you never made it. I didn't know what to think. I mean … couldn't you have called me?"

Mark shakes his head, not taking his eyes off her. "I'm sorry. Things have been . . . crazy. I . . . just . . ."

"Can we go somewhere else and talk?"

Mark looks down. "No. That's not a good idea."

Alicia looks at Mark with tears in her eyes. "What has she done to you?" She feels on Mark's forehead the scar from when Jade hit him. Mark pulls away. He looks her straight in the eyes.

"We, you and I, have made some mistakes as of late. I've made plenty more, but we both know . . . we both know we can't continue on the way that we have been. There's no way something like this can work. You're a married woman. I'm a married man . . . I'm married to Jade . . . and I love her."

Alicia nods. "So what about me? I don't mean anything to you?"

"I didn't say that. I'm just saying that we have fallen into something we shouldn't have . . . and there's only one way to make things right."

"Mark, she's in your head now. Ju—"

"She is my wife, Alicia." Mark raises his voice. "She isn't some random woman off the streets."

"Neither am I. I . . . me . . . I was supposed to be your wife," Alicia's tone changes.

"I'm sorry. But I think we should have left the past in the past. I cannot see you anymore. I have to . . . I have to fight for my marriage."

"No! If you think I'm letting you go again . . . no! It's not going to happen this way . . . not again."

"I'm sorry, Alicia. I truly am. But I think it is way past time that you move on. I know I am."

Mark gets up from the machine and walks to grab his things in the back, leaving Alicia standing there staring at the wall. Her eyes are wide and filled with tears. Mark nervously grabs his bags from a locker and starts to leave the locker room. Standing right at the doorway is Alicia, who is now crying.

"What did she do, Mark? Threaten to take everything? Threaten to take your kids? Whatever it is, we can fight through it." She steps into the locker room. Mark takes a step back. "I know the way we did things isn't conventional . . . but . . . I love you . . . you love me. Please, don't do this." She gently grabs Mark's arm and pulls him close to her. She grabs his face and gently kisses him. Mark does nothing but stand there trying to will himself to walk away.

"My lips, Mark," she whispers. "My lips tell you a story . . . our story . . . our unfinished story. You remember that night, Mark? Do you remember when you came over to my place, the two of us laying in the bed, our skin touching?" She goes in to kiss Mark deeper.

Mark steps back away from Alicia, away from her grasps, away from her lips. "I can't." Mark rubs his head. "I can't. I won't. Call me a fool . . . curse me out . . . do what you want. I'm sure after all this, I deserve it . . . but I have prepared myself to go through hell and high waters . . . for Jade."

"But God—"

"God," Mark raises his voice. "God didn't do this. We did. He didn't lead you here to me . . . you came here. God didn't force Jade to cheat on me or me to cheat on Jade. We chose that path ourselves. Now, I must correct my mistakes . . . somehow." Mark looks at Alicia and fully understands what he has gotten himself into and what he has to do to fix it. She advances again but Mark stops her. "I lied. I told you that I loved you . . . but I don't. I did back then . . . but I left you then for a reason."

"What are you talking about?"

"I never wanted to marry you. That's why I cheated on you back then. That's the real reason I cheated on you. Nothing has changed. Nothing ever will."

Alicia stands, staring at Mark with tear filled eyes. Mark knows he hit her hard and he takes the brief moment to leave the locker room. He rushes out of the gym and starts down the street. A tear rolls down his cheek. He never wanted to hurt her. And he definitely didn't want to see the hurt expression on her face that he just saw, but he had to hurt her. He had to say something that would push her away, even if it was a lie.

Craig is just coming out of the church when Mark walks up to him.

"We got to go," Mark says.

"What's up, man? I take too long?"

"No. We have to go, now."

"You cool?"

"No. Alicia showed up. We have to get out of here."

Craig matches Mark's urgency and springs to his car. "How would she know to show up here?"

"It's the only place she knows that I go to regularly, other than the school."

Both men get into the car. "How would she know that?"

Mark stops to look at Craig. "I messed up big time." He looks out the window. "Do you mind if I crash at your place?"

"Not at all. I wasn't going to do anything but sulk for the rest of the night."

Mark thanks Craig and pulls out his cell phone. He slowly and shakily dials Jade's cell phone.

"Jade."

"Yes, Mark?" Jade says plainly.

"I . . . I'm staying over at Craig's tonight. We just came from the gym."

Mark doesn't say any more. Instead he attempts to hold back tears.

"Okay. Thanks for telling me," Jade says in a confused tone.

"How are the kids?"

"They're fine. Kalina has been beating up on everyone in the house in chess. And for Charles . . . he thinks this place is a big amusement park."

Mark wants to smile, but the more he feels himself doing so, the more he wants to cry. "Can you tell them that I love them?"

Jade pauses and her tone becomes gentler. "I do every day . . . and every night."

"I have to go," Mark interrupts. "But I'll call you back when I get to Craig's place. We have to talk."

"Okay. I'll be up."

Mark gets off the phone and hangs his head.

"You okay?" Craig asks.

"Not really."

Craig gives Mark a tough pat on the shoulder. "Everything will be all right. Just keep pressing on."

"Yeah," Mark says.

His phone beeps from an incoming text message. He reads the message three times before setting his phone down and shaking his head. "Craig, man, what do you suppose I should do now?"

"What do you mean?"

"She's threatening to go to the school board."

"Jade?"

"No, Alicia. She's going to try to get me fired."

"She can't do that."

"If she makes enough noise . . . anything can happen."

"Sounds like revenge or something."

"Maybe."

Mark stares out the window. Every so often, Craig peers over at Mark and sees him wiping tears from his face.

෴

Later in the night, Jade lays in bed awaiting Mark's call. She's nervous about the way he was talking earlier. Part of her thinks that he's set to bail out on her, to give up all hope of a successful marriage. More thoughts of divorce and what life would be like creep into her head. All thoughts cease when her phone buzzes next to her head. She scoops it up.

"Hey."

"Hi."

Long silence.

"I ran into Alicia at the gym today," Mark says.

Jade's heart sinks but her voice remains steady. "Did you?"

"Yeah. She came on to me again . . . even after I told her we had to stop."

Jade starts to feel relieved that Mark told her they had to stop. "And?"

"I hurt her feelings . . . bad."

"Are you okay?"

"I'm fine, I guess. She is now threatening to go to the school board to try to get me fired."

"She can't do anything but make noise. Don't worry about it."

"Yeah, I guess." Mark gets quiet.

"You think she can really do something?"

"Maybe, no . . . I don't know."

"Mark, this all went on in your personal life. That's where the responsibility to the kids stops. Did anything happen on school grounds?"

Mark sighs.

"Mark, are you serious?" Jade raises her voice but still tries to whisper. "What did you do on school grounds?"

"My classroom is where most of everything started."

"I don't believe you. I do not believe you. How could you? Not only do you jeopardize your marriage but your job . . . your dream."

"She wants to have dinner."

"No."

"She said she deserves at least that."

"No."

"It's either I go to the dinner or risk losing my job."

"No. No. No. Mark, do you understand what you are saying? Do you even care about what you are saying? Do you care about our marriage? Do you care about fixing our marriage?"

"I just wanted to talk to you about it . . . to see what you thought."

"For what? If it were as easy as you telling her no, you wouldn't need to call me. That tells me you are considering it."

"Of course, I'm considering it. My job is at stake."

"And that's more important than your marriage? Because I can tell you for sure, if you go to this dinner, your marriage is over."

"What are you saying?"

"If you feel the need to go to dinner with her and Lord knows what . . . go ahead . . . but don't expect to be able to run to me . . . or the kids. We will move on."

"First, you are not taking my kids away from me. Don't ever talk like that. Ever. Second, rethink how you are coming at this. Remember, you had plenty of time to deal with any fallout from your mess. How long was it, Jade? Three months? Four?"

Jade remains silent.

"So stop for a second . . ." Mark sighs. "Jade, this isn't supposed to go this way. We shouldn't be doing this, about to go at each other's throats again."

Jade still remains silent.

"I'm backed up against a wall here, and I don't know what to do. The truth is that I need you. I need you by my side, now more than ever."

Jade begins to speak but pauses. She then softens her tone. "I'm uncomfortable with this whole situation. I don't think you have to go out to dinner with her to save your job. Even if you do lose your job, you can get another one. I can work again easily. Financially, we would be fine. But our marriage . . . it wouldn't make it through that. Somewhere, the line has to be drawn . . . maybe some line should have been drawn before, but either way, I'm not staying for that. Contrary to what goes on outside our door, marriages aren't expendable . . . they aren't easily transferable . . . even if it is biblically okay to bail out. You talk about need. I need you more than you ever could know . . . and I know I've done some wrong things before . . . but I can make them right. I know I can make them right. I know we can make this right."

Mark doesn't say anything.

"Mark?"

"I . . . I won't go. And we'll let the chips fall . . . the way they will fall."

Long silence.

"Did you do your homework yet?" Mark asks.

"What?"

"Homework. Pastor Brentwood gave us homework."

"Oh. Yes, I did it. Did you?"

"Nope."

"Well, you better get to it."

"Yeah. I'll talk to you later."

"Okay. Have a good night."

"You too."

Jade gets off the phone and sets it on the nightstand next to her. Immediately, she realizes how odd it is to end a conversation with Mark without telling him she loves him. She quickly calls back but gets his voicemail. He must have turned his phone off for the night. Jade sets her phone back and tries to go to sleep.

CHAPTER THIRTY TWO

IT has been almost a week since Berta said good-bye to Craig. Each subsequent day has become easier for her, easier to forget him, easier to move on with her life. She sits relaxing on the balcony of her brand-new luxury condominium. She didn't have to move out of her apartment and across the state, but she decided to anyway. She knew many people that would look for her there, at her apartment, and she doesn't quite want anyone to find her. She now laughs at the thought that she could have been in Houston at this moment, trying to play house with a lying snake named Daniel. Daniel called a few times, but all calls stopped once the weekend was over. She told him that she never wanted to see him or hear from him again. Of course, Daniel tried to talk his way out of things, saying that this Justine woman is crazy and is a woman from his past. *We'll see just how crazy she is,* Berta thought. She took this woman's address from the envelope she stuffed in her purse and sent her a letter. In it, she explained everything that went on between her and him. During that time, Berta couldn't help but feel like some sort of a mistress, like she intruded on Daniel and Justine's relationship. Either way, Justine should know everything on what Daniel is really about. She described what Daniel told her, and determined that wherever his job takes him, he goes and finds a woman for the area. Usually, they're church women. He acts holy and trustworthy, but really he wants to get in their pants. It's all a game to him, one he played off extremely well. He probably didn't expect her to move with him after four months, and that's where his game faltered. No sane person would, she realizes. Berta sent that letter off a couple days ago, not leaving any way for the woman to contact her back. Again, she doesn't want anyone to find her; anyone, no matter who they are.

So the plan is to start a new life. Although, she didn't move out of state, she moved far enough not to run into anyone she once knew, and that included Craig. Yesterday was the first day she went out since moving into her new place. She had two job interviews that seem to be sure-fire jobs. She just has to pick which of the two is the best opportunity. She plans to tell everyone she once knew what happened to her eventually; but for now, she wants to remain hidden. There's a huge church not too far from where she lives. She plans on attending, but hasn't had the chance to yet. She hears her doorbell ring. She twists her face up in confusion wondering who would come to her door and gets up from her seat on the balcony. Her immediate thought is that it is the nice old woman she met the day she moved in who lives in the condo across from hers. She wraps her shawl over her shoulders even tighter and opens the door. As she opens the door, the first thing she sees are a man's feet. To her surprise, she opens the door all the way to see Craig. The sight of him takes her breath away. Craig, seemingly feeling the same things, says nothing. He looks her up and down to see if it is really her. Berta immediately afterwards slams the door in Craig's face. A few moments later, Craig rings the doorbell again. This time Berta ignores it, or at least attempts to do so. Craig rings again. Berta sits on her couch thinking to herself how hard she has tried to forget him and how easy it was to feel what she felt for him again. She gets up from the couch and walks to the door. Reluctantly, she opens it.

"Okay," Craig says, "I understand you may be a little angry with me."

"How did you find me?"

"Can I come in?"

"How did you find me?"

Craig stares into Berta's eyes. "I woke up this morning and prayed —"

"Craig, how did you find me?"

"Okay, okay. Look, can I come in?" Craig almost pleads with his eyes.

Berta allows Craig to come in and gently closes the door behind him. "Talk."

Craig sighs. "At first, I went to your apartment . . . this was under Candace's orders. She ordered me to stop you from leaving. Obviously, I failed. I go through some things and I wake up this morning with you on my mind . . . even more than what became my usual. I hoped everything was okay with you . . . because there's no way of telling what happened to you. By the way, it is mean to disappear off the face of the planet without telling anyone anything . . . especially those who really care." Berta folds her arms. Craig continues. "Anyway, I feel that I was led back to your empty apartment this morning." Berta closes the balcony door as a rush of warm wind blows through the area.

"Like I said, I was thinking about you this morning, and I prayed for you. In the middle of my prayers, bam, as clear as day, I heard something. It wasn't exactly a voice, but it was something . . . something telling me to go back to the apartment. So I went . . . and found nothing . . . again. But on my way out, I ran into your old landlord. Very nice guy. I start talking to him and he gives me a name . . . the name of this beautiful development. So I travel two hours across the state to get here. Then I see your car . . . and I knew it was yours because it still has that scratch on it from years ago. From there . . . I think it's pretty easy to figure out everything else."

Berta stares at Craig, part of her admiring his determination.

"So the Lord led you to me?" Berta asks, with a wry smile.

"Yes."

Berta chuckles. "Right," she says sarcastically.

"So now that I answered your question, how about mine. Why?"

Berta continues to stare at Craig. She then looks out the window.

"Why, Berta? Why let everyone believe you were gone . . . or worse?"

Berta shakes her head. "You don't get to ask questions. This is my home . . . and you should go. I'm sorry you came all this way."

"Berta, I have gone through pure agony this past week since you supposedly left. You don't understand."

"Don't go down this road, Craig."

"No. If you want to kick me out of your house, fine, but it isn't happening until I tell you what I have to tell you. I spent days torn up over you leaving. I mean ... part of me is so relieved that you didn't go with that guy . . . but another part is angry. Who would do something like this?"

"You really should go."

"Candace told me that you love me. Is that true?"

Berta begins to push Craig out of her home.

"Is it true Berta? Do you love me?"

Berta gets Craig out her home and slams the door. Craig yells through the door.

"Berta, I love you. And maybe you don't love me anymore, but I'm going to keep coming back to this very place until you do."

Berta leans on the other side of the door and stares out in space defiantly. Eventually, Craig leaves.

⋘⋙

The next morning, Berta opens her door to go out and grab her mail and sees Craig standing there. He has a chair next to her door and a briefcase. She stares at him for a second and then closes and locks her door. She walks down the hall as he quickly packs up and follows closely behind her.

"Good morning," he says.

She ignores him and continues on her way. She gets to the lobby and greets everyone she sees. Craig does the same. The receptionist smiles at Berta and then at Craig. Berta gets to the desk and retrieves her mail. She then greets a few more people and goes outside to her car. Craig still follows.

"What did you do? Make out with the receptionist to get where I lived?" she asks.

"Ouch, Berta," Craig says chuckling. "Actually, I told her that I was your man."

Berta stops and turns around. "My man?"

Craig nods vigorously. Berta rolls her eyes and gets into her car. Craig stands there smiling as he watches her leave.

Berta goes to the market to do her weekly shopping, thinking of Craig the entire time. She has built up a form of resistance to him, like he is some form of infectious disease. She still is angry with him, but she isn't so sure why anymore. She tries hard to remember exactly what it was that made her so angry but determines everything to be trivial. For a reason unknown to her, she can't help but feel happy that he's around.

She gets back to the development to see her assigned parking space taken but not with another car. Berta pulls up close to her space without parking and gets out of her car. She walks over to the space to see it almost completely covered with long stemmed roses. She kneels down and picks one up, noticing none of them have any thorns. She can't help but smile as she looks at more than four dozen red and deep pink roses covering her space. She grabs one and gets back into her car. She carefully parks into the space even though she knows that she is likely to crush many of the roses. She gets out and grabs her bags. Once in the lobby, the receptionist calls her over.

"Ms. DeVries, I have a package for you. I can have it delivered up to you. It's rather large."

"Who dropped it off?"

"Your boyfriend."

"I'm sorry, but he isn't my boyfriend. He is barely a friend."

"Oh, I'm sorry. I thought . . . I apologize. He told me—"

"I know what he told you. But listen to what I tell you. He isn't my man."

"Would you have me get rid of the package then?"

Berta thinks for a second. "How big is it?"

The short and skinny woman goes under her desk and pulls out a long box, a dress box. Berta stares at it for a second. "Actually, can you have that delivered to my door?"

The receptionist smiles. "I sure can." She leans in a bit more. "If you don't mind my intrusion, he seems to be a very nice man."

"I know. I've known him for eight years. This is nothing new. He does this for all the women he wanted to date. Which is exactly why he isn't my man."

"I see. Well, I will have the package right up to you in a few minutes."

"Okay, thank you."

Berta carries her bags up to her place and stops at the door. Taped to the door is a single white rose. She unlocks the door and kicks it open carrying the bags to her kitchen. She then goes back to the door and pulls off the rose. She sets it on her coffee table and starts to put the food away. A few moments later, someone comes up with her package. She grabs it and thanks the young man who brought it up to her. She sets it on her couch and opens the box. Digging through the tissue paper, she comes to a piece of deep purple cloth. She pulls on the cloth to get the rest out of the box to see a beautiful purple dress. She holds it up and stares at it, shaking her head. She throws the dress over a chair. She looks back at the box to see a card. She opens it and only one word is written on it.

Friday????

Berta throws the card down and grabs her cell phone. She calls Craig.

"What do you think you are doing?"

Craig sounds happy. "What do you mean?"

"You can't buy my love, Craig. I'm not one of those other women you dated, those numerous women you dated, who just fall for the first gift that you give them."

"Berta, I'm not trying to buy your love. I just want to see you. I just want one more chance."

"A chance at what?"

"A chance at spending the rest of my life with you."

Berta gets silent.

"Berta, God has renewed my spirit. I asked for forgiveness . . . and I forgave, but not only that, I realized something important. Not only is His grace enough to cover me . . . but it's enough to cover us . . . enough to revive something that could be potentially dead. I love you. I'm not afraid to say it, and no matter how long it takes, I want to make sure you know that. You saw things in me that no other woman saw. You stayed next to me when I wanted no one next to me. You let God use you . . . to get to me. So at the very least, I'm asking you out to dinner to thank you for being you."

Berta plops on the couch. "I really don't get you."

"That's fine. I can explain everything over dinner on Friday. Do you like the dress?"

"I never agreed to dinner, Craig."

"Yes, you did. So, the dress—"

"No, I didn't."

"Okay. So what do you suppose we do?"

"Nothing."

Silence.

"Let me ask you this. We can scratch the dinner if you want, but can you answer this?"

"What?"

"How much did this guy hurt you for you to act so cold towards me?"

Berta pauses. "Daniel didn't hurt me. It was you who hurt me."

"How?"

"I've already answered your one question, Craig."

"Fine." Craig sighs. "Whatever it is that I did, just know that I am sorry. For hurting you, I am sorry. I wish there was more I could do to show you. But I guess there isn't anything that I can do. Look, do what you want with the picture and the dress, and you might want to call Candace she . . ."

"Wait, what picture?"

". . . and she's been calling me almost every day now to see if I heard from you . . ."

"Craig, there wasn't a picture in the box."

". . . I would say something but I'm not sure if that's my place to say anything."

"Craig?"

"Yeah?"

"There wasn't a picture in the box."

"You sure? Check it again. I know I put it in there."

Berta starts sifting through the pieces of tissue paper and finds the picture that Craig meant. She observes the picture carefully. In it, Craig and Berta are standing on opposite sides of Mr. Valencia. The husky light skinned man in a suit has his hands on both Craig and Berta's shoulders. He smiles a wide smile, seemingly brimming with pride. Both Berta and Craig look so young in the picture.

"Where did you get this picture?"

"I always had it . . . sitting in my desk drawer."

Berta continues to stare at the picture with worn edges.

"Do you remember when this is?" Craig asks.

"I know it's from a long time ago."

"It's the first day he took me under his wing. The first day me and you met."

Berta continues to stare at the picture, allowing tears to flow from her eyes. The picture brings back a bunch of memories, including sitting at Raul Valencia's bedside as he took his last breaths.

"Berta?"

Berta sniffs. "You are such a jerk."

"Well, that isn't the reaction I was looking for. Actually, none of this is going the way I hoped it would."

"Well, if you weren't such a jerk . . . things . . . things would have gone differently."

"So I'm a jerk now?" Craig asks chuckling.

"Yes. A big one. Look, I've got to go . . . I'll see you Friday."

Craig pauses. "So that means you will go out with me?"

"I guess so. What time?"

"I'll be at your place at seven."

"Fine. I'll see you then."

"Hey, Berta?"

"What, Craig?"

"It's good to hear your voice again."

"Yeah, yeah. Stop with all the mushy stuff. I'll see you later."

Berta gets off the phone and lies back on the couch. Her emotions are bubbling over and it's hard to contain them. On one hand she is still mad, but on the other, she is excited. Finally Craig sees in her what she has been showing him for years, a woman with much love to give, a woman waiting to be loved the same, a woman that even her stepfather saw was for Craig.

CHAPTER THIRTY THREE

"SO how have you two been?"

Pastor Brentwood smiles at Mark and Jade, who sit in front of him. This time, he doesn't sit behind a desk but rather sits in a wooden chair in the middle of the room. Mark and Jade sit on the opposite ends of a long sofa.

"As good as we can be, I guess," Jade says.

Mark nods in agreement. The pastor smiles. "Okay. Well, let's get started for today. First, did you guys do what I sent you home with?"

Both nod.

"Good. Good. Mark, when we talked earlier in the week you told me a little about a new situation that has come up."

"Yes."

Jade looks over at Mark, not knowing that he talked to the pastor outside their counseling sessions.

"Now that you both are here, fill me in on what's going on."

"Well," Mark starts, "Alicia just popped up at the gym I go to. It was creepy the way she just stood behind me."

"And how did she know she would find you there?"

"That's where she picked me up the one day." Mark looks down. "The night we had . . . a date is what I guess you can call it."

Pastor Brentwood nods. "Okay. Go on."

"I left the gym . . . but after telling her that we can't do what we were doing anymore. Needless to say, she took it bad. Now she wants to get me fired from my job . . . either that or have dinner with me."

"Are you're saying that she is blackmailing you . . . for a dinner?"

"Yes. I have the text messages still to prove it."

"What is this dinner for, you suppose?"

"I don't know."

"Hmm. Okay, continue."

"I immediately called Jade afterwards . . . and I told her what happened later in the night."

"And?"

"And we started to argue . . . but we got that under control fast."

"What were you arguing about?"

"I was considering going to the dinner."

The pastor begins to chuckle. "I must say, Mark, there aren't too many wives who will go for something like that. I can understand how the argument started."

"I know. I can understand that too. I just . . . I mean . . . this is my job at stake. She could easily go to the school board and say something. Even the slightest whisper could get me fired. That's what happened to a few great teachers in the district. They got the boot for things that weren't even their fault. That's the way this school district is . . . at the slightest hint of scandal, they go into a panic."

"Jade, what was your take on the situation?"

Jade shakes her head. "I didn't like any bit of what he was telling me. I definitely don't think he should have dinner with this lowlife."

Mark shakes his head. Jade continues.

"I can simply get a job that will have us both covered. With my experience, I could easily do that. He could teach in another district."

"You know I can't," Mark says. "And you haven't even bothered to pick up a job yet."

Jade sighs. "I don't see why you can't teach in another district."

"In what district? The one with the spoiled rich kids? There's a specific reason I wanted to teach in the district that I am in. Those kids . . . they need me."

"I understand that, Mark."

"You don't. Don't try to save face in front of the pastor. You never asked me about my job . . . maybe once or twice . . . but how could you know the inner working of something you never asked about?"

"Excuse me?"

"Mark, Jade, please."

Jade looks at Pastor Brentwood and then over at a painting on the wall. Mark grits his teeth.

"Pastor, my job is important to me. It is my dream. I live it every day . . . to teach them kids . . . to give them the hope that their parents refuse to give."

"But Mark, Jade may have a point, don't you think? Couldn't you get another job? You were teacher of the year how many times now?"

"That doesn't matter. One scandal, just one, and all of that goes away, simply because it makes the board question my integrity. It all goes away just like that." Mark snaps his fingers loud enough to startle Jade.

The pastor nods. "So your job is worth your marriage?" He looks at Mark plainly.

Mark sits back. "It's not . . . I . . . I . . . things wouldn't be okay like Jade thinks. Who knows when I would be able to pick up another job? Who even knows when she could pick up another job? Right now, things are fine financially. We're eating up our savings like no other, but we can make it for another few months … just long enough for Jade to find another job."

Pastor Brentwood nods. "You said it was your dream, teaching. Because of Bernard?"

Mark nods. "A child shouldn't have to go through what I went through. They shouldn't end up like Bernard because of crappy parents who shouldn't have had any kids. Selfish parents who don't care what happens to their kids make me sick. Sick to my stomach."

"So this dream . . . a dream you have no plan of sacrificing? Because it almost sounds like you don't want this to work."

Mark sighs. "It's not that. I've sacrificed so much already. I sacrificed my entire being . . . for our marriage to work. I got nothing more than 'you need to change more.'"

"Are you saying you don't feel appreciated?"

"Yes. I never did. At my job . . . that's where I am appreciated. By my kids . . . I am appreciated, but by Jade . . . she always wants to change who I am . . . to fit her. It's always about her . . . never about me. It took her committing adultery and attempting to cover it up for her to treat me with some more respect, some more appreciation. Sometimes I wonder if she actually loves me or if she is doing all of this just to look better."

Jade continues to stare at the painting, now allowing the tears to flow freely. Pastor Brentwood offers her a tissue but she declines. Instead, she fiddles with the cross on her necklace.

"Jade?"

Jade puts her hand up and shakes her head. She begins weeping. Mark looks down, not knowing what to do. Part of him wants to hold her, but another feels that it would be an awkward thing to do at this point. Jade gets up and hurries out the room.

Mark waits for a few seconds before going after her. When he catches up to her, she is walking in the parking lot heading towards her car.

"Jade."

Jade keeps walking.

"Jade, wait."

Jade snaps around. "What?"

"What are you doing?"

"What do you mean? What are we doing? That's the question."

"What do y—"

"It's clear this isn't going to work."

"What are you talking about?"

"Leave me, Mark. Just leave me. Go to Alicia."

"Stop it." Mark goes to grab her hand.

In a knee jerk reaction, Jade pulls away. "Don't touch me." She marches to her car. Mark runs in front of her, blocking her way to the car. Jade simply walks away from him towards a field of grass. Mark follows her again but this time grabs her and pulls her close to him.

"Leave me, Mark. Leave me . . . please. You would be happier . . . if I wasn't around. I messed everything up." Jade's sobs become louder. She pushes Mark away. "You hear that everyone?" she cries. "I messed everything up. My marriage has gone to hell because of me. It isn't as good as it seems. You hear me? Do you?" Jade releases a loud primal scream into the air though no one but Mark hears her. He cringes at the sound of the scream, feeling the emotion and anguish behind it. Jade stumbles to the ground and continues to wail. Mark walks up to her and puts his arms around her. This time, she doesn't him push away.

"I'm sorry, Mark. I'm so, so sorry. I wish I could have been a better wife to you."

Mark embraces her as she continues to cry into his chest. He rocks back and forth and caresses the back of her head. He wants to say that he is as guilty as she is, but her sobs allow for no other sound. She shivers in his arms as she cries although it isn't cold outside. It takes only a few seconds of rocking her back and forth for Mark to begin crying as well. Mark can't help thinking that this is it for them; their marriage is over. He shakes his head to shake out those thoughts and ends up staring at Jade. She still cries, letting out months maybe even years of frustrations. Mark then looks up at the sky.

Eventually, both Mark and Jade make it back into the pastor's office, where he was waiting patiently for them to return. For the rest of the day neither said more than a few words but rather listened to Pastor Brentwood as he went over seemingly every verse on marriage in the Bible. He broke each one down, one by one, explaining to both of them how God set marriage up to be. The last thing he mentions is a group counseling session for Mark and Jade to consider. He wants them to be guest speakers, letting the world in on their struggles and victories as a married couple. Both are quite skeptical on the idea.

CHAPTER THIRTY FOUR

THE session ran three hours over what Pastor Brentwood had scheduled so by the time Jade gets to dropping Mark off, it's already dinnertime. She pulls up into the garage and parks the car, leaving it running. They both sit in the car staring at each other.

"So what do you think of this group session?" Mark asks.

"I don't know. I'm sure it could help. I just don't know if it would help us. I mean, what's the point in doing the group thing if we don't make it?"

"Are you saying we won't make it?"

"No. I'm saying it's too early to call it either way."

Mark nods and slides out the car. "You going to be all right? Going back to your parents', I mean."

"I'll be fine."

Mark observes Jade for a bit longer. "I don't want you to go."

Jade looks away feeling tears well up in her eyes. "Don't do this, Mark."

"I'll make dinner."

"Please."

"Stay the night . . . leave in the morning after you are rested."

"Mark, I can't."

"Please, Jade. Don't leave me in the house by myself for another night. I can't take it. I want you back. I want the kids back. I want our family back."

"I can't stay the night with you, Mark."

"Okay, fine. Have dinner with me. Please."

Jade looks at Mark. "I don't think that is a good idea."

Mark looks down. He scuffles his way around to the other side of the car. "I understand. Call me when you get back . . . so I know you got back safely?"

Jade brushes her hair behind her ear. "I will."

Mark nods and steps away from the car. He looks at Jade for a few seconds more before going into the house. Jade pulls out of the garage and drives away.

Mark ambles his way through the house, takes out what he needs to make dinner, and heads upstairs to take a shower. Just as he gets to the top step, he hears the garage door opening again. He waits to hear anything else and hears keys going into the door. He walks downstairs to see Jade standing at the door. She doesn't say anything and neither does he. He smirks and walks to the kitchen.

"I was making some lemon chicken . . . rice . . . broccoli," he says.

Jade walks to the kitchen and washes her hands. "Let me help. It will get done faster."

"And it will probably taste better."

Jade looks over to Mark and gives a weak smile.

An hour or so later, Mark and Jade sit at the dining room table eating dinner in complete silence. Every now and again, Mark would look up at Jade and Jade would look up at Mark but neither caught each other's eye. Eventually, Jade says something.

"Mark, can I ask you a question?"

Mark looks up. "Sure."

Jade looks at her plate. "Did you really sleep with her?"

Mark sits up in his chair and answers almost too quickly. "No."

"Then what happened? Why was she so excited about that night?"

Mark puts his fork down on the plate and leans back into the chair. "We kissed . . . and we ended up in her bed . . . naked."

"But you didn't sleep with her?"

"No. Right when things were about to happen, I stopped. I just froze. Completely."

"Why?"

"It wasn't right. It just didn't feel right."

"So?"

"So we ended up just holding each other until I knew I had to leave." Mark looks down and stabs the food on his plate. "Can I ask you a question?"

Jade nods.

"All those times that we made love after you left your job . . . was it me you were making love to?"

"Of course. Of course, it was you."

"What about before you left your job?"

Jade hesitates. "It . . . wasn't you."

"So it was him then?"

Jade nods. Mark looks around the room for a second and ends up focusing on a family picture hanging in the living room.

"Did you ever sleep with him?"

She shakes her head. "I was torn. I wanted to be with Boley ... but I loved—I love you." She rubs the sides of her shoulders as if she were cold. "Why didn't you say anything about your brother?"

"Could you?" Mark asks.

Jade looks down. Mark starts to eat again.

"I'm sorry," Jade says.

Mark slowly turns back towards Jade. "Me too. I'm sorry for everything."

Suddenly, Mark's cell phone beeps from behind Jade. They stare at each other for a second before Mark insists that Jade grab it for him. Jade looks at it and sees two new text messages.

"They're from Alicia," she says. "She's going to the principal of the school next week."

Jade hands the phone to Mark and stares at him, awaiting his next move. He sets the phone down on the table and starts picking at his food again. The phone rings this time and Mark stares at it. He looks to see who's calling. It is Alicia again. Mark grips the phone while it still rings and with all his might, hurls it at the wall. It hits the wall and shatters into many pieces. He looks at Jade with tears in his eyes and gives her a wry smile. Jade stares at Mark as he continues to pick at his food. He stares at the plate as if it is telling him something and realizes that next week marks the ends of a dream he has held since childhood.

"Maybe we should reconsider the dinner thing," Jade says.

"No. No matter what I do, she's going to go to them. I hope they don't believe her. I don't want to lose my job . . . but you know what . . . I can only blame myself." Mark sits up in his chair. After a few moments of an awkward silence, Jade gets up and grabs their plates. She takes the dishes to the kitchen and washes them while Mark still sits at the table.

ଔ৪

Jade comes out of the kitchen and sees that Mark isn't at the table anymore. She steps over the shattered remains of his cell phone and walks the entire floor looking for him but still doesn't find him.

"Mark, I'm going to go."

Jade goes upstairs. "Mark?"

No answer.

She goes to the bedroom but doesn't find him there either. "Mark, where are you?" She takes one last glance at the bedroom, noticing that it hasn't changed much since she left. Actually, it hasn't changed at all. Jade notices the shirt she left on the bed days ago. She leaves the room and looks in Charles's room. Nothing. She goes to Kalina's room to see Mark sitting at her chessboard looking drained. Jade steps into the room. The first thing she notices is a stack of pillows right next to Kalina's bed, as if someone was sleeping on the floor. She determines that this is where Mark has been sleeping all this time. She looks at the board and notices that the pieces are arranged on the board as if two people were playing, but only Mark sits there. Jade sits across from him and stares at him for a bit longer. Tears stream down his face and his chin quivers every so often. He fights hard to not cry in front of someone else, even if it is his wife. Jade looks down at the board and notices that neither side has its queen, but there aren't any openings for it to move. It appears that the game was being played without the queens on the board from the start. The two queens sit on the side of the table, the only pieces that have been taken thus far.

"Whose turn is it?"

Mark looks Jade in the eyes. "That's a good question."

"You've been playing this by yourself, right?"

Mark nods. "Every day. One move a day."

"So where did you leave off?"

Mark smirks. "I don't remember."

Jade looks at the board and moves one of the pieces. Mark keeps his smirk on his face. He grabs the two queens and places them back on the board. "I learned a lot from chess. Got a few key life lessons from this game."

Jade continues to stare at the board. "Like what?"

Mark moves a piece. "The queen. It's the most powerful piece on the board. It can go virtually anywhere on the board. It takes a combination of pieces to match up to what the queen can do; so if you happen to get your queen captured, you have lost a great asset."

Jade makes a move. She then looks up at Mark. "But like the other pieces, if the queen gets captured, the game continues. If you capture the king, the game is over."

Mark looks away from her. "That's true, but the king is simple. It moves simply. It isn't as powerful as the queen; so if you lose your queen, loss of the entire game is next to inevitable."

Jade sits up in her chair. "It depends on what you think power is. Every piece on the board has a job to protect the king while defeating the enemy. That includes the queen. The queen's job is to attack and protect for the king. That's power. No matter how strong the queen is, the king cannot fall or the enemy wins."

"Who is the enemy, Jade?" Mark moves.

"Whoever your opponent is."

Mark leans back in his chair. "What about in this game? I've been playing for both sides."

Jade moves her queen to the center of the board. "I don't know. Check."

Mark looks down at the board. He stares at it for a few seconds before realizing the game is over. "I don't know either." He moves his hand over his king and gently tips it over.

"That's it?" Jade asks. "You have at least two moves."

"I don't see it."

"And you still have your queen."

"Do I?"

Jade stares at Mark for a long time before answering. She brushes her hair behind her ear. "You do. I wouldn't be here if you didn't." She looks him in the eyes. "Is there still a king to fight for?"

"Of course. In heaven."

"You know what I mean."

"I know." Mark runs his hand over the top of his head. "Yes, there is a king to fight for."

Jade looks down at the board. "Then we fight."

"I thought that was what we were doing."

"There was always that question, though. Right? At least in the back of my mind, there was a question of if it will work. Now . . . there isn't any room for questioning. It will work."

"I see."

"Whatever the enemy throws at us."

"He's throwing a lot."

"But we can make it. We just need to get back to the basics."

Mark nods and looks down again. Jade gets up from her seat. "I have to go. It's already pretty late."

Mark follows Jade downstairs and walks her to her car. They stare at each other for a few moments before Mark opens her door for her. She gets in and stares up at him, blinking her eyes a few times. Mark smiles, but she can tell his mind is filled with stress. She grabs his hand and pulls him close to so that she can grab his face. She kisses him and continues to hold his face close to hers, staring at him. She can't tell if it is Mark who shivers or herself. She holds his face with such care, as if she's holding a priceless vase, looking into his eyes. She reads that he's unsure of himself, and in fact, she's quite unsure of herself. In a few short seconds, Mark takes over. He kisses her and grabs her hand, leading her out the car.

Eventually, they make it back upstairs to the bedroom. Mark lays Jade on her back on the bed. Suddenly, memories of the last time they were both in the room flood her mind. She tenses and Mark hops off of her.

"I can't," she says. "I'm sorry." She gets off the bed and stands at the dresser.

He walks over to her and stares into her eyes. She looks away at first, but every time she does, Mark kisses her. She looks deep into his eyes. In his eyes, she sees more than she saw that night when they were battling eachother. She sees hope. She sees love. She keeps her focus on his eyes, not allowing herself to look anywhere else and moves back towards the bed. With a slight touch, Mark lifts Jade's head up so she looks at the ceiling and places his lips on her neck. He kisses her neck and whispers, "I'm sorry," into her ear. He continues to kiss her and whisper in her ear and Jade cries. She holds tight to Mark as he lays her down and starts to slide her clothes off her body. For the rest of the night and into the morning, they make love, apologizing to each other many times over, not just for what they have done, but for those things they allowed to happen to the other.

CHAPTER THIRTY FIVE

BERTA stands in front of a mirror going over her own checklist of how she looks. She has tried on several outfits, none of them being the deep purple cocktail dress that Craig bought for her to wear. It still sits in the box on her coffee table. She sucks her teeth, flips off her shoes, and changes her clothes again. She changes into a long evening gown but doesn't get it fully zipped up before she flings that off and throws it on the bed. She looks back at the box on the table and stomps her way over to open it. She pulls out the dress again and slides it on. The dress is close fitting but loose enough for her to move freely. She stomps back to the mirror and looks at herself. To her surprise, Craig bought her a dress that is a perfect fit. It doesn't come up too high when she sits, and it is long enough for her to look like she's going somewhere other than a club or lounge. She grabs a different pair of shoes and puts them on her feet. After a few more moments of her spraying perfume on and brushing her teeth, she hears a knock on her door. She opens it to see Craig in a suit, likely to be custom made. The first thing she notices is that his tie is the same color as her dress. Berta smirks a bit.

"You're late," she says.

"I know. I thought you may need a bit more time to get yourself situated," Craig says smiling.

"Well, I didn't. I sat here and waited for you for half an hour."

"I'm sorry . . . you look great . . . absolutely great."

"Yeah, thanks. Where are we going?"

"Nowhere overly special."

"That doesn't tell me where."

"You'll see."

Berta grabs her purse and leaves her home, closing and locking the door behind her. Craig observes her every move.

"Did you call Candace?"

"Yes, I did."

"Good, because she was borderline stalking me. She kept asking if I heard from you."

Craig and Berta step into the elevator and remain in complete silence. The cheesy music playing makes Craig smile.

"What did she say?" Craig asks.

"What do you think she said? She was mad, of course, but I explained everything to her . . . and she understood."

"Really?"

"Does that sound outlandish to you?"

"It does. But it is what it is, I guess."

The elevator doors open and they both step out into the lobby. A few moments later, they get into Craig's car and drive out of the complex.

"So what is this dinner about?" Berta asks.

"You know what it's about."

"No, I don't."

"Well, I think a better question is why you are going to this dinner without knowing what it's about . . . wearing a dress I bought you, no less."

"Just shut up."

Craig looks over at Berta and smiles. She looks out the window, angry. "Okay. Shutting up now."

For the rest of the short five minute drive, Craig remains silent and Berta stares out the window. He pulls up in front of a small restaurant.

"I hope you're ready to eat," Craig says.

"Actually, I'm not that hungry."

"That's fine. We may work up an appetite dancing."

"There's nowhere to dance. That place looks too small."

"Who said we are eating there?" Craig smiles. "Stay here." He gets out of the car and runs into the small restaurant. He soon comes out with two bags presumably full of food. He folds down the back bench seat, sets the bags in, and drives off again.

"Craig, where are we going?"

"Hold on a sec. We will be there in another five minutes."

On the way, Craig asks a question that he wanted to ask for a while since seeing Berta again. "So what happened between you and Daniel?"

Berta looks at Craig for a few moments before answering. "He's a liar and a cheater. That's it."

"How did you figure that?"

"I found one of his letters. He has some woman by the name of Justine waiting on him down in Houston."

"But he wanted you to go with him?"

"No. He never expected me to say that I would go with him. He was trying to set things up so that if he had to come back up here, he would have a woman to play around with."

"You being that woman?"

"Yeah." Berta looks out the window. "But his luck ran out."

"So now he's in Texas a—" Craig stops himself. Something clicks in his mind. Berta stares at him. "Maya told me she was leaving to one of her new stores in Texas."

Berta shifts in her seat. "Texas, huh?"

"Do you think t—"

"I wouldn't doubt it. I wouldn't doubt it at all." Berta shakes her head. "I knew it was weird, his reaction to Maya when he first knew who she was."

Craig chuckles. "Yeah. But good luck to them … a cheater and a person always looking to catch a cheater."

A few moments later, Craig pulls up into Berta's development again. Berta gives him a strange face.

"Here we are," Craig says.

"Very funny, Craig. Where are we going?"

"Just follow me." Craig gets out of the car and grabs the two bags of food. Berta sits in the car for a second before getting out and following Craig. They both go back into the building and up to Berta's floor, but Craig keeps walking past her door and to another.

"Craig, that doesn't lead to anywhere but the roof."

"I know," he says as he holds open the door for Berta to walk through. She walks past Craig and up the steps to the door leading to the roof. Craig intentionally lags behind her. Once she gets to the next door, she looks at Craig.

"We aren't doing anything illegal, are we?"

Craig shakes his head. "I don't think so."

Craig pushes open the door. Berta adjusts her eyes to the setting sun and scans the roof, a place that doesn't look much like a roof at all. She walks out to see a table in the middle of the roof and all around the table lay roses arranged in the same way the roses in her parking space had been. She moseys her way to the table by way of a small path outlined in more roses. Two small plates sit on the table with an unlit candle.

"Please, have a seat," Craig says excitedly.

Berta sits down and stares out at the landscape. The development has its own golf course that is always perfectly accented by the setting sun. Although, she isn't much of a golf fan, she loves the scene. A light and warm breeze swirls through lifting up the edge of her skirt. She places her hand in her lap to smooth her dress down.

"I find it hard to believe that the association let you do this."

"For the most part, they don't know about it, but that doesn't matter. So what do you think?" Craig starts placing food onto their plates.

"It's nice," Berta says unenthusiastically.

Craig looks at Berta for a second, still trying to read her. He sets the container he was holding down onto the table. "Okay, Berta, you are killing me here. Do you want to be here or don't you? You didn't have to say yes to me. I mean, what's going on here?"

Berta looks at the last sliver of sunlight as it disappears behind the ground. "What is this dinner about?"

"What do you mean?"

"Why are we on my roof about to have dinner? What is the purpose in this? What is the purpose in anything you have done over the past couple days?"

"To sum it all up, it goes back to what I said before. I love you."

Berta faces Craig. "Why?"

Craig sits down. "Well, that's simple . . . sort of. I've come to this realization that God has never left me. It's not an earth shattering epiphany, but it was enough to realize a few more things. He set two people in my life . . . just two that helped heal all the wounds I had. Just two that brought me back around to Him again. One was Mark . . . and the other is you. And when I think of you . . . when I see you, I see the only woman in my life who has stood next to me, no matter the circumstances . . . even when I believed there was no God. I searched all over the place for a woman who would stand by me, even after knowing my past." Craig looks to the side. "So when I finally got it . . . you were already gone. I felt that I had made the worst mistake in my entire life."

"So what do you get now?"

"I get that you are someday going to be my wife. I know that is why God set you in my life, and if I wasn't so hard headed, we may already be married by now."

"You are very bold with your words."

"When haven't I been?"

Berta looks down at her hands.

"All my cards are on the table, Berta. If you want me gone . . . then I will leave, and you can move on. I will just have to deal with missing the greatest opportunity of my life. I, of course, will still love you. But if there is something there . . . please don't let it go. We can take baby steps if necessary, but please don't let it go."

Berta smirks and shakes her head. "Could you wait for eight years?"

"I would wait for twenty."

"Stop it with the smooth talk, Craig. Could you wait eight years? Could you wait eight years for me to come around while I date a bunch of men that you know don't compare to you? Could you wait eight years for me to realize who I am and the power that I hold? Tell me; could you wait eight years in the shadow of a promise?"

Craig looks at Berta, whose eyes pierce him through his heart. "For you, yes, I could."

Berta looks away from Craig and shakes her head. She chuckles and mumbles something to herself. "No, you couldn't, Craig."

Craig sighs and looks up at the purple sky. For a while, neither one says anything to the other. Craig leans back in his seat and continues to stare up at the sky. Berta gets up from her seat and pushes in her chair.

"Thanks for setting this up," she says. "Everything was beautiful."

"What promise?"

"Huh?"

"What shadow of a promise? What are you talking about?"

Berta sits back down. She crosses her legs and shakes her foot vigorously. It takes her some time to speak. "You know that I was with Daddy during his last moments."

"Yeah."

"We talked for hours before . . . about everything." Berta pauses. She looks at Craig, trying to find a way to say everything. "At one point, he looked at me . . . and he smiled. In a soft voice, he said 'I guess it's time for me to stop running from God, huh?' I nodded and he grabbed my hand. We prayed together and Daddy gave his life back to Christ."

"Back to? I thought Mr. V never believed in God."

Berta shakes her head and looks down. A bit of fear creeps up on her and she tightens her throat. "He was once a very religious man, a very religious husband."

"Husband?"

Berta nods. "He was married. I know he told you that he wasn't . . . that he was always by himself. I'm sure that's the way he felt."

"Why would he tell me otherwise?"

"Because he . . . his wife . . . her name was Emily." Berta reaches into her purse, pulls out a picture, and places it on the table. Craig takes the picture and stares at a beautiful older woman standing in front of a tree. He notices her smile, the same smile Berta used to give him that left him speechless. He looks up at Berta still trying to understand.

"She died . . . rather, she was murdered. For a couple of dollars, some kid shot her. Daddy . . . he lost all faith then . . . he lost all hope . . . and he mentally erased everything that happened . . . even his relationship with God. He didn't get it until he was lying in that hospital bed, what God was doing. I didn't get it either until he made me promise . . . he made me promise him that I would take care of you when he was gone."

"What?"

"He made me promise that I would help you see God for whom He really is . . . for who I see Him as . . . for who he finally saw Him as. He felt so bad for misleading you . . . especially because in you, he saw himself."

Craig leans back in his chair, setting the picture of Emily back onto the table.

"He always said I had her eyes . . . that's why he took me in. I reminded him of her." Berta shows a far off expression. "He started to shake, and I knew . . . it was about time. He kept smiling at me, though. His last words? 'You two are destined to be together.'" Berta nods her head slightly. "So ever since then, I lived my life according to this promise that I made."

"Because to him, we are Emily and himself."

Berta nods.

"I have spent a long time trying to keep my end of the promise. I have spent a long time waiting on you, Craig. I spent a long time believing in this. I look like a fool for waiting on someone for so long. Can you imagine what it felt like to hear that you rededicated your life to Christ, but you saw potential in Maya? Maya, Craig, you still saw potential in Maya."

"Why didn't you tell me this stuff before? You had eight years to tell me that you believe that I am the one for you."

"That doesn't matter if you didn't believe that I was the one for you. I wanted you to *find* me, Craig. I waited on you to *find* me; but for almost a decade, you didn't even see me. I was always right under your nose and you didn't see me. I was there, yes, but I wanted you to *see* me, Craig." Berta tears up. "You didn't see me."

"But I see you now."

"It doesn't matter. I'm not even supposed to be here. I'm supposed to be with a snake who likes to have sex with church women all across America."

Craig looks down. "Maybe it took me a long time to figure this thing out. I understand that you are angry it took so long, but don't give up on me. Don't give up on us. It's like walking off the track a few feet from the finish line. Please, Berta, give us a shot."

"I can't." Berta gets up from her seat again but this time walks past Craig.

"I do love you and if you don't see it . . . then I'll wait until you do. I would wait eight years, Berta. If I had to I would wait until my last breath, just for you to say that you love me too. Many women were a perfect fit for who I was . . . but you are the only one that fits the great man I hope to be. So when you see that . . . I'll be there." Craig continues to stare at the landscape as Berta leaves the rooftop. Craig hears the door creak open and finally shut. He sits at the table unable to watch her leave. This moment hurts him more than he thought it would. He bangs his fist on the table and looks up at the sky. After a few moments, he gets up and starts to gather the food.

Berta leaves the roof and storms into her home. She slams the door shut and leans on it. She slides down the door and sits on the floor. She coaches herself, as she has done many times before. *There it is. There he is. Why are you running now? After a long, long time, he is finally here. You ran away, and he came for you. He came for you! He found you. What is the problem?* She gets up and takes the picture of Emily from her purse. She grabs her Bible and stuffs it in right behind the picture of her, her Dad, and Craig. She stops to look at both pictures. *We do look like Daddy and Emily.* Berta slams the Bible shut and sets it on the table.

The door to the roof creaks open again and Craig stops in his tracks. He looks up to see Berta standing by the door. She looks unsure of herself but walks towards him anyway. Craig puts the containers of food down and makes his way to Berta.

"No matter how many times I say it," Berta says, "I can't not love you." She smiles shyly. "Destiny finally stares me in the face . . . and I run because I'm scared and angry."

They finally are close to each other, standing in the middle of the rooftop. Craig looks at her.

"I love you, Craig."

"Do you know what those words sound like to me? Do you know what they feel like?" Craig asks.

Berta shakes her head.

"They sound sweet. They feel . . . perfect."

"Well, I gu—"

And before Berta could finish her sentence, Craig kisses her. He kisses her deeply. He kisses her passionately, tasting her soft lips. His heart races and he begins to pull away, but Berta pulls his face in more, continuing to kiss him.

Berta feels a jolt in her body when Craig first kisses her. She feels so many emotions at once that it causes her to cry. As she holds Craig's face to hers, she starts to feel a cooling sensation over her entire body. She stops kissing Craig and allows him to hold her. Against her wishes, tears continue to fall from her eyes. She looks up and sees Craig doing the same.

"Are you crying?" she asks.

"No." Craig looks away. "It's the pollen."

"You don't have any allergies."

"Dust."

"We're on a roof."

"The moonlight is burning out my retinas."

Berta stares into Craig's tear filled eyes. They both smile big smiles.

"I'm hungry, Craig."

"Well, that's why I bought the food. Come on, take a seat."

Craig grabs her hand and leads her back to the table.

CHAPTER THIRTY SIX

ON a warm and bright Saturday afternoon, Jade sits outside with her mother while her father and the kids play in the grass.

"So today is the day?" Jade's mother asks.

"Sure is. It's about time."

"Everything packed?"

"Everything is packed."

Jade's mother gets silent.

"You don't want us to go, do you?"

"I would be lying if I said I did. Things have been different with you and the kids around. Your father has been different with you and the kids around."

Both look at him playing with the kids.

"I haven't seen him smile this much in some time."

Jade looks over to her mother. "Why don't you talk to him? Maybe even go to Pastor Brentwood?"

Jade's mother scoffs at Jade's comment. "He doesn't talk to me. He shuts down. And I'm sure he won't be up for counseling."

"Mama, it's been like this for years. Something has to change."

"It will change. I have faith."

"And if it doesn't?"

"It will."

Jade looks away from her mother, who seems to be in another place.

"It takes a bit more than blind faith to get through something. You two ought to talk. There are a lot of things that have probably gone unsaid . . . things that should have been said a long time ago."

"Jade, leave it be."

"I'm just saying."

"Jade."

Jade becomes silent. Her parents' issues sadden her. Neither wants to be the first to admit they were wrong on anything; so they continue, hoping that what they are trying to say will reach the other without ever saying anything. It reminds her of how her and Mark used to be.

ଓଞ୍ଚ

Mark paces back and forth across the living room as he awaits Jade's arrival. He has the jitters and pats his hand on the side of his leg. At every car driving down the street, Mark looks out the window to see if it is Jade and the kids. He notices the sun beaming on their home. He begins to coach himself. *Calm down, Mark. Everything is okay. It's just you and the kids together . . . for the first time in weeks. No big deal. Breathe. There you go, breathe.* At that instant, he hears a car pull up into the driveway, but he doesn't hear the garage door opening. He stops breathing altogether. He goes to the window and sees Jade helping Charles out of the car. As soon as his feet hit the ground, Charles runs to the front door and tries the doorknob. Jade tells him to slow down. Mark looks at Charles and smiles. He goes to open the door but stops in his tracks once he sees Kalina get out of the car. A tear comes to his eye but he uses his shirt to wipe it away. He then takes a second look at Jade, back at Kalina, and then back at Jade again. His heart races at the sight of Jade. He finds her to be beyond gorgeous. She's heavenly. She wears sunglasses and a yellow floral print sundress that blows in the wind. Her hair is tied back into a ponytail. She stares at the window as if she knows that Mark is watching them. He goes to the door and opens it. Charles opens his mouth wide, drops his suitcase, and runs right to Mark. Mark lifts him up and hugs him.

"Daddy!"

"What's up, little big man?"

"Everything. I tackle like the pros and we were in the closet and we ate weird looking rice . . . and we . . . and we . . . ."

Charles keeps talking as Jade and Kalina come into the house. Jade smiles at Mark. Kalina stands behind Jade and looks at Mark for a few seconds before dropping her suitcase and running upstairs. Jade calls for Kalina but Mark stops her. He puts Charles down and kisses Jade.

"Is there anything else in the car?"

"No."

"I'm going to talk to her." Mark starts going upstairs. "Hey, when is the last time I told you that you were beautiful?"

Jade looks at Mark and smirks. "I don't know."

"Well, maybe I should say it more often. You are the most beautiful creature I have ever seen."

"Thank you."

Mark smiles and goes upstairs.

⋈

Jade walks away smiling. It amazes her how one comment from Mark can make the whole world great. She never noticed this earlier. Rather, she never took the time to notice. *Things will be different now,* she thinks. She knows there are still some more counseling sessions with Pastor Brentwood, but she has a lot more confidence that they will make it. She walks to the kitchen and grabs the phone to let her mother know that she and the kids made it back safely. She looks and sees there are eight missed calls and six new messages. Two messages were saved. She looks through the phone and finds the missed calls are from the same number. Jade listens to the two messages saved messages. The first is Alicia almost begging Mark to call her back. The second is her telling Mark where she is going to be, waiting for him. *Why were these two saved?* Jade listens to the rest of the messages of Alicia doing everything from making more threats to go to the school board to going over more memories that the two of them have. Jade erases all the messages and hangs up the phone. She isn't sure of what to think. Part of her isn't concerned, but a larger portion of her is worried all over again. She doesn't understand why Mark saved those two messages, one of which gives him an idea of where she will be. Learning some hard lessons from before their new relationship, she isn't going to hide her knowledge. Instead, she plans to talk to Mark about it tonight. Ironically, tonight is when Alicia set this forced dinner.

⊰⊱

Mark gets upstairs and stands by the doorway to Kalina's room. She ignores him and lies in her bed throwing a ball against the wall. Mark goes in and grabs a chair. He sits next to her bed.

"I don't really know what to say," Mark starts. "All I can do is explain how I feel . . . about you . . . about your brother . . . about your mother."

Kalina turns her back towards Mark.

"I know you're angry, and you have every right to be. What I did was despicable and completely uncalled for. I am ashamed for what I have done to your mother . . . to our family." Mark leans back in his chair and thinks. "Do you know what it was first like when I finally got to hold you?" He pauses. "It was heaven on earth. Never in my life did I feel so many emotions at the same time. I was scared, I was mad, I was hurt . . . but you looked at me . . . and grabbed my nose . . . and you laughed, and I was happy. From that point on, your laugh got me through some rough times. But at one point, I stopped listening to your laughter. I stopped listening to everyone's laughter. I became selfish. I forgot who I was. But if there was ever a thing to trust me on, it's this: I will make it up to all of you. I will spend the rest of my days making sure that you, your brother, and your mother know that I love you all very much." Mark stares at the back of Kalina's head for a few moments before getting up.

"Mom cheated?"

Mark is caught off guard by the question. "Uh. Who told you that?"

"No one. I heard Mom talking to Grandma about it."

Mark pauses. "We both did some things to each other that we shouldn't have."

Kalina finally gets up and turns towards Mark. Her eyes are red and her cheeks are wet with tears. "Why?"

Looking at her breaks his heart. "We both lost sight of what was important. We fell into our own selfishness. Someday, probably sooner than later, you will understand a bit more . . . and you're going to have questions. I'll be here to answer."

"You aren't getting a divorce?"

"No."

Kalina lies back down. "Good."

Mark looks at her. "You know you can still come to me for any-thing, right?"

"Yup."

"And you don't have to be scared to do so."

"I'm not scared to."

Mark nods and starts out the door.

"White still could have won the game."

Mark turns around to see Kalina pointing behind her at the chess-board. "What?"

"There were three moves that white had . . . at least three that I could see."

"I know. I just gave up. I didn't feel like playing much."

"How many times did you tell me not to give up even if I felt like giving up?"

"Tons."

"So why did you give up?"

Mark smirks. "No good reason. Maybe we'll start a new game later?"

Silence.

"I'm not sure you're much of a challenge . . . but we can play."

Mark smiles. "Trash talk, huh? Don't forget who taught you."

Kalina gets up from the bed and walks over to Mark. She gives him a hug. "I love you, Daddy."

"I love you too, baby girl." Mark kneels down and wipes her face dry. He then kisses her on the top of her head.

CHAPTER THIRTY SEVEN

L ATER in the night, Mark stands in front of a restaurant that is a good distance from town. He wears a pained expression as he strides his way to the front door. He enters and talks to the maître de confirming the reservations that he didn't make. Everyone in the restaurant is dressed up, men in blazers and dress shoes, women in evening gowns. Within a few minutes, a tall young woman directs him to a table on the upper level, a seemingly private and cozy section of the place. Apparently, the upstairs section is for important people as everyone he passes looks at him with an interested but jealous look.

She's the only one on the floor. In a short and tight black mini dress, Alicia sits with her legs crossed, facing the city nightline. She already has a drink in her hand and sips on it with ease. She sees Mark approaching and sets her drink on the table. She stands to greet him. It is then that Mark notices just how revealing Alicia's dress really is. It's fashionable with a deep V down the front of it to draw attention to her chest, which Mark notices shimmers under the lights. He hates to admit it, but he still finds her attractive. A diamond bracelet on her wrist sends beams of light in every direction as she goes to give him a hug. Mark steps away to avoid the hug. Alicia smiles weakly and sits down, her back facing the window.

"I'm glad you decided to come," she says.

Mark says nothing and sits down. He stares at her, trying to read her intentions. She looks back at him innocently.

"I set this rendezvous up for us about a month ago. The whole floor is ours . . . well, at least for another hour."

"What is this about?" Mark leans back into his chair and folds his arms.

Alicia doesn't look phased. "Tim was accepted into Delori. Your glowing recommendation helped, I'm sure."

"Alicia."

Alicia stares at Mark for a second. "Right to the chase, I see. This isn't about anything really. We are just two friends having dinner together. What's wrong with that?"

"You threatened my job . . . my livelihood . . . my kids' livelihood . . . my family."

"You don't understand; I had to. You weren't going to show up any other way. Plus, I figured that witch at home has a one up on you . . . maybe dealing with your kids. I don't know. Why else would you run to her?"

"I love her . . . and she loves me. She wouldn't do something like use my kids against me."

"No, you're right. She's much better at cheating on you. I forgot."

Mark grits his teeth. "What do you want?"

"That's a simple question with an even simpler answer. You. I want you."

"I thought I made myself clear at the gym."

"What? Are you talking about that forced speech? I'm sure Jade wrote that one for you and had you recite it ten times before you were ready. I know that wasn't real. After all, you still came to this dinner."

Mark looks around him. He leans in over the table. "I want my job. That's why I came to the dinner."

"How bad do you want it?"

"What?"

"Your job." She flips her hair back away from her face and smiles at Mark with a devilish grin. "How bad do you want your job?"

"Stop playing games."

"I'm not playing any games. You want your job. I want you. We can both get what we want. Life would be so great that way."

Mark looks at Alicia in confusion. "But that requires me to what?"

"Leave her."

Mark smiles and shakes his head. "And if I go to the school board myself?"

"You won't do that."

"You're wrong about that . . . and you know it." He leans back in his chair again.

Alicia stares at the table. She takes a sip of her drink and swishes it around in her mouth. She swallows hard and shoots a look over to Mark. "You're trying to do it again, aren't you?"

"What?"

She looks him in the eyes. "You left my life in shambles, Mark. You managed to make me love you again. You are trying to leave me devastated again. You can't just jerk people around at will. That's what you did to me. That's what you are about to do again."

"That was not my intention then. It isn't now either, but I don't like being made into a puppet."

"So instead, you make me your puppet?"

"No. I—"

"Mark, did you love me, really? Back then, when we were engaged, did you love me?"

"I didn't know what love was back then."

Alicia takes another sip of her drink. "Okay, so now, the older and wiser Mark. The version that knows what love is. Does he love me?"

"Alicia, stop this."

"No. Did you f—"

"Alicia."

"Tell me."

"No."

Alicia slams her fist on the table. "Tell me the truth." A scowl comes over her face as her cheeks become reddened.

"No. I don't love you. The older and wiser Mark that knows what love is . . . loves Jade."

Alicia nods. "Then what was I?" she asks, changing her tone.

"I don't know."

"I was your escape . . . your cheap slut on the side. You didn't intend to try to get back what you had foolishly thrown away. You just wanted to do me and get what your wife wasn't giving you. Is that right?"

"It's not like that."

"Then what is it like?"

Mark finds himself at a loss for words. Alicia's eyes become glassy. She digs into her purse and pulls something out, slamming it onto the table. She then gets up and leaves.

"Good-bye, Mark."

Mark stares at the table and sees a glistening diamond ring. He shakes his head and looks at the ring in disgust; he knows that it is the same ring he gave to her when he asked for her hand in marriage. He gets up from the table and grabs the ring. As he heads back downstairs, he throws it in the trash and walks to another table in the corner of the first floor. Sitting at the table and looking over the menu is Jade. She looks up at him and smiles.

"How did it go?"

Mark sits. "As expected. I think she got the point, though."

"You sure?"

"I hope so."

Jade continues to stare at the menu. "This chick blocked off the entire upper level for you." She looks up at Mark. "So much for me blending in to make sure things are okay." Jade continues to look at Mark. "Are you okay?"

"I'm fine. I just hope that it's all over with . . . that we can move on."

"Me too."

Mark grabs a menu. "I have to admit, I thought you had gone crazy when you suggested doing this."

"I know. Part of me thought I had lost it too. Part of me still thinks I'm crazy. But maybe she will back off now."

Mark smiles. "You know this could have changed nothing."

"I know. But you know how I am. I'd rather try to change it instead of sitting back and taking it as it comes. Plus, she said so herself, the only way she would stay away from you is if you told her to do so."

Mark looks down, continuing to read the menu. "You know, I started to get the feeling that it was more about beating you than it was being with me . . . for her, I mean."

"Yeah?"

"For a quick moment." Mark sets his menu down. "She thought you were controlling me by using the kids against me."

"So in turn, she threatens your job?"

"To have a one up on you I suppose . . . so I would have no choice but to run into her arms."

Jade looks at Mark with a disgusted expression. "You sure know how to pick them."

Mark chuckles and quickly changes the subject. "Did you really want to eat here?"

Jade sets her menu down. "I didn't get all dressed up for nothing."

"I know, but it's really stuffy in here to me. It's a nice night out. Let's go to the park or something. I'm sure an outdoor concert is playing somewhere."

"You want to go outside to a park? With me looking like this? With these shoes on?"

"Yes."

Jade thinks for a moment. Then she smiles and stands up from the table. "Don't try anything fresh while we're there."

"I might. You do look quite tasty," Mark says while standing up with her.

"Oh, stop it." Jade grabs his hand and they walk out of the restaurant together. Just as they get out of the building, Mark pulls Jade in close to him.

"I love you," he says. "I love you more than words can explain at the moment. I promise I will make up for those things I have torn down in our marriage."

Jade looks into his eyes and feels the raw honesty coming from Mark. "You can rest assured knowing that I will be there for you to lift you up, not tear you down. I made some big mistakes, but I thank you and I thank God for giving me another shot at this. I will do right by you, Mark. Just you wait and see." She presses her body against Mark's. "Let's go to the park."

Mark and Jade get in the car. They kiss before Mark starts the car and drives off to find a park.

"Real tasty," Mark says out of nowhere.

"What?"

"You look real tasty. You see, before I said you look quite tasty. That means I can wait until later tonight to make things happen. But you are real tasty. That means I am considering pulling the car over right now."

Jade smiles and decides to play along. "I wanna bite your chest."

Mark laughs. "I didn't expect that one." He continues to laugh as he stops at a red light.

"I know you—"

BANG!

The car jerks forward into the middle of the intersection causing both Mark and Jade to slam their heads on the headrests of the car. Mark's vision is blurry, but he recognizes the dusty smell of the airbags after they have deployed.

"Mark," Jade says, being able to muster up only a faint whisper. "What happened?"

"We . . . we were rear ended. Everything . . ." Mark sees bright headlights and hears another car horn.

CRASH!

Another car hits them on Jade's side, sending them twirling into a pole. Mark hits his head on the steering wheel hard. Still dazed, he feels around to take off his seat belt. He feels something warm dripping off his chin and knows that it's blood. He pushes open the car door and flops out onto the ground. A bunch of other cars must have pulled over as all he can see are bright lights. Directly in his line of vision is the black SUV that rear-ended them. He looks to see Alicia stumble out of the vehicle and fall to the ground. Mark tries to stand but a few people who are trying to help tell him to be still. He hears a bunch of people yelling, most of them asking someone to call the police. He looks back into the car to see Jade still sitting there, her body lying in an awkward position. Mark pushes people away to get to her, but he doesn't have the strength to make it. He stumbles and falls flat to the concrete.

"Jade," he whispers. "Jade."

CHAPTER THIRTY EIGHT

WEEKS after his rooftop date, Craig stands in front of a headstone in a cemetery. It's a bright and sunny day, one that brings the chirpings of birds. Kneeling down at the headstone is Berta, who meticulously wipes the headstone of any dirt and debris.

"Who keeps up with this place?" she asks annoyed. She turns back and looks at Craig. "You okay?"

He nods. "I haven't been here since his funeral. A bunch of thoughts . . . ."

Berta turns to look at the headstone as Craig trails off somberly. She eventually stands up and walks over to Craig. He puts his arm around her and they both stare in silence.

"How do you think he knew?" Berta asks.

Craig thinks for a second. "Knew what?"

"Us. That we were going to end like this."

"Honestly . . . I don't think he knew . . . I think he saw things . . . in us both. I think he saw what God was doing with us . . . he simply acted as the confirmation to that movement."

Berta looks at Craig. "Look at you, talking all spiritual and stuff." She pats him on the chest. "It kinda turns me on." She leans in closer to him.

Craig laughs. "Oh, yeah. Well, here's one for you." He clears his throat. "The Lord is my shepherd. I shall not want . . . ."

"Don't you do it," Berta says smiling.

"He maketh me to lie down—"

"Where?"

"In green pastures." Craig starts sounding like he's preaching. "He lead-eth me, ah, beside the still waters."

"Ooooh."

"He restor-eth my soul. He lead-eth me in the paths of righteousness for His name's sake. Yea, though I walk through the valley of the shadow of death, I will fear no evil."

"Don't you fear that evil. Don't you do it." She stomps her foot.

"For thou art—"

"With me."

"Say it again. For thou art—"

"With me." Berta flings herself into Craig's arms pretending to faint. "Take me now."

Craig catches her, leaning over as if they were doing a dance move. "Why are you so silly?"

"Why do you entertain my silliness?"

"I'm still trying to figure that out."

"Nice one. It looks like you finally have a sense of humor."

"Thanks."

For a few moments more, Craig holds Berta as he looks into her eyes.

"Kiss me," she says. "You know you want to."

Craig smiles and kisses Berta but stops abruptly. "Why are we about to make out in a cemetery?" He lifts her back up to her feet.

"Because Craig, that's what people who are in love do. They make out in cemeteries." She laughs.

"Come on, let's get out of here."

"Where are we going?"

"To grab some lunch. Bible study is tonight at your church, isn't it?"

"Yeah, it is. I wasn't going, though."

"Why not?"

"I thought we were going to your church tomorrow?"

"We are."

"Wait, so you want to go to Bible study at my church tonight, Saturday service at your church, and then Sunday service back at my church?"

"No. Sunday, I cleared off."

"For what?"

"Something special."

"Something special like what?"

"You'll see." Craig smiles. "Look, you go ahead back to the car. I'll be there in a few seconds."

Berta looks at Craig and gives him a smile. She looks past him at Mr. Valencia's headstone. She blows a kiss in that direction and walks to the car.

Craig stands alone by Mr. Valencia's headstone. He kneels down and smiles as he fumbles with something in his pocket.

"Sir," he says. "It has been a while. I uhhh . . ." He pauses and looks down. "Thanks for everything. Thanks for taking care of her . . . thanks for being the one who God used to rescue her . . . thanks for being the one God used to bring her to me . . . thanks for being the one who God used to bring me . . . back to me." He nods his head a bit before pulling his hand out of his pocket holding a little box. "I got this yesterday. Now, I know this may be too soon . . . or maybe not. I don't know. Either way, I wanted to ask you . . . I wanted to ask you if I could take your daughter's hand in marriage." Craig pauses and feels the sun beaming down on the back of his neck. He stands up. "I'm going to ask her on Sunday." He waits for a bit more. A few moments later, he smiles. He gives an informal salute to the grave and walks back to the car.

"Hey, Craig," Berta says while leaning on the car. "Who did you get to fill my position?"

"No one."

"What? You're doing everything by yourself?"

"Nope."

"So?"

"This guy came into the church last week. He just got out of jail."

"Are you serious or are you joking?"

"I'm being serious. He came in needing help . . . and a job. The young guy has some skills." Craig leans on the car next to Berta. "So I'm putting him through school . . . like Mr. V. did for me."

Berta nods. She smiles at Craig, who stares in the direction of Mr. Valencia's grave with a determined look on his face.

"Why do you ask? You want your job back?"

"No way. My boss was a jerk."

Craig looks over to her and smiles. "Yeah, he was."

"But he did take me to this jazz club in Philly." Berta leans into Craig. "I think he was coming on to me then."

Craig laughs. "Maybe he was."

"Or maybe he was really trying to take me to the club down the street." Berta begins dancing around Craig. "To see my moves."

"Hey, hey, now. Church girls don't do that."

"What do you think I was before I was a church girl?"

"The way you're dancing, I'd say a stripper?"

Berta cuts short her dance and snaps a jab into Craig's arm.

"Just kidding," Craig says laughing while holding his arm.

Berta continues to stare him down, lips pursed.

"Just a joke." Craig still smiles. "Tell you what, if you were a stripper, I'd make it rain all the time, just for you."

Berta smirks, though her lips are still pursed. "You'd better."

Craig opens up his arms and allows Berta to lean back on him.

"Okay, so seriously, on a scale of one to ten, how scared were you that you weren't ever going to see me again?"

"I'd say about two and a half," Craig quickly answers.

"Stop lying. It had to be somewhere around nine."

"Nope. Two and a half."

"Craig, it's okay. You can tell the truth," Berta says laughing.

Craig squeezes her arm and turns her around.

"Are you trying to make out at the cemetery again?"

"Yup."

Craig kisses Berta again, this time with more zeal. Clutching the sides of her waist, he thanks God in his head and vows to never let her go. Indeed, Craig has "found" the one. He has found the one who sees him for whom he could be, the one who has always seen great potential in him, the one who doesn't see the present day money or the not so good past. Indeed Craig has finally found Berta. As for Berta, she has had a face to face encounter with one thing, that moment when everything falls into place, when much hard work and patience finally pays off. Berta has come face to face with and now dwells in her destiny.

CHAPTER THIRTY NINE

MARK sits in front of Pastor Brentwood and stares at the empty seat next to him. His eyes are glassy.

"Neither one of us thought it was going to end like this."

"I thought it was agreed that you wouldn't go. Quite honestly, Mark, I don't understand why you did . . . or why Jade persuaded you to do so."

"She figured that we shouldn't take it lying down. We had to fight somehow."

The pastor leans back in his chair. He shakes his head. "You two ran a great risk."

"I know. We know."

"Your job is safe?"

Mark nods. "From my understanding, yes. For right now, anyway. The full story isn't out yet, either."

"And when it does get out?"

"The board will have questions . . . a lot of questions, but I'm prepared for whichever way it goes."

The pastor nods. "And what of her?"

Mark shifts in his seat. He knows exactly who he is asking about. "She's in the psyche ward. I put out a restraining order on her. I overheard some of the cops talking about some jail time for her."

Pastor Brentwood looks at Mark. "So, what of her son?"

"He is with his father now . . . back up north."

"No music school?"

Mark looks at the floor with a pained expression. "No. His father enrolled him in a private school."

"How does that make you feel?"

Mark doesn't move. "I feel nothing, really. His dad has full custody over him . . . apparently, he isn't who Alicia made him out to be . . . and the private school is a great school. I just . . . I don't know." He leans back in his chair and looks up at the ceiling. "I just don't know." Mark pauses for a while and looks at the pastor. "She was abusing him, sir." Mark shakes his head and looks embarrassed. "I normally pick up on things like that. I bet I would have if I wasn't so caught up in the situation."

"Abusing him?"

"Yeah. That's why the kid was so quiet . . . so shy." Mark places his cupped hands behind his head. "She lied about everything."

"Well, what do you expect from a woman who knowingly and actively pursues a married man?"

"I guess. I just wish ... I ju—"

"What's done is done, Mark. Now, you need to find the strength to move on."

"But what do you think things would have been like if I didn't mess up?"

"I don't know. There's no way of telling. But I'm going to tell you the same thing that I told Jade a long time ago. You may make a wrong choice or two along the way, but you can always make another choice to make things right. You always have the freedom to make another choice, no matter how bleak the circumstances may seem. Jesus made sure of that." The pastor gets up from his seat. "We can continue this later." He starts to walk out of the office with Mark following. "But for now, we have a bunch of people waiting on us."

They walk to the front door of a large conference room. Pastor Brentwood walks in and starts talking to his wife. People talk and mingle. In the middle of the crowd, Mark sees Jade talking and laughing with a group of women. For Mark, time slows down. He notices every movement she makes, her brushing her hair back behind her ear, her strong yet dainty stance, her modest giggle that erupts into laughter, and finds her to be the most elegant woman he has ever known. Mark stays at the door, staring into the room. *Today is the day,* he thinks. He looks out into the crowd of people, all broken couples wanting to repair their marriages.

As soon as Mark and Jade entered his office, Pastor Brentwood told them that God's light would shine through both of them, bright enough for others to see. Mark chuckles thinking that he believes God told him that some time ago. He just never thought it would be after falling so far. Jade sees him and makes her way through the crowd to his side. Her arm is in a sling, but she wears a huge, bright smile.

"Everything okay?" she asks.

Mark kisses her on the forehead. "Of course it is."

Jade looks around. "Can I talk to you for a second?"

"You have cold feet?"

"Yes." Jade says anxiously. Her and Mark walk away from the door and down the hall. "I don't know if I can do this."

"Why?"

"Everyone that I talked to in there . . . everyone . . . they are so shocked like we were Mary and Joseph or something."

"Well, our story is a different one."

"Yeah, I know. And I know we agreed to this but—"

Mark cups her face and kisses her. "We can do this."

Jade nods and looks down. "Mark, I have something else to tell you. Something important."

"I'm all ears."

"I love you. I love you with all my heart. I know that after all we have been through, things won't be the same, and I don't want them to be. I hope for them to be better. You are a strong man, a caring man, a man that God has given to me even in my ignorance. I know for me and our *three* kids, you will continue to be just that."

Mark hugs Jade and then peels away from her. "Three kids?"

Jade looks Mark in the eyes and nods. "Three kids."

Mark smiles. He takes a deep breath and exhales slowly. He hugs Jade again.

"Found out in the hospital," Jade says. "The doctors want me back for a checkup next week; but for now, everything is fine."

"Well in that case, we better get this over with so you can get off your feet."

"I was thinking that we could go dancing tonight instead. The neighbors are picking the kids up from summer camp. They are staying with them."

"Dancing?"

Jade smiles. "Yes, dancing. We could turn the living room into our own ballroom . . . you know . . . like before. Don't let the broken arm fool ya. I can still move."

Mark grabs Jade by her waist. "Well, dancing it is."

He grabs her free hand and holds it, looking into her eyes. For a while, he just stands there, drinking her in with his eyes, and Jade doesn't flinch one bit.

"My queen," Mark says, kissing her hand.

Jade smiles and holds his hand to her face, indulging in his warm touch. A tear falls from her eye.

"My king," she says, still holding his hand.

Mark wipes away the tear from her face and leads the way back into the conference room.

THANK YOU FOR READING
THIS J. EVAN JOHNSON BOOK

Sign up for his FREE newsletter and be first to get updates on
new releases, sneak peeks of future stories,
completely free books and short stories, bonus content,
AND MORE!

Visit him online to sign up at
www.thejejstory.com